S0-DOP-726

The Legend of Phoenix Mountain

鳳山傳奇

tinabot

Ninja Pueblo Publishing

The Legend of Phoenix Mountain
Copyright © Tina Tsai
All rights reserved.
Printed in the United States of America.
No part of this book may be used or reproduced in any manner whatsoever without written permission except in the case of brief quotations embodied in critical articles and reviews.
For information address Ninja Pueblo Publishing, P.O. Box 36125
Los Angeles, CA 90036

First Edition

ISBN 978-0-9846077-2-3

Visit www.ninjapueblo.com

To my dearest Carlo
for the paradigm shifts
every moment with you
has been a gift

To Mom and Dad
for teaching me
the best of all worlds
is what I must be

To my brother Ben
for sticking with me
when doors were locked
you were my key

To all the friends
who helped me out
invaluable perspectives
without a doubt

To all my students
for being so smart
you made this story
from the heart

Table of Contents

Chapter

Chapter 1
Suburban Attack

Her hair always glistened in the sunlight like a precious metal, perfectly gold in its blond glory. Her eyes were a crystal clear blue, forever sparkling like sapphires. He always yearned to reach out and touch her smooth, porcelain skin as she smiled up at him while hugging her school books to her chest. Today she had worn a perfectly fitted pair of blue jeans that went well with the pink, flowing blouse that was slit at the shoulders and loose in the collar exposing her slender neck. In his eyes, Rose Tracy was the perfect girl.

Kyle Lin knew he could never have her. She was his best friend's girlfriend, and he also felt that someone like her could never fall for someone like him. But the way she smiled at him sometimes tempted him to believe otherwise. Then again, she smiled that way at a lot of people. She was just being nice.

The image of Rose Tracy and his best friend, Matt Lee, going off on a date to the mall after school today stuck in his head. Kyle, Matt, and Rose had grown up together in the same Los Angeles county suburban landscape. They had been friends since kindergarten, and Kyle had had a crush on Rose since 2nd grade, but of course he had always been too chicken to do anything about it. And Matt, Matt was like his brother. Both friendly and out-going, Matt and Rose were a perfect match for each other. Kyle knew that.

He walked up to the front door of his bright and warm home nestled between cheerful green hills. He fumbled in his duffle bag for his keys while balancing the weight of his textbook laden backpack. He shook his head at himself. He felt pathetic for having a crush on his best bud's girlfriend, especially when there were other available pretty girls

at his high school. There was Mandy Yamada, Mercedes Lopez, Robin Jackson, Soo Kim, Kyra Lu…all friends of Rose and all on the cheerleading squad with her. They were always done up in perfectly matched clothes of the latest styles and were honors students, kids with more than decent grades and lots of school spirit. With this sweet and pretty all-American girl next door look, they were the most sought after girls at school. Boys wanted to date them, and girls wanted to be like them, which meant Kyle had no chance with any of them. He didn't have his friend Matt's confidence and charm with the ladies, and although both were athletic, he didn't feel he was as good looking as his friend, either.

Matt always had this sparkle to his smile and sureness in his walk that Kyle couldn't imitate. Matt always wore designer clothes that his fashionable mother would pick out for him. Both Matt and Kyle had black hair, almond-shaped brown eyes, and the same healthy Southern Californian tan, but Kyle still had a bit of that lanky boyhood in him whereas Matt already had the broad shoulders and solid build of a young man. Every hair on Matt's head was always perfectly in place, even during basketball practice. He always had the newest, hottest sneakers, the current model being black with red trim. Looking down at his own worn out shoes and non-descript wholesale clothes, Kyle heaved a sigh. His family wasn't poor, but they weren't rich. His parents weren't the fashion savvy types either, and their strict practical nature deterred Kyle from asking for new clothes.

"Yours don't have holes in them yet," he could imagine his mother saying. He had ten t-shirts and ten pairs of jeans that were exactly like the ones he was wearing. His parents just didn't understand what it was like to be in an American high school. They had grown up at schools in Asia. Everyone wore uniforms to school there.

Kyle unlocked his door, and as it swung open, a clenched fist unexpectedly came flying at his face out of the shadows of his home. His eyes grew wide as he ducked out of the way. The hostile fist struck into the empty sunlight outside the door where Kyle's head had been just a split second earlier, and then it withdrew back into the shadows. Kyle had just caught his balance when a foot replaced the fist and came flying at his head again. This time, Kyle let his duffle bag slip off his shoulder and fall to the ground as he raised a hand to push the assaulting foot aside with his forearm in a skilled block. That foot pulled back and another came flying out at him. He barely avoided this third strike by leaning backwards and tilting his head back away from the blow. The weight of his backpack, though, was his undoing. The sudden shift pulled him off balance, and Kyle fell backwards onto his backpack. He let out a grunt and gasp of surprise, but he was unhurt. He was now like a turtle stuck on its back. Two hands reached out of the house's darkness and grabbed onto his two ankles. With a quick swishing sound, he was dragged into the house by his assailant. Then, the attacking fist reached back out into the sunlight and grabbed Kyle's fallen duffle bag. The door closed quickly with a sure click as soon as the duffle bag was pulled into the house.

"Not bad, but still not nearly good enough for the one destined to save the world."

As Kyle blinked to adjust to the dimly lit inside of his house, the sight of a familiar face took form.

"Ah-gong (Grandpa), you're back already?" Kyle said while still blinking.

"Don't sound so disappointed," his grandfather said as he held out a firm hand to the grandson he had just attacked. Slipping his backpack straps off his shoulders, Kyle took his grandfather's hand and felt himself pulled effortlessly up from the ground. His grandfather was strong.

"You know, I don't know how things are in Asia, but in America, it's not a normal thing for grandparents to attack their grandchildren," Kyle said throwing a mild glare of annoyance at his grandfather. He also looked away in disgust as he noticed his grandfather was wearing the same old blue mandarin-collared button-down vest, baggy black pants, and white socks that contrasted noticeably with his black shoes. White hair flowed sagaciously off his face and chin. Ah-gong looked like he had stepped out of one of those English dubbed 70s kung fu movies. *Why does he always have to look like a walking stereotype?* Kyle wondered with annoyance. He cringed at the thought of having his grandpa show up at his high school.

"Stop being so dramatic."

"*I'm* being dramatic? You're the one that keeps calling me the savior of the world," Kyle retorted. It was the first time he had seen his grandfather in a year and already they were quarreling.

"I'm just stating fact. You, my grandson…" Ah-gong paused for dramatic effect, "…are the Chosen One."

Kyle rolled his eyes so far back up into his head he was surprised he could still see. *How clichéd*...he thought to himself. He heaved an exasperated sigh.

"I am not part of your cult—"

"Tian Yi Society," Ah-gong corrected.

"Whatever. I'm just not part of it okay?"

His grandfather stared at him seriously as if scrutinizing every muscle and sinew in his body. Kyle tried to hold his ground and stare back, but it was hard to hold up spirit against his grandfather's overbearing demeanor. That and he didn't like being examined so closely. He felt self-consciousness enough every day in school.

"Have you been practicing your calligraphy?" Ah-gong asked.

"No."

"I emailed you reminders to practice. I even attached images of the works of great calligraphers from all over Asia. You have no excuse."

"I'm not making any excuses! I just didn't want to, okay?"

"That's not a good excuse."

Kyle was about to tear his hair out in frustration.

"How is calligraphy supposed to help me save the world?!"

"Good question! All of your power is in the spirit of your soul, and calligraphy is a fine way to hone your mind and soul just as martial arts is fit for preparing your mind and body."

"I'm sorry I asked," Kyle shook his head.

"Let's train now. I'll let you choose. Tsai Li Fo Fist or the calligraphy of Japanese masters. I had an extended stay in both Southern China and Kyoto this spring."

"I have an A.P. Biology test to study for tomorrow, Ah-gong. I don't have time for this nonsense."

"You can study after training. The sun is still out, and we have to make up for lost time."

His grandfather, as usual, wouldn't take no for an answer and quickly grabbed Kyle's heavy backpack and duffle bag with little effort and headed for the back yard. Kyle grabbed instantly for his confiscated backpack where his A.P. Biology textbook was. He knew full well that his grandfather was going to hold it ransom until Kyle finished training with him. The young teen tried to pull the backpack away from his grandfather, but he only got pulled forward with it.

"Ah-gong! Will you stop? I really have to study for my test tomorrow! It's the final A.P. test! I paid money to take it! I'm serious! Let go!" Kyle said as he was dragged down the hallway clutching his backpack. Ah-gong didn't heed his pleas.

Finally, Kyle let go of his backpack. He was fed up with it all.

"I don't need calligraphy! I need to score a five on the A.P. test! I need a new hair cut! I…I need new sneakers!"

His grandfather stopped and turned around to face him. First he raised an eyebrow. Then he spoke.

"You have grown up to be a shallow, failure of a grandson. Your trip to Asia this summer will be your last chance to fulfill your destiny. Hopefully it will do your soul some good."

With that, Ah-gong swiftly turned around and continued away with Kyle's study materials.

Kyle stood in the hallway alone with his mouth agape. When he had come to his senses and processed some of what his grandfather had said, he sputtered out some outrage.

"Failure?" he said, "I've got a 4.88 GPA! And…and…WHAT TRIP TO ASIA?"

Chapter 2

Flight to Phoenix Mountain

Kyle's parents consented to Ah-gong's request to take him on a summer trip to Asia, and less than a month after he had finished all of his Advanced Placement exams for the year, Kyle sat disgruntled on the airplane in mid-flight trying hard to focus on the large test prep book open on the plastic serving tray connected to the back of the seat in front of him. Outside the window next to him were vast vistas of deep blue oceans and pristine sunlit white clouds billowing across a cerulean sky. He took no notice of any of it.

"Aberration – not normal. Admonish – to warn. Apocalyptic – of or like the end of the world."

Kyle muttered the test prep vocabulary words and their meanings out loud in an attempt to keep his mind on studying. Going on to his junior year of high school, rumored as the most critical and difficult year in an American kid's high school career, he was supposed to be taking test prep courses over the summer. The tests for getting into college were coming up, and if he did well on them, he could get a nice scholarship for college. He wasn't going to let a trip to Asia forced upon him by an incorrigibly eccentric grandfather get in the way of a potential college scholarship. The digital media player tucked next to his passport was full of test prep audio and video files. He tried to make sentences with the vocabulary words he had just gone over.

"Ah-gong is an *aberration* of nature. He constantly *admonishes* me about an *apocalyptic* event predicted by his cult."

"Tian Yi Society," his grandfather corrected again as he sat back down in the seat next to him. Kyle put his hands up to the side of his head and lightly massaged his temples in irritation. He decided to get back to his studying and ignore his grandfather.

"Abhor – to extremely hate. Arduous – difficult. Adulate – to flatter, to adore."

He was tempted to make a sentence using 'adulate' and 'Rose Tracy' but decided he should stop being a pathetic idiot.

"Busy?" his grandfather said as he stuck his head in front of Kyle's face to closely examine the book his grandson was so intent on staring at. Kyle pushed his grandfather's head out of his view.

"Yes, very."

"No wonder you've become so shallow. You're reading books that have no substance, no soul."

Kyle felt another wave of annoyance wash over him.

"You just don't understand how important this is for my future."

Ah-gong raised an eyebrow.

"I understand what you're doing better than *you* do," he said, leaning back with a self-confidence that infuriated Kyle.

"HOW could you POSSIBLY understand?"

His grandfather didn't grow up in the United States. He didn't understand the college entrance system there. He didn't know that tests, grades, and extracurricular activities could make or break your future. How could he possibly know the system better than Kyle?

Ah-gong cleared his throat, threw him a sideways glance with a purposefully patronizing expression on his face, and then said,

"Even if I explained it to you, you wouldn't understand."

"TRY ME."

Ah-gong shrugged his shoulders.

"It's one of those things you have to figure out for yourself. You just go back to looking at your nice little book there because I'm sure becoming really good at multiple choice questions will be critical to your survival in this world."

Kyle shook his head in disbelief.

"Ah-gong, how am I supposed to get into college without good test scores? How am I supposed to get a good job without a college degree?"

"I'm not saying studying for tests or going to college is bad. I just think you follow that system without questioning it. It's like you're…in a cult or something," Ah-gong said with a sarcastically contrived look of puzzlement.

"Chicken or steak?"

The voice of the flight attendant interrupted their little argument. Kyle was a bit relieved that the serving of lunch had interrupted their discussion because he couldn't think of a good come back to his grandfather's sarcasm. He turned to look up at the source of the voice and found himself looking at one of the most beautiful women he had ever laid eyes on. She had a velvety brown skin tone and luminous brown eyes framed by black silken hair. She smiled brightly down at him with luscious red lips.

"Chicken or steak?" she asked again.

"Uh, um, steak, please. Thank you," Kyle stammered a bit as he put away his test practice book to make room for the food.

She pulled out a tray from the cart in the aisle and handed it over to him. Then she turned her attention to Ah-gong who ordered chicken. His grandfather then proceeded to ask her in Indonesian whether she was from Jakarta, and she smiled with delight because she was indeed from Jakarta. They had a friendly little exchange that Kyle couldn't understand at all. The lady suddenly laughed at something Ah-gong had said, and he chuckled along with her. Then she turned and gave Kyle another smile and a wink. Kyle promptly flushed a bit red while she turned her attention back to serving the other passengers.

They started on their meal in silence and all was peaceful until Ah-

gong spoke again.

"You think that lady was pretty huh?"

Kyle shrugged, hoping that if he didn't say anything, his Ah-gong would just let the subject drop.

"I told her that you had a crush on her."

Kyle turned to look at his grandfather with disbelief.

"WHAT?"

"Well, it's the truth, isn't it?" Ah-gong said with a feigned look of innocence.

Kyle closed his eyes and leaned back into his chair with a breath of exasperation. That's why she had winked at him.

"Can you stop embarrassing me? Please? Just for a minute?" Kyle said while emphatically holding his hands up in front of him in a halting gesture.

"Eleanor Roosevelt said 'Nobody can make a fool out of you without your consent.' You do know who Eleanor Roosevelt is, don't you?" his grandfather pressed.

"Of course I know!" Kyle said irritably. He had, after all, just finished an A.P. U.S. History course.

"Then obviously there's a difference between knowing who she is and knowing what she meant."

"I'd just like to finish my food in peace please."

They both fell into another silence as they continued their meal.

"I only think one girl is pretty."

Kyle looked at Ah-gong genuinely a bit puzzled by why his grandfather was sharing information about his taste in women with him. He wasn't sure if Ah-gong was baiting another hook that would yet again drag him into a bothersome and pointless conversation. Ah-gong pulled out the leather wallet he had bought at the mall near Kyle's home. He flipped it open and for the first time showed Kyle a picture of himself and Kyle's grandmother when they were still young.

Kyle looked at the picture. The younger version of his grandfather had his arm unabashedly around the younger version of Kyle's deceased grandmother. Both were smiling broadly, clearly a happy couple full of life and joy. In the young woman's face Kyle could recognize the familiar features of the grandmother who used to care for him when he was little while his parents were at work. There was nothing silken about her braided black, rather coarse-looking hair nor was there anything velvety about her natural skin, but there was a radiance in her smile and an intelligent sparkle in her eyes that gave even this two-dimensional rendition of her likeness captivating. He remembered the tenderness with which she had placed a calligraphy brush into his small hand and the patience in her kind face as she taught him the first strokes of his Chinese name. Ah-gong handed the picture over to Kyle as he leaned back contentedly into his seat. He looked up slightly as nostalgia spread across his face in the form of a peaceful smile.

"I knew she was the one for me when she broke through my defenses and gave me a black eye."

"Ah-ma (Grandmother) gave you a black eye?" Kyle said with a laugh despite himself.

"Yeah, she hit me right here," Ah-gong said as he held a fist up and pointed it at his right eye. "No one in my class was able to beat me in a sparring match. But your Ah-ma was something else. It was a draw. I gave her quite a bruise on her left cheek, you know." Ah-gong chuckled at the memory. "She had a mean left hook, but, ayoh, she always had trouble guarding her own left side."

Kyle stared at the picture some more in silence. His grandmother had taught him Chinese writing, calligraphy, and painting. She had told him the best stories full of dragons, demons, and mystical heroes. She had always seemed like a serene and peaceful artist, not a martial arts

warrior.

"I didn't know Ah-ma could fight."

"Yes, well, she was diagnosed with cancer when you were very young, so she had to progressively limit her physical activity as you grew older. Chemotherapy left her especially weak."

An image of his grandmother's kind smile flashed through his mind. He had always wondered as a child why she always looked kind of sad. He understood now that it was because she knew early on that she didn't have much time left. And she had spent the bulk of her remaining time on Earth teaching him.

"Your Ah-ma wasn't afraid of death. She was just sad to leave us behind. But she told me she was glad she lasted long enough to be able to spend some time with you. She was both proud and worried that you were born as the Chosen One."

Kyle flipped the wallet with the picture inside it closed and returned it to his grandfather. He still couldn't understand the superstitious beliefs of his grandparents. They were so farfetched, so unbelievable. Apparently, he was this 'chosen one' because of the time and date of his birth. Something about the stars being auspiciously aligned at the moment he was born. He wasn't in the mood to argue with his grandfather about it all again.

"Where did you say we were going?"

"Phoenix Mountain."

Chapter 3

Through Chitou Forest

Kyle stepped off the rusty, creaky public bus and found himself in the middle of Chitou Forest on a mountainside in the heart of Taiwan, the island of legendary beauty. The stone pathway off to the side of the asphalt road was damp, and a mist filled the air, thick with the fragrance of a variety of plant life, stones, and minerals. There was a pleasant rushing sound of water that came from hidden water sources and the flow of air between the foliage. All around were towering trees with slender yet sturdy trunks, and the canopy above allowed only streams of sunlight to slip through. Although it was about noon, it felt like it was perpetually early morning in the peaceful mountain forest.

The place felt like a different world altogether compared to the sunny suburban American landscape Kyle had been born and raised in. But he was incredibly exhausted from the trip, and he didn't really have the energy to feel energized by the freshness of the new environment.

Heaving his backpack heavy with study aid books and his rolling suitcase full of the rest of his belongings, Kyle followed his grandfather, half alive and barely aware of his surroundings. He just focused on putting one foot in front of the other and hoped there was a soft bed at the end of it all.

Ah-gong looked like a mystic sage walking along the path flanked on either side by towering bamboo trees with their green and sleek leaves waving pleasantly in the light, breezy mist. He had a simple cloth messenger bag slung over his shoulder.

They went on like this for a couple of hours.

Kyle couldn't stand it anymore.

"ARE WE THERE YET?"

Ah-gong glanced back over at him and then gave a disappointed shake of the head. At that point, Kyle couldn't care less if Ah-gong thought he was a failure. In fact, he didn't care if the whole world thought he was a failure. He just wanted a place to lie down, and the moss covered soil on either side of their path was beginning to look quite inviting. To Kyle's surprise, his Ah-gong answered, "We're here."

The path took a sharp turn, and when Kyle rounded the corner, he found himself staring up a steep stone stairway that seemed to go straight up to the top of the mountain. The top was obscured by clouds that billowed lazily by.

"YOU HAVE GOT TO BE KIDDING ME."

Kyle threw down his backpack and luggage, rolled to the ground, and sprawled himself on the damp, stone path. Ah-gong was already up a few of the steps, and he looked back down on his sprawling starfish of a grandson with a dry expression on his face.

"I'm going on ahead. I'll see you at the top."

Kyle waved one of his hands weakly to show that he had heard. Ah-gong turned and ran up the stairs as energetic as a young college athlete.

"Try not to embarrass me too much when you meet everyone," he yelled to Kyle as he left.

Everyone...? Kyle pondered faintly as he tried to catch his breath and rest his aching body. Despite all the talking Ah-gong did on their trip here, he had said very little about exactly where they were headed and what they were going to do when they got there. Kyle figured the stone stairway was going up Phoenix Mountain.

As he lay on his back, he looked up at the forest top and the bamboo that towered above him. For the first time he noticed the grace, peace, and beauty in the way these amazing plants carried themselves. They were at the same time dreamy and solid, swaying and still.

Involuntarily he took in a deep breath of the rich mountain forest air, immediately felt better, and continued this deep breathing until he felt ready to get up.

When he finally pulled himself to his feet, he realized that his clothes were clinging uncomfortably to his body from the dampness caused by his own perspiration and the moist air of the forest. He then hoped there was a shower at the top of this stone stairway. Heaving his heavy backpack onto his shoulders again and pulling on his luggage, Kyle heaved an equally heavy sigh as he began his long trek up the steep stone steps. To call the task painstaking was an understatement. Take a step, pull the luggage up. Take a step, pull the luggage up. Take a step...Kyle's mind was going numb, and his muscles often refused his commands. Each step seemed higher and harder than the one before. There were hundreds of them.

Hasn't anyone here ever heard of an escalator? Kyle thought painfully. It wasn't his first trip to Taiwan. He'd visited the modern, high-tech city areas before. Even on this trip, he had seen escalators at the airport and through the large windows of department stores on the streets of Taichung City as he had passed by in the bus. He had gone by skyscrapers, sleek modern apartments, and cities enveloped in wireless internet. He thought wistfully of the stores full of the latest electronic gadgets and video games, the clubs packed with young people having a good time, and the streets lined with shops and restaurants, and he heaved a sigh, wishing that they had stayed in civilization.

When he finally reached the top, he let go of his luggage, dropped his backpack, and sprawled on the ground again with his feet pointing at the stairway that he had just conquered. As he caught his breath again, he looked up and above his reclined head and saw, upside down, a massive temple with green trimmings and red tiled roof tops that curved up at the edges and corners, buttressed by thick, red columns on all sides. Tall walls panned out from both sides of the building, enclosing a larger space in the confines of the complex. There was a large stone placed out in front with Chinese characters carved into it.

别有洞天

"(Another World Lies Beyond)," Kyle read out loud in Mandarin Chinese, surprised at his ability to decipher the code. His grandmother's teachings were still strong in him.

He had not expected such a large complex to be at the top of this small mountain. He got to his feet again and made it up a few more flights of stairs to reach the massive front doors of the temple. Being awe-struck with what he was looking at, he made no complaint about having to climb more steps.

Not quite knowing what to do for sure when he reached the entrance, he held up a tentative hand to the large door and knocked lightly. The impact of his small hand on thick wood made little sound, and his knocking sound thinned out quickly as if it came from far away. He stood about one fifth as high as the doors. They were huge.

"Hello?" he called out.

Kyle looked behind him, then to either side looking for some clue as to what he was to do next. All was quiet and still as if there were no one else on this mountain top besides himself. He began to wonder if his Ah-gong was playing a prank on him. He wouldn't be surprised. Finally, with a shrug of the shoulders, Kyle placed both hands on one of the wooden doors and pushed.

The door opened smoothly without creaking despite its enormity. Kyle stepped inside, dragging his belongings in with him, and shut the door behind him. The inside was dimly lit with a few candles, but Kyle could tell it was a vast hall. On the other side, he saw an open doorway, and through it he could hear the bustling noise of people busy with preparations for something. It sounded much like the kitchen of a large Chinese restaurant. He headed towards the light.

As he emerged from the empty and dark hall, he found himself looking at a large, beautiful courtyard covered in rectangular stone slabs lined with grass. The edges of the courtyard were embellished with lush, carefully trimmed and designed gardens of trees, flowers, and rocks, and in one corner a large rock formation seemed to be embedded into the building itself. Water flowed pleasantly down over the rocks filling the courtyard with its soothing sounds. All around people in t-shirts and blue jeans were moving here and there, doing this and that, preparing what looked like a grand feast. Kyle's stomach rumbled loudly as the delicious smells of a cooking dinner reached him. He realized he hadn't eaten a thing since the meager meal on the airplane.

He looked down at his stomach as he put a hand on it, and when he looked back up, he found everyone in the courtyard had stopped what they were doing to look directly at him. Apparently his growling stomach had just announced his presence. At first they were curious, but it looked to Kyle as if they slowly recognized him.

He felt more awkward and self-conscious than he ever had in his entire life. He was about to open his mouth and ask about his grandfather to break the silence, when a young girl about his age came up to him. She had luminous dark eyes and shiny black flowing hair cascading over her simple pink t-shirt. Her unremarkable clothes and those of the others struck him as strange matched against the backdrop of this magnificent structure of Chinese architectural style. She smiled sweetly with unfettered excitement and said in a delicate voice,

"You must be 林神銳!" The girl spoke in English with a heavy accent.

"Yes," Kyle answered to his Chinese name with a timid nod. He was not used to being called by his full Chinese name.

"We've been waiting for you! Come with me. Your grandfather is already in his quarters. I will show you to yours. My name is 玫 (Mei)."

Kyle smiled in thanks to Mei, a little weirded out that her name meant 'Rose', and was relieved to hear that he would have his own separate room. She tried to get his luggage for him, but he insisted on carrying it himself. With another sweet and rather coy approving smile, she led him down what seemed like a maze of long hallways and walkways that passed by smaller courtyards and rows of rooms of various sizes before they arrived at his living quarters.

It was a good sized room that was decorated with ornate furniture and art. He had a study desk with a complete set of calligraphy brushes, ink, and ink stone and plenty of blank papers in a stack to the side. Opposite the desk was the bed which was enclosed in a wooden frame and draped with fabric. The silk sheets and comforter that covered the bed looked soft, smooth, and inviting. His guide pulled open the windows at the end of his quarters to let in the sunlight and to reveal a pleasant surprise. Outside was a small pool of steaming hot water surrounded by a cascading rock formation. It was a natural hot spring bath. A doorway to the left of the window led out to it.

She then opened the doors to the top half of a large dresser and, to Kyle's surprise, inside was a large flat screen T.V., a fancy cable box that boasted 200+ channels, and multiple game consoles with an assortment of the latest game releases. *In a temple?* Kyle thought to himself. There was also a large basket of various fruits, breads, cheeses, and drinks on ice for him to enjoy.

"Please make yourself comfortable and rest up. We are doing our best to prepare a grand feast in your honor tonight."

Mei smiled at him, lightly bit her lower lip as if contemplating something, and then gave Kyle a peck on the cheek.

"That is for good luck on your journey."

She bowed, gave him a flirtatious wink of the eye, and closed the door as she left.

Kyle was too shocked to say anything as she left. He was a bit glad she had left so quickly because he could feel his face burning red by the time she had shut the door. He looked around at his room in a daze and tried to sort it all out.

He had expected to live the life of an monk up here on the mountain with his grandfather and a handful of withered old men. Instead, he got what ended up being luxury hotel lodgings with young, pretty girls kissing him on the cheek. It was too weird for him to comprehend. The way his grandfather was, he never would have expected all of this. He looked at the basket of food, the flat screen TV, the video games, the silk covered bed…it was too good to be true. There had to be a catch.

Kyle decided he would figure it out later. Despite all the excitement, he was still exhausted from the journey, and he was extremely grateful that he had such rich comforts to enjoy after such a long trip. He wiped his hands on a hot wet towel by the basket of food and ravenously stuffed his face until his cheeks puffed out, making him look much like a gluttonous chipmunk. As he chewed a mouthful of cheese and bread, he undressed and went outside to his own private hot spring, bringing a can of soda and a bottle of water with him. After a quick shower in the small restroom he found on the side, he luxuriated in the pool for a good while, sipping his beverages at leisure while nursing his aching muscles. When he was done, he noticed that two sets of clothing were folded neatly in the shelving by the pool. One apparently was for sleeping. Too tired to pull clothes out of his own luggage, Kyle didn't think twice about putting on the silk blue pajamas. He lay down on the cushy bed and passed out as soon as his head hit the pillow.

Chapter 4

Enter the Dragon

When Kyle awoke, the sun had fully set, and it was almost completely dark inside his room. The only light came from some of the lamps that lit the hallways outside. Kyle was disoriented when he awoke. He didn't know where he was at first, but as he sat up and got his bearings, it all started coming back to him. He got out of bed, stretched his legs, and turned on the lights, wondering if he might have missed the banquet. He pulled some more food out of the still chilled basket and munched on that as he turned on the television. Flipping from channel to channel, images of Asian, American, Middle Eastern, and European pop stars pranced across the screen. He watched a bit of Korean drama, some movies from India, music videos from the Philippines, and anime from Japan.

Then a knock came on his door. It was Mei. When he opened his door, he found her bowing and smiling sweetly up at him. She wore a red mandarin-collared, sleeveless silk dress with flower patterns. Her face glowed with newly applied make-up that made her look dreamy and glamorous.

"Dinner will begin shortly. I hope you had a good rest."

"Yeah, thanks."

Mei smiled demurely, "When you are ready, I will show you to…"

Just then another girl came running up to her and explained something frantically in a language that Kyle could not understand. Mei listened intently, and then turned to Kyle.

"I'm so sorry. There is an emergency in the kitchen that I must attend to. Will you be able to find your way back to the main courtyard?"

"I'm sure I can figure it out, thanks," Kyle said. Though he felt a little disappointed he wouldn't be able to spend more time with the lovely Mei, he figured it might be nice to be able to explore a bit on his own before he was caught up in his grandfather's games again.

Mei bowed and left with the other girl.

Kyle changed into the other set of clothes, deciding that it would probably be best not to stick out too much. Though he had expected to wear something very traditional Chinese, he found that the clothes laid out for him were just a simple button down blue mandarin-collared cotton shirt with a pair of comfortable, boot cut black pants. They were not so formal, and aside from the mandarin collar, the shirt looked just like a plain old Western button down shirt. He was pleased with that. He didn't want to look flamboyantly ethnic like his grandfather.

He left his room and began his way back to the front courtyard. Though he had been tired, Kyle was good with directions and knew he was at least generally headed in the right way.

As he walked down a pathway that ran along the perimeter of one of the smaller courtyards, he passed by an open door to a small room with a large piece of white, cotton paper hanging on the wall. On it was a single Chinese character written in black-ink calligraphy. It was lit by a single candle that flickered beneath it. He couldn't help but stop to look at it.

It was the character for endurance or tolerance, and the calligraphy showed the work of a steady hand and a sure heart. The lines curved like powerful ocean waves in a storm, and they ended on razor sharp points. They were solid yet elegant, like the bamboo covering the mountain area Kyle had passed by earlier in the day. Kyle's study of Chinese calligraphy from childhood resurfaced as he examined the word

with his trained eye.

"好字(great penmanship)," he said out loud, involuntarily using the standard Chinese language that his grandma always used with him when he was little. She always said this to compliment him when he did a good job on his calligraphy.

"謝了(thanks)," a voice said from behind him.

Kyle turned around and saw a girl his age wearing a red, vest-like top with one side folded over the other and tied together at the back. He could see that her torso was bandaged in white wraps underneath, and her wrists were similarly bandaged. Her shoulders, arms, and face shone sun-browned skin in the lamp light. She was an inch or two shorter than Kyle and wore loose, baggy brown pants; her black hair was pulled up into a high pony-tail. Folding her arms across her chest with her hands in fists, she looked at Kyle with serious and challenging light brown eyes. She looked like she had popped right out of a video game.

"It's really good, I mean, uh..." Kyle realized he couldn't assume that she spoke English, and he stuttered out some of his very rusty Mandarin Chinese as he tried to explain his thoughts about the calligraphy piece that was apparently written by her.

She listened intently but didn't respond. Kyle finally faltered to a stop and decided he should probably just shut up. For a moment, she simply stared at him in silence, and then she spoke.

"來，比武 (Come, let's fight)," she challenged him to a duel and then turned away from him, clearly expecting him to follow her. Kyle looked down the hall on both sides half expecting to see his grandfather hiding in the shadows somewhere with a goofy grin of satisfaction on his face. Why else would a random girl suddenly show up and challenge him to a sparring match? But to his puzzlement, Kyle saw no one else in the courtyard but himself and this severe looking girl.

Stupidly, he followed her out to the courtyard, and as they left the

lighted walkways, the lamplight was replaced by soft lights of night. Everything was a silvery blue under a full moon making Kyle feel more than ever that he was in another world altogether. He was amazed at how many stars there were in the sky. In the city and suburbs where he grew up, he could only see a few meager ones twinkling in the massive dark space above. Here, the sky was bursting with diamonds.

He looked back at the strange girl that had just challenged him to fight. He was about to ask her why in the world she wanted to fight him and whether she was in cahoots with his grandfather when he realized the bottom of her foot was headed for his throat. Instinctively, he crossed his forearms in front of him to block the attack. Her foot struck his arms, and he was pushed back a few steps and almost off his feet. She punched next, aiming for his solar plexus, a gathering of nerves behind the stomach. His right arm blocked it, knocking her attacking fist off of its mark, and it harmlessly grazed his waist. That was when he saw the palm of her other hand coming up towards his face. He leaned back away from the attack and at the same time threw a kick up at her as he did a deft back flip. He was rusty, but he still had *some* skills.

As he landed on his feet again, he saw that she had done a back flip as well to avoid the strike from his foot. The sharp look in her eye told him that she wasn't going to explain herself until this fight was over. Kyle was bewildered and said under his breath,

"Okay…"

He sunk into a solid t-stance, where his left foot was planted firmly out in front of him perpendicular to his right foot that was solidly dug into the ground behind him. He held his fists up with his left in front of his right and prepared for the fight.

The girl took a cat stance, which was much like his except her front foot only lightly touched the ground at the toe. Her hands came up in front of her, and her fingers curled into fists. She looked like a tiger ready to pounce, and in the next moment she did indeed pounce in a most surprising way. From her position, she jumped and spun through the air like a tornado, swinging her leg in a horizontal circle that came crashing down at him, and Kyle barely had time to dodge this strike that came from above. He was surprised at both her agility and strength, but he was tired of being on the defensive.

He went at her with some hard hits to the face, but she easily dodged them leaning just enough out of the way for his strikes to slide right past her without making any contact. He tried another series of punches and kicks all to no avail. Trying to hit her was like trying to hit a blade of grass. She would just bend away making his efforts fruitless. He grew more and more frustrated as the battle went on.

Fed up, Kyle gathered up everything he had and threw one more solid punch at her, hoping that if he punched with a heavy enough hit, he would be able to strike her decisively despite her fluid evasions. The next thing he knew, she had jumped up over his strike, and her foot landed on his shoulder. He felt a rude push towards the earth as she jumped off of his shoulder, flipped in the air over him, and landed behind him.

Alarmed that his opponent was now behind him and out of his sight, he turned quickly to face her and was promptly punched in his right eye.

"OWW!"

He held his hand up to his throbbing eye, and the throbbing was quickly spreading throughout his skull. That was one hard hit.

The girl stood there with fists on her hips and stared without remorse at him as he nursed his injured eye.

"Pathetic."

Kyle thought he had imagined her speaking English, but as he got a little used to the throbbing and shook off some of the dizziness, he realized she really had spoken an English word.

"What did you call me?"

"Pathetic," she repeated without hesitation, "Not much of a Chosen One, are you?"

"Dude, who do you think you are? And…and how come you speak English?"

Mei had spoken her English with a heavy accent, making it pretty clear that she had learned her English later on in her life and that she had probably grown up in Taiwan or Asia somewhere. This girl, on the other hand, despite her shao-lin like attire, had perfect Southern Californian flavored American English.

"Because, Kyle Lin, I'm from Los Angeles."

"What? From…How do you know my name?"

The girl rolled her eyes.

"Because I go to the same high school as you. Idiot."

Chapter 5

The Real Chosen One

"Who are you?" Kyle asked again. He tried to look at her through both eyes at first and then gave up. He kept his hand over his injured eye and peered at her through his remaining good eye.

"My name's 譚泰努(Tan Tai Nu). People just call me Tai. You seriously don't know me, huh?"

"Tai? What year are you?"

"Same as you. Just finished 10th grade."

"Our high school has like two thousand students. You can't expect me to know everyone there," Kyle said, fully annoyed at being called an idiot. He got enough of that from his grandfather.

"I was in your A.P. Biology class."

"There're like 40 of us in there."

"I sat behind you."

"Okay, okay, fine. Look, I'm sorry I don't know you even though you sat behind me in A.P. Bio, okay? But did you really have to punch my eye out? I mean, geez, why are you so violent? You remind me of my grandpa."

"You should have been able to defend yourself. You should have been able to defeat me, if you're everything everyone says you are."

"Look, I don't know what's going on here, okay?"

One of Tai's eyebrow rose. She was genuinely surprised.

"You don't know that you're the Chosen One?"

"Well, yeah, I know that. At least that's what my Ah-gong keeps calling me."

"You don't know that you're destined to save the world?"

"Um, well, yeah, he told me that part, too…"

"Well, then you do know what's going on here."

"No, I don't. I'm just here because my grandpa dragged me here. I should be safe and sound sitting in a test prep course right now studying for college entrance exams, but no, here I am in a freakish Chinese cult temple on top of a mountain with my eye punched out."

Kyle's frustrations were spilling out unfettered.

"So you don't know what tomorrow is?"

Kyle looked at her with his one good eye and made an exasperated gesture with his free hand.

"NO! Feel like filling me in?"

He had no patience for anything anymore.

"Tomorrow is the day when the Chosen One travels to the other world, to Tian, to maintain the balance of worlds, the balance of Earth and Sky."

"Travel? To another world?"

Suddenly, what Mei had said earlier hit Kyle. She had kissed him for good luck on his journey. He had been so affected by being kissed on the cheek that he didn't think to ask what journey she was talking about.

"Yes."

"How? Where?"

"Where is difficult to pinpoint. How is even more inexplicable."

"Oh great. Wait, does this involve cutting out my beating heart and setting it on fire or something?" Kyle said a little alarmed.

He knew his Ah-gong was a little insane, but he didn't think he would actually bring him to any harm. Then again, crazy things were happening to him, like strange kung fu girls punching his eye out.

"You watch too many movies," Tai said, sighing.

"Yeah, and traveling to another world by unknown means is totally reality TV."

Tai gave him another disparaging look.

"No one ever told you did they? About me?"

"What about you?"

Tai glanced down at the ground for a moment, and then looked back up into Kyle's one good eye.

"The Chosen One is 'the chosen one' based on an auspicious date and time of birth."

"Yeah, yeah, I know that much. What about it?"

"I was born when you were born. Exact same date. Exact same time. Exact same place. You and I were both born here at this place, side by side."

It took a moment for the new information to sink in for Kyle. He stood there a little dumbfounded.

"Wait, what?"

Tai shifted her weight from one leg to the other. Kyle was still processing the information. He knew he had been born on this island and that he had immigrated with his parents to the United States when he was still just an infant, but he'd always thought he had been born at some local hospital…not in a vast temple on the top of a mountain. His grandfather had been nagging *him* about being the Chosen One for so long that he was also having a little difficulty understanding the meaning of Tai's existence.

"So that means…that means you're the Chosen One? You and I are the Chosen One? There are two Chosen Ones? Wait, what?"

Kyle felt the throbbing in his head regain momentum. Ah-gong never told him anything about this, and Kyle suspected there were a lot more surprises Ah-gong didn't bother to warn him about.

"Doesn't that defeat the purpose of being a Chosen *One* if there are two of us?" Kyle puzzled some more.

"Well, there's some controversy over which one of us is the *real*

Chosen One. As you probably figured out already, most people think it's you."

"Me? Why me?"

Kyle thought of how everyone had quieted down when they had seen him. He thought of Mei and her good luck kiss. He thought of the hot spring bath and flat screen TV in his nice room.

Tai folded her arms across her chest, her hands still in fists as she looked him up and down as she sized him up.

"Beats me."

"Ha ha. Very funny."

Kyle felt the dizziness coming back, and he swayed a little to the side feeling like he was about to fall over. Tai made no effort to help him.

"I need some ice," Kyle groaned.

Unmoved, Tai said dryly, "They'll have some at the banquet."

With that, she briskly turned and started walking away. Kyle stared after her with a look of disbelief spreading across his face. She was the rudest, most insensitive and coldhearted girl he had ever met.

On top of that, she seemed to have a personal vendetta against him. He thought she was being thoroughly unfair. It's not like he actively went around currying people's favor. He didn't want to be the Chosen One. He just wanted to live his normal American high school life.

He followed her down the hallway, hoping she wasn't ill-spirited enough to lead him astray on purpose. In his current state, he couldn't remember which way was which and had to rely on her to lead the way. When he had steady footing, he caught up to her and walked almost by her side.

"Hey, look, I don't care about being the Chosen One. This is all my grandpa's idea. I mean, you can be the Chosen One if you want. I don't want it."

"Wow, you're so generous," Tai said with a roll of her eyes.

"I didn't mean it that way. I'm just saying I'm not in on any of this. I don't want to be in on any of it. I mean do you *want* to be the Chosen One?"

Tai walked on in silence for a moment.

"Well, after our little match back there, I think I am the better choice."

"Okay then, it's settled. You're the Chosen One, and I'm just a regular high school junior studying for college entrance exams."

Kyle looked at her expectantly, hoping that she would be just thrilled to hear what he had just said. It was wishful thinking. Her severe expression showed no signs of waning.

"That's not a decision you can make."

Tai walked on ahead of him at a faster pace, and Kyle took the hint that she didn't want to talk about it anymore. In silence, they made their way to the main courtyard where the banquet was to be held.

When they arrived, they found themselves awash in the smells of a delicious meal and all around them people were settling in and beginning to taste their food with exclamations of how delightful it all tasted.

Lanterns glowing with different colors hung all around and across the large space giving it a festive ambiance. The clinking of chopsticks on plates and tea pots against cups was cheerfully cacophonous.

"Oh no! What happened to your eye?"

Mei's voice cut through the hum of conversation as she ran frantically towards Kyle with a look of concern in her luminous eyes. Her flattering red silk dress showed off the contours of her curvaceous figure, and her silken hair was tied up in a bun with a splash of curls hanging down that danced around and teased at her smooth, pale skin. Her lips were rosy red with lipstick, and her long eyelashes batted playfully with every blink. Kyle was blinking his one good eye nervously at the sight of her.

"Oh this?" he pointed to his hurt eye. "It's not a big deal. Tai here and I were just sparring…"

He watched as Mei threw a thoroughly disapproving look at Tai who stood a few steps to Kyle's left. He looked over at Tai to see what her reaction would be, and he wasn't too surprised to see that she wasn't at all fazed or apologetic.

Mei said something in another unknown language to a nearby girl serving some tea, and the girl quickly left and promptly returned with a plastic zip lock bag full of ice.

"Here, put this on your eye to ease the swelling," Mei said tenderly with concern.

"Thanks, but really, I'm fine. The ice helps, but it's really nothing…"

Kyle continued to downplay his knocked out eye as she proceeded to lead him to his seat with Tai following silently behind them. They walked by table after table full of people enjoying their feast. He noticed a few people give him meaningful and curious stares as he crossed the courtyard. There was a motley fashion about the night with some people in what looked like more traditional clothing while others were in gowns and still more were in casual wear. It was like everyone had come here from all different walks of life, from different countries and jobs and lifestyles.

Kyle noticed he was being led to the front of the event, the northernmost wall of the large open-air space, and his Ah-gong sat there fully decked out in golden mandarin collared, knot-buttoned down long sleeved robe that reached down to his ankles. Kyle realized he was not looking forward to his Ah-gong seeing his punched out eye.

"Tai! Kyle! I see the two of you have met! Sit down! Sit down!

The meal's just begun!" Ah-gong said full of good spirits as he motioned to their seats.

Kyle took his seat to his grandfather's right, surprised that Ah-gong hadn't made public comment on his injury. As soon as he sat down in the seat, the table in front of him was filled with delicious foods of all sorts. There was whole fried milk fish and fresh cold sashimi, garlic fried rice and palak paneer, roti canai and sticky rice mango, steak and pasta. There was no end to the staggering variety of food. Kyle felt his mouth water.

"Please, what would you like?" Mei asked but began to fill Kyle's plate without waiting for a reply. Tai sat to Ah-gong's left and was helping herself to the food with no one fawning over her. Kyle felt uncomfortable about that.

"It's okay, I can get it myself, thank you Mei," Kyle said quickly and reached for the serving utensils Mei had in her hand.

"No, no, please, it is my pleasure," Mei insisted with another sweet smile of her glossy red, mesmerizing lips.

Not knowing what to do, Kyle just let Mei serve him, expressing gratitude at every morsel of food that was placed on his plate. Then to his further discomfort, Mei picked up his chopsticks and proceeded to feed him.

"Here," she said.

"Um, I'm…it's okay…um…I'd feel more comfortable if I fed myself," Kyle stammered out. Although being spoon fed delicious food by a beautiful girl sounded like a great idea to Kyle, he got the sudden impression that Tai would disapprove and refused Mei's offer. As soon as he thought that, though, he wondered why he even cared whether Tai approved or disapproved of his actions. She just seemed to have a judgmental quality about her, the kind of person who often disproves of much of what others do.

"Oh, I see, very well," Mei said, her voice still charming as she handed over the chopsticks to him.

"I will be performing with the dance tonight. I hope you enjoy it," Mei said.

"Oh? You dance? That's…that's really great. Yeah, I'm looking forward to it, then. What kind of dance is it?"

"It's called the 'Assassin's Charm.' It's a dance that has been handed down for generations since The Crossover."

"The…The Crossover?" Kyle wondered out loud.

"Yes, the day when your ancestors came to our world from the other, from Tian," Mei explained.

Kyle couldn't help widen his eyes a bit skeptically and wondered if this dazzling maiden in front of him had all her wits about her. *Other world?* He had to remind himself that no matter how pretty and charming Mei was, he was in his grandfather's cult territory.

"Oh, you do not know? I see, well, I'm sure the Grandmaster has his reasons," Mei seemed to think out loud.

"What?"

"Nothing, nothing. I'm sure your grandfather will explain everything to you when he sees fit. You are very special Kyle Lin. That's all you need to know for now. How is your eye by the way?"

"Oh this?" Kyle lifted the ice pack from his eye a bit and then put it back, "It's fine. Just a little bruise. It happens when you spar and stuff." He stuffed some food into his mouth to keep it busy.

"Did she start the fight with you?" Mei pressed.

Kyle swallowed his food and said, "Huh? Oh, well, yeah, she challenged me, but I accepted, so, you know, we were just sparring."

Mei threw another disdainful look over at Tai, then turned her attention back to Kyle.

"You know, I don't believe in the whole soul mate idea. I think people should be able to choose who they spend the rest of their lives with, don't you?" Mei said with a few meaningful bats of her pretty lashes.

"Huh? What?" Kyle was not following the flow of the conversation at all. Why were they suddenly talking about soul mates?

"Soul mates. I don't think they exist. I think you just choose someone to love," Mei continued.

"Oh, uh, yeah, I guess so," Kyle said as he stuffed food into his mouth again.

"Hmm…I'm glad you agree," Mei said smiling, "I can't imagine how you must feel then with people saying that that disagreeable girl is your soul mate."

The food Kyle had just chewed up suddenly splattered back down on Kyle's plate and he sputtered in surprise.

"Oh dear, let me get you a new plate," Mei said and in the blink of an eye, she had that plate taken away and began filling a new plate for him.

"What do you mean my soul mate?" Kyle said.

"You do not know? Oh, well, it is not important, all that silliness. I must go prepare for the performance. You will watch me, won't you?"

Kyle nodded dumbly, still not sure what to do with himself. He watched as Mei walked away and then turned to his grandfather and hissed in his ear, "Ah-gong, what's going on here? What other world? What Crossover? What soul mate?"

Ah-gong gave an exaggeratedly furtive look around the courtyard, then hissed back, "A banquet, a parallel world to this one, when your ancestors six generations back came from that world to this world, and Tai."

Kyle stared at him with a strange expression on his face. His eyebrows were partly furrowed but his eyes were wide open, his mouth was slightly open, and he'd forgotten to keep breathing. It looked like he couldn't decide between being confused, furious, or flabbergasted so he was all three at the same time.

His grandpa, on the other hand, went back to enjoying his meal. The grandson looked down at his hands and slowly counted with his fingers the four questions he asked and carefully matched them up to the four answers his grandfather had given him. He made a mental note not to ask multiple questions at the same time in the future and counted through those four one more time to make sure he had got it all right. Tai was supposedly his…soul mate? His imagination went wild.

"AH-GONG! WHA—"

He was about to demand more details and follow that with a demand that he be allowed to go home, back to normal land, back to America, back to his comfortable, sunny suburban life. But his protests were stopped abruptly when Ah-gong held a firm finger up in front of him indicating for him to shut up.

"The dance is about to start. Don't be rude."

Kyle had to hold in his outburst as the courtyard broke into applause welcoming a group of about twenty young women who were now taking their places on a large and red raised platform stage in the center of the courtyard. Kyle noticed also that a group of musicians were at the foot of the stage, each holding instruments that he only vaguely recognized.

The girls were all decorated in flowing garments of different shades of pink that hung like liquid silk off of their youthful bodies. In their right hand they held a dark pink, thin sheer scarf, and the light pink sleeve of their left hand reach far past their fingertips. These soft and flowing cloth extensions of their arms gave them an ethereal look. Each girl had dazzling eyes and charming red-lipped smiles. Despite his indignity, Kyle couldn't help but be thoroughly entranced by the spectacle.

He nearly forgot all his worries when the melodious sounds of those unfamiliar instruments began to fill the courtyard with their delicate winds and strings and the performers began their dance. Their movements were elegantly smooth, and they floated across the stage as coy and alluring faeries. Their long sleeves and loose scarves whipped and sailed through the air as they danced.

It wasn't until a minute into the performance did Kyle notice Mei and that she was staring meaningfully at him. Then he realized the reason why he hadn't noticed her earlier was because all of the girls were staring meaningfully at him. As soon as he realized this fact, he felt that old wave of self-consciousness drowning him again. He wanted to crawl under the table but knew it would be rude to look away, so he tried to relax and enjoy the rest of the dance. He succeeded in keeping his eyes on all the performers that were batting their eyelashes at him at every tilt of their heads, but he didn't succeed in keeping his face from turning red.

When the dance finished, the audience burst into applause and cheers, and the dancers demurely bowed in thanks. Kyle was clapping, too, the embarrassment of having the beautiful performers stare at him had wiped his outrage from his mind, but some of it began to resurface as he noticed his grandpa stand up when the applause died down. Kyle decided that no matter what new surprise his Ah-gong had for him next, he was going home on the next flight back to the States.

"It's so wonderful for us all to unite tonight as a community, enjoying good food and beautiful art while we celebrate the coming of the long awaited Crossover to Tian."

There was widespread, enthusiastic applause in response to this.

"I must inform you of the wishes of my grandson, the seventh generation descendant of the original Crosser."

A hush fell over the crowd, and Kyle could feel his heart beating up into his throat. What was his grandfather going to say next?

"Kyle does not wish to Crossover."

The hush quickly became a burst into talk, gasps of surprise, and wide eyes. Kyle's heart felt like it was about to come out of his nose. He had no part in all of this, yet he apparently was the central piece of everything. More than ever he wished he was back home sitting in familiar classrooms and walking down the clean, neat and predictable suburban streets of his neighborhood. Ah-gong put up his hands indicating for everyone to calm down.

"I understand that we all feel strongly about this, but we must be prepared to accept what destiny may hand down to us. We cannot force someone to Crossover against his own will, but clearly, all is not lost, for as you all know, we have two candidates for the Crossover, and the other, Tai, is prepared to undergo Crossover tomorrow morning."

There was a lackluster applause at this. For a moment, Kyle forgot his own discomfort and remembered the girl who had so ruthlessly punched him in the eye less than an hour earlier. He craned his neck a bit to look over at Tai who was sitting on the other side of his grandfather. She stared out at the disapproving people, her face expressionless, calm and serious. Kyle detected the slightest hint of contempt in her eyes.

Ah-gong sat back down and leaned over to Kyle.

"Happy now? You're off the hook. After tomorrow's Crossover ceremony for Tai, you can go home and do whatever you'd like."

Kyle couldn't help but feel a little deflated. He had built up all this energy to fight Ah-gong for the right to go home, and now he was being told that he was getting exactly what he wanted. He knew he should be feeling relieved, but there was something anticlimactic about it all.

Chapter 6
The Crossover

Kyle shifted uncomfortably on the flat, gray pillow he sat on. He was sitting in a large hall that was dark on all sides except for a single beam of sunlight that came in through a circular oculus in the ceiling at the center of the room. All of the participants from the previous night's celebration were seated around him in a massive circular formation that began at the edge of the circle of sunlight on the hard stone floor, and people in black robes fanned out across the dark floor. He was next to his Ah-gong and, with about ten other people, they made up the first inner circle. Behind them was another row and then another. It went on to the walls of the room, but since the people farthest from the center were in the dark, it felt like the circles of seated people went on forever and ever into a black abyss.

The stone floor upon which the sunlight shone was unoccupied save for Tai, the Chosen One, who sat as the only one illuminated at the center of the circle of light. She wore robes of white that glowed with the reflected rays of the sun.

They had been sitting like this for about two hours already. Early in the morning, Ah-gong had woken Kyle up and brought him to the ceremony. Kyle had obliged since he couldn't think of a reason to say no. After the ceremony, he would be free to go home if he wanted. There was nothing to it.

When they had all assembled in this large hall, he was handed a simple, long black robe that looked like a bathrobe but made of tougher material. It felt starched and stiff as Kyle slipped his arms into its sleeves and covered over his regular clothes with its black folds. Unlike Tai and her luminous white robes, everyone else in the hall wore the same black robe as Kyle over their clothes.

Ah-gong had given the simple direction, "Let us begin." Everyone took their place as if they had rehearsed this ceremony a dozen times over, and Kyle had simply followed his grandfather until he was told where to sit. Then the Crossover ceremony began, and it was, as much as Kyle could figure out, a sort of extensive meditation. Everyone had taken a seat with legs crossed and then closed their eyes.

Now that they were about to hit the two hour mark, Kyle, who had opened his eyes from time to time to look around him, was growing very weary of just sitting. He had to admit, he was amazed at everyone's discipline in keeping this up for so long, but he didn't know how long he could go on without knowing how long it would keep going.

He reached a hand out and lightly tapped his grandfather's shoulder. It was completely silent in the large hall, and as usual Kyle didn't want to make a spectacle of himself. He hoped his grandfather wouldn't make a big fuss.

Ah-gong opened his eyes and turned to his grandson who gave him a questioning look. Then he reached over unexpectedly and put his hand on Kyle's shoulder with a sad smile on his face. In his eyes was a faraway look that was focused clearly on his grandson, and Kyle was immediately filled with nostalgia. He remembered only one other time his grandfather had given him this look. Three years earlier, Kyle had been sitting in a hospital waiting room with his mother and father. Ah-gong had come out to them with a weary look on his face. Kyle's mother and father had broken into tears of grief, and Kyle had stared up at his grandfather in shock at the news of his grandmother's death.

Kyle didn't understand why Ah-gong would give him this look now, but he nodded in response to his grandfather's solemn expression and settled himself back into the meditation. Giving one last glance to the very still Tai sitting with full and serene concentration at the middle of the sunlit circle, he closed his eyes again and let the darkness envelope him. He tried to empty his mind of thoughts, but what arose in his mind repeatedly were memories of his grandmother. Images of her smiles, her laughing and loving eyes, her patient and instructive voice as she taught him calligraphy played in his thoughts, and a small, peaceful smile spread across his face.

The memories brought him back to the happy and simpler moments of his childhood when the sun seemed it would shine forever and the soft, gentle summer winds flowed eternally. In fact, it felt like a soft, cool breeze was brushing past his cheeks as he sat there on the meditation pillow. Then Kyle noticed warmth on his face, as if he were sitting in direct sunlight. At first he brushed off these sensations as side effects of meditation or of just sitting there for too long. When sunlight seemed to be coming through his closed eyelids as blurry red blotches, he decided to open his eyes and check out what was going on.

At first he blinked in the bright sunlight, a bit blinded. He guessed that the unseen windows in the dark hall must have somehow been silently opened. As his vision cleared, though, he realized that he was no longer in the hall, or in any hall for that matter. He sat at the top of a grassy hill. The sky above his head was perfectly blue with a gorgeously shining sun, and the tall green grass under and around him seemed to go on and on. He saw Tai sitting in front of him as she had been in the hallway just moments earlier, only now there was some rather long bunches of green grass that obstructed his full view of her.

Tai was looking back at him with a scowl on her face. Her stare seemed to press a silent demand at him asking "What are *you* doing here?"

Kyle couldn't help but feel panic mounting in his chest, and it heaved a bit, threatening hyperventilation as if he were afraid he would suddenly run out of air to breath. Moments ago he had been in the large, dark hall full of people, and in what seemed like only seconds, he had somehow transported to his current location, a place that felt far, far, far removed from where he had been. He stared back at Tai with wide eyes and mouth agape and could only watch in shocked silence as she sighed discontentedly, got up and surveyed the landscape.

"Where are we?" Kyle finally managed to croak out as if he hadn't used his voice in centuries.

Tai shot him another look of disdain.

"We are probably in the parallel world. The world your ancestors came from. Tian."

"In the…what?"

Tai shrugged her shoulders in a matter-of-fact way, as if instant transport to another world was no big deal.

Now Kyle really felt suffocated with panic.

"Are we even on *Earth* anymore?!"

Tai shrugged her shoulders again. "Maybe. It's hard to say."

"Come on Tai! Stop messing with me! Where the heck are we? This is a really bad joke!"

Tai now heaved a sigh of deep irritation.

"Look, no joke. I'm not messing with you, and I've answered your questions to the best of my knowledge."

Kyle stood up. He still wore the black robe that covered over his entire body, and Tai contrasted with him, wrapped in her white robes. They looked like young scholars from opposing schools.

As he looked more carefully, he saw land forms in the distance beyond the hills upon hills of green grass. As his mind attempted to comprehend his present situation, events and words from the previous evening emerged in his consciousness.

"Did I…did we…Crossover?"

"Looks like it," Tai said as she turned away from him and rolled her eyes.

A mountain range in the distance caught her attention. She decided to check it out and set out for them without a word to Kyle.

"Where are you going?" Kyle said, unable to hide the cracking panic in his voice. He sounded not unlike a puppy about to be left to sleep alone in the dark for the first time.

"I'm going to investigate those mountains over there," Tai said without turning back to face him, her voice faded in the open air. She advanced towards the range with sure footing through the tall green grass.

Kyle took another horrified look around at his beautiful surroundings before running off after Tai in silence. In this vast, unknown world he had been thrown in, the ill-tempered and violent girl who had punched his eye the night before was the only familiar element, and he couldn't help but feel the need to cling to her presence. He stumbled after her.

"Why are you going towards those mountains?"

"To investigate."

"Yeah, but why those mountains?"

"I don't know. I just thought I'd start there and move on to something else if there's nothing there."

"Are we looking for something?"

Tai rolled her eyes again. She didn't like how he was using "we" while she was explicitly and purposefully using "I" in her speech.

"I don't know what to expect. I only know that I'm here to stop a great danger, and I'll search every inch of this land until I find whatever it is I'm supposed to stop."

They went along in silence for a while through the pleasant weather with only the sound of the crisp and fresh grass underneath their feet to fill the quiet space between them. It was a long ways from where they had been to the mountains in the distance.

By the time they had reached the foot of the mountains, it looked as if it were late in the afternoon in this foreign land. Sun, grass, blue sky, and cool breezes…Kyle wondered how a land that wasn't Earth could have so much in common with it. He became frightfully aware of the air he was breathing and guessed there must be oxygen in it if he was able to breathe it so normally.

The shadows of mountains were growing long and the sunlight was slowly warming down to an orange glow as the atmosphere filtered through its wavelengths. Tai was walking briskly towards what looked like a vertical crack in a steep drop of the mountain range, as if the solid rock edifices had been split in some tectonic movements long since passed. Trailing behind her, Kyle wondered at her still energetic movements after a long day of all walking and no rest. He was hungry, tired, and deathly thirsty, but he quickened his pace as she disappeared into the crack in the mountainside.

When he entered into the opening, he looked up to see that the crack partly opened straight up to the sky letting what was left of the daylight stream into the darkness between the stone walls jutting up on either side of him. Ahead of him, though, was a massive dark cavern that dug deep into the mountain. A few stray strands of light bounced here and there to reveal sharp stalactites and stalagmites wet with unseen mountain streams that Kyle could hear whispering in the black unknown.

Tai was standing on the last patch of grass that was left before the ground transitioned into the moist, gray cave floor. Kyle was just a few steps behind her when he noticed something in the darkness. There were two gleaming points of light in the darkness, too well spaced, it seemed, to be random reflections of light.

Kyle stood mesmerized by the pair of lights and distinctly felt that they were staring right back at him. Then they moved forward, shifting in unison as they advanced, until features began to form around them. The eyes were framed by a roughly triangular face with the sharp edge jutting forwards menacingly towards him and Tai. Multiple pairs of horns jutted out bilaterally on either side of the face, and the texture of the face was almost identical to that of the black cave walls, so much so that Kyle was confused at first into thinking that he was only imagining this advancing draconian face, confused that is until the entirety of the dragon, with its massive black wings folded on either side, emerged from the darkness and was clearly illuminated by the waning sunlight. The beast was the length of two school buses, and with its head held up, it was three stories high.

A scream was caught in Kyle's throat, and he made a pathetic choking sound as he turned and high-tailed it out of the mountain crevice. Quickly assessing that he would be an easy meal running across the open grass hills, he immediately turned the corner and started running alongside the foot of the sheer mountain cliffs looking for some place to hide. He ran for a bit until it occurred to him to look behind him to see if Tai was close at his heels. When he saw that she was not, another sort of panic washed over him. He realized he had just run off without her.

Chapter 7
The Forest of Ghosts

Kyle jumped behind a nearby rock roughly twice his size in length and width before he crept carefully back towards the crevice opening, moving from behind one rock to another. When he reached the opening, he carefully and very slowly peered into it, expecting at any moment to have large black dragon claws make a swipe at his head. What he saw at first made him think that Tai must be loonier than he had first thought.

Tai was walking towards the monster with her arms outstretched towards it like a child reaching for a stuffed animal. The creature could probably gobble her up whole or snap her in half with its granite-like jaws. It sported five talons the length of a grown man on each claw, and its invincible looking scales looked like they could slice human flesh quite easily if touched in any way. And there Tai was, reaching out to it as if it were a harmless little bunny.

To Kyle's surprise, the monster lowered its head delicately to her, and she touched its deadly jaws under the fearsome horns framing its face. Kyle couldn't see her face, but he could tell from her movements that she was in awe. And he couldn't believe the dragon was acting like a gentle old dog.

The creature suddenly opened its mouth, and Kyle felt panic shoot through him again as he thought it had decided that she would make a nice evening snack, but instead it spoke with the tone and voice of a kind yet strong old woman.

"Welcome, Chosen One."

The dragon looked down at her gently and then lifted its head and looked straight at Kyle. Kyle's eyes promptly disappeared behind the rock wall. Still in full shock that there was a real live dragon just a few

yards away from him, he had no time to be ashamed of his cowardly behavior.

"Welcome, Chosen One, to Tian," the dragon said again and added, "Do not be frightened. I will not harm you. My name is 飛龍 (Fei Long). I guard these mountains and the realm around it."

Kyle's eyes peaked back around from behind the rock and met Fei Long's eyes with continued trepidation. He then noticed that Tai was glaring at him and suddenly felt that she was more threatening than the large, docile dragon next to her. Her angry eyes commanded him to come forward and address the dragon, and though he was still struggling to calm the terror of being face to face with a living and breathing dragon, he felt guilty enough about running off without her earlier that he complied with her silent request.

"Um…I'm Kyle…and…we just got here…" Kyle stammered out as he slowly and awkwardly made his way to Tai's side.

"Yes. I know you are from another world, from the Earth. I am honored to be the first to welcome the Chosen One here." The dragon looked at them both, and she seemed to be calling both of them the Chosen One.

Kyle couldn't help but glance at Tai as Fei Long mentioned the whole Chosen One deal again. He couldn't shake the grammatical weirdness of the dragon speaking in a singular sense when there were two of them. Tai didn't look happy at all.

"Come. This place is not accommodated to your needs. I will take you to the Forest of Ghosts."

Kyle did not like the sound of going to a forest full of ghosts, but he only watched silently as the dragon bowed her head. Then she reached out her claw and wrapped her five talons around Tai who had raised her arms to allow herself to be picked up. Before he knew it, Fei Long reached her other claw out at Kyle, and he hurriedly copied Tai and lifted his arms just before the claw closed in around him. He couldn't help but brace himself to be crushed in Fei Long's strong grip, but her deadly claws were unexpectedly gentle.

Without giving Kyle a chance to catch his breath, the dragon spread its massive black wings, leapt up off the ground, and began to rise up through the opening in the mountainside to the evening sky above them. The air twirled and rushed passed Kyle and Tai, ruffling their clothes and tossing up loose hair. Kyle tried not to hyperventilate as they rose higher and higher and began to move forward, away from the mountain home of Fei Long.

When they were going at a steady speed flying high above this unknown world, Kyle was able to regain a certain amount of internal composure, and he realized the experience wasn't half bad. There was a peaceful silence all around him save for the calming sound of the wind that flowed by and the gliding of the wings over the currents of air. He looked below him and saw that they were quickly nearing the edge of the grassy plain that he and Tai had appeared in that morning, and the black mountain range they had walked towards all day was growing small behind them. Past the fields of tall green grass, the plant life transitioned to a shoreline which introduced a massive ocean beyond. They seemed to be traveling west as they appeared to be chasing after the sun that was setting in the ocean.

Kyle tried not to let the looming ocean bring him to panic again and took deep breaths. As his breathing exercise succeeded in keeping him calm, Kyle noticed Tai hanging quite comfortably in the dragon's claw adjacent to his own. She had her arms crossed and resting on the dragon claw as if she were looking off a high balcony instead of flying in the clutches of a mystical monster with her feet dangling above clouds. He realized that his own hands and arms were holding the dragon claw as if he would fall if he didn't do so. His knuckles were

turning white. He loosened his grip a bit.

Tai was looking out at the scenery that passed below them, and they were fully over the ocean now. Suddenly a tear escaped the corner of her eye that was immediately blown off by the wind. It happened so quickly that Kyle couldn't help but wonder if he had imagined it. Then he noticed that there was a hint of emotion in her otherwise stoic face. What emotion it was was hard to say, but he was pretty sure he was seeing something. She looked somehow at peace.

They soon passed over the great ocean and came upon another shore at the other side which yielded to another spread of grassland, and that transitioned to another vast mountain range. The setting sun now only half peeked over the horizon and began slowly to hang to their left as they turned north. Rivers streamed through the land as large bodies of inland water came and went under them like inconsequential puddles of rain water.

As the last of the sun's red glow ebbed away, they watched as the stars began to appear with a few shy twinkles. Soon the night was awash in the glimmering splendor of millions of stars, and the full moon glowed like an incandescent pendant hung in the vast darkness. If Kyle didn't know better, he would have thought he was still on Earth. Being carried across the skies by a dragon told him otherwise.

What came next was the most breathtaking sight so far on their voyage. Sparkling as if its leaves were made of gems instead of greenery, a vast oceanic forest suddenly leaped at them over the horizon. The trees spread over successions of hills and flatlands. The foliage fluttered in the wind, the whole mass of leaves undulating much the way ripples would run through water.

Fei Long began her descent as they made their way to what looked like the deepest, darkest center of the vast forest.

To Kyle, one part of the forest looked like any other part of the forest, so he could imagine how easy it would be to get lost in it. Fei Long, however, seemed to know exactly where she was going.

The dragon folded her wings in. They dipped in through the tree tops, and they disappeared into the forest as the trees swung back and covered over their point of entry as if it had never happened. Kyle felt the light brushing of leaves and twigs against his shoes, clothes, hands and face. At first he could see nothing but the leaves and branches all around them. When that cleared up, he realized that they were lowering to a sizable clearing on the forest floor, just large enough for Fei Long to comfortably land with some breathing space.

She alighted on the ground, some dead leaves and dust swirling up as her wings spread to ease into the landing. Gently she placed Tai and Kyle on the ground. Tai turned around, placed her fisted right hand cupped in her left palm in front of her chest, and bowed.

"Thank you Fei Long. You've honored us with your help."

Kyle thought it impolite not to do the same and made the same gesture and bow but decided to let Tai do all the talking. There was a muted silence in the forest. The trees around them were massive beings, thick and full of time. The leaves above almost blocked the night sky out completely.

"The honor is all mine," Fei Long said. "Your hosts will show you the way from here on."

"You're leaving?" Tai asked, unable to hide the disappointment in her voice.

"Yes, little one. All will be explained to you in the Ghost Village here in their forest. May we meet again. Good winds on your journey, Chosen One," she said as she looked at the two of them. Then Fei Long, the black dragon of the sky, spread her wings again and rose steadily up out of the clearing, burst through the leafy canopy above, and was gone.

All fell silent again in the dark forest. Kyle looked around him.

There were dark shadows everywhere and very little light coming from the streams of moonlight that made it through the thick overhang. He wasn't at all thrilled to be meeting the inhabitants of a Ghost Village and felt a chill run up his spine just thinking about it. He imagined a dead, old village of some sort with white, transparent apparitions floating aimlessly around in a melancholy procession of hopelessness. With this in mind, Kyle thought maybe they had been better off with the dragon.

"What do we do now?" Kyle asked Tai.

"Follow our hosts to their village."

Kyle put his hands on his waist thoughtfully and turned to look around at their surroundings. The forest continued to be dark, quiet, and empty.

"I wonder when they'll get here."

"They're already here."

Kyle shot Tai a surprised look.

"Already here? Where?" He looked frantically into the darkness, half expecting to see a sea of ghostly white faces staring back at him.

"Didn't you know?" Tai said dryly. She crossed her arms and looked around nonchalantly at the shadows around them. "We're surrounded."

Chapter 8

The Lin Gui Village

"Surrounded?" Kyle's voice cracked.

His eyes frantically searched the darkness but he couldn't see anything. To his terror, he heard scratching sounds against wood and saw large, dark oval-shelled creatures start to crawl down the sides of the massive tree trunks around them. They looked like huge beetles the size of large dogs scampering down the trees. The sight of them made Kyle sick to his stomach, but he saw that Tai was largely unaffected by the onslaught of giant bugs, and he unsuccessfully tried to take some comfort in her calm.

When the creatures reached the bottom of the tree trunks, they suddenly stopped, and their stillness now made them look like large mushrooms growing out from the foot of the trees. Kyle thought maybe they were pausing to assess the situation before they picked the flesh clean off of his bones. His hands turned to fists. Tai continued to stand at ease with her arms folded loosely across her chest.

The large beetle-like beings resumed their crawl, coming down over the roots of the old trees that protruded from the ground and onto the grass of the small clearing on the forest floor where Kyle and Tai stood. They came from all sides, and there were at least a hundred of them.

Kyle took a fighting stance, fists and feet ready to start knocking these large insects away since they showed no signs of stopping, but the whole swarm of them stopped abruptly about a yard away from Kyle and Tai, fully surrounding them in a ring of their shelled bodies.

Then they spoke.

"Welcome Chosen One!" It was a chorus of children's voices.

Kyle found this very creepy. Then to his great surprise, the creatures stood up to reveal that they were in fact human children, ranging in age from about seven to eleven, all wearing black shells on their backs that had served as their disguise. Their hands, elbows, knees, and feet were fitted with what looked like sturdy iron claws that must have been the source of the scratching sound he had heard when they came down the tree trunks.

The tallest and eldest looking one of them stepped forward.

"I am Bao. We are Lin Gui. Welcome to the Forest of Ghosts. We will be your guide to the Ghost Village."

The small boy spoke and stood with an air of maturity far beyond his years. He had a bright twinkle in his brown eyes and a wide smile to match.

"I am Tai."

"Uh, I'm Kyle…"

"Come on!" Bao suddenly yelled with a gesture of his hand for them to follow him. He broke out into a run, and the rest of the children burst after him. Tai followed suit, and Kyle was at her heels soon after. Some of the children at the front of the pack jumped up quite high into the air and rolled up with their shells into balls like large roly-poly pill bugs. With their built up momentum, they would roll for a while across the forest floor, stand up, run, jump and roll again. Some of the children climbed up the trees and started jumping from trunk to trunk, branch to branch. They seemed barely human or super human—Kyle couldn't decide which.

After a while of travel, it didn't seem like they were getting anywhere. The forest continued on and on, one sequence of trees looking like all others. It would be more than easy to get lost forever in this forest, perishing on a journey in circles with no direction, but the children seemed to know clearly where they were going, and they sprinted on into the unending darkness.

Suddenly, Kyle noticed that they all started to head towards one patch of darkness that didn't seem to be particularly different from the thousands of other patches of darkness around them. Yet child after child with shelled back jumped towards it and disappeared into its untouched abyss. Tai jumped in, and then, not knowing what else to do, Kyle jumped in after her. He immediately regretted the hasty act. Not only was he now surrounded by complete and utter darkness, he was plummeting uncontrollably down what felt like a very long water slide of some sort, minus the water. All he could hear was the echoing wooshing sound as he slid down to who knew where.

He burst through some sort of foliage into a bright place that blinded him at first. He landed rather roughly on a patch of exposed soil. Before his eyes adjusted, he was pulled to his feet and out of the way just as he felt someone else land in the spot where he had just fallen. When he could see, he found Tai's hand firmly grasping the cloth that covered his chest. Twisting quickly to look behind him, he saw child after child burst through a dark patch of leaves and vines, land expertly with feet first on some soft earthy ground, and scamper away with a bright smile full of joy.

"Thanks," he said to Tai, knowing that he would have gotten a face full of dirt-covered kids feet if she hadn't pulled him out of the way.

With a mild look of disapproval on her face that said much about what she thought of having to help him, she let go of his clothes and, without a word, turned and followed the stream of children that were scampering down a dirt path. Kyle stared after her indignantly. He felt her animosity toward him was totally unwarranted. Whatever she was angry at, it wasn't his fault, he was sure of it. He'd never even met her before the previous night. Kyle looked away from Tai's leaving figure and was distracted from his irritation with her when he feasted his eyes

for the first time on the Ghost Village.

It was far from what he had imagined. The place was burning with light and life amid the earthy colors of the forest. From every direction there seemed to be the dancing glow of firelight with reds, oranges, and yellows blending into each other like a perpetual flow of dawn that played upon the muted browns and greens. The smells of a grand feast mingled with the fresh forest night air, and above them the canopy was thicker than ever, probably keeping any of the warm light from escaping or allowing any of the pale star light above to enter. The building structures were made of wood, some built in the trees and some on the ground, and wooden walkways and bridges connected it all in a complicated network. Carvings, paintings, embroidered cloth, and even fresh flowers adorned every windowsill, doorway, and railing.

People were bustling about carrying this here and that there, pouring this and filling that. Some were swinging from the trees on ropes or climbing across nets connecting one tree loft structure to another. Through the center of the Ghost Village ran a mid-sized river that sparkled and reflected the images of the lively place on its mercurial surface.

"My father and mother want to see you first. This way!" Bao said with his youthful and cheerful voice. He led them down past busy people, steaming pots, and whistling tea kettles to the river bank. Across it were some floating wooden boards the size of skateboards fashioned like large leaves. They seemed to be anchored to their spots in the river, and they bobbed as the water flowed under them. Bao leapt onto them nimbly, hopping from one to the other, one foot at a time, and began his crossing of the river over this most unstable of paths. Tai followed after him, impressing even Kyle with her ability to balance as she crossed the bridge of drifting wooden leaves. As her foot landed on one after another, the floating wood sunk slightly into the water and then wobbled around just a bit after she'd launched to the next step. It seemed the trick was not to spend too much time on any one leaf and to keep a quick pace all the way through.

Kyle heaved an exasperated sigh as he stared at the task before him with wide and incredulous eyes. *Why me?* was his passing thought. He scooted to the edge of the river bank, his toes just centimeters away from the rushing river water as the first wooden leaf bobbed and dared him to take his first step. Tai and Bao had reached the river bank on the other side and turned to face him expectantly. He waved uneasily to them with a nervous laugh and smile.

The river was about six freeway lanes wide, and he counted out that there were forty wooden leaves. Bracing himself and taking a few deep breaths, he leapt off the solid earth. His right foot landed on the first leaf, and he was able to push off of it quite stably onto the next leaf. However, his step on the second leaf was not as well angled as the first, and that wooden leaf slipped a good six inches to the left. This led into an even more poorly angled third step, and although Kyle made a heroic attempt to try and push off to his fourth step, the third leaf slipped completely out from under him, and he plunged gloriously into the ice cold water.

The next few moments, Kyle was helplessly tossed about the river, and though he knew the basics of swimming and keeping afloat, he was not at all good enough at swimming to deal with the strong river currents. He pushed his face above water only enough to gulp some air before being pulled under again. When he came back up for air, a wave splashed right into his face, just when he was about the breath some more air, and he choked on the water that partially invaded his trachea. He was pulled under again by a twirling current and lost all sense of which direction gravity might be pulling him; he couldn't even figure out in which direction he should swim to get to air. He fought to keep from breathing in the water as his lungs fought to inhale. He felt sure he was a goner until he felt something take a firm grasp of the back of his collar at the nape of his neck and pull him in what he figured must be the direction "up". His head broke through the surface, and he gasped loudly as he inhaled the precious air now within his reach. He was firmly held at the back of the neck with his face directed upwards as he was pulled across the surface of the river. While coughing out water, he tried his best to command his hands and legs to push through the water in a feeble attempt to help his rescuer along with the task of saving him. All he could see was the foliage of the trees that hung thickly over the river.

Finally, he felt himself dragged onto solid, dry earth, and as he coughed some more, he found himself looking up into the faces of Bao, a man, and a woman. The two adults were unremarkable in appearance, and they wore plain brown long-sleeved shirts and pants that made them look like simple village peasants. He tried to stave off the embarrassment that welled up inside him.

"Are you okay?" Bao asked, still as friendly as ever.

"Yeah, I'm fine, thanks."

"My name is Ting, and this is my soul mate, Xiang. We are Bao's parents and leaders of the Ghost Village and its inhabitants," the woman with dark hair and eyes said with a gentle smile.

"We apologize for the difficult river crossing. We incorporate such little challenges into our daily lives as part of our training. Your attempt was most courageous," Xiang said with no mockery in his dark eyes that were framed by black hair. He held a hand out to Kyle, and when Kyle took it, he felt the warmth and strength of Xiang's firm grip as he was pulled up.

"Come, you should warm up and dry off with some tea and blankets," Ting added.

Kyle finally realized that Tai stood next to him, and her white robes and clothes underneath were as soaked and dripping wet as his. She had been the one who had jumped in after him and pulled him to safety. The family turned and led them up a small worn path in the lush grass that stretched to a net of ropes that hung from a good-sized wooden building constructed in a tree above. Kyle watched as Tai followed them, and he reached a hand out and grabbed her shoulder to stop her. He felt it would be rude to delay his thanks for her saving him until later and took this transitory moment to do so. She turned to look at him over her shoulder.

"Hey, thanks for saving me," he said sincerely. He took his hand off her shoulder, and she sighed and seemed to stare at him for a small pensive moment before she slightly shook her head as she turned and followed after Bao and the village leaders.

As Kyle followed after, he looked down at his black robes and felt the uncomfortable squishiness of his wet clothes against his skin. He came to the realization that whatever issues Tai had with him from before they met, there was one thing clear here and now—he was a burden to her. He shook his head at himself, wondering if this whole journey with her to where ever they were going was going to be filled with scenarios of her saving him from his own incompetence over and over again. When they reached the netted ropes, Kyle climbed up after the others, making a face at the soggy clothes that restricted his movements. He immediately felt better when he reached the top and pulled himself into the warm room.

"Here are some clothes for you to change into. You can take turns using that room to change. Once you're comfortable, I'll serve the tea," Xiang said.

"You first," Kyle said to Tai. He felt that since she was soaked on his account, the least he could do was to let her get out of her discomfort

first. Tai looked at him, blinked and looked away, and then went in with her new clothes held carefully away from her wet ones. Kyle took the chance to look around the room. It was about as big as his living room at home but lit by oil lamps and candlelight. There was what looked like a low coffee table near the back of the room that was long and wide enough for about six people, and indeed there were six pillows lined around it for seating. The wooden walls around him were covered in hanging scrolls of calligraphy. Kyle admired them. He knew his Ah-gong would have enjoyed having an extended conversation with the authors of these pieces. They were exquisite.

Thinking of his grandfather, Kyle thought of his home, the rolling green hills of suburbia, the solid red-bricked walls of his high school, and the bright clearness of the Southern California sky. A pang of homesickness hit him.

"Not that I don't think your village here isn't amazing, but do you know how I can get home?" he finally asked hopefully.

Ting smiled again and nodded, "Forward is the only way home."

Kyle looked at her with confused eyes. "I see…" he said, though he really didn't.

"Don't worry. You will."

Chapter 9

The Legend of Phoenix Mountain

"Let us begin with the Legend of Phoenix Mountain," Ting said as all settled down around the table.

"The Legend of Phoenix Mountain?" Kyle asked. He looked at Tai to see if she knew what they were talking about, but she surprised him by shrugging her shoulders.

"Yes, we believe it is the reason why you are here," Xiang responded.

Bao set the small, brown tea cups on a raised wooden tray with spaces between the wooden panels that lined it. He prepared and served the tea. There was also a plate of round, brown cookies that Bao placed within easy reach of all present at the table.

The new, dry clothes that Tai and Kyle wore were simple, earthy brown long sleeved shirts and matching pants. They looked just like the other villagers now.

"We shall start at the beginning of the story," Xiang followed his soul mate's beginning. "It is said that the goddess Nu Wa loved the beauty of this world but became lonely in her enjoyment of its wonders. With enchanted hands, she molded a young girl in her own image out of clay, and the enchantment gave that young girl life. The girl and her mother, the goddess, enjoyed the world together, dancing in the beautiful scenery always to the natural musical sounds around them. The girl was often mischievous, but they passed their days in happiness. One day, when the girl was playing, she followed a small white rabbit into the Phoenix Mountain and was never found by Nu Wa again. The goddess despaired, searching the entirety of the world for her child, but to no avail. Finally, she decided to create the whole of humankind in this world in the same manner, bringing to life the clay sculptures she fashioned with her enchanted hands. Those were the first human inhabitants of Tian, including the Lin Gui. We are the warriors of this world."

Ting continued the tale.

"When Tian was in peril because of the battles of gods, Nu Wa painstakingly mended the broken sky using a five colored stone that she melted into an opalescent liquid. The task was so straining that it took her life. Humanity was grateful to the kind and compassionate goddess for her great sacrifice and laid her remains to rest on Phoenix Mountain where she had last seen her first beloved child. Soon after, tales of a growing disturbance in those mountains slowly began to spread. At first they were just dismissible reports of tricks and frights that travelers and inhabitants near the mountains shared over tea at inns. Over the centuries, though, those small tricks grew slowly but surely to terrifying tales of demons, ghosts, and malevolent spirits, and finally, disappearances and deaths began to alarm all. We, the Lin Gui, have sent investigative teams to determine the source of these disturbing tidings over the last few generations."

"And we have found," Xiang flawlessly picked up where Ting stopped, "that the perpetrator of these cruelties is none other than the long lost first daughter of the goddess. Her cruelties are no longer confined to the locale of Phoenix Mountain. She has recently been mounting erratic attacks on inhabitants all over. Many other Lin Gui villages in other parts of Tian have been attacked. As the most deeply hidden village, we have been taking in refugees from many of them."

"And that," Ting looked at Kyle and Tai meaningfully, "is why we believe that you, the Chosen One, are here, come to us from another world. We have tried to stop the First Child demon, but we are no match for her."

Kyle looked back into her kind yet sad eyes as she looked upon him with an untold heavy burden on her shoulders.

"Then it is my duty to stop this demon," Tai said with sureness in her voice and a firmly held head.

"It was foretold that the Chosen One would arrive from another world, and that it would be the duty of the Chosen One to face the First Child," Xiang said, looking from Kyle to Tai and back to Kyle again. Kyle felt very confused by this acknowledgement, and in his confusion, he forgot his self-consciousness and asked a question.

"Wait, Tai is the Chosen One, right? What does this have to do with me? Why am I here?"

"You are also the Chosen One," Ting said with a glimmer of laughter in her eyes. Kyle was further perplexed by her amusement. He looked over at Tai, and she was visibly displeased but said nothing in response. Kyle turned back to Xiang and Ting.

"Doesn't that contradict the idea of a Chosen *One*? Wouldn't that make us the Chosen Two or something?"

Bao picked up one of the round, brown cookies with his small hands and held it up for all to see. Kyle had to admire the almost perfect circularity of the cookie despite its rough edges. The Lin Gui boy then placed the fingers of both of his hands on the cookie and broke it in half straight down the middle.

He held up one half, "This is one cookie," and then he held up the other, "and this is one cookie."

Then he placed the two halves together to make the cookie whole again.

"And this is also one cookie."

The young boy smiled brightly and then took a bite out of the two halves held together.

Kyle threw Tai a glance, and though she now appeared

expressionless, he could still somehow sense she was not happy with the news that the both of them were somehow chosen, somehow two halves of the same cookie, according to Bao's little analogy.

"Wait, who 'foretold' all of this?" Kyle couldn't help asking.

"A great elder who consulted the spirit of the goddess. He has long since passed from this world. He used to say that the swirling currents of the heavens all meet at a key time and place producing an equal reaction to every action. For the First Child's existence and actions, there will be a reaction, and that reaction is you," Ting said, again looking at both of them despite her use of a singular pronoun.

"What must we do?" It was Tai who spoke this time which surprised Kyle. It was the first time he heard her include him with herself in her speech, using 'we' instead of just 'I'. He looked over at her and saw a flash of determination in her eyes.

"We will begin training first thing tomorrow morning. But tonight, we feast, celebrate your coming and all of our lives," Xiang said with a warm smile.

"Do you know the Assassin's Charm?" Ting asked Tai. Kyle recognized it as the name of the dance that Mei had performed the night before back on Earth, where ever that was. Tai nodded in response.

"Excellent, will you join us for our performance then?"

"Yes, of course," Tai said politely.

Ting held up a friendly hand to Tai, and with a little hesitation, Tai took her hand and was pulled effortlessly to her feet.

"We'll be off to prepare for the dance then," Ting said cheerfully. Bao jumped up and gave his mother a desperate hug, as if he couldn't bear her leaving his side even for a moment. Despite being quite mature for his age, he was still just a little boy. Ting smiled gently down at him.

"I'll clean up here," Bao offered, returning his mother's loving look.

"Come, Kyle, you can help us set up," Xiang directed.

The next hour or so passed busily as Kyle helped with preparations for the feast. Kyle was instructed by Bao and Xiang to carry a large, rolled up grass mat to the river bank and unfurl it out there. All around him, other Lin Gui families were doing the same. Bao came bounding out with baskets of fruits and breads, hot buns filled with cooked morsels, pots of aromatic soups, and plenty of freshly brewed tea for everyone. Kyle's stomach growled involuntarily again as he realized he had not eaten anything since the morning breakfast he had had with his grandfather before his arrival here on this strange new world. Bao smiled and tossed him a mantao, a large and round, white and fluffy, lightly sweet tasting bread. It felt warm and soft in his hand like a soft plush pillow fresh out of the dryer.

"Thanks!" Kyle said gratefully as Bao smiled in return, watching happily as Kyle sunk his teeth into the bread. It was the softest, most delectable mantao Kyle had ever tasted, and he soon devoured the whole of it.

"That was delicious!" he couldn't help exclaiming. He turned to look hungrily at the rest of the food which looked just as delicious as the mantao he had just inhaled.

"Come help me bring more stuff and I'll toss you another one," Bao said with laughter in his voice. Kyle chuckled as he ran after the lively young boy.

When they were all settled down, Kyle was ready to dig in when Ting joined their group.

"Where's Tai?" Kyle asked.

"Oh, she'll be part of the performance," Ting replied with a bit of mischief in her smile.

He was then handed a completely white, fold-up fan by Xiang who settled down next to him on the mat. Father, mother and son began fanning themselves with their own white fans in an expectant way, and Kyle pulled open his white fan and began fanning himself, too, although he didn't feel warm enough to warrant such action. He simply followed so as not to look out of place, since he saw that everyone around them had also begun doing the same with identical white fans. Seated on both sides of the river, everyone seemed to be looking at the waterfall, and Kyle looked in the same direction, not sure what was going to happen.

Then the music began. It echoed off of all the trees and buildings, so much so that it took Kyle a moment to figure out where the musicians were. They were perched with instruments in the tree branches above scattered all around them, creating a surround sound effect. The song began with the light plucking of soothing strings, aurally sprinkling the air with delicate vibrations, and then the beginning of a lonely, slightly high pitched wind sound which was later joined by a deeper one. The music blended perfectly with the sounds of the waterfall, and the whole effect was so dreamy that it sent shivers through Kyle as his mind seemed to even out like a troubled pool settled by a single expanding ring.

From the waterfall emerged a large floating platform that reached the length of the river, and on it stood about twenty young girls hidden under large umbrellas that kept the waterfall water from soaking them. The sound of the falling water on their sap-coated paper umbrellas added to a crescendo in the song. When they had cleared the waterfall, the dancers shifted their umbrellas in unison and began to twirl them, artfully throwing off the spray in a crisscrossed pattern that left all of them still untouched by the moisture. Each of the girls had a soft smile on their make-up coated faces as they danced with the umbrellas swaying, twirling, and swinging in unison, forming flowery patterns and displays. The umbrellas were then closed up and placed on the perimeter of the floating platform, leaving their lovely costumes in full view of the appreciating audience on the river banks. They wore a flowing cloth of different shades of pink similar to what Mei had worn before, but both of the sleeves were flowing long with the occasional slim arm peeking out of them like the stamen hidden among the petals of silken flowers. Their hair fell in profuse curls from a sparkling ornament that tied their locks up into a cascading ponytail. The slender midsections of their bodies were uncovered with mid-drift tops. The bottom part of their costume was a long and sinuous dress of the same material as the sleeves, and it covered their feet so that they appeared to be floating across the platform in their dance, bending and drifting to the sound of the music like spring blossoms in a gentle breeze. The platform floated slowly and steadily down the river as they danced. Their dance was exponentially more mesmerizing than the one performed by Mei and her troop the night before, and Kyle could tell this was because of the heightened skill and artistry of the Lin Gui performers. It was as if the one that Kyle had seen the previous night was just a watered down version of the one he was witnessing right now.

Kyle found himself looking for Tai amongst the dancers, and since they were all identically dressed with matching facial embellishments, it took him a moment to find her. She was of course done up like the rest, but there was a sharpness to her curving movements, a sureness that surpassed the others ever so slightly yet clearly enough to set her apart. Though Kyle was no connoisseur of dance, he had studied enough martial arts with his grandfather to be able to appreciate the highly skilled calisthenics of Tai's movements. Her dance was not only aesthetically captivating to the eye but also revealing of her skill and control over her own body in speed, flexibility, and precision. Kyle imagined if all of the girls on the platform suddenly attacked her, she would be more than a match for all of them at once, which was saying a lot because it was clear the rest of them were highly skilled as well. He realized that she had gone easy on him in their little bout the night before in the courtyard. If she had been serious from the get-go, he would have been fully knocked out with one strike.

As the dance came to a close and the sounds of the music finished their last echoes, the crowds of people around the river burst into applause and yelps of appreciation for the excellent performance. The girls lined up at the edges of the platform and bowed graciously, and then they jumped off the platform onto the riverbanks and ran to their respective families to join in on the feast. The large platform was pulled by an invisible source back up the river, and it soon disappeared under the waterfall.

Kyle watched as Tai made her way towards them. He couldn't help but stare down at her exposed slender waist and blushed lightly at the sight of her in such fantastic and lovely attire. She looked like a totally different girl from the surly one who had punched him in the eye the night before. As she came near him, she looked down at him with luminous yet puzzled eyes, which he noticed for the first time were light brown with a hint of glimmering amber gold. Her brow furrowed at first as if she were trying to decide what to do next, and then her dainty lips covered in luscious red broke out into a genuine smile that, with all the make-up, made her even more unrecognizable to Kyle. Then Tai started to laugh lightly, and Kyle realized that Bao, Xiang, and Ting were also chuckling at him. At first he thought it was because he was blushing at the sight of Tai done up as an enchanting maiden sprite, but then he realized that on the white fans that Bao and his parents held were splashed patterns of multicolored paint that still looked wet to the touch. He was about to ask how the once plain white fans had become so decorated when he looked down and saw that his simple brown clothing was covered in a cacophonous array of colors. His plain white fan was still crisp, clean, and untouched.

"What…?" Kyle was too confused to let his embarrassment fully sink in.

Xiang put a steadying hand on his shoulder.

"Remember how I said we incorporate little challenges into our daily lives as part of our training? Our leisure activities are no exception. The Assassin's Charm is a dance not just of the performing girls but one between the audience and the dancers as well. As they dance, they intermittently throw out tiny pellets full of colored paint targeted at members of the audience. That's what the plain white fans are for, to block their 'attacks' during their performance. Don't worry, the colors will wash out easily."

"Oh…I see," Kyle said as the embarrassment finally sunk in. He was meant to block the 'attacks' of paint pellets with his white fan. To his partial relief, the music started up again, and the meal began with haste. The delicious food pushed aside some of the awkwardness of his situation, but the dinner went on pleasantly with no further mention of his failure to participate in the Assassin's Charm performance. They talked of the weather, of the wonderful food, of fond memories, and of the artfulness of the fans that each had their own distinctive pattern based on the angle of the blocks used by respective owners. Tai smiled and chatted with Bao and his parents in such a friendly manner full of pleasantries that she had never offered him. She was obviously very capable of being 'nice'. He stole glances at her here and there, wondering what it was about him that made her so angry. After all, they had only just met the day before.

When all had been eaten, all the Lin Gui began to pack up their things and clean up for the night. Bao and his parents walked off with arms full of their dinner implements leaving Tai and Kyle to roll up the mat and pick up the rest. As Tai worked, the silken fabric accentuated the curves of her young, athletic body and her bare waist was still a source of distraction for Kyle. He decided he should say something nice as was customary to do when girls dressed up.

"Uh…you look really nice tonight," he stammered out. Suddenly, she shot him a glare that told him he had said the wrong thing. The amber gold in her eyes were more apparent now than ever. Kyle was so baffled by her reaction to his compliment that he could only stare back blankly at first. Tai went back to work.

"What?" Kyle blurted out exasperated and indignant. "What did I say? I was just trying to be nice!"

Tai gave him an impatient look, rolled her eyes, and went back to cleaning.

He way the amber glint in her light brown eyes pierced through him lingered as he slowly tried to comprehend why she was so upset at him. Tai began to roll up the mat, and Kyle jumped instinctively to help her with it. However, before he was able to help, she hoisted the rolled up mat onto her shoulder and began to walk away, leaving him to pick up the remaining items.

After washing up in some public baths, Kyle and Tai were to share the plain room that they had changed in earlier. The prospect of sleeping in the same room with a girl alarmed Kyle quite a bit, but he tried to play it off as nothing. Still, the extraordinary tension between them made it extra uncomfortable. They took turns changing in the room while the other waited outside, and soon he was lying down in clean and soft black sleepwear on a futon-like mattress positioned on the floor with Tai's a few feet away. She moved about the room to extinguish the series of candles lining the window and tables that kept their humble sleeping quarters lit. He watched her as she moved from candle to candle, the flame light playing across her features each time she came up to one to put it out. All the make-up she had worn earlier was removed. Her black hair hung loose and straight about her shoulders, and she wore the same, plain black soft long sleeved shirt and long pants that he wore. No more flowing silk, no more dainty red lips, no more elegantly curled hair, and no more feigned smiles for the stage. It was just her, plain and simple. She was not a remarkable looking girl, and would be judged as plain in the eyes of most, but the energy of her presence and the spirit that emanated from her every movement showed everything but plain and simple to the discerning eye. As Kyle watched her, he had an inkling of why she might have been upset at his complimenting her when she was all done up.

She blew the last of the candles out and settled down into her bed. The room was dark save for a few streams of light from torches outside that were quickly diminishing in number as they were put out for a night. Soon, the only light was some faint moonlight that escaped through the thick foliage above the village, sparkling off of the river outside. The waterfall was a soft lull in the distance from where they were.

"Tai?"

There was a pause of loud silence.

"Yes."

Kyle found that his words were all jumbled up in his incomplete understanding.

"Nevermind. Goodnight."

Again the loud silence filled the air. Through the quiet dark, Kyle could still feel irritation emanating from her direction. He held back a sigh and tried to clear his mind for sleep. He had a long day of 'training' tomorrow, whatever that meant.

Being thoroughly exhausted, Kyle fell asleep quickly, and he slept like a log the whole night, except that even when he slept like a log, he had a tendency to move around in his sleep. He was snoring lightly with the top half of his body off of his futon bed and on the wooden floor when Tai woke up in the middle of the night. He remained unbothered as she sat up and looked over at him, observing in the moonlight that his blanket now only covered the bottom half of his body and that his arms were spread out over his head, making him look like a starfish that had passed out half buried in sand. She stared at him for a moment as if contemplating something, and then she leaned over and pulled the blanket up so that it comfortably covered his body. Then her eyes drifted to a lock of Kyle's hair that curved over his forehead and poked into his eye. Again, she hesitated, staring at the lock of hair and his eye before she reached out a hand and brushed the hair gently away from his face with steady fingers. A look of exasperation spread across her face as she sighed loudly and lay back down in bed, turning away so that her back faced Kyle as he slept on, oblivious.

Chapter 10

Synchronicity

Kyle was about to pass out. He stood at the foot of the waterfall with Tai awaiting their instructions on their last day of training. It had been one heck of a week full of intense physical training, and Kyle was exhausted beyond belief. Nevertheless, mingled in with the fatigue and dread was a sense of accomplishment at having gone through probably one of the most intense physical training regimens in existence.

He had spent the entire first day by Tai's side learning the Eight Essential Forms of Lin Gui, all very long and complicated sequences of martial arts forms. He was amazed to recognize in it the styles of many different types of martial arts, both modern and ancient, from the fluidity of tai chi to the rhythmics of capoeira to the hard strikes of classic karate. At the same time, it was not a frankenstein combination of styles and was instead a cogent and coherent unity of all. Kyle couldn't decide whether the Lin Gui martial style was a combination of existing fighting arts that he knew of or a primary source style that the rest had derived from.

In any case, it wasn't something a beginner of martial arts could learn all in one day, and even though Kyle had only been trained intermittently by his grandfather all his life, he was well versed enough to be able to follow along and somewhat keep up with the insane pace Ting, Xiang, and Bao were putting them through. Tai, as usual, picked it all up with much more ease than he did. The form sequences were clearly new to her, but her efforts were only minor pauses as the new routines were incorporated into her existing knowledge. She clearly knew a lot more about martial arts than he did.

Kyle, on the other hand, occasionally got completely lost which required them to start from the beginning and considerably slowed down the progress of the instruction.

The second day was another full day of the Eight Lin Gui Weapons Forms: sword, spear, sticks, staff, sections, chain, dagger, and needles. Kyle was especially terrified of the sharp weapons and was glad to have made it through the day without slicing any part of himself off. The third, fourth, fifth, and sixth days were spent on speed, strength, agility, and reflex respectively. Speed and strength training were quite straight forward, but agility and reflex were another story.

For agility, he found himself running across a track that was made entirely of three yard-high bamboo poles embedded in the ground. It brought back unpleasant memories of when his grandfather used to line the backyard with unevenly spaced soda cans and force him to run across them without touching his foot to a single blade of grass. A number of the still unopened cans had exploded under his weight leaving quite a mess in the yard and permanently staining whatever clothes he had on. After he could cross the path of bamboo poles without faltering, he also mastered running across the wooden leaves floating across the river, but not without falling into the water a few more times.

Reflex training started with the children of the village throwing light, hollow grass-woven spheres at him. His task was to block them with his hands and feet. When he was able to successfully block or duck from about 90% of the hollow spheres, he graduated to having small cloth sacks filled with dirt thrown at him. Then he was handed a pair of half a meter long bamboo sticks which he quickly figured out were for blocking the rocks they started to throw at him. At the end of that day, he found himself with two plain white fold up fans in his hands and a rain of paint pellets flying his way much like during his first night at the Ghost Village during Tai's performance of the Assasin's Charm. He didn't escape completely unscathed by paint, but he surprised even himself with how much color he had managed to fill his fan up with. Even Tai had a few stains of paint pellets that had managed to get past her defenses, and Kyle had noticed this with guilt-ridden satisfaction.

Every night after dinner, he and Tai were supervised by the young Bao to go through all the forms they had memorized, and to do all of them at once took a good three hours. They practiced by firelight, went to bed exhausted, and woke up every morning before dawn to be dragged out for a warm-up jog before breakfast and a new day of training. He was lucky to have been in good athletic condition or none of this training would have helped him improve much.

They had two more days of training left, and he had no idea what the topic of focus was on the seventh day.

"Synchronicity."

Xiang and Ting's voice chimed in from behind them. Tai and Kyle turned and bowed respectfully at their teachers. Bao scrambled up behind his parents.

"Today you will focus on synchronicity," Ting added.

"A single cloud does not make a storm and a single drop of water cannot constitute a whirlpool. In a synchronized dance, *two* can become a very powerful and dynamic *one*."

In Kyle's mind emerged a silly image of him dancing the waltz with Tai and Tai purposefully stepping on his tender feet out of spite. He glanced at Tai who didn't look too thrilled at the prospect of 'synchronizing' with him.

"Synchronicity is by far the most difficult aspect of your training. You will need an open mind today more than any of the other days we have spent training," Xiang said.

"Through this waterfall is a labyrinth of tunnels and puzzles. Your task is to retrieve a text from the hidden Library of the Ancients," Ting instructed.

Kyle imagined a dusty old Egyptian tomb full of rotting scrolls.

"Which scroll are we supposed to retrieve?" he asked.

"Your choice," Bao said with a smile.

"My choice?" Kyle said pointing at himself, but then he realized. "Oh, I see, you mean *our* choice. We'll have to pick one together."

Bao's exuberant little nod of the head answered his question.

"You should choose something that you think will be of help on your journey," Xiang instructed.

"Oh…kay…"

Kyle almost said, "Oh boy…" but had caught himself. The labyrinth itself had sounded difficult, but now he realized that choosing with Tai was going to be even more of a challenge. He could just go with what she chooses, but something told him that she wouldn't be happy with that.

"You have until sundown to complete your task," Ting said.

Kyle and Tai began their little mini-quest, heading towards the waterfall entrance. At first, it seemed that there was no way into the cave behind the waterfall except by swimming upstream into it, but as they got closer, they saw that there were a series of large rocks situated like huge steps up to a little opening on the side of the waterfall near its top. The large stone stairway was blended in so that it was difficult to realize they were there from afar. Each step was too high for a single person to get over, and they were smooth with no grips anywhere for a sturdy climber. The mist from the waterfall and varying layers of moss patches also made the rock slippery.

"Synchronicity…huh?" Tai thought out loud.

"Hm?" Kyle said as he was still trying to figure out how they were going to climb these giant stairs.

"Here," Tai said as she stood with her back to the first huge stone step and her hands held together in front of her as if she were getting ready to play some volleyball.

"Oh, good thinking," Kyle understood, silently chiding himself for not figuring it out before her. He walked up to her and stood facing her, pausing for just a moment. She was still looking down at her hands, preparing to hoist his weight up, and then she looked up at him, the flash of gold in her eyes asking him why he was hesitating.

"You ready?" he asked.

"Yes," she said.

"So, um, are you gonna throw me over or…"

"Use my hands as a boost so that you can use my shoulders as a steady step up. It may be slippery on the rock because of all the moisture, so watch your step."

"Okay, got it," Kyle said, still feeling really uncomfortable being so close to her. He put his hands on her shoulders, which were unexpectedly warm, and placed his right foot on her hands. He pushed up, found footing on her shoulders, and then found himself looking over the ledge of the first step. With his arms, he pulled himself up securely onto that first stone step, and then quickly turned around and reached his hand back down out to Tai. She, too, hesitated for a moment before she took his hand and allowed herself to be pulled up. The strength training had helped, but, that didn't mean pulling Tai up was easily. She was a lot heavier than she looked. He tried to use some speed and momentum to make the most of what strength he had, and Tai was quick to steady herself on the step, too, as soon as she could get more of a grip on it.

Kyle looked up and counted nine more steep steps and took a deep breath. He decided it would be best if they took turns and took the same position against the second step that Tai had taken with the first one.

"Ready?" he asked again.

She nodded and put her right foot on his hands and climbed up the same way. Then it was Kyle's turn to be pulled up. He took Tai's hand

and was appreciative of the strength with which she pulled him up. Each subsequent step went more smoothly as they grew accustomed to their little system of climbing and to each other's strengths and weights. They became surer of their footing and of each other. They found themselves at the entrance and took the opportunity to look back down at Bao and his parents. They smiled and waved up at them encouragingly, and Kyle and Tai waved back before disappearing behind the curtain of water.

The sound of the rushing water was even louder in the cave behind the waterfall as the acoustics of the place magnified every splash and splatter. Kyle stared precipitously down at the large pool that extended behind the waterfall. The large platform Tai had performed on was floating there in the water, awaiting its next use. They made their way along a ledge path that led to an opening in the back of the cave. The opening was dark, and the sunlight that came through the falling water could not pierce it. They looked around and found some torches, which they took some time to light with some flint next to the pile, and began making their way down a long hall of stone walls with the fire light flickering on their path. Soon, they reached a fork in the path as the one hall split off into two. They paused as they considered their options.

"They both look the same to me," Kyle thought out loud.

"Yes. Why don't we each go down one to explore and then meet back here."

Kyle looked over at her wondering if this was just her way of getting rid of him, but her suggestion did make sense.

"Alright."

Kyle took the right path, and Tai took the left. The new path Kyle was on looked identical to the one he had been on before with Tai. It then crossed his mind that they didn't decide just how far they would go before doubling back to meet at the fork again.

"I guess when I find something different," he said out loud to himself.

In the darkness ahead, he perceived a flicker of firelight, and he quickened his pace. When he finally reached the firelight that wasn't emitting from his own torch, it spoke to him.

"Took you long enough."

To his left there was a small horizontal slit in the wall where he could see Tai's eyes staring back at him.

"There's a stone door a little ways down and a lever next to it, but when I pull mine, it doesn't open my door. Instead, I hear something else slide away. You must have a similar contraption on your side. Your door is probably opened already, but I'm guessing you'll have to open mine from your side."

"I see," Kyle said. "I'll head there now."

He turned away from the slit in the wall and made his way further down his tunnel. Sure enough, there was an opened stone door and a lever next to it. He pulled on it and heard the sliding of the stone door in the adjacent tunnel.

"Keep going?" he called out to Tai. He heard a muffled reply, figured she had said yes, and then shrugged his shoulders as he continued on.

Again he saw the flickering light ahead, and this time, Tai showed up in front of him in full view. Their paths had merged again. She met his eyes and then turned around to look at something. When he reached her, he found himself standing in a large circular room with openings all around.

"One, two, three…" he started counting the doors, "seven, eight, nine, ten. Not counting the two openings we came from."

Tai was staring intently down each one in turn.

"Should we check each one like we did before?"

"No time," she said with certainty, and then asked, "What's your lucky number?"

"Um…eight I guess," Kyle said. Not really having a lucky number, he chose the universal Chinese lucky number.

"This way," Tai said, pointing to a doorway to his right. She plowed ahead, and he followed.

"Are you picking at random?"

"Sort of. We're going down the way that you labeled as 'eight' when you were counting the doors."

"Ah, okay."

After a while, they came to an empty, square-shaped room that looked like a dead end.

"Hmm…" Tai looked at the wall intensely for a moment while thinking of her next move. Something caught the corner of Kyle's eye.

"Look, there's a ladder over here," he moved his torch in that direction to light it.

The sturdy looking structure was the same color as the wall and was hard to pick out without close attention.

"There's one on this side, too," Tai said, going to the opposite wall. They looked upwards and realized their torch light could not reach very far up. The tops of the two ladders disappeared into the darkness above.

"Let's go," Tai said with confidence as she began to climb the ladder she was next to. Kyle took the cue and began to climb up his own. Climbing with a torch in hand was slow going. When they reached the top, they climbed onto walled paths that lead in opposite directions. Both turned to look at each other across the deadly fall that was too far to make a safe jump.

"I guess we have to go our separate ways again," Kyle observed out loud.

"Yes, it would seem so," Tai added.

"Let's meet back here when we find something," Kyle suggested.

"Agreed. It is possible the paths will cross again," Tai said. Kyle nodded in response, and the two walked on in their respective directions.

After some time, Kyle's path started to curve to the left and slope upwards. It evened out again and Kyle could see a light ahead again, but this time it wasn't fire light; it was a strange blue glow of some sort. When he reached it, he realized he was standing on what looked like a high balcony walkway overlooking a large cavernous area. On the rocks above and all over the area were small blue points of light in the darkness that made the place look like a night sky full of sparkling blue stars. If he didn't feel the ground solidly under him, Kyle could have imagined himself floating in space and staring into infinity. He looked closely at the stone near his torchlight and realized what the source of the strange blue light was. The rock near him was covered with worms, each with a point of blue light emanating from its end. The night sky effect was kind of cool; the worms, however, were pretty nasty looking. He made a face and moved away from the walls.

Firelight emerged on the opposite side of the cavern, and he saw the small figure of Tai emerge onto a similar balcony walkway about a hundred yards away with the large and dark cavern separating them. Kyle waved his torch at her, and she waved back and then signaled for him to keep walking forward. He continued on until the walkway curved to the left again, and he was facing Tai across a gap about as long as the room where they had found the ladders. There was a thick and heavy rope dangling on either side of the drop. Almost simultaneously, they both raised their torches up to look at what the rope was attached to at the top and saw that the rope was strung through a very large pulley contraption. Tai reached out a hand and grabbed the rope and gave it an experimental tug down. Sure enough, Kyle's rope pulled up in response, and Kyle instinctively reached out to grab it to keep it steady. They both

looked around but found no place to tie the ropes.

"This is like playing co-op," he said to himself out loud.

"Like what?" Tai asked with a raised voice because their voices tended to fade off into echoes in the cavern.

"I said this is like co-op."

"Co-op? As in cooperative?"

"Yeah, like in video games."

"I don't play video games."

"Oh yeah? Well, you should try it sometime. Co-op games are a lot like this maze. Two players or more have to work together in order to get through the game." He looked at the rope. "I half expect to find some kind of puzzle we'll have to solve together. I guess we'll have to put our weight on the rope at the same time or, uh, one of us will fall."

"If one of us falls, so will the other. It's all or nothing," Tai said heaving a sigh. Kyle felt she was expecting him to somehow mess up and send them both to their deaths. Tai looked at the torch in her hand. "We should leave our torches up here. I doubt we can make it down safely with a torch in one hand."

They both looked around and found crevices in the rock where they could stick their torches firmly in place so as not to have to put them out. Kyle had a thought.

"Why can't one of us just hold onto the rope while the other descends?"

"Synchronicity, right? Plus we don't know how far down this goes and what's waiting at the bottom."

"Okay, let's ease into it then, yeah?" Kyle said apprehensively as he took the rope firmly in two hands.

"Yes, let's."

The two of them began by gently pulling down on their respective rope ends to get a sense for the force of the other person pulling on the rope. Then they began to lean back a bit to test their weights against each other.

"Ready?" Tai asked.

"Yeah, I'm ready," Kyle said, though he didn't feel ready.

"On three. One…two…three."

The two of them fully put their weight onto the rope and hung for a moment, swinging slightly from side to side, a pair of giant pendulums. Kyle was already flinching as if waiting for something to snap or break.

When it became clear that they were clearly and stably balancing each other's weights and there was no sign of anything breaking or snapping, Tai said, "We should climb down the rope at the same speed with our weights balanced on it, like on a scale. Our force on the pulley needs to be changing at the same rate or else we'll be out of balance and we'll fall."

"Got it," Kyle said, trying not to sound as nervous as he felt.

"Ready?"

"Yeah."

"Start now."

Kyle felt the rough surface of the rope rubbing unpleasantly against his hands which were firmly gripping them. The two inched down slowly, or more accurately, Kyle inched down his rope slowly and Tai was trying to carefully match his cautious pace.

Suddenly, Kyle felt the weight on Tai's side lighten, and he free-fell for a second and yelped in panic.

"We're at the bottom now. You can get off the rope."

Kyle looked down and saw nothing but blackness. He looked over at Tai who still had her hands on the rope, but even in the dim light, it was clear that she was standing and pulling, not just hanging her weight on the rope. Tentatively stretching out a foot, he felt for solid ground, found it, and quickly stepped off onto it, and Tai let go of the rope she was pulling to keep him suspended. Kyle looked around and saw that there were hundreds of thousands of tiny blue lights emanating from the glow worms. A shiver ran up his spine both because of the strange way in which the site mimicked the endless vastness of space and because he knew that there was a squirmy, slimy little worm for every point of light out there. The worms kept to the walls and ceiling and remained off the ground, which suited Kyle just fine since he did not want to cover the bottom of his Lin Gui sandals with smooshed worm guts.

As he looked toward what appeared to be the end of the cavern, which was only apparent because it was covered in glowing blue lights, he noticed a shimmer of something else on the rock wall. The two of them began to move towards it. Something seemed to be reflecting the blue light of the glow worms, and the closer they got, the clearer the pattern became. Finally, when they stood looking right up at it, they saw that the pattern on the stone wall was that of two crystalline butterflies frozen in position as if they were about to commence swirling in unison up into the blue twinkling space around them. Unsure of what to do, Kyle reached a hand out to touch the crystalline material that marked the images of the butterflies onto the rock.

"It's warm," Kyle said, surprised. Tai reached out her hand and touched the material, too, and inadvertently, they each had a hand on one of the butterflies. The fluttering images suddenly began to glow brighter, and the two retracted their hands in instinctive alarm and watched with awe as the two images began to flap their crystalline wings and flutter upon the rock's surface as if it were some sort of liquid crystal display instead of simple, solid rock. Then the rock seemed to melt into a fluid that stayed in place, and it soon became as clear as spring water, allowing them the ability to see a well lit room beyond the liquid-like space between that had just been solid rock a moment earlier. Kyle had to put aside all reason in order to accept what he was seeing. It made no sense for rock to suddenly turn into clear water and even less sense for it to stay in place instead of splash away. He couldn't decide if it was magic or very advanced technology. Then again, he reasoned with himself, there was no explanation for him even being in this strange world in the first place. And he had seen a dragon the other day. He put aside his human need for a rational explanation for everything in order to keep his functional sanity, if only for the time being.

It was Tai that dared to reach a hand out to touch the liquid barrier first, and it rippled like a vertical pool to the motions of her fingers against it.

"What is it?" Kyle asked in amazement.

"It's somehow not wet, but it's substantial. I can feel it, but at the same time it feels like it's not there."

"Weird."

"Yes, well, I think we need to walk through it."

"Walk through it?"

"Yes. The room beyond, it's full of books and scrolls. That must be the library we're meant to find."

The lit room beyond was a good five yards through the strange clear substance. Kyle pressed his lips together as he thought seriously about walking through what was solid rock just moments before.

"What if it turns back to rock when we're half way through?"

Tai shrugged. Kyle tried to imagine what kind of pain he would feel if he were half way or all the way stuck inside a rock. He couldn't, but that didn't make the prospect of it happening any less terrifying. He felt a little paralyzed in place, and Tai could sense it.

"Do you want me to pull you through?"

"Huh? What? No, I'll do it myself."

"We should do it at the same time just to be safe."

"Why at the same time?"

"Well, since today is all about synchronicity, it may be safer to follow that rule. Like with the ropes."

Kyle saw her point. What if the liquid solidifies if only one of them jumps through? He was suddenly more afraid for Tai than himself.

"On second thought, here," he said as he held out a hand to her.

"What?" she stared dubiously at his dimly lit, outstretched hand.

"Here, take my hand."

"What? Why?"

"I'm just afraid I'm gonna chicken out at the last minute. Just take my hand. This way you can yank me through if I hesitate."

"Are you sure?"

"Yeah, I'm positive."

Tai reached out at first to grab his shirt, but the clothing hanging comfortably on his frame suddenly looked like such a flimsy thing, so she took his outstretched hand instead and gripped it firmly.

"I'm just going to pull you through, then, okay? No matter what, yes?"

"Yeah, okay, I'm ready."

"Just try to relax and go with me."

"Okay, I'm relaxed."

"Are you sure?"

"Yeah. No, wait, we should probably hold our breath while we go through."

"That would be advisable."

"Okay, okay." Kyle took a few deep breaths.

"Ready now?"

"Yes."

"Alright, on three then. Ready? One, two, THREE!"

Chapter 11

Library of the Ancients

Kyle couldn't decide what state the matter he was passing through was in. It flowed like liquid, felt insubstantial like gas, but was at the same time quite solid. He tried to keep his eye on the glowing light emanating from their destination. Although Tai's firm grip on his hand was reassuring, his cheeks puffed out as the urge to exhale began to build, and then they were through. He breathed out in a burst as Tai released his hand. Then he looked around. To his mild horror, the clearness behind them suddenly changed back to stone.

The room was a rather large, a square shape cut out of the rock, and there were shelves full of books and scrolls of all shapes and sizes. Everything looked very old but not dusty with disuse. In the middle of the room was a large, heavy looking tortoise shell about the size of a coffee table. It looked like the oldest relic in the room. Kyle recalled from his old social studies book that such shells were often used in ancient times to carve on or as oracle mediums. He figured it must be covered in record-keeping marks on the inside.

The warm, yellow hued light in the enclosed room emanated from pieces of paper that had the character for "light".

Kyle walked up to one of the papers to see if they were covering a recessed lamp of some sort, but upon examination of the papers, he found that they were just papers on a wall, aside from the glowing part that is.

"How is this possible?" Kyle said out loud to himself.

"How…is…anything…possible?" a very old sounding voice asked

back very, very slowly.

Kyle first swirled around looking for the source of the voice and met Tai's eyes which told him that she had no idea either. Their silent questions were answered with what sounded like stone grating slowly against stone, and finally they noticed that the large, very old tortoise shell in the middle of the room was stirring. Slowly out of its openings stretched dry and rough looking skin of a dusty grayish color, and to their amazement, a large head with droopy but lively old eyes turned up and looked at them over the shell. He looked very much like a regular giant tortoise, except that when his mouth opened, he spoke with a slow and ancient voice.

"Welcome, Chosen One, to the Library of the Ancients. I am Cai, the librarian."

A talking turtle...was all Kyle could manage to run through his mind.

"It is good to meet you, Librarian Cai. I am Tai, and this is Kyle."

It's a talking librarian turtle...Kyle tried to keep his mind running with rudimentary thoughts so that it wouldn't go into an automatic shutdown sequence in response to the strangeness of coming face to face with a sentient reptile.

"Hi," he finally managed to squeeze out of his vocal chords.

"Yes, so which text shall it be?" Cai said as he turned his shell and body around to face them.

"Which scroll?" Kyle asked before he remembered why they had come to this library in the first place.

"Do we pick from any of the ones here?"

"Yes," Cai said as his body and shell slowly completed a hundred and eighty degree turn around. Kyle looked around again at all the books and scrolls.

"Do you have any suggestions?" Kyle asked.

"Hmm, well, yes, as a matter of fact I do."

"You do?" Tai asked. She had been prepared to scour all the books as quickly as possible in order to meet their sunset deadline. The prospect of having some help to cut down the time wasted caught her interest.

"Yes," Cai nodded very slowly, so slowly in fact that Kyle could tell Tai had wished she had asked a more pertinent question.

"I understand that you will be going on a perilous journey, and to prepare for that, you must have a text that will help you with your difficult task. What you choose must be powerful and resilient, inspiring and expanding. As the Librarian, I would suggest you choose from the Three Treasures."

Kyle and Tai watched as the very old tortoise turned its large, heavy body back around again and began heaving himself slowly toward the bookshelves. Tai and Kyle followed behind carefully, taking small measured steps to match the librarian's pace. Old Cai stopped at one of the bookcases, heaved himself up onto his back feet while placing his large forefeet gently against the bookshelf, which creaked but did not fall over or break under the tortoise's weight. Nevertheless, Kyle and Tai both stepped forward at the same time to catch whatever might fall. Cai's neck stretched out far up to the top shelf, and when his neck was retracting, he had a cloth bundle hanging from his mouth. He returned to the ground just as delicately as he had rose despite his heavy weight. He turned again to face them, dropping the bundle he held in his mouth at their feet. Tai kneeled down to open it.

"These are the scrolls of the Three Treasures."

Tai undid the knot to reveal three blue scrolls that were identical in every way except that each had a single character written on a white label that was different from the rest.

慈

compassion

moderation

modesty

Kyle felt a little disappointed in those choices. Instinctively he looked around the room for another scroll. If he and Tai were to go up against an evil demon girl, he thought maybe a scroll that said 'power overwhelming' or 'megaton punch' or 'extra health' might be more useful. Then he realized Cai was looking at him with amusement in his beady tortoise eyes. He felt embarrassed and looked back at the three that Cai had recommended.

"Which should we choose?" Kyle asked Tai.

Tai gave him a strange look of uncertainty, like she wasn't really uncertain about which scroll to choose so much as she was uncertain of what *he* might choose.

"Which do you think is the most important?" she asked.

"Good question," Cai approved.

Kyle looked at each of the three scrolls in turn, examining the strokes of the elegant calligraphy used to write the characters hoping for a clue.

"Um, compassion?" Kyle asked instead of stated.

"You should say things with more conviction," Tai reprimanded him. "Why did you pick that one? You didn't pick it randomly didn't you?"

"No," Kyle responded indignantly. "Of course not. I picked it because it's the hardest out of the three."

"Good answer," Cai approved.

"Alright, compassion it is," Tai said.

"You agree with me?" Kyle asked.

"No, I had my mind set on picking compassion already. I just wanted to make sure you were genuinely choosing it and not just picking what I pick."

"Which means you agree with me," Kyle said with a dash of victory in his voice.

Tai gave him a stubborn look.

"Fine, yes, I agree with you."

She picked up the compassion scroll and handed it sharply to Kyle who took it with as much smugness as he dared to give his ill-humored partner in crime. He looked down at it again.

"Compassion, huh?" he wondered out loud.

Tai tied up the remaining two scrolls and placed them back in their original location on the top shelf.

"Thank you, Librarian Cai," Tai said with a polite bow which Kyle rushed to imitate with a last minute 'thank you' of his own.

The old tortoise nodded his head in acknowledgement. Then Kyle found himself in a new dilemma.

"Um, how do we get out of here?"

The rock wall that was their entrance was now more solid than ever, and there were no butterflies to 'activate' on this side.

"Write your way out," Cai said.

"What?" It was Tai's turn to be confused. Cai looked towards the corner of the room, and Kyle and Tai followed his gaze to what looked like two poles stuck in a pot leaning against the wall. Tai stepped forward, grabbed one of the poles, and pulled it up. It turned out to be a very large brush, but the pot it lay in was empty of ink or any type of liquid. She looked at the brush and then at the wall.

"What ink do we write with?"

"Your soul, universal life force, qi."

"Okay..." Kyle said dubiously.

"How do we do that?" Tai asked.

"It is no different than the writing you do on a regular basis. Just put your heart into it," Cai said as a wide tortoise smile of encouragement spread across his ancient face.

"Alright then," Tai said with some conviction but then her gaze shifted to the blank wall, and it was Kyle who asked her unspoken question.

"What do we write?"

"Open," Cai said.

開

"Open," Tai said, and she started immediately to write the character with the large brush on to the wall leaving no mark on the wall. When she finished, nothing happened. She turned to look at Cai, and then she looked at Kyle and let out a loud sigh. With her eyes and a nod of her head, she signaled for Kyle to get the other brush.

"Do you know how to write this character?" Tai asked with a dash of mockery as Kyle pulled the other brush out.

"Yeah, like in first grade," Kyle threw back with as much sass as he dared. He turned his attention to the solid rock wall and tried to 'put his heart into' the writing he was about to do. They both lifted their brushes to the wall.

"Let's try to match our stroke speed. Ready, go."

In large, fluid movements, the both of them wrote out all eleven strokes of the character in proper order, left before right, top before bottom, and so forth. To write such a large version of the character with a brush the size of a mop and a whole wall for a canvas, they looked as if they were engaged in a choreographed, synchronized dance. Cai followed their efforts with approving grin. When they finished, the two writings of the same character suddenly glowed on the rock the way the butterflies had, as if the strokes of their brushes had left crystal on the rock. The glowing strokes of the Chinese writing began to thicken and spread over the rock, and once again it was the same insubstantial, clear liquid they had passed through before. The two placed the brushes back into the pot in the corner.

"Thank you again, Librarian Cai," Tai said, this time placing her fisted right hand into the palm of her left hand as she bowed to him.

"Thank you," Kyle said with the same gesture.

"May your road have smooth winds," Librarian Cai said.

With scroll in one hand, Kyle then unexpectedly held his other hand out to Tai. She looked at his hand with a do-I-really-have-to look on her face.

"It's for your own good," Kyle said with a mildly goofy grin, half joking, half dead-serious. He didn't exactly want either of them to be stuck in solid rock due to his hesitant nature.

With a roll of the eyes, Tai took his hand again, and they went back through the wall, leaving the librarian turtle behind them smiling with approval.

When Kyle and Tai showed the scroll they had retrieved to Xiang and Ting, their teachers were immensely pleased. Even Bao gave them a thumbs up and a toothy grin. After a hearty early evening meal, their host Lin Gui family excused themselves, mentioning that Bao was due for some private training, and that they shouldn't wait up for them if the training took longer than expected. The two teens were a little surprised to be left alone to their own devices.

Kyle sat at the low table tapping his brown tea cup nervously. Tai

sat across from him, holding her cup, steadily and serenely sipping from it in silence. She was looking at the dark, wooden table almost meditatively as he stole awkward glances at her, trying to decide what to do next. He had a whole evening alone with Tai, and he didn't know how he should start it. Should he suggest some activity? Or maybe leave her alone and go off on his own?

Every moment since that first day they had arrived at the Ghost Village had been so jam-packed with events, information, and training that there was scarcely a moment of quiet for them, and when they got back to their shared room at night, they were so exhausted that they had pretty much just passed out as soon as their heads hit their pillows. Now that they had leisure time and were not worn out from a day of intense training, Kyle felt the full blast of the awkwardness between them.

"Let's take a walk around the village, yes?" Tai said.

Kyle looked over at her with slightly raised eyebrows.

"Uh, sure."

Needless to say, he was surprised by Tai's invitation. He thought most likely she would be so sick of having him around her that leisure time would be a great time to take a break from him.

As they cleaned up the tea cups and stood up, Tai added, "Tomorrow's our last day of training here. We'll probably leave soon."

Kyle nodded in agreement. He hadn't thought of that. It would be nice to explore the village on their own before they had to leave.

The night air was fresh and scented with jasmine flowers that blossomed nearby. Each of the village homes glowed with an inner fire, the calm figures within all engaged in quiet activities. Through the windows, Tai and Kyle could see parents engaged in conversations with their children, the young ones gazing up at the adults with attentiveness and adoration. In one home, a mother taught her children how to clean and maintain weapons. A pair in the adjacent home was showing their little ones how to weave cloth. Through another window, an aunt was teaching a young nephew how to string an instrument. In yet another home, a father read from a book to his children as they held tiny calligraphy brushes upright in their small yet skilled hands, making meticulous strokes on the papers before them. The village was a rich and solid community, a sense of love and belonging emanating from every warmly lit dwelling.

Kyle couldn't help but be reminded of the many quiet evenings he had spent with his grandmother working on reading and writing calligraphy. His parents often worked late at their respective offices, and his grandmother was the one who watched over him while they worked.

Tai stood by his side on the river bank, the space between and around them filled with the gentle roar of the rushing water as they looked at the village before them. For a long while they stood silent, letting the river speak for them as they contemplated where they were, how they got there, and why they were there.

"Why us?" Kyle wondered out loud. In the rush of training, this question kept bothering him, but it kept getting pushed aside as each new task or activity arose to occupy his time and thoughts. Xiang and Ting's answer was cryptic at best and hadn't clarified anything for him. He didn't really expect an answer now; he just felt the need to ask it out loud again.

"There's something that needs to be done," Tai responded, more to herself than to him, "and I'm here to do it. That's all I need to know."

Kyle looked at her, a bit puzzled. Although Tai had spoken with some determination, he noticed that she also sounded as if she were resigned to her apparent role in this world. Now he spoke directly to her.

"Why do it though? I mean, do we even have a choice?"

Tai looked over at him, her eyes meeting his before she looked away again. He noticed the way stray hairs escaped her high pony tail and floated by her face. She shrugged as she stared out into the rushing river waters.

"What else are we going to do?"

Kyle had no answer to that. A big part of him wanted to return to his normal life, but at the same time, he wasn't sure if he could fully walk away from all of this. Nevertheless, this First Child Demon still seemed an abstract concept to him, an insubstantial boogieman that he'd only heard second-hand accounts of. At the same time, the quest to face and defeat this adversary seemed the only way home. It was frustrating.

"It's getting late. We should rest," Tai said as she turned and headed back towards the Lin Gui home they stayed at. Kyle followed close behind her.

Their host family still hadn't come back yet, so the two of them prepared to turn in for the night. In their shared room, Tai began her nightly ritual of putting out the candles that lit their room. In the dark, they both settled in their futon beds that were on the floor.

Unlike previous nights where he had been all too grateful to lie down after an exhausting day and fall immediately to sleep, Kyle was wide awake tonight, and Tai's presence next to him made him fidgety. First of all, he was an only child who was used to sleeping in his own room by himself. To make things worse, the person who was lying down next to him less than a yard away was a young girl. The more he thought about it, the more anxious he got, and the more anxious he got, the more he fidgeted, tossing and turning intermittently trying to find a relaxing position and tapping his fingers when he wasn't shifting and changing positions.

"What's wrong?"

Oh great, now he had gotten her attention. He was surprised, however, that she didn't sound thoroughly annoyed with him. In fact, she even sounded a little genuinely concerned.

"Oh, nothing, just anxious I guess." He looked over at her and could see her nodding and sighing in understanding.

"Try this. Count backwards silently in your head, starting from one hundred. With each number, take a deep breath, and don't move on to the next number until you've totally breathed in and out once."

"Okay, thanks."

"Try not to think of anything. Just focus on your breathing and on counting."

Kyle nodded and lay down on his back staring up at the ceiling at first before closing his eyes. He took a deep breath in, feeling the cool air enter his lungs.

One hundred.

He breathed in slowly and deeply and then breathed out.

Ninety-nine.

Again he breathed, then counted, then breathed again and repeated. By eighty-nine, he had already drifted off into sleep and was breathing steadily. Next to him, Tai was lying down on her back as well, but her head was turned facing him as she looked at him, an amused smile spreading across her face before she, too, closed her eyes and fell asleep.

Chapter 12

Qi Script

Kyle held the brush vertically positioned in his fingers with the firmness and gentleness that his grandmother had taught him as a child. It was a grip that was just tight enough to control movements, yet loose enough to allow for flexibility and grace. Writing with a brush again like this was sadly nostalgic for him. He hadn't picked one up since before his grandmother had passed away in junior high. He looked at the ink he had made by grounding the ink stick with water in the ink stone, a sort of stone plate. His particular ink stone had the beautiful image of a black dragon carved into its perimeter. Tai, who had a phoenix carved into hers, had clearly thrown an envious glance at his when they sat down. He guessed she might have insisted that they trade places if Bao, Xiang, and Ting hadn't been present. They had left them to warm up in their calligraphy skills before lessons began.

The scroll of compassion they had picked out at the library hung unfurled from the roof edge. On it was the character for 'compassion'.

慈

Somehow, Kyle had expected there to be more written in the scroll, like a secret incantation of some sort that promised to destroy or bind the First Child demon forever, or something like that. But it was just the character itself, written so that it filled up the white space of the scroll with its dark strokes.

Kyle had already used up a few sheets practicing just that character as Tai had, but now he felt he was done with that one and was trying to come up with something else to write. Tai had been filling page after page with writing, creating an impressive pile for an hour's worth of work. Kyle's pile, on the other hand, was only two sheets high, and his latest paper had been sitting blank for quite a while. He looked over at Tai who was finishing up yet another page and had a look on her face that said she had plenty more where that came from. Heaving a sigh, he looked back at his own, and then his gaze wandered up to the scenery before them.

They were at adjacent low tables sitting on flat pillows that were neatly placed on a grass mat flooring. The structure they sat in was a platform constructed in a tree that hung over the river running through the Ghost Village. Under them the river hummed and roared along, and the structure had no walls, so their panoramic surroundings were the browns and greens of the forest scenery.

In the quiet of the moment, thoughts of his home and his normal life came to mind. He had a load of summer assignments to complete for his advanced placement classes and college entrance exams to study for. Those obligations seemed rather distant now, and he wondered if he would ever get home again. Sitting here, so far away from it all, he wondered a little about why all of those old obligations seemed so urgent and all engrossing before. He had bigger problems now. He tried to focus on getting home, but, like Ting had said, all he could do was move forward with his quest. It was the only lead he had to getting back to the life he knew, to the sunny suburbia, the perfect GPA, the testing, and the pre-determined road to college and a successful career.

Without much thought, he wrote a character that floated to the surface of his consciousness as his mind had wandered to this and that.

"Lost," he read his own writing out loud.

"Eh?" Tai said in response, looking away from her work at him.

"Huh? Oh, nothing," Kyle said, throwing her a self-conscious glance as he quickly pulled that paper away and placed a fresh new

blank one in its place. To throw Tai off the scent, he started to write whatever Chinese characters came to mind.

口 mouth	東 east
人 person	西 west
大 big	南 south
小 small	北 north

It was a string of some of the simplest and most basic characters that were often learned in the first few lessons of Chinese language instruction. Tai raised an eyebrow in an unrestrained questioning of his literary mastery before turning back to her own work.

Kyle was about to commence writing numbers one to ten in Chinese character form when he was interrupted.

"We're back!" Bao called from the tree that he had climbed up to reach them. Behind him were his mother and father, also climbing up the tree. Kyle took note of how over the past week, Bao seemed pained to leave his parents' side. He was not a baby, but he definitely seemed to cling to them. Kyle couldn't help but be reminded of when he was younger, being the only child and clinging to his parents and his grandmother.

A pile of golden papers were placed on each of their desks.

"These papers are made from the feathers of phoenix. They will enhance the aura of your writing," Ting explained.

"And these," Xiang said as he handed them each a slim, black box, "are brushes with handles made from the wood of the tree that bears the Peach of Immortality and bristles made from the fur of white tigers. All the materials were gifts from noble creatures, imbued with their strength and spirit."

The slim boxes were quickly clicked open, and in each lay a beautifully crafted calligraphy brush with wood of a dark, calming brown and bristles as soft and white as newly fallen snow. Both Kyle and Tai breathed out in almost a whistle as they admired the craftsmanship and the quality of the materials. These were definitely not ordinary tools for calligraphy. They both looked at the remaining ink in their respective ink stones and loathed to dip the pristine brush tip into the black liquid.

"Writing is an expression of the soul, and calligraphy, as a form of writing, is no different. Each of the characters you write is full of centuries of meaning poured into them from the hearts, minds, and souls of the living, and in recreating those characters, you summon forth all that energy reborn in your own life force," Ting explained.

"Bao will demonstrate for you," said Xiang.

With a toothy grin, Bao pulled out a slim box from a leather bag slung across his body and opened it to reveal a brush almost identical to the ones that Tai and Kyle had been handed. He pulled one of the golden papers from Kyle's table and wrote on the paper surface without dipping his brush in any ink. Both Kyle and Tai could see that Bao was quite masterful with the calligraphy brush and not just for his age. The tiger's fur caressed the golden strands of the phoenix feather paper and left not a single mark. It was not until Bao had finished and lifted his brush up from the paper that what he had written began to show itself in a crystalline glow much like what Tai and Kyle had seen on the entrance and exit of the Library of the Ancients deep in the caves under the waterfall of the Ghost Village. Then it glowed golden like sunlight. Bao had written "butterfly".

蝴蝶兒

The light emanating from the characters engulfed the entire sheet of paper like a white flame, and then as the light faded, an explosion of fluttering blue and gold butterflies burst forth from where the paper had been and flew out in all directions, the tiny gusts of air from the flapping wings brushing against their cheeks, showing Kyle and Tai that they were not just images but rather substantial manifestations of what Bao wrote. Just as quickly as they had formed, the butterflies dissolved into what looked like sparkling stardust.

"Wow," they both said in unison.

"Now you try," Bao encouraged.

Tai set to work right away, pulling a golden sheet out and writing something quickly with a sure hand.

Her writing of the 'double-edged sword' character began to glow and expand as Bao's writing had, and as the white flaming light subsided, there was an elegantly forged double-edged blade complete with sheath and handle all decorated with golden dragons and a red, Chinese knotted tassel hanging from the end.

"Amazing!" Tai exclaimed as she took a hold of the sword, one hand on handle and the other on sheath. With an effortless tug, she unsheathed the weapon, and her face glowed with approval at the quality.

Not knowing what to write, Kyle decided to follow Tai and write the same character. With relief, he watched as his own writing went through the same glowing process, but when the white flame had subsided, there was not a long, elegant sword on the table like Tai's. Instead, it was a small plain, dagger-sized version of the double-edged sword. On top of that, it was made out of a flimsy plastic instead of metal. It looked like a children's toy from some souvenir shop in a Chinatown.

"What?" Kyle exclaimed, feeling deflated.

"It seems you wrote that character half-heartedly," Ting said gently. “You must really believe in what you write for it to reach its full potential.”

“I see,” Kyle said, remembering that he had only written the character because Tai had written it. Putting the dagger sized sword aside, he took a deep breath and tried to think of something he wanted to whole-heartedly write. Since he knew he would be up against a powerful demon girl, he focused his attention on a weapon that he could use in battle. As soon as one came to mind, the small, toy sword he had just created vaporized into white particles. After recovering from the mild surprise from this, he placed his brush against a new sheet of golden phoenix paper and wrote.

棍

The character for ‘staff’ glowed, and finally there was a very solid, very sturdy staff made of strong bamboo. Kyle picked up the weapon, felt its heavy presence, and had an urge to break out in the Lin Gui staff form.

“Excellent,” Bao exclaimed and nodded in approval.

“Now, eat this,” Xiang said as he handed each of the three youngsters a slice of hearty grain bread.

“Now?” Tai asked, clearly eager to try her hand at more of those phoenix papers with her new brush. They did have breakfast after all, and it wasn't lunch time. “I'm not hungry yet.”

“Yes, but you will be quite soon. Qi script is very draining, and it literally uses your life force as its ink. So you best not take your energy for granted and keep in mind that your ability to create using this sort of writing is limited,” Ting said.

“Drink some of this as well,” he placed a large cup of tea in front of each of them. Kyle picked up the large cup and sipped some of its hot contents and then made a face at its bitterness. It was the strongest tea he had ever had. Tai had a similar look on her face.

"To clear your mind," Xiang laughed at both Kyle's and Tai's reactions.

"So as long as we keep eating, we can keep doing this…Qi Script?" Kyle asked.

"No, it's not as easy as that. Eating and drinking will raise your endurance and overall energy so that you can write more, but you should still be careful not to do too much at once. You still have a limit, and the complete transfer of those things external, like food and ideas and music, into something internal takes time," Xiang said.

"Yes," Ting continued, "think of it as blood. It takes time for your body to convert food into making blood, so you can live after losing some blood because your body can replace it, but lose too much at once, and no amount of food can bring you back."

Kyle looked down at his brush now with a bit more awe, respect, and even some fear. The item suddenly seemed parasitic, and he exchanged a cautious look with Tai as they realized they could not go around making swords and staffs frivolously. Kyle looked back at the heavy staff in his hand and realized that it was a physical manifestation of his life force, like an arm or a leg, the way written words were a physical manifestation of the abstract concepts of the mind. He put the staff carefully back down.

"Now, you guys are good at objects. Let's try something living, like the butterflies I created. Start small," Bao said.

Kyle eventually created a little brown puppy while Tai made a fluffy gray kitten that started chasing the puppy around the platform to everyone's amusement. Next, they moved on to abstract concepts.

力

power

快

swift

明

clear

Xiang continued the lesson, "Power can increase your strength temporarily. 'Swift' can increase speed, and 'clear' can heighten your perception to understand a situation or object more clearly. But it doesn't last very long, so you can't rely on it all the time. Plus, you feel the exact opposite right after, because everything must balance out in the end. So if you use 'power', right when it wears out you'll be weaker than you were before you used that qi script. Same applies to all the others. And it'll take a bit to recover depending on the level of qi you put into your writing. The more effective the qi script is, the longer the recovery time."

"Qi script…" Tai said thoughtfully. "Are there only certain characters that will work? Is it only the ones we've done today that will work?"

"Well, in theory, any character ever created and ever will be created is supposed to manifest in some way, but the older the word and the more it's used, the stronger it usually is. Maybe it has something to do with the 'life force' poured into them. It also depends on the writer and how much he or she has put into the writing," Bao said.

"Complicated," Kyle said.

"Yup," Bao said, and they continued their lesson.

The sun had already climbed through the sky and was heading for the other horizon when they finished their lesson. All the while, Xiang and Ting had been patiently sitting by and watching, handing them food now and then to keep up their stamina.

"Excellent progress! You'll be wielding qi script effortlessly in no time. Well, then, this calls for another feast!" Xiang exclaimed as they finished. They all returned up river to the heart of the village and set up things the way they were the first night Kyle and Tai were there, only this time, the sun was still up, and slowly reddening rays were filtering through the foliage. There was no dancing during this early dinner feast, and Kyle and Tai could sense a solemnity among all the village folk, and the young did not seem to pay much attention to their food as they seemed hastily engaged in conversation and other tender exchanges with their parents. Kyle leaned over to Tai in a quiet moment and whispered,

"Do you think the kids are coming with us?"

Tai looked around, acknowledging that she felt the same strange sense of farewell and somber ambience of this feast, especially compared to the festive one on their first night in the village. They both suddenly noticed a few of the Lin Gui children wiping away tears here and there as their parents spoke to them in hushed yet gentle voices. Giving each other a meaningful look, Tai and Kyle turned back to their food, feeling as if they were intruding upon private moments of farewell.

Bao sat between his mother and father, a brave smile on his face as he gobbled down his food and gulped his tea. Xiang and Ting smiled down at him happily, and he gave a crumb covered toothy grin in response.

"Tai, Kyle," Ting said in a releasing tone that caught their immediate attention, "I'm afraid we've been deceiving you up to this point, and I have to apologize for it."

The two teens widened their eyes with alarm at these words. *Lied to us? About what?* Kyle thought as a whole host of possibilities flooded through his mind. They had in fact allowed themselves to follow a black dragon's direction to a hidden village of warriors buried deep in a dark, impenetrable forest. He was at the mercy of these people, and yet, he wondered why they would have spent so much time training them to become stronger, faster, and smarter if they meant them ill will. He decided to suppress his fight-or-flight reactions as he suspected there was more to all of this than he could figure out on his own.

"You see, we decided it might be for your own good if you didn't know, so that it wouldn't distract you from your training," Xiang added.

"Do you remember when we told you that the First Child had been attacking Lin Gui villages and we had been taking in refugees from other villages?"

Kyle and Tai nodded slowly in answer to Ting's question.

"Well, that much was true. We had been taking refugees from other villages…that is, until the First Child attacked our village."

"Attacked? This village?" Kyle blurted out. He had seen no signs of such an attack.

"It happened about a month before you arrived," Bao said, suddenly looking smaller and more fragile than Kyle and Tai had ever seen him before. "We were able to repair all of the physical damages to the village by ourselves before your arrival."

"What do you mean 'by yourselves'?" Tai pointedly asked.

"The other kids and I," Bao said with a slightly visible shiver in his body. "You see, we…we were the only survivors."

Kyle could only look at Bao bewildered, unable to comprehend what the young boy was communicating to him. Xiang stepped in to help clarify.

"Our village was called the Ghost Village because of all the Lin Gui villages, we were the most skilled in stealth and the hardest to find or track. However, now that name is more fitting than ever."

Ting continued with a sad smile.

"When the First Child attacked, all of the children were sent to take refuge in the Library of Ancients with Cai. As you know, the library is well hidden and hard to get to, and only a pair of soul mates can open the entrance to it by touching the crystal butterflies."

Kyle avoided throwing Tai an uncomfortable glance.

"Everyone outside perished," Xiang finished.

There was a pause of silence in which Tai and Kyle were trying to stomach the news. In that moment, Bao slipped his little hands into the warm ones of his parents. The sunlight began to wane.

"What do you mean everyone?" Kyle had to ask.

"Xiang and I, we have both passed on," Ting said.

"What? But how? You're still here, in flesh and blood," Kyle said in a partly hysterical voice, the strain of the news starting to show at the corners of his eyes.

"With the help of phoenix paper, Bao and the other children have brought our spirits back for a short time with his qi script for the purpose of your training. It was what we had instructed him to do, and he has done a magnificent job," Ting said, smoothing the hair on her son's young head before she continued on.

"We knew that an attack on our village was coming when the refugees started pouring in, and we were afraid that we would not be able to survive long enough to greet and train The Chosen One, the only one who can defeat the First Child. Ting and I both wrote our names in layers of contained qi script on phoenix paper, infusing it with as much of our life force as was possible early on in preparation for the attack we knew was coming, an attack we could not fend off. We taught Bao how to infuse his own energy into our writing with a final layer of qi script that activated the rest, and thus, with his help, we were able to manifest ourselves for a short time in order to carry out your training. The same was done by all the villagers who both wanted to make you feel welcome and comfortable as well as say a final farewell to their children and give them some last teachings to help them carry on the Lin Gui tradition on their own."

Kyle and Tai were too dumbfounded to say anything.

"It is the eighth day," Xiang said, "and your training is complete, and our manifestation time is coming to an end."

"Good bye, Chosen One," Ting said, her eyes brimming with emotion as she then turned her attention to her son. "We are so proud of you Bao." Both parents gave their son a warm embrace, and it was then that Kyle noticed the slight transparency in their form.

"Thank you," Kyle and Tai said quickly and simultaneously. Apparently, Tai had become aware of the transparency at the same time and felt the same urgency to show gratitude. With right fist held in left palm, they respectfully gave a small bow from their sitting position.

Ting and Xiang gave them a kind smile as their faces became even more transparent and the mingling of qi script and golden phoenix paper began to unravel in a sparkling nebula of silver and gold.

"Please defeat the First Child. Her unfettered rage is all-consuming," Xiang made the final request.

With what little countenance they had left, they looked down at Bao with eyes still bursting with parental love for the child they had left behind.

"We will always be with you."

And with a last glimmer, they were gone.

Kyle and Tai were too stunned to move or breath. They could only stare speechlessly at Bao who sat in a kneeling position in front of them alone, staring down at the ground in front of him, his fingers digging into his legs as he grabbed the light cloth that covered them. It was clear he was trying not to burst out in tears, but the tears gathering at the edges of his eyes were too heavy to hold, and they began to spill down his face. He held a forearm up to cover his eyes and face, and his body began to shake as small sobs escaped from him.

Tai moved forward to put a tender arm around Bao's small frame, her own face wet with tears. Bao pressed his face into her shoulder. It was then that Kyle heard the sounds of grief coming from all the other children of the Ghost Village, and he turned to look around at all the other families surrounding them on either side of the river bank only to see that all the adults had indeed vanished, and all that was left in their place were the bereaved children, some of them holding onto each other for comfort while others were reduced to sobbing bundles huddled on the ground. The sights and sounds caused Kyle's emotions to freeze, and he couldn't understand why he didn't shed a single tear.

Chapter 13
Dragon of the Earth

"We should go," Kyle said to Tai. Outside the window, the brisk morning air of the Forest of Ghosts was filled with mist floating peacefully among its branches with streams of sunlight illuminating the wisps in a soft dance of light and vapor. This beautiful sight was lost to Kyle, as he felt only the urge to leave this place and forget the experience of the night before.

Tai responded with a questioning look and watched as Kyle busied himself with packing up for the journey. She then shifted her gaze to Bao who was also busily packing provisions for the two of them.

"Are you sure you will all be all right here on your own?" Tai asked with concern. She didn't want to bring the children with her on their perilous journey, but she couldn't shake the uneasiness of leaving them here on their own either.

Bao managed a brave smile, "Yes. In fact, we're actually safer here. We have Librarian Cai to watch over us and teach us, and the library to retreat to if there is an attack. Plus, with you on your way to defeat the First Child, we'll be safer than ever."

Bao tossed her the bag of food he had packed for her, and Tai thanked him as she stuffed the provisions and a tiny pot and utensils into the sack she had fashioned into a backpack and slung it over her back.

"Don't worry," Tai said with confidence and a dash of vengeful hate, "we'll take care of her. Is there anything more you can tell us about the First Child?"

Bao was still for a moment as he seemingly retreated into himself and the sadness underneath showed in his eyes.

"I only know as much as my parents have told you. I've never seen her myself," Bao said. He then looked around at his home and heaved a heavy sigh. "I don't understand why she didn't totally destroy our village."

Unable to make anymore sense of it, Bao shook his head and went back to preparing Kyle's provisions. Among the travel foods were white bread mantao, dried fish and squid strips, salted eggs, pickled tofu and vegetables, rice cakes, onigiri rice balls, and cookies. When he was done, he also tossed the bag to Kyle who mumbled a thanks without making any eye contact. Bao gave him a confused look, and then threw Tai a questioning glance, and she responded with an assuring smile.

"I brewed some honey lemon ginger and ginseng tea for you to take along with you! Let me get it!" Bao said, mustering as much cheer as he could at the moment, and he headed away to the kitchen.

Tai turned to Kyle in great annoyance.

"What's wrong with you?" she asked angrily.

He mumbled something that sounded like a "Nothing" and shuffled stuff around in his bag as if busy with rearranging it. He didn't look up at her and didn't answer her demand for a real answer. Tai waited impatiently and was about to lay a heavy reprimand on him for his sour attitude when Bao came back in.

"This stuff is tasty and will keep you guys healthy and energetic for the whole trip! I made it concentrated so that you can add it to water you find along the way if you want and have more to drink!" Bao said with a smile as he held the two corked gourds up for them.

"Thank you," Tai said as she took them from him. She shoved one in front of Kyle, and he took it without a word and stuffed it into his bag. This infuriated Tai, but she kept the smile on her face for Bao's sake.

"Do you have some extra cookies? I'd love to have more for the trip," she asked.

"SURE!" Bao said, happy to oblige. He bounded back towards the kitchen.

"Hey," Tai called to Kyle. When he wouldn't look up and acknowledge her, she smacked him on the shoulder with the back of her hand. Slightly louder but much more force, she said again, "Hey!"

"What?" Kyle irritably responded as he looked up at her with open annoyance flashing in his eyes.

"Whatever your problem is, you deal with your issues and don't make others deal with them, especially not recently orphaned little boys," Tai scolded sharply.

He looked away from her again. Kyle wouldn't let go of his anger because it was his shield, but guilt and shame definitely made its way into his emotional mix.

Bao came back with more cookies than anyone could carry, and with consciously enhanced eagerness, Tai filled her bag to maximum capacity with them and even put one in her mouth for immediate consumption. Then Bao brought the bowl of cookies over to Kyle and offered them to him with bright eyes. When Kyle looked up to meet Bao's hopeful face, shame and guilt overtook his other emotions. He realized how self-centered and ungrateful he had been all morning.

"Thanks Bao, this'll help out a lot," Kyle finally managed with a weak smile.

Bao's face beamed with satisfaction. He then disappeared into his parents' bedroom and reappeared with the scroll of "Compassion" that they had borrowed from the Library of Ancients.

"Here," Bao said as he handed it to Kyle, who felt even worse about his behavior over the morning upon seeing the scroll.

"Do you know when or how we're supposed to use this?" Tai asked.

Bao shook his little head. "I guess you'll just find out when the time comes."

Kyle put the scroll into his bag, tucking it next to the roll of phoenix paper.

"Let's go," Tai said.

They made their way down to the river that cut through the village, and there were all the village children, dressed in their beetle-like garb again in an almost ceremonial manner. Kyle and Tai stood towering over them as the only teenagers around, but though they were small, they carried themselves with a sense of responsibility, a maturity and poise beyond their years, so much so that Kyle could almost imagine what they would look like when they were fully grown adults carrying on the torch of their village.

There was a large, wood-carved leaf curled up in a way that artfully made it into a small boat. A rope anchored to the shore was tied to the large, wooden stem of the leaf-boat and held it from being carried away by the strong river current. It bobbed and swayed, impatient to begin its journey. Bao gave them what directions he could to help them reach their destination.

"The river will take you out of the Forest of Ghosts so you won't get lost. When you're out of the forest, you'll need to land on the southern shore, which is on your left. Beyond that, I don't know much except that there are many mountains, rivers, and oceans to cross before you get to the Phoenix Mountain of the First Child. You're heading west, so just follow the sun. From what I've heard, Phoenix Mountain isn't hard to miss."

"Here." Some of the children came up Tai and Kyle to hand them two long, bamboo poles that towered a foot or two above their heads.

"You can use them to help you steer down the river and also for protection," Bao said.

"Protection?" Kyle perked to the implication of danger.

"Well, there's kind of a lot of dangerous creatures around, so keep alert," Bao said.

"Creatures? Like what?" Kyle pressed on.

Bao took a deep breath and looked like he was about to begin a dissertation on the subject when Tai jumped in.

"We'll just have to find out along the way. We shouldn't waste anymore daylight."

Kyle and Tai boarded the small boat. Tai indicated for Kyle to untie the rope that held the boat at bay. As soon as the rope was loosened and falling from the stem, Tai bowed respectfully to the Lin Gui children with right fist cupped in left palm, and Kyle hastily did the same.

"Thank you," Tai spoke for the two of them, "for everything."

"一路順風 May you have a smooth journey!" the children chimed in unison as they began to wave enthusiastically with smiles on their faces and tears sparkling in their eyes. The sight of the Chosen One setting off on their journey was one they wanted to cherish for their parents' sake. They began to run down the river following the wooden leaf boat as it bobbed out to the middle of the river and began to pick up speed in the rushing current. They continued to chant the well-wishing idiom, some yelling it exuberantly out of unison, wishing the pair a road with smooth winds on their way to face the First Child.

The ride down the river was at first uneventful and silent save for the sound of rushing water and birds and animal calls in the trees. Tai and Kyle were busy monitoring their respective halves of the boat. Whenever they wandered too close to one shore or the other, one or both of them would use their handy bamboo poles to push their little vessel back on track. Kyle's attention focused on this back and forth stewarding of their little vessel.

"So what's with you anyway?"

Tai's sudden interjection into his quiet absorption in this task startled him a bit.

"What do you mean?"

He avoided looking up at her.

"I mean, yesterday, when Xiang and Ting…left us, and this morning, with Bao. Your reaction isn't exactly normal."

"What's not normal about it?" Kyle responded with a level of annoyance in his voice that surprised even himself.

"Well, I don't know, Xiang and Ting took us in, fed us, taught us," Tai said without hiding some of the sarcasm that surfaced in her voice. "I would think you'd have some…some compassion…feel some sadness for the children. Or maybe anger at the First Child for causing so much pain. But you, you seemed like you were just annoyed that you had to deal with the situation."

"Well of course I'm annoyed! I'm here in this godforsaken lala-land with dragons and ghosts and whatevers, all against my will," Kyle poured out his frustrations, still not looking at Tai and paying more attention than he needed to his bamboo stick and steering. "I just want to get home, back to school, back to *normal*."

"That's not what I'm talking about. You're changing the subject," Tai accused, to which Kyle responded with more silent steering.

"In any case," Tai continued, ignoring his silent unwillingness to respond, "let's just make this clear. Normally, I wouldn't care what your issues are because I work alone. But since we're supposed to work as a team to defeat the First Child demon, it's of strategic importance that I understand your psyche."

Kyle lifted his bamboo stick out of the water, placed the tip securely against the shore of the river that their boat was floating towards, and pushed back off into the main flow of the river.

"Does this have to do with your grandmother?"

That caught his undivided attention. Kyle turned looked up at Tai, eyes wide with surprise and indignation. She didn't turn to meet his gaze.

"How do you know about my grandmother?" he asked with a tinge of anger.

Tai took the opportunity to look away, ignore him, and give him a taste of his own avoidance medicine. Then, nonchalantly, as if it were just inconsequential fact, she shrugged her shoulders and said, "Your grandfather told me."

Kyle mulled over her answer for a quiet moment. Suddenly, some of the old questions that had swirled in his mind back when he had first met Tai at the Tian Yi Society gathering sprang to the surface.

"How do you know my grandfather anyway?"

"He's my teacher."

"Your teacher?"

"Yes, he taught me calligraphy, history, philosophy, and martial arts."

"What?!" Kyle didn't understand why, but he felt a little betrayed by his grandfather.

"You thought you were his only student or something?" Tai mocked.

"No, I…I just…he never told me about you, about there being two of us…the two of us being the Chosen One."

"Well, don't you think it's interesting that we've gone to the same high school, the same middle school, and the same elementary school, and you've never even noticed I existed even though your grandfather has been training me this whole time?"

Kyle started to wonder if his grandfather had really gone off on trips around the world as often as he claimed. Then he puzzled over the new information she had just revealed to him.

"We were in the same elementary school and middle school?" He examined her face for any sign of impish deception, but Tai just nodded with a dry expression on her face that told him she thought of him as a nincompoop for not knowing.

"And you knew about me this whole time? Have you…have you been *spying* on me?"

"I guess you could say that. Your grandfather often asked me about how you were doing at school. So yeah, I was spying on you and relaying the information to him."

No wonder he always had that smug smile on his face, like he knew more about me than I did, Kyle thought to himself.

"It was your failure for not noticing," Tai said.

"What?"

"Since we were very young, your grandfather told me that I was to play a game with you. The game was that I would keep myself from being noticed by you, and your job was to notice me. I guess I won by a landslide. You didn't even recognize me when you first saw me."

"Well, you were dressed differently. How was I supposed to recognize you if you dressed differently?" Kyle said defensively.

"That's a lame excuse and you know it. A true warrior is always aware of her surroundings."

"You sound like my grandfather."

"Well, now you know why."

It was Tai's turn to use her bamboo to push their leaf-shaped boat from the shore, and they were well back in the middle of the river again when they hit something. The collision caused their small craft to sway somewhat wildly back and forth, putting it in danger of capsizing altogether. Kyle knew that if he hadn't received all that training in agility and balance over the past week, he probably would have easily fallen off the boat.

As their boat stabilized, they both saw a dreadful sight at the same time. Rolling out and then back into the water was the massive body of some large serpent-like creature. The creature's body was at least three yards in diameter and who knew how long in length. Kyle suddenly wished he'd never watched all those movies about giant snakes.

The water began to whirl instead of flow forward, and their boat began to turn with the change. Again and again, portions of the creature's body emerged out of the water only to turn back into the water like a slimy waterwheel, and it seemed their boat was surrounded in turning masses of scaled flesh that trapped them from moving forward.

Just when Kyle felt he was about to pass out from the intensity of it all, his adrenaline shot to new heights as the head of the massive creature finally emerged from the whirlpool. First to appear was its wide-set snout with flaring nostrils and two long, fleshy mustache-like extensions that would have made the creature look sage-like if it hadn't been for the sharp and vicious fangs in its mouth and the pair of large wild-looking, forward-facing eyes. On the back of its round serpent's body were spiky ridges that looked like razor teeth on the edge of a saw. Its scales were dark green, and it had two arms with menacing claws at the end of each, and Kyle figured it must have two more of such unfriendly appendages on the other end of its body.

Kyle could only grab his bamboo pole tightly as he waited for the creature's next move. The bamboo had felt rather reassuring when it was first put in his hand, but now it seemed like it would only be good as a toothpick for the massive creature they faced.

It was Tai who spoke up for the both of them again.

"Great dragon! My name is Tai, and this is Kyle. We are on our way to Phoenix Mountain to face the First Child! Can you give us any assistance?"

"I am 地龍, Dragon of the Earth," the creature's deep voice boomed.

Di Long looked at them for a long, silent while. The swirling of their boat had abated, but they were still turning slightly, and he seemed to be sizing them up as they revolved slowly like a new car on display in a dealer's lot.

"Hmm…*you* are going to face the First?" the dragon glistening with water said with doubt. It was in fact the first time anyone had expressed doubt in the powers of The Chosen One.

"Yes," Tai answered firmly.

"You will fail," was Di Long's flat response to Tai's confidence. Even Tai was at first shocked to silence at the finality in his voice. Despite being terribly frightened, Kyle was curious enough to brave a question.

"How do you know?"

"I can tell that you are no match for me, and I," Di Long seemed to gather what was left of his pride together before answering, "I am no match for her."

Chapter 14

Clash of the Dragons

Before Kyle had a chance to say anything else, Tai spoke up for the both of them.

"Then we challenge you Di Long!"

"WHAT?!"

Kyle couldn't comprehend Tai's impatient audacity when he himself couldn't see how they would be able to defeat such a humungous and powerful-looking creature. He could only conclude that she must be insane with pride.

"Very well," the Dragon of the Earth boomed in response as it craned its neck for its first strike.

Kyle realized he was going to have to back up Tai's challenge whether he wanted to or not. The dragon's head shot forward without warning, heading straight for them. Kyle and Tai had only a split second to jump off of the little wooden leaf boat before it was smashed to splinters by Di Long's powerful strike.

Feeling the spray of water and occasional bits of splintered boat against him, Kyle had a moment to be surprised at how high he had jumped, attributed it to his adrenaline rush, and then look frantically for a place to land his feet. He realized that his trajectory wasn't headed for dry land or tumultuous waters; he was heading straight for a part of the dragon's body which was swirling and churning in the water in a sickening, worm-like manner. As his feet made contact with Di Long's solid and scaly body, Kyle landed running, trying to keep from falling into the water or being pulled in the undertow of the dragon's momentum. His bamboo staff still in hand, he used it as a balancing aide as he tried to keep his footing on the moving dragon.

A yard or two ahead of him, he saw another part of the dragon's body, and another, and another, its writhing form creating churning stepping stones to the shore. Steadying his footing, Kyle made a leap for the nearest part of twisting dragon flesh, barely keeping his balance and yet not falling into the abyss of water and scales. Still working to keep with the movement of the dragon's body, Kyle made another successful jump and another, and finally made his way to solid ground.

Glad to be on steady earth again, he turned to survey the scene he had just escaped and saw that Tai was standing on the opposite shore, and he figured she must have gotten there the same way he had. Her bamboo staff was held defensively in her hands, and Kyle's heart almost stopped as he saw Di Long plunge at her the way he had attacked their helpless little boat. He watched in shock as she disappeared under the dragon's attack, and earth, grass, and roots flew up in the air at the impact, but he breathed in relief when he saw her reappear above the tumultuous crash. She had jumped up, barely avoiding this second strike, and then she landed a clear blow on the dragon's head with her bamboo staff, but it was like hitting wood against stone; the bamboo staff broke into splinters as a result, and the impact flung it painfully out of her hand.

Kyle watched on for a moment as Tai dodged strike after strike of the dragon's attacks; he was too far away to help, but before he could figure out a way to get across the river to Tai, his unconscious senses told him to look up just in time to see the dragon's tail come shooting towards him. He jumped out of the way, and the tale speared itself into the ground at the spot where he had been standing just a split second earlier. It rose up and shot at him again, a sharp, gigantic spike whose sole purpose was to impale him. Avoiding death by a hair again and again, Kyle was surprised he wasn't simply petrified with fear. In fact, he felt almost nothing at all with all of his mental and physical resources strained and focused on his evasive maneuvers.

The dragon tail suddenly retreated, which gave Kyle a chance to see that Tai was still in one piece on the other shore, staring at the reeling dragon's head as it rose up away from her, appearing to halt its assault on her as well. The dragon tail that had been attacking Kyle suddenly shot out of the water to match the height of its head, and then the spearheaded point was plunged into the water. It began to move around in the water, stirring up the river like so much soup, but Kyle soon realized the dragon tail was actually *writing* something in the water. He recognized it was the character for "bubble".

"Wha—?" he mouthed in confusion. Why would the dragon write the word "bubble" in the water?

Almost in immediate response to his near silent question, two round spheres of water burst out of the river surface, one flying towards Tai and the other towards Kyle. Tai and Kyle moved to evade the liquid missile, but the attacking spheres were homed in on each of them respectively like smart bombs. Kyle was barely turning to run when he felt the wet mass meet with his back, but instead of being thrown forward, he was engulfed in the watery ball.

Inside the ball of water, he strained and moved his arms and kicked his feet randomly and frantically at first, losing all sense of direction of up or down, and then he was trying to breast stroke himself out of his liquid prison, but it was no use. The liquid that made up the sphere was swirling continuously, and he was spinning with it, all his efforts to go anywhere redirected back into the center of it all. Kyle was overwhelmed with dizziness and disorientation, and not having been prepared to be submerged like this, he had not taken a proper deep breath and was on the verge of inhaling a lungful of water.

Just when he thought he was a goner, Kyle felt the water suddenly drain away from him, and he gasped painfully for the life giving air that was unexpectedly available to him. When he had regained some control over his breathing, he looked up to see that he was standing in a ball of water that was now hollow on the inside, which explained the sudden availability of air. Through the shell of liquid, he could see a distorted view of the Tai next to him, who also appeared to be encased in a similar prison. Then Kyle saw that they were both floating in front of the dragon's face, and dread sunk in as he expected the worse. If they were hovering this close to Di Long's face, he might be considering having these two worthless humans as a mid-afternoon snack. It crossed Kyle's mind that he didn't want to die as a water dumpling.

The sphere of water suddenly lost its cogency, and the fluid splashed back down to join again with the river waters. Kyle expected to fall, but instead found himself standing on the scaly mass of a part of the dragon's body, which was no longer churning the waters. Looking down, he saw that each of the dragon's scales was roughly equivalent to both of his feet put together. The scales glimmered with the water and reflected sunlight, and Kyle would have found them beautiful if they hadn't been attached to a dragon that had just tried to obliterate him and his companion.

"You have lost," boomed Di Long's voice with a surprising tinge of disappointment.

The Dragon of the Earth lowered the two humans perched on his body to the ground, and they stepped off, bedraggled like a defeated pair of half-drowned alley cats. Breathing heavily and slightly erratically, the two dropped their soaking bags on the ground and collapsed upon reaching the solid earth, having still to fully recover from their near drowning.

"As I said before, you are no match for the First Child. Relinquish your quest."

On that depressing note, the dragon lowered itself back into the river water, sinking into it like an old battleship damaged beyond repair, apparently taking no joy in his victory over the two humans.

Chapter 15
Goddess of Mercy

Kyle lay back on the ground, mostly just glad he was alive. Tai stayed sitting up, her arms draped over her knees. Then she pulled herself up to a standing position. Curiosity caused Kyle to turn and watch what his companion was doing, and he watched as she stumbled a bit on her way to a bush nearby. From behind it, she pulled out the remains of her bamboo staff and then shocked Kyle by smashing what was left against a nearby tree. The splinters and bits sprayed out under the impact. Then Tai took off into the thick forest and quickly disappeared out of sight.

The sudden burst of violent anger from his companion and her sudden disappearance into the forest had given Kyle enough of a jolt to come back to his senses from his fatigue. He got to his feet, picked up both of their packs, and followed her. If he was aware of anything, he at least knew that the two of them getting separated wasn't a good idea.

"Tai?" he called out as he entered the forest, too, with the roar of the river beginning to fade behind him as he went. There was a moment of panic as he scanned for her, but he soon spotted her brown clad back, the simple clothing they had been given by the Lin Gui making her blend with the environment.

"Tai!" he called out to her, but she didn't respond, she just kept walking away from him in silence. Though his limbs ached both from the battle they had just lost and the weeklong Lin Gui training, he broke out into a trot after her. When he caught up to her, he called her name again, but still she didn't respond. For a moment he just followed behind her in silence, but in that silence, he realized he could barely hear the roar of the river behind them, which worried him. He realized too that if they lost the river, they may be lost in the Forest of Ghosts forever. His new panic was heightened some more as he looked around and saw that every direction looked like every other direction.

"Hey, Tai, I think we should get back to the river," Kyle said. He was only a few paces behind her, so he knew she could hear him. The calls of some unseen birds filled the silence between them.

"Hey, Tai, we should get back before we get lost," Kyle tried again, this time trying to appeal to her logical side, but still she just kept on walking.

Finally, Kyle decided to take a bolder approach. He put a hand on her shoulder and pulled her around to talk to her face to face.

"Hey, Tai, come on—"

He was stopped short when he saw her face. Her cheeks were wet from tears, and she had a look of intense anger and frustration mixed in with a good amount of shame and embarrassment. She didn't look up directly into his eyes, but instead looked to the side away from him even though she now stood facing him. He wasn't quite sure how to deal with her upset.

"Um, look, everything's going to be okay," he started unconvincingly. "We just need to get back to the river and keep going."

Tai just continued to stare silently at the ground. It seemed to Kyle that she was afraid to talk, as if opening her mouth would reveal more than she wanted to share.

"Come on, we can't stay here. We just gotta keep moving forward," Kyle gestured to the forest around them as he attempted again to appeal to her logical side. Having never been any good with girls, Kyle looked around at the labyrinth of a forest that surrounded them and thought for a moment about how ironic it was that his life currently depended on his being able to soothe the bruised pride of a girl.

"Not all is lost," a woman's voice broke into their silence.

Kyle and Tai were suddenly pulled out of their current, awkward stalemate to look for the source of the voice.

"Up here," said the kind sounding voice.

They both looked up and saw a woman in flowing white robes sitting on a tree branch. Her left foot hung loose while her right was resting up on the branch causing her knee to jut up, and her arm rested on that knee at the elbow. In her right hand was a thin green branch of a willow tree with slender thin leaves, and in her left hand was a small, porcelain vase-like container. Her long black hair was covered with a white cloth, and her face was unremarkable. If not done up the way she was or perched in a tree, they may have just thought she was some simple, local inhabitant. However, the calming steadiness of the light in her eye and her kind smile made her radiate with the white robes she wore, giving her a beauty that told Kyle and Tai she was no ordinary being.

She hopped down from her perch and alighted on the ground near them, a gentle breeze emanating from the place where she landed and stood. She walked towards them, and as she came closer, they felt that they were enveloped in a soothing calm.

"My name is Guan Yin. I am here because I heard your call for help."

"I'm sorry, what…who are you?" Kyle asked.

"I am as you see. Just a woman who was passing by, answering someone's call for help."

Kyle looked at Tai looked down in silence. She appeared ashamed of something.

"Well, we do kind of need some help," Kyle said.

"Oh? Then I am glad that the winds have brought me to a place where I might be of some assistance. What is it that you need?" Guan Yin asked, her voice simple yet melodious at the same time. She had a purity to her soul that made everything about her extraordinary precisely because she was so ordinary.

Kyle gave Tai another glance. Seeing no open protest to his divulging their identity and exploits to a perfect stranger, he continued on.

"My name is Kyle, and this is Tai. We are…supposedly the Chosen One. We're on a mission to stop the First Child from causing more trouble in this world. But we just met with a dragon named Di Long, Dragon of the Earth, and he basically told us we won't be able to stop the First Child. So here we are…uh…trying to figure out what to do next."

"I see, I see," Guan Yin said, nodding her head in comprehension, but Kyle got the distinct feeling that she already knew everything he had just told her and had only listened quietly out of politeness. Her kind eyes examined Kyle carefully, like a kindergarten teacher checking a student carefully for any bruises or cuts, and then she shifted her gaze to Tai and did the same thing.

"Well, Di Long is right, you two are currently not capable of defeating the First Child." A sadness fell over her eyes as her thoughts drifted over the First Child. "She is indeed a formidable opponent, and her soul…her soul is Twisted beyond imagination." Guan Yin flinched at those last words, as if she were burned by a flame in her memory.

"What do you mean…twisted?" Kyle was both curious and worried.

"The First Child is called a demon for a reason. But I cannot paint out her soul's landscape for you. It is something you will have to explore for yourselves in order to fully understand it."

"Why can't you tell us more? If you are a Guan Yin, you are the Goddess of Mercy, are you not?" Tai pressed. Kyle's eyes widened. Although he didn't know who the Goddess of Mercy was, the title sounded faintly familiar to him.

"I am no goddess," Guan Yin said with another kind smile and a soft shake of her head. "I am just a woman who wanders about listening to people's troubles. And that is the answer to your question Tai. I am like you, like Kyle, and even like the First Child. Only human."

Tai breathed in and out a little deeper than usual, as if she were coming partially to terms with something.

"What can we do to defeat the First Child?" Tai asked, sounding more like her old self again, to Kyle's uncertain relief. The 'goddess' smiled again, but this time with hope and even some joy mixed in with her kindness.

"There is something that can give you some strength against the First Child. The Peach of Immortality."

"Immortality?" Kyle questioned. He wasn't sure he liked the sound of this.

"Yes."

"Where can we find it?" Tai asked impatiently.

"To the east."

"Wait, but isn't that opposite the direction of where we're trying to go?" Kyle asked, unable to mask his dismay. Back tracking just didn't sound like the fastest way home.

"Sometimes the way backwards is the way forwards," Guan Yin said with a twinkle in her eye. Kyle's brow furrowed pensively.

"Is this like that whole deal where it's not about the destination, it's about the journey?" Kyle puzzled.

The 'goddess' tilted her head slightly in a curious manner and said, "Who says the journey and the destination are two separate things?"

Kyle felt even more confused.

"I see," Tai said a bit hastily. "Where in the east is this Peach?"

"The tree that bears the Peach of Immortality grows on the lush green tops of Jade Mountain. If you wish to defeat the First Child, then you must go there first."

"How many mountains are there in this place anyways?" Kyle said, still feeling exasperated at the news that they would have to basically go back the way they had come, eat something mystical and probably unsanitary, and then turn around and go all the way back the other way and then some.

"Life is full of mountains to climb and pebbles in your shoe," Guan Yin said cheerfully. "Here, take these."

She handed the small white porcelain, vase-like container to Kyle and the evergreen willow branch to Tai.

"This jar will always be full of pure water to sustain you on your journey, and this willow, when held up, will always blow in the direction you need to go."

Kyle and Tai each received their respective gifts politely with both hands.

"Thank you," they both said and bowed in gratitude.

"Well, then, we'd all best be on our way again then," the 'goddess' said cheerfully. "May you have smooth winds on your journey."

"Where are you going?" Kyle asked out of curiosity.

"Wherever the wind blows. Don't worry, I'll be listening," Guan Yin said with a friendly wink. With that, she turned and took off through the forest, heading in no particular direction, as her path naturally curved this way at this point and that way at that point like a butterfly's jagged flight from one flower to another.

Kyle and Tai watched transfixed by the image of the Goddess of Mercy taking a stroll through the forest, both expecting to see her poof out of existence or suddenly float up towards the sky on a mystical cloud, but Guan Yin simply walked and walked and walked until she was out of sight.

"That was kind of weird," Kyle thought out loud.

"Yeah, well, let's check our supplies before we go on," Tai said, back to business as usual. Kyle looked over at her, seeing that her cheek was dry and her face determined again, the only evidence of her earlier upset found in the slight redness around her eyes. Tai held a hand out to Kyle, and he stared at it stupidly.

"My bag?" Tai asked impatiently.

"Oh yeah, here," Kyle snapped out of his confusion and handed her bag to her.

"Thanks for bringing it for me," she said, "and I'm sorry about my behavior earlier." She looked him straight in the eyes with sincerity.

Kyle froze for a moment. He'd never seen eyes so full of clarity. He decided at that moment that he liked her eyes.

"Uh…nah, don't worry about it. No big," he said, and then after a moment of thought, he added, "I'm sorry about my behavior this morning, too."

Suddenly, Tai did something that Kyle definitely wouldn't have expected in a million years—she smiled at him with approval. It was a smile that didn't hide any hidden agendas. He decided he liked her smile.

They both proceeded to look through the contents of their bags with amazement. Despite their ordeal and the soaking exterior of the bag, the contents inside were dry and undamaged thanks to good craftsmanship of the Lin Gui. Tai carefully checked the phoenix papers, the Scroll of Compassion, and the brushes and finally breathed a sigh of relief to see that they were definitely undamaged. She put them carefully back.

"We should eat while we walk," Tai said, looking up at the late afternoon sun. She pulled out three rice onigiri and some cookies and then slung the pack on her back again. Kyle did the same, and when they had their food securely in hand, Tai held the evergreen willow up, and though they felt no wind, it fluttered in an eastward direction.

“Let’s go,” Tai said and then took a big bite out of her rice onigiri before heading east.

Chapter 16

The Orphan

"So you're ranked first in class, too?" Kyle asked.

They had spent the rest of the day walking through forest, forest, and more forest. It seemed unending. It was night now, and though their little directional willow branch could help them find their way despite the dark, they had decided to camp out for the night and move again before dawn. Kyle was trying to make small talk to find out more about this girl who had apparently lurked in the shadows of his life all this time undetected by him.

"There are like twelve people ranked first in our class," Tai shrugged.

"Are you planning on taking the exams this fall, too?" Kyle asked.

"Probably," Tai shrugged again.

"Have you taken a practice test yet?"

"Yes."

"How did you do?"

"Perfect score."

"WHAT?!"

Tai added wood to the fire that crackled under the little metal pot in which she was cooking the rice porridge that they were going to eat with the dried fish and pickled vegetables that Kyle was pulling out of their sacks. They had the cookies, too.

"What?" Tai responded to his surprise nonchalantly as she ate a couple of cookies.

"Perfect score? Wow, I'm scoring high, but not PERFECT. You're going to get a scholarship for sure."

Tai shrugged again as she stirred the rice porridge. "Well, I've always been a quick study."

Kyle sat back, looked up and sighed. A quick study was something he never was. Every grade, every high score, every point was worked for with long nights under a small desk lamp in the dark of his little cave of a room. Nothing ever came quick and easy for him.

"And I'm missing all this time to study this summer. I'm never going to catch up," Kyle worried out loud. "So what classes are you going to take next year?" Even though Kyle really wasn't sure if he wasn't going to get back home, he pushed that nagging fear to the back of his mind. Acting like going back to school was going to be a definite future outcome helped him to hold that fear at bay.

"All the classes you're planning to take," Tai said matter-of-factly.

"All of them?"

"Yeah, that's usually how I pick my classes. I look at what you're taking and I sign up for all the same classes."

"What? Why?"

Tai filled his metal bowl with porridge and handed it to him and then filled her own. The two picked up their metallic chopsticks and began picking up pieces of dried fish or pickled vegetables and shoveling them into their mouths with the rice porridge.

"It's just easier that way," Tai said with another shrug. She finished one bowl and served herself another.

"It always takes me a long time to figure out which classes to take," Kyle said. He paused a moment as he looked at the white jar, wary of the fact that clean water was flowing continuously from some unseen source, but finally he just poured some into his mouth, careful not to touch the rim of the container to his lips.

"I know, that's why it's easier for me just to copy your schedule," Tai said.

"Well, aren't you worried about which classes you need to get into

certain colleges? Optimize your GPA?"

"They're just classes, Kyle," Tai said. "Besides, you figured all that out already, so why do I need to spend my precious time on it?"

"Wait a minute, how do you find out what classes I'm planning to take?" Kyle asked, eyeing her with suspicion again.

"I just look at what you mark down on your paper. You don't exactly plan your schedule in a top secret room." Tai stuffed a pickled vegetable in her mouth and followed that with the rice porridge. She held her hand out to Kyle, and he handed her the white jar of water. "Besides, you mumble out loud to yourself when you're thinking really hard."

"No!"

"Yes."

Kyle sat there trying to remember. Tai drank some of the water the way he had, pouring the pure fluid into her mouth without touching the rim to her lips, but she had no hesitation in drinking it.

"You know, it's kinda creepy to me that you've been watching me this whole time without my knowing," Kyle changed his angle of argument.

"Direct your complaints to your grandfather. It's not like I would have paid any attention to you if I hadn't been asked to by him."

Kyle felt more annoyed by what she had just said than by anything else she had said so far. He emptied the rest of the porridge in his bowl into his mouth. He refilled his bowl.

"Well, it's not fair."

"What's not fair?" Tai said as she ate and drank some more.

"I feel like you know so much about me, but I know almost nothing about you. It just seems unbalanced, like you always have the upper hand on me."

Kyle finished his second serving of porridge, picked up a cookie, and began nibbling on it. Tai finished up the rest of her meal in a big gulp, turning her bowl almost totally bottom-side-up as she poured every last bit of porridge into her mouth.

"Okay, fine, what do you want to know about me?"

He thought through what he did know about her. She was born on the same day as he was. She went to his high school, middle school, and elementary school. She took all the same classes he did. She had trained under his grandfather.

"Do you know where I live?" Kyle asked.

"Yes."

"Okay then, where do you live?"

"Down the street from you."

Kyle let out an exasperated sigh.

"Really?"

"Really."

"Which house?"

"The one with the two cycads in front, eight houses away."

Kyle had no idea which one she was talking about. He figured he could check it when he went back home and went on to think about his next question.

"Um…uh…what's your favorite color?" He knew it was a lame question, but he couldn't think of anything better.

"Black."

"Black's not a color."

"Black is my favorite color."

"Black is the absence of color."

"Black is the absence of light, and it's my favorite color."

"Okay fine, fine. Um…what are your hobbies?"

"I don't have any."

"No hobbies? What about martial arts?"

"The term 'hobbies' denotes an *extra* activity. Everything I do is central to my life, *not* extra. Thus, I have no hobbies."

Tai's voice took on the tone of a lecturer, and Kyle gave her a dry look in response.

"Fine. Then what are the *central* activities of your life?"

"Training, studying, learning."

"What do you study?"

"Everything."

"What do you mean by everything?"

"I mean everything. What else could I mean?"

"So math, science, language arts, social studies…everything?"

"Those categories are superfluous and limiting. 'Everything' just means 'everything'. If I say I like fruits, it's redundant to name out all of them, right? The superordinate category already has it all covered."

"Alright, alright." Kyle let out a breath of mild exasperation. He never thought such simple questions could have such complicated answers. He decided to steer back to more concrete questions.

"Do you know my parents' names?"

"Yes, John and Mary Lin."

"What are your parent's names?"

"I don't know."

"What?"

"I don't know what my parent's names are."

Kyle's attempt to veer back towards more 'concrete' questions had just backfired. Apparently, he had asked the most complicated question of them all. Silence suddenly poured into the space between them. Tai picked up some cookies and started to munch away on them and drink from the white jar. Kyle wasn't sure how to proceed. Finally, he decided to go with the most obvious question.

"Why don't you know their names?"

"Because I don't know who my parents are."

After another pause, Kyle finished with a heavy breath, "I see."

Feeling his discomfort, Tai offered some more information.

"I was told that my mother came into the Tian Yi Society pregnant with me. After she had me, she left. The house I live in down the street from you is my foster home."

Unfortunately, that extra information only served to make Kyle feel even more uncomfortable. He didn't know what to say and had no concept of how to approach the topic. So he decided to go for the most generic response.

"I'm sorry."

"Why?" Tai said with an eyebrow raised.

"I dunno, I just am. Like I wish it wasn't like that with you."

"It is no big deal. It's just what is. I've been well fed and always had a roof over my head. So no big," Tai shrugged her shoulders. "Look, we should get some sleep. We've got a long day tomorrow."

Tai began to clean up and pack up unneeded items. Kyle moved silently to help her. They put enough wood into the fire to keep it running for a while, and finally, each pulled out a large, light, yet sturdy blanket made by the Lin Gui and using their packs as pillows, they turned in for the night.

Kyle lay facing the crackling fire and watched the flames dancing and driving away the darkness. Tai lay on the other side of the fire with her back to burning embers. He stared at her back and wondered what it must have been like to grow up in her life instead of his own.

Chapter 17

Swift

Kyle woke up in a black and blue world, with the unseen sun only barely lighting the edges of a dark sky. Some night time insects buzzed about, and the cold, still silence of an early morning outdoors brought him quickly out of sleep. He saw Tai sitting up already on the other side of the dead fire with her back turned to him, and a golden glow was emanating from in front of her, as if she had captured a little piece of the morning sun in her lap. This stimulated enough curiosity in Kyle for him to break out of his warm cocoon of a blanket and sit up.

"What are you doing?" he asked, stretching some of the stiffness of sleep out of his joints.

"I think I figured out a way to quicken our pace."

Kyle was out of bed at this. A way to get home faster was definitely something he was interested in.

"Really? How?"

He looked over her shoulder to see what she was doing. She had before her a piece of wood, some phoenix paper, and her brush. The moist earth around her was upturned, and Kyle could see that this was because Tai had been using the stick to practice writing a Chinese character over and over again into the soil. On the phoenix paper, the word she had written with the brush and her own life energy qi as the ink glowed with life. It was the Chinese character for 'swift'.

"If I'm right, the phoenix paper should enhance the qi energy in the character I've written here, and if I reabsorb this energy back into myself, it should manifest in my body making me capable of greater physical speed," Tai explained her logic to him. He squatted down next to her, listening and watching intently. She looked up at him, and the glow of her qi script bounced off her light brown eyes, emphasizing the hint of amber in them more than ever. The steadiness of the dawn-like glow in her eyes hypnotized him for a moment before her voice broke into his mild trance. "Kind of like E equals MC squared."

"Huh?"

"Einstein's equation."

"What about it?"

"Nevermind," Tai said looking away impatiently.

"No really, what about it?" Kyle pressed on. He was both weirded out and curious at how Tai could see something 'scientific' in something 'magical' like qi writing. Tai looked back up at him.

"Energy and mass are interchangeable. I'm trying to transform energy into written matter, transform that written matter back into enhanced energy, and then make that enhanced energy increase the speed of my physical matter."

"Hmm…" Kyle thought a bit, but though he wasn't totally sure what she was talking about, he was feeling as impatient as Tai to try this out. The glowing Chinese writing waited for their next move. "Okay then, try it out."

Trying to steady her eagerness, she held out her right hand over the phoenix paper with her palm faced down towards the glowing character, and then slowly she lowered her hand till her skin was pressed down against it. The character glowed brighter under the pressure of her hand, and then the phoenix paper began to burn up in a golden fire. Kyle watched with wide eyes as the light crept up Tai's hand, causing her arm to glow under the simple brown, long sleeve of her shirt that matched his own, and then spread to the rest of her body. Tai's eyes grew wide, and she sat there in perfect stillness, emanating light silently and illuminating some of the dark of the night that still remained. The sun had lightened most of the sky into a mild blue, but it had not thrown its blazing rays over the horizon yet. Tai was still and quiet long enough to worry Kyle.

"Tai? Are you okay?" Instinctively, he put a hand up to her forehead to feel her temperature. As soon as his skin made contact with hers, he felt a rush of warmth surge into him. The world around him slowed. The leaves of the trees and bushes that had been moving in a light breeze were practically at a standstill, and suddenly Kyle was aware of a tiny wasp that hung in mid-flight and midair in front of his eyes. He removed his hand from Tai's forehead, and she looked up at him with as much amazement in her expression as he felt.

"I think…I think it worked," she said, breathing a little harder than usual in her surprise.

Kyle noticed that Tai was the only physical entity that moved at what seemed like a normal speed to him.

"Wait, I thought this was supposed to give us speed, not slow everything else down…Oh!" Kyle answered his own question. "Everything's slow because we're faster!"

"Exactly," Tai said. "And the qi script must have spread to you, too, when you touched my forehead. Why were you touching my forehead?" A little indignity crept into her voice.

"You were glowing, so I was just checking your temperature," Kyle said with a shrug.

"Oh," Tai said.

"How long is this going to last?" Kyle said, looking at his own hands in disbelief, and then looking back up at the suspended world around him.

"I don't know, but maybe we should make use of it while it lasts and get going."

"Good idea," Kyle said. Both of them packed up their things and set off. The walking seemed normal enough, aside from the fact that everything around them was moving at a snail's pace and they had to try to avoid walking into poor insects and small birds flying across their path. As time passed, everything around them returned slowly to its normal speed—at least that's what it looked like from their perspective. They were slowing down, and as they slowed down, it looked like everything else was speeding up. When everything was pretty much back to normal, the two of them were pretty exhausted. To them, they had been walking for hours and hours, but the sun had only just made it over the horizon indicating they had been traveling for only less than an hour's time.

Kyle was walking behind Tai when he felt his stomach growl. He was feeling slightly woozy from not having eaten for so long and from exerting himself. He was about to suggest to Tai that they take a break when she suddenly fell forward. The sound of her body hitting the earth told him it wasn't a soft landing.

"Woah! Tai! Are you okay?"

He rushed to her side and tried his best to help her sit up even though she was batting at his hands and weakly trying to push them away from her.

"I'm...fine…I'm just feeling a little dizzy." The way she was blinking her eyes to fight off an onslaught of unconsciousness and the slight lolling of her head told him that it was more than just a little dizziness.

"Here," he pulled out the white jar for her. She held up a weak hand to try to hold it, but thinking better of it, he pushed her hand aside and held one hand behind her head to help her steady it and poured water into her mouth for her.

"It'd be a pain if you dropped it," he said to her as he poured the water in her mouth and sensed her irritation at being nursed. She gulped down the water and then wiped the extra drops from the corner of her mouth with the back of her hand.

"I suppose the qi script took more out of me than I had thought," she said, closing her eyes and resting for a moment.

"That's right, you were the one who wrote it. No wonder you're so out of it right now. We should have stopped to rest ages ago," Kyle said. "You're pretty stubborn, aren't you? Here." He took her pack from her, pulled out her blanket, and laid it on the ground. "Lie down and rest."

Tai was in such a feeble state, she could only swallow her headstrong pride and roll herself onto the blanket. Kyle pulled out his small pot from his pack and set about making a new pot of rice porridge. Using a flint and knife given to them by Bao, he gathered some wood and started another fire. After the rice was on its way to boiling, he pulled out the other small pot from Tai's pack and a flask from his own that was full of the rich tea that Bao had prepared for them. Pouring some of the contents of the flask in the pot first, he then filled the rest of the pot up with the pure water from the white jar.

"Xiang and Ting had told us that qi script uses our life energy as the 'ink'. You should be more careful next time," he lightly chided Tai for her stubbornness. "You dying from over exertion doesn't help anyone. Least of all me," Kyle admitted.

Tai was too fatigued to be fully irritated at being lectured by Kyle, but she still asked, "What do you mean?"

"Dude, I can't get through all of this by myself," Kyle said as he gestured to the whole forest which was only a physical representation of the predicament they were in. "Besides, there's a better chance of survival if there are two of us."

The sun was almost halfway up in the sky by the time the food was ready. Kyle propped Tai up on both of their packs and then used the large wooden spoon used for cooking to feed Tai porridge with dried fish and pickled vegetables. She was still too weak to hold up the bowl by herself.

"How do you feel?" Kyle said after he had finished feeding her two bowls full of porridge.

"A lot better…thanks," Tai replied hesitantly.

"Good."

Kyle gave her some of the tea and then placed a few cookies and rice onigiris next to her with a fully refilled bowl of the tea before diving into his own meal.

"The use of qi script should be saved for when we really need it, especially with phoenix paper. Using speed will probably be useful for getting past people undetected," Tai wondered out loud.

"Yeah, but you'll be exhausted afterwards, so you'd have to take care of everything right away before it wears out," Kyle warned.

"Not if one of us writes it for the other. You're fine, and you were traveling just as fast as I was," Tai said.

"Well, I'm not about to pass out like you are, but I'm still pretty exhausted."

"Maybe if I wrote it without the phoenix paper. Maybe that can help boost our speed without such an extreme effect," Tai pondered.

"Yeah, well, let's try that later when you've fully regained your strength. It doesn't even feel like we went faster or gained much ground really. I mean, we got here in less 'time' than we would have with the qi script, but we're still as tired as we would have been if we had walked the entire day."

"It still saved us some time," Tai said with slight defiance.

"But you're so worn out that we'll probably have to take it easy for the rest of the day before we move again," Kyle pointed out.

"No, just give me a couple of hours and I'll be up again. We can't waste the daylight," Tai pressed.

"Okay, whatever, we'll see. You'd better eat more food if you're planning to recover faster," Kyle said as he indicated to the food he had placed next to her before turning his attention back to his own meal.

Tai looked down at the food, and then, with a steadier hand and a look of determination, she picked up one of the rice onigiri and stuffed it into her mouth, chewing with more force than needed. Kyle smiled inwardly at her comically resolute consumption of food.

"Slow down, you're going to end up choking to death instead if you keep that up," he said with some humor. He shook his head at her stubborn nature.

As a testament to both Tai's stubbornness and her resilience, they were up and moving again in about two hours, though they were moving slower and with more care than before. In essence, they were walking two days' worth of travel in this one, so their efficiency naturally decreased as they continued. But at the end of the day, when dusk was upon then, they reached the end of the forest. To their surprise, the forest opened up to a small strip of grass which faded into the sandy shore, and beyond that, the ocean, vast, cold and uninviting in the waning light.

Nevertheless, the change of scenery was a relief as it was a sign that they were moving forward and making progress. They paused for a moment at the edge of the sand, listening to the hum of millions of rolling and churning waves and the wind rushing through the open air and sky which was no longer obstructed by an endless roof of treetops. Turning to exchange glances, Kyle couldn't help but feel pleased to see a satisfied smile spread across Tai's face.

It was in the midst of such a peaceful musing that Kyle suddenly felt a cold shiver run up his spine. He could feel Tai tensing up the same way next to him, and just when he felt the urge to grab her arm and make a run for it, they heard a low growl behind them. There was nowhere to run. The ocean blocked off their best direction of escape, and the open sands to their left and right promised only a slow, laborious run. They had little choice but to turn slowly around to face whatever it was that had made that menacing growl.

Chapter 18

Yehren

The first thing Tai and Kyle saw was its teeth. Those horrible, awful, long and sharp rows of teeth that were never meant for the humanoid shape of the creature they belonged to. And that was the second thing they noticed, that the creature was oddly human-shaped, but with a torso that was too triangular and limbs that were too long and skinny with fingers and toes that arched into cruel, claw-like flesh digits. It was hairless, and looked as if it had a pig skin (they dared not think of it as human skin) stretched over its bony frame. The rank of rotting flesh thickened the air around them. Something about the twisted familiarity of the creature made their stomachs turn and inspired an exquisite mix of horror and revulsion that they had never experienced before.

Its fleshy claws were curled menacingly, its black vapid eyes stared widely and wildly at them, and a disgustingly viscous saliva dripped from the corners of its mouth. The chest in the center of its angled torso heaved as the creature breathed heavily, apparently from a physical exertion of some sort, possibly from running. It may have come after them after sniffing out their presence; Kyle couldn't know for sure, but what was clear was the thing looked hungry or angry or both. Either way, it looked deranged enough to signal a full rush of fear and panic. The creature gave another feral growl and took another step towards them, advancing from the forest only a few yards away.

Without warning it crouched quickly and leapt up into the air, sharp teeth parting in a scream, and as its over six foot long body fell upon them, arched and predatory, Tai jumped to one side to avoid it and Kyle to the other. They didn't have a chance to be dismayed at being separated as the vicious creature turned towards Kyle and moved to pounce on him. Kyle brought his arms up instinctively in front of him, ready to protect himself from the onslaught though he didn't know what his puny little arms could do against such a powerhouse of malevolence. Before the creature had a chance to launch fully into another jump, Kyle was surprised to see its terrifying face suddenly covered by a cloth. He was even more surprised to see Tai suddenly emerge above its head with an arm wrapped around the monster's neck.

The cloth she had used to cover the monster was her own blanket, and it was large enough to cover up the top half of the monster's body and confuse some of its arm movements for a moment. For a second, Kyle could only watch in shock as Tai smashed her fist down again and again on the monster's head with no success in knocking it out as it continued to move and flail. The only thing she was able to do was keep the blanket securely wrapped around its head, but its arms were soon freeing themselves of the blanket's confines and the fleshy claws were reaching wildly for her.

It was on one of such close calls, where one of the creature's claws swiped close to taking off Tai's head that Kyle snapped out of his daze and did the only thing he could think of doing. With adrenaline pumping through his whole being, he ran forward, jumped, twisted his body and launched a vicious and heavy flying side kick. His foot made contact with the monster's head, there was a sickening dull thud and crack, and the next thing he knew, the gargantuan figure was falling to the ground, taking Tai with it.

Miraculously unhurt, Tai got up, still staring warily at the fallen figure. Both breathing heavily, they stood on either side of the monster, looking down on its fallen form, and unwilling to pull Tai's blanket off.

"Not bad for a couple of newbies," a male voice said out of nowhere.

Kyle and Tai looked around and were startled to see a young man

walking towards them out of the ocean that sparkled in the waning sunlight. He had dark green hair and wore a long, dark green, slick-looking jacket that was gleaming wet from ocean water. A strap wrapped diagonally across his torso. Even in the dim light, they could see his emerald eyes, and he wore black pants and no shirt. His chest and abdomen were tone and cut; he looked immensely athletic and fit, so much so that Kyle couldn't help but feel like a feeble little boy in comparison.

"My name is Jade. I am a Dragon Prince," the stranger introduced himself with a handsome smile that revealed some canines that looked a little sharper and longer than was normal.

Of course you're a prince, Kyle thought sardonically to himself, and then he wondered why this 'dragon' was in human form. Tai, on the other hand, was unfazed.

"I am Tai, and this is Kyle. We're—"

"The Chosen One, I know. Word about you has spread throughout the dragon world. You give us hope in these dark times. I've been sent by my father, one of the Dragon Kings, to come lead you to the palace. And that," Jade indicated a nod to the creature they had just downed, "is one of the First Child's twisted Yehren."

"Yehren?" Kyle repeated as he looked at the fallen creature between him and Tai. "Is that what this thing is called?"

"Yeah. They are the First's…henchmen in a way." Jade sniffed the air and his eyes sudden widened. "Hey, is that…it is! I see you've been paid a visit by the Guan Yin. Here, can I borrow the white jar?" Jade walked up to him and held his large, strong hand out to Kyle, and Kyle pulled out the white jar reluctantly and handed it to him. The Dragon Prince then pulled the blanket off the creature, revealing its now lifeless form that was still as revolting as ever, and he poured the purified water over its body. The body started to shimmer, as if it had suddenly turned into millions of tiny little diamond fragments, and it reduced from its grotesque overgrown body form to what looked like a normally proportioned human body. Then the glittering form dispersed, as if blown away by the sea wind. Kyle's heart suddenly froze.

"Was that a…a person?" he asked, the image of himself kicking the monster's head playing over again in his mind.

"Yes," the Dragon Prince said with tangible sadness, "yes it was. The Yehren are people that have met a fate worse than death at the hands of the First. She has twisted their bodies and souls for her own cruel purposes."

"You mean I just…" Kyle couldn't finish the sentence. It was too overwhelming to even conceive what he had just done. Jade put a steadying hand on his shoulder.

"You did what you had to do. If you hadn't, both you and Tai would have been ripped to shreds by this creature. And that's what it was when it attacked you, really, just a creature. Now, at least, the soul of the person it once was can rest in peace, with some help of the purity from this water jar."

Kyle fell to his knees as that dull cracking sound from his kick to the creature's head torturously played itself over and over again in his head. He put his hands up to hold his head, as if doing that could clear his mind of this affliction or at least stave off its onslaught. At this moment, more than ever, he wished he could go back home, wake up and find that all of this was just a dream.

"Kyle."

He felt a small hand on his shoulder. He kept his eyes closed. *Just a dream*, he wished desperately. The gentle hand gave him a gentle shake.

"Kyle."

He opened his eyes and found himself face to face with Tai who had knelt down in front of him and was looking intently into his eyes. Her eyes left his for just a moment to look at another part of his face, and then, to both of their surprise, her hand came up and her fingers gently wiped some moisture from his face, a gesture that brought a measure of comfort to Kyle, however small it was compared to the overwhelming rush of other emotions he was feeling. Kyle realized his cheek was wet with tears.

"We both did this. We both take responsibility. Got it?" Tai said with an earnestness he hadn't heard in her voice before. "We both did this," Tai repeated again.

Finally, he nodded in silence and allowed Tai to help him to his feet. He looked away from the spot where Tai's blanket now lay and focused his vision on a dark spot in the sand. The sun had fully set, and only a faint glow in the sky was the remaining evidence of the day that had just passed, and soon that was gone, too.

Tai looked down at her blanket, then looked around and saw a piece of driftwood. She picked it up and began to dig a hole in the half-sand, half-earth ground that they stood on. Jade seemed to understand what was on Tai's mind. He unstrapped something from his back, and he held it out to Kyle who noticed it only when it was shoved in front of his face. It was a straight, double-edged sword in a dark green leather sheath. The hilt had a glimmering, green eyed dragon entwined around it, and the sheath had a similar dragon on it.

Jade motioned for Kyle to grab a hold of the sheath, and when Kyle did, Jade pulled the blade out in a swift motion, and then the Dragon Prince got down on his knees next to Tai and started digging as well. Kyle at first watched dumbly as they dug, holding the empty sheath in his hand. Then, understanding snapped him out of his stupor, and he, too, got down on his knees and began to dig.

When the hole was large enough, Tai folded up her blanket and placed it respectfully into the freshly dug hole, and then covered it up. When the blanket was fully buried, Tai shoved the piece of driftwood she had found into the ground to mark the spot. Then she kneeled, held her hands together and closed her eyes in a quick prayer before she stood back up. Kyle still felt numb and shaken up, but the act of burying the blanket did bring him some feeling of closure.

"Well, that's that," Jade said, trying to be upbeat despite the situation as he sheathed his sword. "Now, my father awaits your audience."

Jade turned and started walking out towards the ocean. The two teenagers looked at each other, wondering whether they could trust this new stranger, but they shrugged and started towards the ocean. What choice did they have? At first, Tai and Kyle followed him out, sloshing clumsily through the sea water that the Dragon Prince seemed to glide through as if it were as thin as air. Jade kept on walking and walking until finally he had disappeared completely into the water.

Tai and Kyle looked at each other while they stood just above knee deep in the ocean, both equally confused.

"Does he want us to swim after him?" Kyle asked Tai out loud.

"I'm not sure," Tai shrugged, although she looked ready to dive in after the Prince.

Jade re-emerged from the dark, night waters.

"Oh, sorry. I forgot you can't breathe water. Air and water are all the same to me, so sometimes I forget that it's not the same for others," Jade smiled both jokingly and apologetically. He pulled a large pearl the size of a baseball out of the pocket of his flowing, dark green coat. It was perfectly spherical and had a soft green glow about its milky whiteness.

"Brace yourself," Jade said and then he drew his hand back and wound up like he was about to throw a fastball. And he did in fact throw a fastball, only it was with the pearl, and it was straight at Tai and Kyle who instinctively put their hands up to block their faces from being hit. The pearl grew exponentially in size as it flew at them, and the next thing they knew, Kyle and Tai were fully encased in a large, glass sphere, dry and breathing.

Jade walked up to their glassy prison and put a hand on the surface. They could hear him clearly enough speaking to them, but his voice was slightly muffled coming from the other side of the glass.

"I'm going to take you down to the Dragon Kingdom at the bottom of the ocean. So sit back, relax, and enjoy the ride!"

With that, Jade's face began to stretch rather grotesquely, and whatever horror Kyle had left in his being bubbled to the surface of his emotions. Tai and Kyle watched with wide eyes as scales sprouted all over the Dragon Prince's body and his coat stretched out and melded with his skin, all dark green. His hair lengthened, flowing like a garden of seaweed, and the pupils in his eyes stretched vertically until they were just black slits in the green of his iris. The clothes he wore smoothed out into scales. The transformation looked painful, yet Jade had a relaxed smile on his face during the whole process.

When he was fully in his dragon form, Jade was about as long and thick as five school buses lined up in a row. His face had wide wide snout that was lined with large, pearly white teeth that he flashed at them in a smile, and after a wink from his emerald eyes, he opened his mouth, took the glass sphere that contained The Chosen One in his deadly jaws, and pounced up into the air into a wingless flight.

Kyle felt like he was going to be sick. He was reminded of this one roller coaster ride where you sat in a little compartment that spun both horizontally and vertically at the same time while speeding through the air. It made your stomach and heart switch places and then switch back again. Jade spun up in the air, apparently reveling in the freedom of being back in his original form, and then, from quite high up in the sky and, without much regard for the terrified passengers he carried in his mouth, nose-dived down into the dark ocean with a thunderous splash.

Chapter 19

The Ocean Palace

The ride to the bottom of the ocean was a relatively peaceful one, considering the circumstances. There wasn't really much to see in the night ocean. The dark waters stretched out endlessly, and the liquid flowed and bubbled against their glass container. They heard the steady rushing of the water around them as Jade's powerful body propelled them forward.

Kyle tried to keep his mind off of the fact that he was being taken deep underwater because thinking about it caused him to feel suffocated and brought about the urge to hyperventilate.

"Why do you think the Dragon King wants to speak to us?" Kyle asked, thinking that conversation would keep his mind off of the dark, murky depths of deep sea.

"I don't know. Maybe he wants to help. It seems like no one's able to stop the First Child, from what I've gathered," Tai said, hugging her knees to herself.

Feeling more than a little tired, Kyle lay down, trying to relax, but when he did, he found himself looking up at the roof of the dragon's mouth, then at his rows of large carnivorous teeth, and then back into the cavernous void of the Dragon Prince's esophagus (or whatever it is a dragon had for a throat), and Kyle decided to sit back up, realizing that the view laying down would only stress him out more. He decided to copy Tai's position and sit with his arms hugging his knees while staring forward into the ocean water.

"There sure are a lot of dragons in this place," Kyle said absentmindedly. Tai smiled at this, and then she broke into a light laughter. This reaction surprised Kyle, but he found himself laughing along with her. He knew it wasn't so much that he had made such a big funny; he never was any good as a comedian. It was a laughter born of the strain of their ordeals that was both light hearted and cathartic yet slightly hysterical at the same time. Kyle could feel that they could easily transition into sobs, but both of them kept their cool and let the moment fade out into a silent calm.

"What's that?" Tai suddenly said.

Kyle squinted his eyes as he tried to make out something in the ocean darkness.

"Yeah, I see it, there's a light there," Kyle said.

The light he saw was at first dim, but as they hurled toward it, it grew and grew, until they saw that it was a massive dome of glowing light spread across the ocean floor. There were blurry images beyond the surface of the dome. Before they knew it, they were upon the dome, bursting through it, and finding themselves flying through the 'sky' of a vast, gorgeous and ancient-looking city full of curved emerald green and cobalt blue rooftops, golden columns, and numerous areas of lush green, perfectly tended Chinese scholar gardens. Walking all over were people dressed in gorgeous, flowing gowns that moved about them as if they were floating in water. It was like an old Chinese scroll painting come to life.

The dazzling sight was so overwhelming, especially after the dull darkness of the ocean ride they had just had, that Kyle and Tai felt dizzy from it all. Jade flew straight for the largest building at the middle of the vast city and landed in a giant courtyard that was more than enough room for even his large dragon body. Carefully, he placed the cargo in his mouth on the ground, and as soon as it was fully out of his mouth, the glass sphere was gone, and Tai and Kyle found themselves standing on a floor that was covered in shells arranged in an ornate pattern of square tiles. When they turned around to look at Jade, he was back in human form and was just putting the large, baseball-sized pearl away in his inner coat pocket.

"Jade! You're back so soon!" A beautiful sprite-like woman with long, black silken hair braided up with hundreds of tiny pearls came running towards them. She had eyes blue enough to match Jade's green, and as she hurried towards them, her robes of soft shades of green floated about making it look as if she were gliding towards them instead of running.

"Well, I found them right away, so it was a quick affair," Jade said gesturing to Kyle and Tai. The woman jumped into his arms and kissed him on the cheek lovingly. Then she turned to look at the two humans before them.

"Oh no!" she exclaimed when she laid eyes on them. "You two look utterly exhausted!"

"I found them after they had brought down a Yehren."

"A Yehren!" she exclaimed, shaking her head at them with eyes wide open. "But you're, you're just children. Come, come, you must rest up before you give audience to the Dragon King."

"But Father's eager to meet them," Jade began to protest.

"Well, he will just have to wait. No productivity in meeting with worn out young ones like this. They'll need a proper bath, meal, and a good night's sleep."

The finality of her statement was enough to stop Jade from going against her recommendation.

"I am Snow," the woman said. "I am a human just like you, so you needn't be afraid, not that you need to be afraid of the dragons here. Welcome to the Ocean Palace. What are your names, Chosen One?"

"My name is Kyle," he said wearily, too tired to feel shy in the presence of such a beautiful woman.

"My name is Tai," Tai introduced herself in the same weary tone.

"This definitely will not do. You two look as if you can barely stand! Jade you take care of Kyle, and I'll see to Tai."

Jade gave Snow a little comedic salute before taking Kyle by the shoulder and marching him forward. Snow took Tai by the arm and gently led her in the opposite direction. Kyle and Tai turned a moment to look at each other, their eyes meeting with some alarm, unwilling to be separated in an unfamiliar new place filled with strangers.

"Don't worry," their respective caretakers told them, "you're both in good hands."

Kyle allowed himself to be led to a place with a large public hot spring. He first went into a small water closet, took off his dirty brown clothes, showered off all of the grime and dirt with some fresh smelling soap, and put on a towel wrapped around his waist. Then he went back out to the large hot spring pool and saw that there were plenty of patrons there; Kyle could not really tell who was human and who was dragon or whatever other types of beings. There was a fragrant smelling steam floating around the entire area, as if the spring water was infused with fresh flowers or wholesome wood. He met up with Jade who was also in a towel ready for a hot spring soak.

"Oh, you're in for a treat. The hot springs here are more amazing than any you've experienced anywhere else, straight from the ocean floor. Only the best for dragon royalty, eh?" Jade laughed heartily and lightly hit Kyle on the back, causing him to stumble forward a bit.

When they reached the edge of the pool, Kyle looked warily at the water. If the water was hot enough to warm up a dragon, wouldn't it cook a mere human like him alive? Jade stepped in without hesitation and sunk into the waters, letting out a satisfied sigh. Kyle decided it would be safe to sacrifice one toe and tested the waters with his left, big toe. When his toe did not burn right off and actually felt soothed by the hot spring waters, he immersed his foot in it. Slowly and steadily, he lowered himself into the hot spring and was finally immersed up to his neck, and a healing relaxation washed over him, calming not only every muscle in his tired body but also clearing his now weary soul of worries, if only for the moment.

"So? What do you think?" Jade said in a lazy voice.

Kyle breathed out a satisfied sigh and said, "This is pretty amazing."

They sat in silence for a while, just soaking in the magical healing properties of the hot springs that sprung from the ocean floor. Kyle had always thought of the ocean floor as a cold, dark, and anaerobic abyss, and what he was experiencing here was the total opposite.

"Who built this palace?" Kyle finally said.

"My father did," Jade said. "The Ocean Palace is a gift for my mother. It's the best place to spend your days lounging, bathing, studying, and listening as you please. I love it here."

"I'll bet," Kyle said. "I could really get used to this." He sunk lower into the water.

"Few humans get to visit this place, so count yourself lucky," Jade said with a smile.

"How many humans actually live down here?" Kyle said.

"About a third of the city's inhabitants are human. They come here only if invited to by a dragon and with the permission of the Dragon King."

"Like Snow?" Kyle said sleepily.

"Yeah, like Snow."

"She's gorgeous…" Kyle mumbled half awake, but as soon as the words left his mouth, he was wide awake again. "I mean, I'm sorry, I was just thinking that…"

"Are you trying to steal my woman?" Jade said with mock-anger playing across his eyes.

"No! No, nothing like that, I was just commenting on…I mean…" Kyle stammered. The last thing he needed was a Dragon Prince upset at him for gawking at his girl. Jade gave him another friendly hit on the shoulder that almost threw Kyle completely into the hot water.

"Man, I'm just joking with you. No worries, no worries," Jade laughed good-naturedly.

Kyle sat back down into the water, determined not to let his guard down again or say anything that would make him a dragon-snack. Jade sunk deeper into the water, sighing.

"You know how I met her?" he looked at Kyle who gave him his attention. "When I was younger, I had gone to the surface to play one day. Being childish and a little ignorant, I was swimming around in the form of a fish when I got caught up in a fisherman's net. A fish out of water, I was weakened to the point where I couldn't defend myself or change myself back. So there I was, lying in the fish stall display and still breathing and alive, which really drew a crowd at the marketplace. Everyone wanted a taste of the largest, freshest fish in the market that day. I thought I was a goner, but the fisherman's youngest daughter took pity on me and snatched me away while everyone was fighting over who was going to get to fry me up first. She ran with me all wet and flapping in her arms to the ocean and threw me back in. Immediately I transformed myself back to my dragon form and swam away. Every chance I got after that, I went back and visited her in my human form, and we had a great time just playing in the forest, in the ocean, in the sky. But I watched as she started to age faster than me, growing into a young woman while I was still just a child. Dragon years and human years don't exactly match up, you see. And even in my tender years, I knew she would die before I even reached adulthood, that her time in this world was even more fleeting than mine, and I couldn't bear to lose her. So I asked my father for permission to bring her to the palace to

live. He was very fond of her, too, knowing that she had saved my life, so it was no question she was welcome to come stay here with us. However, that wouldn't stop her from aging."

"How old are you anyway?" Kyle asked.

"A little over a thousand years old," Jade responded with a shrug. His handsome, chiseled features and athletic body seemed more like twenty years old than a thousand.

"How long to dragons live?"

"Hm, it depends. Pretty long I guess."

"So how old is Snow?"

"About 823 years old," Jade said.

"Wow," Kyle said. "So how did you keep her from growing older?"

"The Peach of Immortality," Jade said with a shrug, as if it were common knowledge. "I took her to my mountain where the peach tree grows under the care of the old immortal ascetic."

"Jade Mountain!" Kyle said, remembering the advice of Guan Yin.

"Yes?" Jade said.

"That's where we're headed! Guan Yin told us we would need the Peach of Immortality if we're going to defeat the First Child."

"Oh, I see. Well, after you meet with my father, I can take you both straight there, if you'd like," Jade shrugged and sat back again.

"That would be great. So, Snow ate the Peach of Immortality?" Kyle brought the topic back, more curious now about it since he was considering eating it himself. He really wasn't sure how he felt about eternal life as a teenager.

"Yes, she did. That's how we are able to be with each other so long."

"Is she your wife?" Kyle couldn't help but be weirded out by the fact that Jade was a dragon and Snow was a human being.

"My what?"

"Your wife. You know, till death do us part?"

"Oh no, we won't ever part, even at death."

"Oh right, because Snow is immortal now, right?"

"No, immortality doesn't mean you don't die. It does help you live longer, but death is a part of life. If you were to be frozen in time, unmoving and unchanging for all of eternity, you'd pretty much be dead. No, there's a difference between not dying and being immortal."

"I don't really get it," Kyle admitted.

Jade laughed. "Don't worry too much about it. Some things just can't be explained, you know? Oh, come on, it's getting late. We'll miss our dinner date."

"Our what?"

"You'll see."

Chapter 20

The Scholar's Garden

It was a bit unnerving for Kyle to look up and see the roof of ocean water arched precariously over them, as if it would come crashing down on the pristine city at any moment. He also wondered how there seemed to be sunlight everywhere despite the fact that they were in the ocean depths. These thoughts made him feel claustrophobic, so he tried to focus on the pleasant scene before him instead.

He was sitting with Jade in a good-sized pavilion on some dark wooden chairs carved with the images of dragons among clouds, and the table before them had a massive wood carved dragon encircling its perimeter. The pavilion of dark wood was in the middle of a small pond connected to the main grounds by an immaculately white bridge with intricate carvings of floral designs. Surrounding the pond were the lush greens of the garden bushes and trees, with each plant having clearly received careful grooming by attentive gardeners. In the pond swam large orange, yellow, and white fish that came up to bob for air now and then. The light sound of flowing water and the chirping of small birds added a measure of perfection to the whole scene.

Kyle was wearing some dark blue silk robes generously embroidered with golden dragons. He felt strange in them, as if the clothes were too regal for him. The fact that they belonged to a Dragon Prince didn't help to alleviate that feeling. Sitting next to the manly Prince simply added to his feeling of deficiency.

"Here they come," Jade said gesturing with a nod to the gleaming white bridge that connected their mid-pond pavilion to the grounds. Over it glided Snow who was glowing radiantly in her soft green robes, and her smile was the shining masterpiece of her whole presence.

"Not bad for a poor little fisherman's daughter, huh?" poked Jade with his elbow.

Indeed, to Kyle, Snow looked like a princess of all princesses. It was hard for him to imagine that she was a poor ocean side peasant girl from the start. Then he wondered if eating the Peach of Immortality had anything to do with her dazzling beauty, which made him wonder if eating the Peach would change him into a stud…

He was torn away from those thoughts when Tai emerged from behind Snow. She was wearing silken white robes that were covered over with sheer black robes that had gray bamboo leaves embroidered all over it. Her hair was tide back in a single bun which was wrapped with a small cloth bearing the Chinese character that meant 'clear, bright, understanding'.

明

Next to Snow's flowery fairy princess look, Tai looked more like a studious examinations student, quite serious and all business. Aside from that, she seemed rather refreshed, no doubt a result of the amazing hot springs.

Snow grabbed Jade by the arm and pulled him to his feet.

"Come on, let's go get the food. It's ready in the kitchen," Snow said, and the two of them left Kyle and Tai to sit alone in the pavilion in the peaceful garden. Out of socially trained habit, Kyle again felt the need to say something about Tai's new clothes, but given her previous negative reaction to the standard compliment of "You look nice", he picked his words a little more carefully this time.

"Uh, nice threads," he said and then winced a bit in anticipation of her angry response.

"Thank you," was Tai's surprising response, "I picked them out myself."

"She let you pick yours?" Kyle lifted his silken blue sleeves with the shining golden dragon embroidery. "Jade just threw this at me."

To Kyle's surprise, Tai smiled and said, "It is a little bit over the top with all the gold dragons."

"Yeah. How are you feeling?" Kyle asked.

"Surprisingly much better. The hot springs they have down here are amazing," Tai breathed, relieved to get back a good measure of her strength.

"I know! Wish I could bottle some up and use it before a test," Kyle mused. Tai rolled her eyes.

"Here we are!" Snow's cheerful voice rang through the yard, and the delicious smells of the food caused both Kyle and Tai's stomachs to growl loudly. They both put a hand to their stomachs and looked at each other with shared embarrassment.

Jade scooped fresh bowls of brown rice that had a refreshing barley-like aroma as Snow placed the plates of entrees in the center of the table. Stir fried green beans, steamed tofu, pickled seaweed, broiled bamboo shoots, and other such vegetarian dishes were spread across the table for them in a hearty display.

"Dig in!" Jade said, seeing the two young ones looking hungrily at the food. They promptly started to cover their bowls of rice with everything they could fit and then proceeded to shovel the food into their faces. Jade and Snow exchanged smiles at their ravenous consumption. Jade poured some rich, steaming green tea for everyone while Snow ladled some of the clear, daikon soup into bowls.

When the meal was well underway, Snow and Jade were discussing which piece of music would best fit the occasion.

"What instruments do you have here?" Tai asked.

"Why? Do you know how to play an instrument?" Snow asked, delight sparkling in her eyes. Kyle looked amazed at Tai. Was there anything she couldn't do?

"I am trained in a number of instruments. I can play a song for you if you'd like, in appreciation for your hospitality," Tai offered.

"That would be absolutely wonderful!" Snow said, clasping her hands in delight.

"Oh, you're really on her good side now. Snow loves music," Jade said with a wink at Tai. Kyle looked at Tai, half expecting that a young girl like her would blush at such attention from such a handsome man, but he was amused to see how unaffected Tai was and figured cows would be jumping over a blue moon before he would see a blush across Tai's face.

"What instrument would you like me to play?" Tai asked.

"I love the guqin, and you're quite perfectly dressed to play the scholar's instrument. I'll go get it right away," Snow said happily. She got up and was away and back in a flash. Under one arm she had tucked a very large case, which held the guqin zither, and in her other hand she held a erhu, a violin-like string instrument, by the neck.

"Here, I can accompany you!" Snow said, as excited as a little girl at a Christmas day family gathering.

"Did my grandfather teach you how to play?" Kyle asked Tai out of curiosity.

"Of course," she said as she placed her utensils down on the porcelain chopsticks holder in the shape of a delicate little sleeping kitten. She got up to take the guqin from Snow, and then turned to Kyle again and added with the corner of her lip curled up a little in an amused half smile, "He also taught me how to dance."

"Ah-gong taught you how to *dance*? No way!" Kyle exclaimed with a laugh of disbelief, and then his brow furrowed at the attempt to imagine his old, long bearded grandfather trying to teach Tai how to twirl a ribbon or walk gracefully in flowing robes. It really conflicted with the macho martial artist warrior scholar that Kyle always felt was his grandfather's projected persona.

"You can *dance*, too?" Snow said with a new degree of sparkle.

"Oh boy, now you've got her wrapped around your little finger," Jade exclaimed as he cleared the table of the dishes and then poured a fresh supply of hot water into the teapot.

"You *have* to join me in a performance for the King then!" Snow implored emphatically.

"I would love to," Tai said with a polite bow of the head that made Kyle distinctly notice he wasn't being as generous and gracious with their guests as Tai was. He thought through what it was that he could offer in return for their kindness, but the only thing that popped up in his mind were vocabulary words for his exams.

Tai took the instrument carefully out of its case and laid it carefully onto the now cleared table. She shook the sleeves away from her hands and then slid her fingers gracefully along each of its strings, plucking here and there and tilting her head slightly as she listened to quality of the sound. After a few minutes of this, she let her finger strum across all the strings, allowing a thrilling succession of notes to pour out of the instrument.

"Excellent," said Snow as she tuned her own instrument.

"I'll play one of my favorites for you," Tai offered.

Kyle suddenly felt strangely more intimidated by Tai than by the manly Jade. There was something very refined about her speech and her movements, as if she were the cultured daughter of an emperor and not an orphan abandoned on someone's doorstep.

Snow readied her instrument and then nodded to Tai. Lowering her head slightly in acknowledgement, Tai's fingers suddenly hovered up above the instrument and began flowing over it like a willow branch dipping into the currents of a rushing river below. Snow had her eyes closed and was listening with her head nodding smoothly at first, and then when she found a place to join in, the bow she held in her hand started to slide across her instrument, adding a perfect harmony and blend with the song.

The song started out with a sprinkle of light notes, like drops of fresh morning dew glistening in a morning sun, and then the main melody began. It was a tune that captured the nostalgia of youthful, springtime innocence with a hint of sadness and longing. More than that, it sunk into Kyle and broke a floodgate that he had ignored for too many years. He realized in shock that he recognized the song, knew it, actually, all too well. Each note of the melody literally felt like a cord in his heart being struck, and it made him weak with its familiarity. He let out a breath.

When Tai and Snow finished, Jade clapped enthusiastically while Kyle clapped politely.

"That was amazing! Really heart felt," Jade said approvingly.

"Lovely," Snow said with a wistful sigh. She took a moment to pack up the instruments. "You two finish up your tea while we put these instruments away and make some arrangements for you."

Snow and Jade left them for another quiet moment, and Tai poured some tea for Kyle and herself. She sipped quietly and looked contemplatively out at the fine scenery. The water of the pond around their pavilion lapped at the rocks gently. There was a gentle breeze with a hint of ocean scent in it that caused the garden plants to sway elegantly in a waving dance, the greenery peacefully backed by the white garden walls topped with soft gray tiles.

"I know that song," Kyle said finally.

"I see," Tai responded casually. "Well, your grandfather wrote it."

"My grandmother used to play it when she had me practice calligraphy. She said it was her favorite song."

Tai glanced at Kyle and noticed his slightly shell-shocked expression. She looked back out at the softly swaying greenery. They sat in another moment of silence, sipping at the comforting tea as another gentle zephyr carried the lightly ocean-scented air to brush across their faces.

"Will you teach me how to play it sometime?" Kyle asked suddenly.

Looking down at the gleaming fish with their gem-like scales sailing this way and that in the sparkling pool, Tai answered, "Sure."

Chapter 21

The Ownership Ceremony

Kyle stood uncomfortably in his simple brown Lin Gui attire. With everyone around him in flowing silken robes and adorned with expensive looking accessories, he felt a little self-conscious about being underdressed. He and Tai had had a good night's sleep, as was insisted upon by Snow, and now they were at a luncheon banquet in the audience of the Dragon King himself.

As instructed to by Jade, he held the white porcelain jar that the Goddess of Mercy had given him carefully in his hands and was going around to every guest at the luncheon in the Dragon King's great hall and dutifully bowing and pouring a cupful of pure water from the jar for each of them. The Dragon King sat at the head of the hall which was awash in the cool marbles of greens and blues. When the lights played upon them, the marble seemed to undulate like the ocean waters.

Too soon, it was time for Kyle to pour a cup of the pure water for the Dragon King himself, and the young teen walked up towards the sagacious man, bowing extra low, and then poured a cup for him. The King was an older looking man, or in man-form at least, and he had long black beard and flowing robes of emerald and cobalt with a matching headpiece embroidered with a single, prominent golden dragon. The Dragon King looked strong and wise but also very, very sad. Kyle could feel this more than he could see it.

"I thank you, Chosen One, for sharing purity with us," the King said courteously. "It will bring all who drink it good health and long life."

"I wish you long life and good health, Dragon King," Kyle repeated what Jade had told him to say and bowed again as the King drank the pure water from his cup.

"I only wish," the King said, a shadow falling across his eyes, "that my Queen could be here to enjoy this precious gift."

Kyle wasn't sure what would be appropriate to say, so he remained quiet but didn't leave. Finally, the Dragon King looked back up at him, the shadow lifting. He looked at Kyle as if he were searching for something.

"Do you know, Chosen One, what it is like to lose someone dear to you?"

The Dragon King's question caught Kyle off guard, and he looked straight into the royal dragon's dark green eyes, then looked away and gave a slight, barely noticeable nod. The Dragon King took a deep breath, closing his eyes on the intake and opening them again as he exhaled. He gave Kyle a sad and kind smile.

"Angered by the heinous acts of the First Child, my beloved had confronted the First Child on one of her trips away from our safe palace, and no one ever saw her alive again. I was sent her cracked pearl in a cruel message from the Demon. A pearl is the heart and soul of a dragon's being. As you can see," the Dragon King pulled out the two broken halves of a large pearl much like the one that Jade had pulled out of his pocket, "my heart is broken."

Kyle didn't know what to say to such a heartfelt confession of grief. Then he thought of the cheerful Jade and realized how much emotion he must be hiding beneath. His mother had been killed by the First Child demon.

"I'm sorry that you must bear the burden of defeating the First Child, but I implore you to stop her. She is destroying so many lives, twisting so many dreams. I only hope you do not fall prey to her cruelties. Take care, Chosen One Kyle."

Kyle bowed deferentially low again to the Dragon King. He moved to his seat at a lower table and sat down next to Jade who welcomed him with a warm smile and a strong pat on the back. Kyle wondered about what sadness Jade might be hiding behind his broad smile as he looked out on the beautiful palace that had been built as a gift for the now dead Dragon Queen.

"The performance is about to start," Jade said, nodding to the center of the great hall.

The group of musicians sat in a formation on the other side of the hall facing them, and they began to play. The music filled the hallway with a sort of flowing liquid sound of deep bells and low twangs and croons of strings. Almost simultaneously with the start of the music came the performing women. They came prancing into the center from either side of the hall, clad in green silken robes with long sinuous sleeves all over light mint-white dresses. They formed in three lines with Snow and Tai in the center of the front line. They moved like seaweed dancing in summer waters. Tai held the willow branch bending and swaying out of one of her long, green sleeves as if it were a lithe extension of her arm.

Kyle noted that their movements were not as coy and flirtatious as the performance at the Lin Gui village, and the sudden memory caused him to look quickly down at his clothes, patting them with his hands to see if it were being covered in blotches of paint.

"What's wrong?" Jade asked.

"Oh nothing," Kyle said.

He turned his attention back to the performance, allowing himself to be lost in the playful and upbeat tempo of their movements and friendly expressions and gestures, and his attention fell on Tai.

The dance ended, and the crowd applauded approvingly with great enthusiasm. The performers bowed off the stage, and Jade nudged Kyle.

"Go on, it's time for the Dragon King to speak to the Chosen

One."

Kyle looked around frantically for Tai and felt relieved when he saw her coming back to the middle of the hall again, having changed back into the same simple brown Lin Gui clothing that he was wearing. Her hair was pulled away from her face and tied in a long, high ponytail. He clambered up and joined her by her side.

They bowed together to the Dragon King who stood up and bowed politely back, and then Kyle wondered what was next, since Jade hadn't told him what the King wanted to speak to them about. The Dragon King's voice echoed strong and firm throughout the hall.

"We are all grateful to the bravery of The Chosen One," he gestured to the entire audience, many of them nodding steadily in agreement. "On behalf of the dragon world, I would like to present to you gifts to help you with your task."

The Dragon King nodded to his son who stood up and strolled casually over to the center of the hall where Tai and Kyle stood looking like peasants in their simple clothes. Snow came out from the opposite side to stand next to Jade facing them; in her hand she held a silver staff with dragons flying through swirling clouds emblazoned all over it. Jade pulled the sword out of the green sheath strapped to his back. Both Jade and Snow held their respective weapons with both hands in presentation. Jade held the sword to Tai, and Snow held the staff to Kyle.

"I give you the Liquid Blade and the Soaring Staff, each forged from ten thousand dragon scales," the Dragon King's regal voice echoed.

Tai and Kyle raised their hands up to accept their gifts, but right when their fingers were about to touch the precious weapons, Jade and Sky retracted their gift.

"Now, let the Ownership Ceremony begin," said the Dragon King.

Puzzled, Kyle looked over at Tai and saw that she didn't know what was going on either. Both turned to look at Snow and Jade who had good-humored smiles on their faces.

"That means…" Snow began.

"…you'll have to take them from us," Jade finished, and the two of them suddenly twirled their weapons from a presentational gesture into a combative one.

Kyle and Tai exchanged incredulous looks. Apparently, they had to wrestle the weapons from their generous host and hostess couple with their bare hands.

"Sorry kids," Jade said with a wink, "but you'll have to prove yourselves worthy of these weapons."

Kyle gave him a slightly annoyed look in response. He would have appreciated a little warning about this, but he figured that they probably wanted to surprise them with the challenge so that they would be empty-handed during the fight. Kyle wished he had at least had his brush and phoenix paper in hand, then maybe he could have made himself an impenetrable bubble and rolled out of there unscathed.

As always, Tai was the first one to make a move. While Kyle stood there with a look of focused panic, she lunged forward with a growing fierceness spreading across her face and dodged a swish of Jade's blade with a deft turn to her left. She then avoided a sweep of Snow's staff with a nimble jump, and as the staff came in a forward thrust towards her, she made a grab for it, but it was quickly twisted out of her reach. Behind her, Jade's blade was quickly coming down on her, looking to make a gash in her back, and Kyle, without having time at being shocked at Jade's overt attempt to harm Tai, found that he had jumped forward and thrown an upward snap kick at Jade's attacking arm and sent him a few steps back, the blade pulled safely back away from Tai's back. Kyle had moved instinctively to protect her.

"Hao!" people in the audience yelled out in approval.

Kyle next found himself back to back to Tai, with Jade and Snow circling the two of them, teasingly brandishing their weapons. When Jade was in front of Tai and Snow was in front of Kyle, the armed pair attacked the two youth in the middle simultaneously, and there was a flurry of flashing blades and jabbing staff ends. Tai and Kyle were only barely avoiding the onslaught of attacks, and there seemed to be no hope of turning the tide. The weaponless youth were only able to barely survive against their more seasoned and armed opponents. Kyle was amazed he could dodge the attacks at all.

Suddenly, an opportunity presented itself to Kyle. Snow made a stab with her pole that Kyle avoided quicker than usual with a turn to the side. He had the time in that split second to grab the pole before it finished its forward thrust motion and pull with that momentum, causing Snow to be pulled forward by Kyle's manipulation of her own forward attack power. For that brief fraction of a second, Snow lost control of both her footing and the staff, and Tai, having noticed Kyle's move, grabbed onto the staff and gave it a good twist and yank forward, simultaneously pulling it completely out of Snow's now unbalanced and loose hands and blocking another one of the deadly slices Jade had just thrown at her. The audience was in an uproar, yelling "Hao!" more times than could be counted.

For a moment, Kyle was at a loss of what to do next. Should he turn his attention to Jade who had his hand on the other weapon they needed to acquire? But Snow's next act forced his decision—she made a grab for the staff that Tai was now using to slowly turn the her defensive battle against Jade's blade to an offensive one.

The clang of dragon steel blade against dragon steel staff echoed like a musical instrument throughout the hall, awing all within hearing range, and Kyle set about in a hand to hand combat against the lovely Snow, who's flowing robes of different green shades rose and fell, swooshed and floated with the graceful movements of her martial display.

Kyle tried to put pressure on her, making his exchanges with her more and more offensive as he attacked more than defended. He figured he'd have his hands full just keeping Snow from getting back her staff or they would be starting this whole deal from square one. He had no time to be amazed that such a gentle lady could take her gracefulness and roll it out into such effective combat. The onlookers were entranced by her dance of movements as she battled with a calm smile on her face; she bent and swayed like a free-floating flower twirling in the wind.

At one point, Snow's robes seem to envelop her, and she disappeared between their silken folds. Kyle was confused for a second, but a second was all she needed, and through the soft fabric came a very hard punch that caught Kyle in the left cheek. Smarting from the strike and trying to shake off the slight dizziness of it, he focused on not getting distracted by her beautiful robes as she was clearly using them as a guise and distraction for her attacks.

Again, another fist came out of the folds and then a graceful high kick that looked dance-like but dropped through the air like a hammer let loose from a rubber spring. Kyle blocked the punch and jumped back just as the drop-kick flew through the space he had just occupied a split-second earlier. Then as a drifting piece of green cloth came close to him when Snow threw another kick at him, Kyle quickly reached a hand up and closed his fingers on the cloth. It slipped through his fingers, but with another series of kicks and punch attacks from Snow, he got his grip around a large piece of her robes, yanked on the fabric, and pulled Snow sharply towards him for a back handed fist strike, but she blocked it expertly with her forearms held up parallel in front of her face.

Then, as Kyle was about to throw another punch, a flowing piece of cloth wrapped around his arm, yanking him to almost fall forward off his feet. He moved to avoid further attempts by Snow to immobilize him

with the very fabric she wore.

Jade's sword moved fluidly, living up to its name as the Liquid Blade, with its metallic point flying sharp and firm but curving and bending to make its striking points hard to predict. Tai, with the Soaring Staff in hand, could parry the cutting attacks, and unlike Snow's flowery and soft style of fighting, she swung and jabbed the staff with the ferocity of a tiger, quite surprising coming from a small girl. She had no qualms about smashing the dragon steel staff onto the floor in an attempt to flatten Jade, and the green and blue marble turned out to be sturdy stuff, or at least enchanted, for it did not crack or chip by the clearly powerful blows it was taking. Jade leapt away, barely avoiding the vicious blow.

"Good speed!" he complimented, smiling like he was playing a game of table hockey instead of being engaged in an intense battle.

Then Tai had an idea, twirled her staff back quickly, and when it was positioned at the right length and distance, she charged forward as if she were holding a spear and running at the frontlines of an army. She accompanied this motion with an extra intense and loud battle cry meant both to disarm her opponent and to signal to Kyle that she was doing something different. She hoped he would get the message.

Kyle heard Tai and so did Snow who glanced over at Tai and Jade, which gave Kyle a slight opening in her defense which he exploited with a heavy hitting forward thrust kick with his right leg, one that slid between Snow's dynamic arms and flowing robes and made a firm contact with her torso, sending her flying back a few yards and falling to the ground with a loud gasp, evidence that the wind had been knocked out of her, if only for the moment. Kyle accompanied his blow on Snow with an equally forceful battle cry to match Tai's, both to sync with hers and let her know that he was ready for whatever it was that had in mind.

Tai, in her running jab forward, caused Jade to move to avoid attack, but it was too close to him and threatened to make a damaging hit to his side, and the Dragon Prince had to flick his sword upward in front of him to give the Soaring Staff a slight change in trajectory, to force it to miss its mark. However, that wasn't what Tai was aiming for. That same instant was when Kyle knocked down Snow, which distracted Jade for another split second after his avoiding Tai's onslaught, and that gave Tai the chance to use her momentum to jump and flip up into the air over Jade and land behind him with both her hands on the staff now pressed horizontally across Jade's chest in a binding position.

With Snow down for the moment, Kyle turned his attention to the now immobilized Jade and, in a run to the side of the Dragon Prince, his hand gripped Jade's hand that held the Liquid Blade. In a strategically applied pressure and twist of the wrist that his grandfather had taught him to disarm a swordsman, the sword fell clanging to the floor. Kyle picked the blade up by its handle, and prepared himself as Jade broke out of Tai's bind and dodged some slashes and attacks by both youth with their weapons. Jade and Snow regrouped, and Tai and Kyle did the same, wielding the weapons in preparation for another attack.

The audience was in an uproar of shouts of approval and applause, and Jade and Snow relaxed from their battle positions and applauded with broad, satisfied grins on their faces.

Kyle and Tai slowly relaxed from the combat stances, too, and then held the two weapons in front in both hands, as if to present it back to the warriors they wrestled them from, and bowed in respect. Snow and Jade bowed in return.

Kyle's heart was pumping with the excitement of both the battle and the victory. He really didn't know he had had it in him. The cheers of the audience added to his energy, and he was suddenly grateful to his grandfather for all of the years of martial tutoring since the moment he could walk, and he was also appreciative of the Lin Gui leaders, Xiang

and Ting as well as Bao and the other children, for their patient instruction and extensive burst of training in his short time there. Suddenly, it crossed his mind that he really might be this Chosen One they've all been talking about. He glanced at Tai. She was breathing a little heavier than usual from the exertion, but she had a suppressed smile on her face. Clearly, she was pleased with the outcome, and, feeling Kyle looking her way, she glanced at him, too, with a nod and smile of approval. He couldn't help but break into a smile himself.

"Excellent synchronicity," the Dragon King complimented with a broad smile and a steady clap of the hands. "You have truly earned the right to wield your gifts."

In the celebratory mood, no one noticed a frantic figure running towards the Dragon King, one of the soldiers from the city's perimeter watch, clad in brick red armor that looked rather like a crab's shell. He quickly delivered a message into the ear of his King. Jade noticed the look of alarm that spread across his father's face, and as awareness of the soldier messenger grew in the hall, the applause died down and all looked eagerly at the Dragon King for explanation.

"Everyone, an urgent situation is upon us. You must remain calm but be prepared for battle. Our city is under attack."

Chapter 22
Jade Mountain

Without so much as a scream or panicked gasp, all of the people in the hall got up and left in a hurry, all headed in different directions with purpose. The only anxious sound was the quick beat of their feet against the floor as they hurried out. Kyle and Tai followed Jade and Snow as they went up to the Dragon King.

"What is it Father?"

"The First Child. An army of Yehren are falling upon our city."

Kyle felt terror shoot up his spine. An entire army of that…that thing they had found at the edge of the forest and ocean.

"I thought they weren't capable of penetrating the depths of the ocean!" Jade exclaimed in alarm.

"That was what we had thought. Tragically, we were wrong. It is possible the First Child is after them," the Dragon King said as he looked meaningfully at Kyle and Tai who were holding their newly acquired weapons. "Quickly, you must take them to Jun Bao."

"I understand Father," Jade said and then motioned for them to follow him.

The Dragon King bowed his head.

Kyle and Tai bowed to the Dragon King one last time and then followed Snow and Jade.

"Get the willow and jar," Snow instructed them as she ripped off strips of her silken robes and fashioned them quickly into sacks for the two of them to place their respective gifts from Guan Yin securely to their body.

With weapons in hand, they left the hall, and the sight that met them was a chaotic taint on the beautiful sea palace. Dropping from the water-domed ceiling over the Ocean Palace were hundreds of pale flesh creatures, the Yehren of the First Child, and they were landing in the gardens, on the rooftops, and some directly onto some of the inhabitants of the palace with their fleshy claws outstretched and gnarling teeth dripping with viscous saliva. The citizens fought bravely, a few turning into dragon form and shooting up into the sky through the dome, apparently to strike at the Yehren before they could reach the palace's dome perimeter.

Just as they fully took in the horrible sight, a dozen Yehren suddenly dropped from the edges of the roof that covered the great hall they had just left, and they plopped sickeningly to the ground, standing up slowly and menacingly to zero in on their new prey. Kyle and Tai almost suffocated under the smell of rotting flesh that came with the Yehren.

Jade and Snow wasted no time in jumping forward in front of the two youths. Snow's soft robes shot out and entwined around the legs of the closest Yehren, pulling his feet out from under him. Then she dragged the Yehren towards herself and began to swing it around, the centrifugal force of her movements enough to lift the beast off of the marbled ground. Tai and Kyle stepped back to avoid being struck by the disgusting creature that flew past them, and then Snow loosed the hold her silk had on the creature's legs as it swung back towards its original position. The Yehren flung through the air in a straight trajectory now, knocking over a number of the other advancing monsters. Snow stepped back and placed herself protectively in front of Kyle and Tai, her arms lifted and sleeves flowing, ready for the next assault.

A larger batch of the monsters dropped from the edge of a roof. Snow was in motion again with Jade fighting as well, but there were too many of them. As three of the Yehren slipped past Jade and Snow, they leapt up into the air at Kyle with mouths wide and teeth slick with saliva, looking much like hyenas hungry to feast on fresh carrion.

Eyes wide with terror as he stared at these human abominations, knowing they were once people, were still people in a sense, Kyle held the Liquid Blade up dumbly in front of him, all the skill he showed in the Ownership Ceremony less than an hour earlier disappeared as panic shot through him, paralyzing him like a deer in headlights. However, before he had a chance to even brace for impact, the terrifying image of the attacking Yehren was suddenly interrupted as Tai slid out in front of him, placing herself squarely between Kyle and the monsters. A new sort of terror filled Kyle as he watched Tai beat aside two of the vile assaulting creatures in a split second with a single powerful swing of her Soaring Staff. The third unchecked Yehren, however, landed on Tai with a vengeful snarl.

Before Tai's cry of pain even reached his ears, Kyle had shot forward and slashed the monster at the shoulder and down its back with his Liquid Blade, and it fell back, spitting and hissing at him while attempting in vain to nurse its new gaping wound that crossed its back. The smell of the creature's blood was even more disgusting, and Kyle was already shaken with the sensation he had felt as his blade had sliced through flesh, flesh that he knew was actually human flesh. It was all he could do to keep from vomiting.

As the Yehren he had cut dragged itself away past the two others lying unconscious on the ground from Tai's blow, a trail of rancid blood staining the beautiful palace floors, Kyle turned quickly to Tai and saw that she had a nasty cut on her shoulder that went down her back, a wound that looked almost identical to the one Kyle had just inflicted on the monster. He shivered even as he rushed to her side.

Tai couldn't speak, her face was contorted in pain as she lay on the ground, trying her best to slow her erratic breathing and calm down despite her injury. Kyle looked at her, his hands hovering above her as he panicked. He had no idea what to do.

"JADE! SNOW!"

He yelled for help. It was all he could think of doing.

But it worked. Immediately, Snow was by them again, the fabric of her robes flowing around them in a sort of protective, silken cloud.

After quickly downing two of the Yehren with his fists and kicks, Jade pulled out his baseball-sized pearl again and threw it at Kyle, Tai, and Snow. The pearl grew again into a large, glass sphere, and the three of them were encased inside. Three more Yehren jumped onto the glass ball, but the creatures were stopped by the glass barrier, thankfully much stronger than it looked. They clawed and scratched at its surface, their saliva dripping repulsively over the glass. Looking up at the sound of the scratching, Kyle was transfixed for a second on the details of the Yehren as he was able to see them up close without fending for his life. What revolted him most was not the fleshy claws, the sharp teeth, or the wild look in their vapidly black eyes; it was the traces of humanity that seemed left in the creatures. What could have been done to turn human beings into such feral monsters?

The Yehren were suddenly swiped off of the glass sphere by a powerful, five-fingered dragon claw, and there was Jade, fully in his dragon form. As before, he took the glass sphere and its precious contents into his powerful jaws and took flight. With Snow's help, Kyle tried his best to hold the injured Tai steady as they moved in flight, every painful breath she took stabbed at his heart. It was his fault she was hurt. She had protected him with her life.

As the rose, Kyle couldn't help but see all around him through the clear glass sphere, and he helplessly watched the beautiful undersea palace being attacked by the soulless Yehren as Jade swirled through the sky, evading the falling monsters the best he could before breaking through the liquid dome ceiling of the city into the ocean waters above.

Looking into the waters, he could see hundreds more of the Yehren making their way towards the city. Jade's growl rumbled into their crystal sphere, for he wanted to stop them all before they reached the city, but he had a more pressing matter to attend to. Then Kyle and Tai noticed that twirling around the waters near them were dragons, almost as massive as Jade himself, clawing and biting at the Yehren as they swam.

It seemed as if the Yehren noticed the presence of Kyle and Tai, for a good number of them suddenly veered away from the city and headed towards Jade who was making his way towards the surface. Though not made for the water, the Yehren were surprisingly good at maneuvering through the ocean, and the few already close by were grabbing onto Jade's body, looking like little fleshy ticks clinging to the majestic dragon's form. Jade had to twist and swirl in an attempt to shake the things off, but as he did so, the others started to close in on them, and more and more were getting a foothold on his body. Snow, Tai, and Kyle were being jostled around inside the glass sphere with Tai crying out in pain when her wound was hit in the tumult. Kyle tried his best to shield her with his body. They held onto each other for lack of anything else to hold onto to steady themselves, and Snow tried her best to hold the two of them firm in her arms as Jade made his maneuvers. The Dragon Prince, however, looked in danger of being covered and suffocated by the monsters like a massive creature downed by relentless siafu ants.

Suddenly, a large, dark blue dragon broke into view and began to claw and bite the Yehren off of Jade. Something about this dragon's long black, fleshy mustache and the kind sadness in his eyes told Kyle that it was in fact the Dragon King in his natural form.

"GO!" yelled the King urgently, and Jade responded by shooting forward towards the surface, the speed of his ascent scraping off the rest of the Yehren left on him.

With Jade now swimming up steadily, Snow quickly began to treat Tai's wound. Given the spherical nature of capsule they were trapped in, there was no place for Tai to lie down comfortably on her stomach since the wound largely stretched across her back. She was also too weak and hurt to hold herself up in a crouching position.

"Here, can you hold her like this?" Snow said to Kyle as she place Tai into his arms so that Tai's forehead rested on his right shoulder. He held her arms near the shoulders to steady her so that her back was facing Snow at a slanted angle. He suddenly noticed that he had a full and close up view of her wound and that Tai's blood stained his hands and his clothes.

"It's shallow," Snow gave Kyle a reassuring nod. He nodded back but didn't feel relieved. There was a lot of blood for what was supposed to be a shallow wound. Snow pulled out the white jar of pure water and poured it over the wound. There was a bit of painful fizzing, and he could feel Tai's body stiffen in pain as she held her breath and then gasped for air again. Then Snow held her hand over the wound, and Kyle watched with surprise as her eyes began to glow with a sort of inner sunlight and the same light glowed in the form of some kind of symbol on her forehead that he couldn't make out because it was obscured by loose locks of her hair.

As Snow was doing whatever it was she was doing, he could feel Tai's breathing even out and her body relax. When Snow had removed her hands, he looked on in amazement as Tai's open wound was now a closed scar on her back. He felt a lot more relieved to see that she was healed and finally allowed himself to breath.

Snow sat back, looking exhausted, and leaned against the wall of the glass sphere, closing her eyes. Kyle stayed there, still holding Tai, her forehead resting on his shoulder, her body limp from exhaustion.

A flood of thoughts rushed through Kyle's head. That Yehren could have torn her to pieces. She was lucky to have gotten away with just one 'scratch'. Tai had just risked her life to save his. He couldn't understand it.

"Why?" he whispered out loud to no one in particular. He was asking her, but not asking her at the same time.

"Why what?" was Tai's weak reply.

He turned slightly to look over at her, only able to look at the back of her head since she still rested her forehead on his shoulder.

"You could have died."

This time he was speaking to her directly. His eyes were wide with incomprehension.

"It was just reflex."

"But we've only just met…"

There was a pause of silence before Tai answered.

"You've only just met me, but I've known you your whole life." She raised a weak hand up to shakily push herself off his shoulder. "I think I can lie on my back now."

Kyle helped her gently lie down on her back; every wince on her face sent a wave of worry through his chest. As soon as she was settled, he moved quickly to pour some of the pure water into her mouth. She drank thirstily and then closed her eyes and rested. He sat kneeling down next to her watchfully, resolving quietly to himself that he would never again allow himself to be so stunned in battle that someone else would have to take the fall in his place. For a good silent while, they sailed through the dark ocean, quiet and relatively peaceful.

The dark waters gradually began to grow lighter and lighter until they could see the glimmering, mirror-like underside of the ocean surface with rays of sunlight reaching down into the depths, looking much more cheerful than they felt. They broke through the surface and met with blue skies filled with comforting white clouds, a peaceful sight that lightened their moods a little despite the dark scene they had left behind. Whimsically, Jade took a soaring wide circular path into the air, and they reveled in the sky's purity for a moment before heading off to Jade Mountain where the Peach of Immortality awaited them.

"Agh!" Tai said suddenly and slapping her hand to her forehead.

"What's wrong?" Kyle said alarmed.

"The phoenix paper, we left it behind," Tai said. He let out a breath of relief. She sounded like her old self again. He couldn't help but marvel at how effective Snow's healing of Tai's wound had been. Tai looked as if she was almost fully recovered; the only evidence of her wound was a scar, dried blood, and some torn clothing. But what Tai had said reminded him of something.

"And the scroll," he said, breathing out in frustration. Although he still didn't know how that scroll was supposed to help them, he felt that whatever had potential to help them fight a demon, especially one capable of changing people into Yehren, would be good to have.

"Have you read the contents of the scroll yet?"

"It just had the character for compassion, 慈," Kyle said.

"Then you do not need the scroll anymore. Keep its contents safe in your soul," Snow said.

Kyle wondered what the point of remembering a single character was. It wasn't like it was hard to do, and it didn't feel particularly impressive, especially because it was supposed to somehow help them defeat a demon child. The thought of the demon First Child brought the image of the terrifying Yehren to Kyle's mind, and he focused his vision on the distant horizon, busying himself with searching for land so that he could keep his mind off the demon and her tortured-human abominations.

"By the way," Tai said, smiling gratefully at Snow, "Thank you.

For healing me."

Snow smiled, looked at Kyle, and said, "I had a little assistance."

Tai turned her smile to Kyle, and he held his hands up in front of himself in a halting gesture, "Hey, it was my fault you were hurt in the first place, so yeah. Thanks for…getting hurt for me."

Both Tai and Snow gave Kyle a weird look.

"Yeah, that didn't really come out right, did it?"

Snow laughed and Tai smiled while shaking her head while Kyle scratched his head in embarrassment. Snow ripped another piece of cloth off of her robes and wet it with pure water, then she helped clean the blood off of Tai. Kyle tried his best clean himself off, too.

After a good while of soaring over the ocean that sparkled beneath them, showing no evidence of the war that raged far in its deepest regions, they saw land again. They passed over some forest area, not nearly as dense as the Forest of Ghosts, and after that, they flew over rocky terrain that dropped off into a breathtaking sight. The flat lands were moist and full of greenery with rice fields spread across areas here and there, peacefully laid out in simple, patchwork patterns, the water in them reflecting the blue sky like giant mirrors across the land. Occasionally, they saw a farmer in tow behind a large ox or workers squat in fields tending to the rice stalks. Jutting out from the flat grounds were sudden, oval shaped mountains that reached up with sheer cliffs past the clouds like skyscrapers made of stone. The sheer sides of these dramatic mountains were marked with the horizontal lines of centuries upon centuries of water recession, adding to their ancient presence. Atop each of these steep mountains grew greenery that seemed to drift in the mist of the clouds floating by.

It was on the largest of these many mountains that Jade landed, clinging as gently as giant dragon's claws could cling to the side of the mountain's delicate formation, the mountain being so massive that his large dragon body seemed like a small worm on a large leaf. He let the glass sphere settle on a safe spot, and as he changed into human form again, the glass sphere shrunk to its baseball size again, leaving its passengers standing on the firm mountaintop ground. They spent some time walking upwards on the mountain, with Kyle wondering how anyone could get up there without some form of flight capability. The air was perpetually brisk and fragrant from some unseen source.

Through a small thicket of trees, they were met with a stunning sight—a modest-sized yet rather thick and ancient looking peach tree, its dark trunk twisted and wrinkled with age but its branches exploding with pink peach blossoms. It hung near the edge of the mountain against a breath-taking view of the valley and mountains that reached out as far as the eye could see.

"This is the first time I've ever seen it in full bloom like this. It's beautiful," Snow whispered to herself as she walked up toward the tree and reach her fingers up to gently touch the pink petals.

Sharing a quick look of amazement with Kyle, Tai followed Snow and did the same thing, delicately brushing a finger against the pink petals, afraid to taint their perfection. Kyle reached a hand up too and touched the nearest petal, and it felt like silk against his skin, each flower seemingly too perfect to be real, but their fragrance and softness attested to their trueness. The beauty of the blossoms felt timeless.

A man in an earthy green robe came out of a wooden building on the other side of the peach blossom tree. Made out of the wood of the surrounding trees, its outline easily blended in with its environment. The man walked out, light in step but with no evidence of weakness, although he did seem quite ancient. His hair and beard were grown quite long, adding to his sage-like appearance. He held in his hand an old staff made of the wood of the peach tree.

"Jun Bao! Has the weather been good to you on this fine mountain

top of mine?" Jade said giving the man a friendly slap on the back.

The old man smiled at the Dragon Prince and nodded, turned his smile to Snow in greeting, and then saw Kyle and Tai.

"Ah, you're here for the Peach of Immortality."

Kyle and Tai came forward to meet him. They nodded to confirm his statement.

"You're extremely late…or maybe extremely early," was the old man's reply.

Chapter 23
Peach of Immortality

"What do you mean by too late?" Kyle asked.

"Just look, the peach tree is in blossom, there will be no more new peaches for another two thousand years," Jun Bao said, pointing his staff towards the flowering tree. Then the old man turned and disappeared back into his modest dwelling.

Kyle and Tai, with mouths agape, looked towards Jade for confirmation, and Jade just shrugged his shoulders and followed the old man in with Snow gliding in after him. Left outside alone for a moment, they looked back up at the peach blossoms, and suddenly the awesomely beautiful flowers were not so awesome.

"What are we going to do?" Kyle asked Tai.

"I don't know. We'll have to figure out something," Tai said with her lips pressed in a serious, straight line.

They followed after the others. Inside the small structure it was warm and cozy, full of the light from a fire and an oven. Also, the air was thick with the smells of something awfully familiar to Kyle, but for some reason, he was having trouble pinpointing the memory of the smell. He felt that the smell was somehow totally out of place, but he couldn't understand why yet.

They sat down at a table made out of the cross section of a massive tree's thick trunk with the segments of a smaller tree's trunk arranged around it as seating stools. In the center of the table were a teapot and a set of five tea cups all arranged on a tray on the table. Jun Bao took a boiling kettle of water off the fire and brought it over to the table. He brewed the tea and served his guests, the small tea cups steaming invitingly in front of each of them.

"The tea leaves grown on this mountain are infused with the taste of the heavens," Jun Bao said with the serious face of a connoisseur. Then gesturing for his guests to enjoy their drinks, he drank his own and got up to go back to the fire. He opened a metal oven, grabbed a thick cloth hanging near the fire and used it to reach in to pull something out. His body blocked the view of the oven's contents, and Kyle craned his neck to see what was inside. Something about the deep familiarity of the smell in the room made him really curious to see what had been cooking.

When Jun Bao turned around, both Tai and Kyle's jaws dropped. In his cloth protected hand he was holding a freshly baked pie. It was the last thing they had expected to see him bring to the table.

"Oh, you like pie, don't you?" said Jun Bao with a twinkling laughter in his eye as he placed the delicacy on the table. He looked at the surprised expressions on their faces and asked in mock confusion, "What's wrong? Not up for pie today?"

Snapping out of the mild shock, they proceed to regain their manners.

"Not at all, it smells delicious," Tai said politely.

"Yeah, I love pie," Kyle added truthfully. His favorite was apple.

"Good, good, I love pie, too," he chuckled. Jade and Snow exchanged a smile which made Kyle and Tai certain they were totally in on whatever joke this strange old man was playing on them.

Jun Bao brought out a box of eating utensils and placed them in the middle of the table.

"Choose your weapon," the old man said. For a second, Tai and Kyle half expected to be challenged to another battle of skill, but Jun Bao just picked up a knife and began cutting the pie into evenly sliced wedges, placing each piece on a plate, and handing one to each guest.

Snow reached into the box of utensils, pulled out a pair of

chopsticks, and started to work on her piece bit by bit. Jun Bao reached in and pulled out a spoon. Jade just dug into his pie with his hands. Finally, Kyle and Tai were passed the box, and they looked into the box, shaking it around a bit to look at what was available. Kyle looked at the piece of pie in front of him, shrugged at Tai, and then pulled a fork out of the box. Tai pulled out a fork as well, and they scooped up a bit of their pie and placed it in their mouths. The pie was warm, moist, and rich with flavor, the double crust perfectly complimenting the sweet tart of the fruit inside. At first, the two of them were enjoying the delicious dessert, but then a passing thought of the fruit inside suddenly caused them to widen their eyes.

"Wait a minute, is this *peach* pie?" Tai asked.

"Yes," Jun Bao said with a small, amused smile.

Exchanging a look of suspicion with Tai, Kyle asked the obvious next question,

"Um, is this a Peach of Immortality pie?"

Jun Bao nodded his head as he placed another spoonful in his mouth and then sipped some tea.

"But you said that we were too late," Kyle said, a little thrown off.

"You are, but the Peach of Immortality, well, it keeps very well you see. You're eating pie made from the last batch of peaches that ripened, oh, about one thousand years ago."

"And why pie?" Kyle queried, bewildered at having something that reminded him so much of home in this faraway place.

"Why not?" Jun Bao replied.

Kyle looked down at the unusual and unexpected pie and gulped a little as he thought to himself, *This is definitely not FDA approved.* He decided to ask the next obvious question.

"So does this mean that, that I'm immortal now?"

"Maybe," Jun Bao said.

"What do you mean 'maybe'?" asked Tai, sounding impatient.

"Well, it depends on what you mean by immortal," Jun Bao responded.

"Everlasting life?" Kyle tried.

"Maybe," Jun Bao said again.

"It doesn't sound like a very good Peach of Immortality if it only works some of the time," Tai said, her impatience turning to indignity.

"No, but it still makes excellent pie," Jun Bao said putting another bite of pie into his mouth and chewing on it happily. Tai bit her bottom lip, as if to keep herself from saying too much more. When Jun Bao swallowed, he took another sip of tea and continued on. "Immortality, like everything else, is a relative thing. Life and death is yet another false dichotomy of human thinking. Time does not move the same for everyone, you see, and a peach blossom that never turns into a peach will never fulfill its destiny."

"I control my own destiny," Tai blurted out.

Jun Bao smiled and nodded.

"Indeed you do, Chosen One, just as your destiny controls you. Destiny has no power or form without freewill to drive it forward. I do hope you decide that your destiny includes finishing that piece of pie. It would be such a waste of good pie if you were to leave it unfinished."

Tai looked down at her pie and dutifully began to shove it into her mouth.

"Slow down, Tai, and enjoy it. There's no joy in scarfing it down and choking on it along the way," Jade said with a pat on Tai's back. She took a deep breath, as if to extinguish a flame inside her chest, and slowed down her chewing with as much grace as she could muster in her irritated state.

Kyle looked down at his piece of pie, pondered its oldness for a moment, and then shrugged and proceeded to finish his slice at a steady pace as well. It tasted okay. After finishing it, he wondered if he was supposed to feel different now, in an immortal sort of way. But he didn't feel any different, really, aside from just being full.

When they were done with their pie eating and tea drinking, Jun Bao stood up and slowly made his way out with his peach wood staff in hand. The other four followed him outside. The old man stood under the peach tree and took a deep breath of the fresh mountain air and smiled peacefully while a breeze blew in, causing just a handful of petals to drift away off the mountain top.

"So the First Child has finally attacked the undersea palace," he said, the smile fading from his face.

"Yes, she has," Jade said with a heavy heart.

"I see," Jun Bao said, stroking his beard pensively as he leaned his staff against the tree. "Come, Chosen One, join me in meditation."

With a nod of encouragement from both Snow and Jade, Tai and Kyle went forward to join Jun Bao under the peach blossoms. Standing on either side of him, they looked at him for further direction, but he just stood there looking out at the scenery. After exchanging a quick look of confusion, they looked out at the scenery as well, which was not an unpleasant thing to do. The clouds were rolling in steadily making the tree covered mountain tops look like islands afloat in an ocean of mist. The bright sunlight reflected brilliantly off the rice paddies where the valley below was visible. Floating on the wind currents nearby was a large, white crane. It curved in its flight and headed west.

After a moment of enjoying the scenery, Kyle and Tai noticed that Jun Bao was actually moving, albeit incredibly slowly. His knees were now bent in 120 degree angles, and his front two arms had raised up in front of him with fingers steadily reaching out. Tai and Kyle moved to match his position and slowly followed his actions. He drew his hands back and, with palms facing forward and fingers slightly bent and relaxed, he gradually pushed forward.

Though they had the need to move fast, they did not know where Jun Bao was going with his movements even though his body was moving so slowly, so they had to settle for the centimeter by centimeter imitation of his form. It was a lesson in patience.

Jun Bao slowly pulled his hands back, forming a circle with his right hand on top with palm facing down and his left hand on the bottom with the palm facing up, a classic yin-yang position, and then he pulled his hands out, making the circle oval, then oblong. As Tai and Kyle imitated Jun Bao, they found that even the movements like punches and kicks that they knew so well were suddenly on a new level of difficulty when they were done at such a reduced speed.

When Jun Bao finished, he said to them, "In movement there is stillness, and in stillness there is motion. A single moment and an eternity can be equivalent if you are open to the possibility."

He took a step forward to the blossoming peach tree and placed a hand on its old trunk.

"The enemy you will face cannot be defeated with your victory," he said, still facing the panoramic view stretching out in front of them. "Remember that a whirlpool is not just made of water but also of the energy that flows through it. Don't seek to destroy but to redirect."

He turned around to face the two youths, a kind smile on his face.

"Wind, water, earth, plants, animals, people, everything is infused with energy."

Jun Bao picked up his staff again and walked to a small patch of dirt nearby, and Tai and Kyle followed him.

"Which scroll did you choose?" Jun Bao asked.

Kyle and Tai looked at each other before saying in unison, "Compassion."

Jun Bao put the tip of his staff to the ground and wrote out the character for compassion, his movements were those of an artist painting a masterpiece with a graceful, full bodied dance that flowed with each of the character strokes. The character lay out on the freshly upturned earth, large and clear for all to see.

"Compassion," Jun Bao read it with a firm and steady voice. Suddenly, it began to glow, as if the grooves in the ground suddenly had liquid sunlight poured into them. It had a steady pulse, like that of a heart beat. All of them suddenly felt a peacefulness wash over them, and a light of hope shone upon the deep recesses of their soul where fear, pain, hate, and anger had been stagnant and foul.

Kyle felt his senses opening wide, and he heard the wooshing sound of a wind blowing against a tree that he could have sworn was miles and miles away. Even more amazing was his next sensation, when he felt the expanse of the entire sky within the reach of his conscious perception.

Tai's eyes grew wide, remembering that their brushes were also made out of the wood of the same peach tree.

"Is this possible because of your staff? Because your staff is made from the wood of the Peach of Immortality's tree?"

Jun Bao held up the staff in both hands at a slanted angle and seemed to examine it as if he were seeing it for the first time.

"Yes and no," he said pensive tilt of the head. "It is true that such ancient entities as the peach tree or the phoenix can enhance the intent of a soul when it is expressed in script, but that is just borrowed qi. Nothing is more powerful than the source of your own will. This is especially true in writing, when you are putting the energy of your soul into a physical expression."

He walked around his handiwork, admiring and analyzing each

curve and stroke. When he came around full circle and was standing next to Tai and Kyle again, he looked up from his writing.

"Writing helps to focus the mind, but once you have mastered the essence of its power, you will not need a brush or a staff."

His eyes suddenly started to glow with a bright light, and on his forehead suddenly glowed the Chinese character for fire, as if someone had marked those strokes on his head with sunlight.

火

He raised his right hand up with its palm up, and to Tai and Kyle's surprise, a red flame suddenly appeared in his palm. Next, the Chinese character for mist replaced the one for fire on his forehead.

瀖

The fire dissipated only to be replaced by a swirling ball of mist, and then that thickened into a swirling ball of water as that Chinese character glowed on his forehead.

水

Jun Bao turned his palm downward and let the water drop to the ground, and it flowed out like a river and encircled the character for compassion he had written, giving it a liquid frame. The character for grass now glowed on his forehead.

草

The old man let his fingers hang loose pointing down, and then he pinched them together and raised his hand as if he were pulling up on an invisible string. The water encircling the writing sunk into the ground and up in its place grew green grass.

Kyle and Tai were breathless. Such power seemed too much for

one person to have. Was this sort of power now possible for them? Would this be the result of their mastery of qi script? Did consuming the Peach of Immortality give them this ability? It seemed too amazing to be true, and the possibilities of this kind of power seemed endless. If they were capable of such acts, they felt they could definitely be a match for the First Child. Jun Bao's voice broke into their excitement.

"It is time for you to go."

Tai and Kyle both looked at each other in surprise and disappointment.

"Wait, aren't you going to teach us how to do that?" Tai asked.

"Yeah, we're going to need it if we have to face that…that demon child," Kyle added.

"You know how to write, do you not?" Jun Bao asked.

"Yes, but—" Tai began but was cut off.

"You've practiced qi script, too, correct?" the old man continued.

"We have—"

"Then there is nothing more I can teach you."

"But it's not enough! We can't do what you just did!" Tai exclaimed. Kyle nodded in fervent agreement.

"What I just demonstrated for you is not something that can be learned from another. It is the power of knowing yourself. Only you can open your eyes to yourself."

"But we don't have time! Isn't there something we can do?" Tai exclaimed.

"Yeah, isn't there some kind of short cut? Or study guide or something?" Kyle added, sharing in Tai's exasperation.

"Time…yes, we are quite out of time here. A short cut? Only as short as you can make it," was Jun Bao's cryptic response.

"Then why can't you stop the First Child?!" Tai said with force.

"Yeah, why does it have to be us when you're obviously so much stronger?" Kyle added loudly. The two of them were caving in to their own frustration, fear, and disappointment.

Jun Bao shook his head in a sad way that made Kyle and Tai instantly regret their outburst.

"Power is not a linear thing. It is not just more or less. There are different kinds of powers, different kinds of souls, different kinds of music fit for different occasions. I am not the one destined to stop the First Child. My winds will only cross paths with yours, not merge with them."

Kyle felt ashamed of his lack of self-control, and he could tell that Tai felt the same way. He felt disappointed. They'd been moving forward on their journey, but the task of facing the First Child and defeating her only seemed to grow more and more impossible. The Lin Gui, the dragons, and Jun Bao…if the most powerful beings in this world could not stop her, they wondered what hope they had to make any difference?

Nevertheless, it was wrong to be unappreciative of whatever help they were receiving. Both teens held their hands in a fist to palm gesture and bowed in silent thanks, apology, and deference.

Snow and Jade came forward and bowed respectfully as well, and Jun Bao bowed back to them all. He gave Kyle and Tai an encouraging smile.

"Have courage, Chosen One, for even the simple flow of water can create mountains like the one you stand on," he gestured to the ground. "Now, be on your way, and I hope you've enjoyed the tea and pie."

Then with a throw of a dragon's pearl, they were back to soaring through the air in a glass sphere safe in Jade's care.

Jun Bao stood by the peach tree and watched silently as they flew on and on until they were just a speck in the distant sky. The sun began its descent behind the horizon, and as darkness reached over the sky, the old man continued to stand there, steadily breathing the mountain top air with a contemplative look in his eyes.

When night was fully upon him, he still stood there. Around him, the trees began to rustle, and feral growls poisoned the calm night air. Stepping out into the open came dozens of Yehren, their pale skin reflecting the starlight in a distorted, ghastly manner, as if everything that touched them, even light, became tainted by their perversion. If Jade was still circling the mountain, Kyle and Tai would have witnessed the horror of seeing hundreds of the Yehren scaling the mountain like ants on an ant hill.

The old man took a deep breath in, and then when he exhaled slowly, a sadness spread across his face that made him look weary and old in a way that he never let others see. The Yehren were the exception, but he knew they no longer saw anything, really, and the sadness in his heart tonight was for them. They attacked him with their fleshy claws, grotesque teeth, and vacant eyes, and with a fluid fighting style, Jun Bao kept them at bay, a lone warrior protecting the sacred peach tree from the madness assaulting it.

Chapter 24

Test

"Are we going straight to the First Child? Straight to the Phoenix Mountain?" Tai asked, looking out over the land with a mixture of worry and determination. She had her arm resting up against the inside wall of the glass sphere, and she pressed her forehead against it.

"Jade has used his pearl's power to conceal us while we are in the sky, but when we get close the Phoenix Mountain, we will need to go on foot," Snow explained. "Before that, we will be making camp for the night. We'll need our rest for tomorrow."

*We'll need a lot more than that...*Kyle thought to himself as he tried to keep from feeling ill from fear of what was coming. More Yehren meant more horror, and they would face the First Child herself. Kyle couldn't help but imagine what such a cruel being capable of such atrocities would look like. Something medusa-like came to mind, probably half serpent with venomously sharp cobra fangs, thousands of grotesque insect-like eyes, and possibly arachnid appendages. Kyle shook his head to make the image disperse. In his fear, he felt his old resentments coming back, and he felt that he hadn't asked for this and wondered why the peril this world was in was any of his business. This wasn't his world. The image of his suburban, American neighborhood with its clean, bright streets and the simple and organized life demands brought his homesickness to an all-time high.

They landed in a forest at the foot of a massive mountain range. Jade transformed back into his human form as the sphere rolled to the ground and released them from its glassy encasing while it turned back into a baseball-sized pearl.

"Phoenix Mountain is just beyond this mountain range," Jade

explained. "Tomorrow, we'll go on foot."

Kyle and Tai made no complaints. Going on foot meant that facing the First Child was delayed a little while longer, and neither of them minded that idea. They gathered some firewood in silence and put it in a pile surrounded by rocks for their campfire. Kyle and Tai sat staring at the unlit pile of wood looking pretty despondent. Snow and Jade took note of their long faces and exchanged knowing looks.

"Jun Bao is correct in saying that you have learned all you need to learn," Snow said, "but I think a little more explanation may be helpful."

Both youths looked up into Snow's radiant, smiling face.

"When you write, you are not really writing with your hand. You're writing with your mind, your heart, your soul. That is where your qi script really comes from. The use of the hand, the brush, and the phoenix paper, they are all just aids to help your mind focus. So what you witnessed Jun Bao performing was qi script in its real form."

"But how?" Tai asked for both of them.

"Well, why don't you start with imagining that you're writing it," Jade suggested. "Imagine that you're carving a character into something with your eyes."

"Here, let us try with something simple, the character for 'fire'. Look at the wood," Snow instructed.

Dutifully, Kyle and Tai did as they were told and stared with concentration at the pile of wood they had gathered.

"Now, imagine that what you are looking at is just a painting and that it has a flat surface. Then imagine carving the groves into the canvas. Now, carve the character for 'fire' into the firewood," Snow explained.

Kyle and Tai stared carefully at the wood, their first try at "carving" the character into the scene failing, but they immediately tried again and again until finally, from their different angles, they saw from their own perspectives the character for fire glow in the air right in front of the fire wood.

To Tai and Kyle's amazement, the wood burst into flames. They burst into smiles, too, but the joy at accomplishing something similar to what Jun Bao had done was tempered by the still ominous prospect of facing the First Child demon. They still didn't know exactly what to expect or how to really prepare. They only knew that it would not be easy.

Snow pulled out a package wrapped in a scarf and opened it to reveal some soft mochi rice cakes, white and pure as if they had been made by heavenly hands. She handed some to each of them, and when they bit into the cake, it melted in their mouths like sweet nectar.

The evening passed by uneventfully with each of the party taking turns to stand watch, but to everyone's relief, there was no sign of Yehren or any other horrid abomination sent by the First Child.

In the morning, Snow revealed that she had been given some peaches by Jun Bao, and she handed one to each, the large, scrumptious peach tasting delicious, juicy, and invigorating mixed with the morning mist.

They began their ascent up to the nearest crevice between the large range of mountains. This path, too, though uphill, was quiet and peaceful, so much so that all in the party started to feel uneasy. It simply made no sense for them to be so close to the First Child's lair and to see no evidence of Yehren or anything else for that matter aside from vast stretches of gorgeous and majestic mountainsides that belied the horror that hid within.

"It's too quiet," Kyle said under his breath at one point, more to himself than to anyone else, but Tai turned to look at him, and he could

tell in her eyes that she felt the same apprehension.

When they finally crossed through the range, it was near evening, and the setting sun was on the other side of the largest mountain of them all, causing it to glow gold in outline as if it were some promise land and not the lair of an evil demon that it was. The mountain needed no introduction by Snow and Jade. Kyle and Tai knew it was the one. They were there—Phoenix Mountain.

A small, rather pretty valley full of flowers of every shade of spring lay between the range they climbed down from and The Phoenix Mountain. Again, it was not what they had expected to see as they progressed into the belly of the beast. The sun fully set and the moon and stars were shining in full force by the time they were crossing the valley. The colorful flowers now shown pale and white in the moon light, and as a gust of night wind rushed through the small valley and brought glowing silver petals flying up towards the sky, Kyle and Tai felt as if they were walking through a dream more beautiful than imagination. It had to be a trick, they thought, as they kept their minds focused. They could not stop to rest for the night, for they were too close now, but Snow had passed around another batch of rice cakes to keep everyone from feeling the pangs of hunger. However, Kyle noted that he had never felt so strong and fully nourished as he did that day, and he wondered if it had something to do with eating the Peach of Immortality.

They reached the foot of Phoenix Mountain and saw that there was a large cave opening at the bottom. Emanating from inside the dark cave was a pulsing glow that looked as if a piece of the moon has fallen and rolled into it, still gleaming with its reflected light.

Although they both wished Snow and Jade would lead the way into the demon's den, Kyle and Tai knew that they had to take the lead. The two youths drew their weapons in preparation. Kyle's Liquid Blade was ready, and Tai had the Soaring Staff firm in both hands, ready for offense or defense, whatever the situation warranted. They moved in carefully.

They reached the source of the eerie glow a ways into the cave. The tunnel ended with a circular section of the wall made of some silvery, mercury-like liquid that reached from the floor to the ceiling in a large, glimmering mass that undulated with small waves and ripples like a vertical pool. On this strange liquid wall was written the Chinese character for ‘desire’.

The strokes of the writing seemed to float on the surface of this strange, fluid wall like fallen blades of grass that bent and undulated with the liquid canvas without losing its form. The liquid acted like a metallic looking mirror, the reflections of Kyle, Tai, Jade, and Snow floating on its surface along with the written character.

“It’s a test,” Jade said.

“A test?” Kyle asked, unable to keep from hoping it was multiple-choice.

“It seems so.” Jade walked up to it and held out a hand to touch the vertical pool’s surface. The tips of his fingers sunk into it. “It’s cold.”

That was enough to send shivers into Kyle as he imagined what he guessed they would have to do next—walk through it.

“What kind of test?” Tai asked.

“Well, the character written here represents ‘desire’. This barrier is also like a mirror. I think this will be a test of our souls, to see if we can resist or face our desires…and ourselves. It is one of the most difficult type of tests,” Snow explained.

Kyle’s brow furrowed with worry in hearing this, wondering what deep, dark desire he would have to face. It may even be one he was not even conscious of, and that unknown variable scared him more than the ones he could come up with. He'd gladly answer a multiple choice grammar question on a standardized test instead of deal with an unknown, dark side of himself. He knew Snow was right; a test like this could reveal more about him than he'd ever want to know.

"Kyle, Tai, we'll go first," Jade said, and then he held out his hand to Snow. "Together."

Snow looked up to meet her Dragon Prince's warm smile with her own, and for a moment, Kyle thought he saw Snow's loveliness become even more radiant than before, and in a passing thought, he wondered if Snow was loved because she was beautiful or beautiful because she was loved.

Kyle and Tai watched as the loving pair entered into the liquid barrier together. It was now their turn. They gathered up whatever courage they could muster to make their own plunge into the cold, fluid wall that looked more and more menacing as they prepared to enter it. In their pause, they wondered what had happened to Snow and Jade, whether they had come out at the other end or if they had drowned and perished in the watery grave. They had no way of knowing except to go forward and follow. Then Kyle remembered how they had passed into the Library of Ancients back in the Village of Ghosts.

"Um…maybe we should hold hands, too, just to be on the safe side," Kyle suggested warily. He held out a hand to Tai. She looked at his hand with a substantially long pause before nodding in agreement and taking it. They held each other's hands firmly, more to reassure themselves than each other, and their weapons were at the ready in their other hand. Then they stepped into the wintry, mercurial wall.

Chapter 25

It's Complicated

The first thing Kyle felt was the overwhelming cold that bit into his skin. He closed his eyes instinctively against it all. Next, he felt Tai's hand pulled out of his own and wondered for a split second if she had let go of him of her own accord or if something had forced her away. Then, he felt something slender and limber wrapping around his neck and a pressure against his lips, and he was being pushed backward.

He burst out of the liquid barrier back the way he had come and found himself in the cave again. When he had got a sense of where he was, he was able to focus on what had attached itself to him and was surprised to look down to see Rose Tracy, his best friend's blonde-haired, blue-eyed girlfriend holding him and pressing her lips against his in a kiss. Disoriented, his first instinct was to push her away.

"Rose! What are you doing here?" he asked with extreme astonishment and held back the question of what she was doing…period. His Liquid Blade fell clanging to the ground.

Wearing a flattering spaghetti strapped, blue summer dress and matching white sandals on her petite feet, her beautiful, sapphire eyes fluttered open, framed by her golden, princess locks as she stared up at him with the look of adoration he had always wanted to see.

"I'm here for you, Kyle. I've missed you," she said in a melodiously sweet voice. In fact, it was more melodious and sweet than he had remembered.

"Why haven't you called me? Didn't you miss me?" Rose said with a heart-melting pleading in her voice.

"Well…I've…uh…what?" Kyle stammered, overwhelmed to say the least, and then Rose approached, reaching her lips up for his again.

"Rose, wait, stop. What about Matt?"

"Matt? Who's Matt?" Rose said, looking up at him with innocently wide eyes and an eye-catching tilt of her lovely head.

Then the sight of the character for desire behind where Rose was standing suddenly caught his eye, and the disorientation he felt suddenly began to clear up a bit as he got his bearings. He also saw himself and the back of Rose reflected in the liquid wall behind her. *A reflection…of my desire,* Kyle realized as he looked back down at Rose, or what he realized was someone or something that looked like Rose.

"Don't you like me Kyle? Don't you like me as much as I like you?" Rose said as she reached her hands up to wrap around the back of his neck. Her arms were warm, and so were her lips, Kyle realized. She felt real. Though he was tempted not to resist, he brought his hands up to pull her arms off of him.

"Rose…I mean…we can't. I can't," Kyle said, pulling away reluctantly. "You're not real."

He felt he wasn't really trying to convince her as much as he was trying to convince himself, but before he could say anything more, something else burst out of the fluid mirror of desire.

It was Tai. Her Soaring Staff fell to the ground with a vibrating clang, and someone…a male someone had his arms around her and was pressing his face firmly into hers in what was apparently a kiss, akin to what Rose had done to Kyle.

Suddenly, all thought of Rose vanished from Kyle's mind as he was consumed in a fire of curiosity in finding out who was kissing Tai. In the relatively short time he had been aware of her existence, Tai had always come off to him as a hard-hearted, unapproachable girl who liked to go it alone if she could have things her way. She was the classic lone wolf, and the thought of her having tender thoughts for anyone had never crossed his mind.

The guy kissing her had his face tilted away so that Kyle could only see his chin. Tai had her arm up against his throat in an attempt to push him off of her. Then, with the staff fallen out of her hand, she brought her other arm up and pried him off. It was then that Kyle got his first good look at Tai's would-be object of desire.

Kyle's jaw dropped. ...*ME?*

There was no mistaking it. The guy who had just been kissing Tai full on the lips was the spitting image of Kyle. The same short and plain black hair, almond-shaped brown eyes, tanned skin, and somewhat high cheekbones that accented his slightly angular face. The same athletic, yet still-gangly looking build, the sign of a youth who was no longer a boy but not quite a man. The only difference was the way in which this facsimile carried himself. He stood with confidence and stared into Tai's face with a sureness that the real Kyle had never known before.

Kyle flinched as Tai smashed the back of her fist against the clone's face and pushed herself out of his embrace. Then she brought the back of her left hand up to wipe her face in a way that showed how disgusted she was with what had just happened. In that moment, the real Kyle's attention was drawn back to Rose who was once again advancing to embrace and kiss him again. He looked down at her, then at his clone copy, and the reality sunk firmly into him.

"You," he said down to the beautiful blue eyes, porcelain-skinned golden blonde before him, "are not Rose."

"What are you saying Kyle?" Rose said, but before she had the chance to feign any more innocence, he began pushing her backwards, and with one sure shove, she fell back into the liquid wall and did not emerge again.

"Stand with me Tai, we are soul mates. It is your destiny."

Kyle heard his own voice say, but it sounded different because it wasn't coming out of his own mouth or echoing in his own skull. The clone was speaking.

Tai, apparently infuriated by his words, charged at him with a striking fist that was easily blocked, and she threw another strike with her other fist, which was also easily parried. Her knee shot up, then her foot, and then a fist again, but all of these were futile and easily dodged or stopped. The clone of Kyle was quite an adept fighter, and, unlike its real counterpart, was superior to Tai in strength, skill, and speed.

Fully angry, Tai picked up her staff and ran at him, letting out a growling battle cry. The clone jumped and avoided every strike of the weapon as easily as he had evaded her hand to hand combat. The two moved as if they were dancing, each movement matched for another. Kyle watched dumbly on the sidelines.

With one swift and solid offensive side kick, the clone sent Tai flying backwards, and she hit the cave wall and fell to the ground. Her staff clanged on the ground again, and she lay face down, looking frighteningly lifeless. That sight snapped Kyle out of his stupor for the moment, and he ran to her limp form. He turned her around and, in a panic, started tapping her face lightly with his fingers.

"Tai! Are you okay? Tai!" he called out to her absent consciousness. Her head lolled on the ground in response. Kyle anxiously increased the force of his slaps a bit and had never felt as relieved as he did to see her eyes open sluggishly as she came to her senses.

Unfortunately, when her vision focused and she saw Kyle, she tried to punch him. He barely dodged the punch aimed for his right eye.

"HEY! It's me, the *real* Kyle! Are you okay?"

He helped her sit up against the cave wall. She gave him a suspicious look the split second before she saw the glimmering wall of liquid with the character for desire still shining mockingly on its surface. In front of that stood Kyle's facsimile, strong and tall with both hands in fists held out at his sides, staring straight at her. Then she focused back on the real Kyle that was next to her and looking at her with all sorts of bewilderment written on his face. Next, she saw her Soaring Staff on the ground, and she reached for it and attempted to prop herself up again in an apparent attempt to resume attack on the clone.

"What are you doing?" Kyle asked as he restrained her.

"None of your business," she said as she tried to struggle against him to get to her feet.

Kyle turned and looked at his clone, and then back to her. With raised eyebrows and a finger pointed at his facsimile, he said pointedly, "*That's* none of *my* business?"

Tai looked at Kyle, then at the clone, then back at Kyle again.

"It's complicated."

"Is that what it says on your profile page?"

Tai brought a hand up to her head and shook it a bit as she fought off the pain and darkness of unconsciousness that still lingered.

"What are you talking about?" she asked.

Kyle shook his head.

"Nothing. Look, you're no match for…for that thing. If you jump back in there against it without a plan, you're just going to get knocked out again, and I can't imagine that being good for your health."

He helped her sit up against the wall and then pulled out the white jar of pure water and managed to pour some of the water into her open mouth. Tai immediately felt better with the refreshing water and was able to shake off most of her dizziness. She got to her feet, with some attentive help from Kyle, and stood to face Kyle's clone. Though reluctant to share her innermost thoughts, she couldn't deny that in their current predicament, it would be tactically wise to explain the situation to him. She pulled her eyes away from the clone to face the real Kyle.

"My deepest desire," she began as Kyle looked intently into her eyes, searching for the explanation before it was given, "is to prove my self-worth. And I think that's why this is here." Tai indicated to the clone of Kyle with a presenting hand.

A flicker of understanding happened somewhere in Kyle's thick head, but it quickly went out before he could really grasp it.

"I'm not sure I understand," he admitted.

"I'm not sure either," Tai said with a shrug of her shoulders, "but I think I have a psychoanalytic theory. Ever since I can remember, I've been compared to you, paired with you, and it always felt like, I don't know, like I wasn't good enough or something."

"Well, you're obviously a lot better than me at like everything," Kyle blurted out, pushing aside his own inferiority complex for the moment. "Doesn't that solve that problem?"

"That is actually the problem," Tai said. Kyle raised his eyebrows in question, showing he definitely didn't get what she was driving at.

"You see," Tai continued, "there's no satisfaction in being better than someone you're already better than. You were kind of a disappointment."

Kyle gave her a dry look and said sarcastically, "Thanks, I really needed that."

Brushing his hurt ego aside, Tai went on, "So my desire was to defeat a worthy opponent, to really prove myself…prove to myself that I was the best."

"Okay…" Kyle said, "so this clone over here is the 'worthy opponent' then?"

"I suppose so."

Kyle wanted to ask what that kissing part was all about but decided to focus on the current, less-embarrassing problem instead.

"So what do we do now?"

"Well, it seems the best course of action would be to somehow push him back into the liquid wall the way you did with Rose Tracy."

Kyle winced at the mention of Rose's name. *So she saw.*

"Sounds like a plan to me," he said, trying to sound unaffected by the fact that she, too, knew what his innermost desire was.

Holding her staff firmly in her hand, she indicated to Kyle that he should probably draw his sword. He drew it reluctantly. The thought of wielding a blade against something that looked exactly like him was unnerving.

"Maybe we can wear him down if we both attack at the same time."

"Could you not refer to that thing as 'him'?" Kyle asked with annoyance.

"Fine, maybe we can wear *it* down if we both attack at the same time."

"Fine, let's go."

Even though Kyle said that, it was Tai who leaped forward without hesitation while he followed a step behind. She struck at the clone with her staff, and as it dodged away from the attack, Kyle jabbed reluctantly at a non-vital part of the clone, too disoriented with fighting himself to really be effective. The copy easily turned to avoid the sharp strike. Again Tai struck followed with an attempt by Kyle, but the clone was untouched. With a deft punch, the clone sent Tai flying back again, clutching her free hand to her shoulder in pain. With another powerful kick, the clone sent Kyle flying back, too, and he would have hit the wall the way Tai had earlier if she hadn't caught his back and slowed his acceleration towards hard cave wall.

"Thanks," Kyle huffed in appreciation. "It's too strong for us."

Tai shrugged as she held her staff ready again, "I guess I have high standards."

Then an idea came to Tai's mind.

"Alternating our attacks doesn't work. If we alternate, then it's like only one of us is really attacking at a time. If we coordinate and unify our strikes, then it would double the power of the impact."

"Okay, so in sync then?" Kyle agreed.

"Yes."

This time they both rushed forward at the same time, step for step, matching their pace, and both simultaneously raised their respective weapons for identical downward strikes. Unable to dodge one way or the other in time since the duel strike covered a broad area of attack, the clone raised his hands and skillfully caught Kyle's slicing blade between his two hands in a prayer like gesture. However, this left Tai's staff unchecked, and it came down on its shoulder, causing its steady stance to give way under the powerful blow.

The clone didn't look so much hurt as it was just giving way to the physics of the situation, its copycat face showing no signs of emotional or physical distress at having been hit so hard. It made him look robotic and soulless.

With his blade caught, Kyle raised his left foot and aimed a thrusting, front kick at the clone's torso, and Tai flipped the staff and thrust it so that the other end of it struck the clone at the same time as Kyle's foot. The clone was pushed back a couple of steps. Next, the both of them, in perfectly synchronized movements, planted their left feet solidly into the ground as both of their right legs shot out in two perfectly unyielding and simultaneous sidekicks that landed their mark on the clone, sending it flying backwards. The Kyle facsimile splashed back into the symbol for desire in the liquid wall from which it had emerged, and the Chinese character for desire dispersed and did not reform.

The two of them stared at the wall for a while, making sure that the clone was indeed defeated. Kyle caught his breath and took a drink from the white jar of pure water to refresh himself. He looked down at the ground and shook his head.

"What is it?" Tai asked curiously.

"Oh, nothing. It's just I suddenly really felt like a chimichanga right now," Kyle said.

Tai let out a laugh.

"Yeah, that sounds pretty good just about now," she agreed. Finally, Tai held out her hand to Kyle. "Ready?"

"Yeah," Kyle affirmed as he took her hand firmly in his, and, with a deep breath, they plunged back into the liquid wall.

Chapter 26

The Vanity Mirror

As soon as they had fully stepped back into the fluid wall, Kyle felt a rushing current of liquid blast against him, pushing him back and pulling his hand clean out of Tai's again. Then the current curved upwards and twirled and swirled with him at its mercy until he had no sense of which way was up and which way was down. Completely disoriented, Kyle could do nothing but keep his hand tightly around the hilt of his sword as he was dragged like a rag-doll in the current, opening his eyes here and there only to see rushing, bubbling darkness.

This went on for quite some time, and Kyle was beginning to reach his limit. He was holding his breath and couldn't do so for much longer. Without warning, he was thrust into open air, and he involuntarily took a loud, gasping breath of air. He found himself standing in what looked like a small pool of water in the middle of a dark cave room illuminated only by the blue, glowing pool he was in. He was soaked to the bone.

He surveyed the room and saw that against the far wall was a mid-sized, dark brown table with curving corners and legs. It had a matching small stool and a large, three paneled vanity mirror on top of it. In front of the mirror was a plethora of bottles, cases, brushes, and all of such cosmetic implements usually seen cluttering a center of feminine vanity. The flowery design of the table was distinctly Victorian in its mixed styles, looking like something that might be found in the Queen of England's personal quarters. The piece of furniture was oddly out of place in every possible way.

"Isn't it lovely?"

He turned with a start at the sound of Tai's voice. She was emerging silently from the pool next to him wearing a sleeveless and long, flattering gown of a soft, silver color. Unlike Kyle, she was coming out of the pool dry, as if she were coming up from air and not water. She stepped out of the pool gracefully and daintily like a ballerina stepping out onto stage. Kyle looked at her, more bewildered than he had ever been with her behavior.

"Tai?" he asked tentatively. She paused for a moment, turned a bit to look at him, her long hair flowing loose around her face and about her shoulders in a silken mass that was both beautiful and alluring, and the way she looked at him was unsettling. It was coy and slightly playful, almost flirtatious. That really shocked Kyle.

"Uh, are you okay? What happened? Where's your staff? Where're your…other clothes?"

She turned away from him again and continued to head towards the vanity mirror. Sitting down on the plush, velvety bench, she began to open a few of the crystal bottles that lined the table and a warm yellow glow began to emanate from each of them, lighting up her face and the mirror at the same time. Her right hand raised and gently touched her own chin with the tips of her fingers as she turned her face slightly this way and that.

"Such a plain, dull, and boring face," she said with a look of distaste. First, she took one of the open bottles, dabbed some material onto a dense sponge, and began to smooth the foundation all over her face. Then she moved her attention to her eyes, applying eyeliner to bring out a doe-eye look and then adding shadow to accentuate her eyes.

As she worked on her eyes, Kyle stepped out of the pool of water, wringing some water from his clothes and shaking off whatever moisture he could to dry himself. He put the sword that he held in his hand back in its sheath that hung across his back. Still dripping though markedly less soaked than before, he approached the vanity mirror where the girl sat busily making up her face.

When he reached her, she had moved to her lips, applying a rich, red color to them. The effect of the mask she now wore made her look like a completely different person.

"Tai? What are you doing? We need to find Jade and Snow."

She finished applying her lipstick, completing the task by pressing lips together, and then she looked up at Kyle, the corner of her stunning, red lips curling up into a mischievous smile.

"Kyle?" she said as she stood up and started to glide across the cave floor towards him like a panther towards its prey.

Kyle looked around, half expecting to find that she was actually talking to another Kyle in the room, perhaps another clone. Something in the way she smiled at him unnerved him. It wasn't just that; the silkiness of the dress she wore…the smoothness of her skin and hair…the allure of her accentuated eyes and now lusciously red lips…the way in which tilted her head down so that she looked up at him…the fragrant scent that now emanated from her…it all made Kyle feel slightly weak in the knees. He wondered why he didn't feel this way in Tai's presence before, wondered why all of these changes made him feel like he was in the presence of a completely different person even though he knew underneath all the makeup, scent, and altered mannerisms was a girl that looked identical to the one he just fought side by side with so effectively just minutes earlier. Pondering all of this grounded him a bit, and he suddenly felt very worried about Tai.

"Tai. Are you okay? Did something happen to you?"

Kyle remembered how the strong current that had caught him had torn his hand from hers, and given that the first time they went through the liquid wall resulted in a battle with a clone of himself, it seemed likely that something else was happening here, perhaps another test. He wondered if this girl standing before him was the real Tai or just another copy. After all, the clone had been quite solid and persuasive. He thought to pull her back in the water, thinking this might end this second test the way it had the first, but the way she had walked out of the water made him think that trying the same thing again would be useless. It was also possible that it was Tai that stood before him, and that the liquid they passed through had done something to her mind. If it could read their deepest desires, then couldn't it also alter them somehow in a fundamental way?

His thoughts were interrupted when the girl's hands reached up, slid over his shoulder, and locked fingers behind his neck. Quickly, he brought his own hands up to pull her arms off of him.

"Look, Tai, I think something happened to you. Here," with his hands still holding her forearms, he lead her back to the vanity table, "why don't you just sit down here and relax for a moment."

When he got her to sit down on the velveteen vanity stool, he suddenly thought of an idea. Pulling out the small white jar of pure water, he handed it to her.

"Drink some water. You'll feel better afterwards."

Looking flirtatiously up at him, she smiled and tipped the jar of water, pouring it into her mouth. Suddenly she was coughing and gagging, spitting out the pure water onto the ground. For a moment, Kyle thought he saw her glaring angrily up at him for a moment, but it passed so quickly that he dismissed it immediately. It wasn't the first time Tai had glared at him, so he figured she was probably just annoyed.

"Are you okay?" Kyle asked, taking the jar from her hand before it fell out of her grasp.

"Yes, I'm fine now," she responded, coughing and spitting, "I just choked on some of it."

Kyle breathed with relief. The familiarity of her tone of voice set him at ease.

"Thank you," she said, "I'm not sure what came over me." She put a hand up to her forehead and appeared to shake off some dizziness.

"Here, do you want some more?" Kyle asked, kneeling down on one knee to offer the jar of pure water to her again.

"No," she said, "I'm fine now."

He put the jar away in his pouch made of a ripped strip of Snow's robes.

"We'd better go find Snow and Jade. They must be somewhere around here," Kyle said.

"Can I rest here for a moment first?" she said, putting her hand back up to apparently nurse her aching forehead.

"Yeah, sure," Kyle said with sincere concern on his face as he looked at her to observe what was wrong.

"Thanks," she said, "thanks for saving me." Then she lifted her hand off her face and gave an appreciative smile.

"Nah, it's not like I did anything," Kyle said.

"No, really, this whole time, you've been by my side and taking care of me. I really appreciate it, and I'm sorry I didn't thank you earlier."

Kyle felt a kind of welling importance in his chest as she smiled at him with submissive eyes.

"Well, it's not like you didn't do anything…"

"I couldn't have done any of it without you. You really turned out to be a knight in shining armor for me. Thanks."

Her hand came up to touch his cheek appreciatively, and he was mesmerized by the look of appreciation and adoration in her eyes, overwhelmed by the emotions that a look like that elicited in him. So he was caught off guard and paralyzed as she leaned in and gently kissed him on the lips. Kyle felt his heart thumping loudly inside his chest, and he wondered how in the world he ended up being kissed twice in the same day by two different girls, and then he remembered the first kiss that day wasn't real. But this one…this one was…

He heard a splash behind him, and the girl that had just kissed him looked up at the source of the splash. He, too, turned to look back at the pool from which he had emerged to see someone soaked and coming out of the pool with bedraggled hair and clothes. The person looked familiar, and as his eyes focused in on the new occupant of the enclosed cave room, someone who wielded a long silver staff in two hands, he realized the person he was looking at, the person who had just burst out of the pool, was Tai.

As that realization dawned on him, he turned back to look down at the girl who had just kissed him, the girl who looked exactly like Tai but wasn't Tai, and her sweet, sincere face from a moment earlier had changed suddenly into a triumphant and malicious looking smile, giving her a sort of cruel beauty, gorgeous and attractive in a thoroughly wicked way. He was looking at her in bafflement as she spoke to Tai.

"You're too late," the girl said with a voice that sounded just like Tai's but that dripped with a malevolence that he had never sensed from the Tai. "He is already mine."

Kyle turned back to look at Tai as she charged towards him with her staff upraised ready to strike down hard. He heard her yell out, saw her lips move, saw her running and getting closer, but the yell dissolved and so did she, the intensity of the moment seemed to fade away as if it were a dream fading into mist.

Somewhere in the hazy miasma of his mind, he knew very certainly that he was in great peril, a prisoner of the infamous First Child Demon.

"Tai…" he breathed, a futile expression of his clouded dread.

Finally, everything faded to a complete darkness.

Chapter 27

Paradigm Shift

Kyle woke up in a dark place. He was lying on something relatively soft and comfortable. As his eyes adjusted to the light around him, he saw that there was a window above him to his right. Outside it he could see a bright, round moon and a few stars sparkling here and there. There was something incredibly familiar about the window and the scene he could see out of it. He sat up and winced as his body ached all over. His clothes and hair were still a little damp, and the sudden sitting up caused the blood to rush from his head a little too quickly, making him slightly dizzy. He shook it off and reached a hand out to feel around him in the dark.

As Kyle groped in the darkness, he felt a wall. It wasn't the rough stone of a cave wall. Instead, it felt something like wood with some kind of slick covering on it. His fingers hit something sticking out of the wall, and light suddenly chased away all the darkness.

Kyle looked around at his surroundings dumbfounded. He was wearing the same simple, brown Lin Gui clothes. He had Snow's strip of robe still slung around his shoulder, the jar still securely bound in its folds, and the Liquid Blade was still tied to this bag. He was sitting on a small, twin-size bed by a window in a small room covered in old, faded sunflower wallpaper. Over the cheerful yet faded wall colors was plastered posters of the top basketball players next to a poster that listed the top universities and the scores you needed to have in order to get into them. Across from the bed was a mid-sized desk with a desktop computer, the tower resting on a platform under the table, the keyboard on a pull out tray, and the mouse and a widescreen monitor on the table. There was a small stack of books comprised of textbooks and study guides. An old basketball sat on the ground next to the chair, and by the table was a backpack that he had last seen at the Tian Yi society temple at the top of a mountain covered in bamboo forest. It was his backpack. It was his room. Kyle was sitting in his own little bed room back at his suburban home in America.

The shock of it all left him numb. He wanted to think that he had simply just woken up from an elaborate and vivid dream, that all that had happened to him was just a dream created by his subconscious mind, but the clothes he was wearing, the sword he was carrying, and even the dampness of his hair told him otherwise. He then wondered if this was some trick of the First Child, another fun-house play room in the mind-teasing labyrinth of Phoenix Mountain.

He did feel like he had woken up from a long, deep sleep, and as he was shaking off the heaviness of slumber, he heard loud voices yelling nearby, muffled as they passed through the walls of his little room. He got up off of his bed and tested out his legs. They were a bit stiff, but they worked. He left his room, padded down the carpeted hallway, and carefully went down the steps of his two-story home's stairs. Everything seemed real enough at least.

"I KNOW! YOU DON'T HAVE TO KEEP REPEATING YOURSELF!" he heard his father yelling. Kyle had never heard his own father sound so angry. John Lin was usually a soft spoken man. The piercing, powerfully angry emotions in his voice blasted away any of the sleepiness left in Kyle. He made his way even more carefully down the steps. If this was a trick, it seemed an exceptionally cruel one. He'd never heard his father so angry.

"It was your father," Mary Lin sobbed and screamed, "YOUR father! And now I don't know where my son is!"

If waking up in his own room hadn't shocked him enough, this conversation definitely did. It's hard for any child to hear the sound of parents yelling at each other. It broke Kyle's heart.

"Mom…" he said as he walked into the kitchen where the yelling had been coming from.

For a moment, his parents just stared at him bewildered, the sight of him just too much for them to comprehend at that moment in time. Both of their brown eyes were red around the edges. Framed by disheveled black hair, their faces were pale, drained from the negative emotions that had clearly been assaulting their sanity for quite some time. They were at a breaking point.

The icy moment of shock melted away.

"KYLE!"

They both almost fell towards him, first touching his face and shoulder tentatively, as if to make sure he really was there standing in front of them. Then they embraced him with a force he never knew they had.

"We…we thought we'd lost you," his mother sobbed into him.

His father was too broken up to be able to muster any words. As they held him, he felt he was holding them up more than anything else, and it suddenly dawned on Kyle that he was old enough and big enough to do something like that.

"Mom, Dad, what happened?" he asked, confused and concerned. He waited patiently for them to calm down. The last time he had been held by both of his parents was when he was a stumbling, tumbling little toddler.

"Where have you been?" his father finally said with as steady a voice as he could manage.

"It's a long story. I'm sure you won't believe it. But first of all, what happened? Why are you two so upset?"

His parents stared at him with wide eyes, showing they couldn't believe how he could ask such a question.

"Kyle," his mother said, her eyes still brimming with fresh tears, "you've been missing for five months!"

Kyle's jaw dropped at the news.

"Five…months? That's impossible!" In his mind, he silently tabulated for himself how long his journey to the other world had been. There was the two days it took just to travel from Los Angeles to the Tian Yi society temple at the top of the mountain and then Crossing Over to the other world, a week of training at the Village of Ghosts, the visit to the dragon palace under the sea, the hermit on the mountain, and then the Phoenix Mountain. All in all, it came out to be less than a month. Five months? No way.

"Yes, five months," his mother insisted.

"Wait, what day is it? I left for Asia June 15th…"

"It's October 10," his father said. "How could you have been unconscious this whole time? And…and how did you end up back at home?"

"You're really not going to believe this…" Kyle shook his head as he tried his best to explain to them what had happened to him. As he told his tale, he pointed down to his strange clothing as evidence. His parents looked at it in disbelief, and exchanged looks with each other, trying to see if the other felt the same sense of incredulity at the strange tale their son, who had been missing for almost half a year, was trying to relay to them. He showed them the Liquid Blade and the jar of pure water. He finished the rest of the tale, his father pulling the Liquid Blade out of its sheath and looking it over with disbelieving eyes while his mother was holding the white jar and experimentally pouring a drop of the water into the palm of her hand and sniffing it.

When it was all said and done, his mother insisted that they all have a decent meal together. His parents had him sitting down at their modest little kitchen table as the two of them silently busied themselves with heating up leftovers of pasta and mashed potatoes, boiling up some water for tea, and pulling out some danta (egg tarts) out for dessert. There was enough for everyone; apparently his parents hadn't eaten yet, and Kyle had seen on the kitchen clock that it was only a couple hours or less until dawn.

As they all sat down to eat, an awkward silence ensued. Only the sounds of clinking silverware against porcelain dishware echoed into the quiet night as they ate their fill. Suddenly his father broke the silence with a tired sigh.

"Oh, Matt wanted me to call him right away if we heard anything about you."

Kyle smiled at the thought of his old friend. They had grown up together, toddlers in the park, kinders in the yard, elementary school buddies, and middle school and high school basketball teammates.

"It's late. Matt's probably asleep," Kyle's mom said as she finished the rest of her mash. "Let him rest. Kyle can give him a call first thing in the morning."

"It's practically morning now," Kyle said, looking out the kitchen window. "You two should get some rest, too. You both look exhausted." They smiled weakly at him, looking relieved to some extent but still worried, and he wondered if they believed a single word of his fantastic tale. His parents exchanged a weary look with each other before turning back to him.

"We're fine…and just so glad to have you safe at home again," his mother assured him.

"How about you, how do you feel?" his father asked.

Kyle took the moment to assess himself and his surroundings. The simple kitchen around him, the environment where he had grown up, pulsed with a clarity and life that he had long forgotten. The old, faded yellow wall paper still had a bit of luster from its heyday, and it glimmered in the faint sunlight that was creeping over the horizon outside. The white tiled counter was clean but worn from the daily use of a busy family. The brown, wooden cabinets were neat and in good condition but in need of some touch up repairs. His parents were hardworking, practical people who expected the same from their only son. The prudent yet homely feel of their residence reflected that attitude and lifestyle.

Kyle used to find this all very boring and uninteresting, embarrassing even, especially when compared to his more affluent and trendy classmates and neighbors, but he looked upon it all now as if for the first time, and yet it was also completely familiar and comforting to him. He suddenly felt like a child who found even the most mundane blade of grass in his backyard a thing of wonderment and miracles. He felt alert and refreshed, as if he'd been asleep for a long time and was only now awakening to recognize the world around him for the first time. Funny how a stint away from home can make clear everything that had been taken for granted.

"I feel fine, actually, really well rested. Look, you two should really get some rest. Do you have work today?"

"Not anymore we don't," his father said with a laugh. "I'm sure work'll understand when we tell them we found you." John glanced over at his exhausted wife, "But you're right, we should rest."

"You should rest, too, Kyle," his mother said, allowing her husband to help her out of her seat. It was a tenderness that was not there a few hours earlier, a fact which made Kyle feel uncomfortable.

"I'm fine, Mom. Don't worry about me," he tried to assure her. "I really feel like I've been resting indoors for days, kinda antsy to get out and move around a bit, you know?"

His parents moved to clear the dishes, and Kyle helped, insisting on doing it all himself. Reluctantly, they let him handle the clean up as he urged them upstairs to their room. As they were leaving, Kyle was allowed to let something that was bugging him in the back of his mind this whole time creep to the front of his consciousness. Where was Tai? Was she okay? The last he saw of her was at the infamous Phoenix Mountain in the other world. He worried for her safety and wondered if she was still stuck in that other land.

"What day is it today?"

"Monday, why?" his dad answered.

"A school day, huh…" Kyle half muttered to himself.

"You're not thinking of going to school, are you?" his mother asked incredulously. "After you've been gone for five months?" She looked completely unwilling to let him leave her sight again, the anxiety creeping back to strain the corners of her weary countenance.

His father put a reassuring hand on her shoulder.

"It's probably best for him to get back to a normal life after everything he's been through."

"And what about Ah-gong? Where is he?"

A dark look mixed with regret fell over his father's eyes.

"I haven't spoken to him since I found out you were missing," his father said. "I…blamed him for your disappearance, for not watching over you. I don't know where he is or what he's doing. Haven't for five months."

"I see…" Kyle responded. "Dad, I know what it seems like, but please don't be angry at Ah-gong. I'm not quite sure I understand what happened, but I know that it couldn't have happened without my consent."

His father sighed heavily. "I understand, but it will take a while for me to get over losing you for five months. Those were the longest five months of my life." There was a catch in his father's voice, as if he were about the break down into tears, but his father simply smiled and said,

"It's good to have you home, son."

"Thanks dad. It's good to be home," Kyle said, unable to remember the last time he and his father had had such a close exchange. His father gave him another hug, and after that, his mother also hugged him.

"Do you really have to go to school?" she asked again.

"Don't worry mom, I'm not planning on going anywhere but to school and back home. I just want to see Matt and let him know I'm okay and all. And…and I wanted to check on a friend."

His mom nodded her head wearily, but then added, "Your cell phone is still on your desk. Could you text me now and then, just to let me know you're okay?"

"Sure Mom."

Her parents turned and went upstairs, leaving Kyle alone with his thoughts in the kitchen. He finished cleaning up quickly and then went up to his own room. Picking up his cell phone from his desk, he turned it on and found that the charge was near full and his service was still going. He smiled sadly, knowing his parents continued to pay for his cell phone despite his disappearance, a small act of hope on their part that he would return even though they had no sign that he would. It made Kyle's heart ache to know how hard it must have been for them while he was out gallivanting in another world.

Kyle changed out of his now-dry, simple brown Lin Gui attire and into a white t-shirt and blue jeans. He took out all of the study guides in his back pack and replaced it with a new binder filled with line paper and dividers, and checked to make sure he had ample writing utensils and other school supplies in the smaller pocket of his bag. He saw his sports duffle bag and unzipped it to find all of his basketball gear and clothes clean and neatly folded and arranged. His parents must have come into his room often.

Suddenly his phone was vibrating off the hook, and he flipped it open to find that it wasn't actually ringing, it was receiving five months' worth of messages. It wasn't just Matt, it was people from his basketball team, people in his honors classes, some teachers, and even Rose and some of her girl friends. All wondering where he was, all hoping he was okay, all hoping he would come back soon. Kyle was amazed. He hadn't thought anyone would have noticed much if he was gone. He wasn't exactly well known at school, just that low-key regular guy that was a good student and involved in sports, someone there but nobody really talks about much. A guy like him was a dime a dozen at his school. And he tended to be on the quiet side, too. But he figured everyone knew and loved Matt, and Matt being worried about him probably brought everyone's attention to Kyle's absence. Nevertheless, it was nice of them all the same to worry.

With his backpack securely in place and the duffle bag slung over one shoulder, Kyle continued to scroll through his messages as he went downstairs, let himself out, locked the door, and walked down the path splitting his front lawn. The early morning sunlight touched everything in sight, and though it was fall, this sunny southern Californian neighborhood was full of the watered greens typical of Los Angeles suburbia, and everything looked almost exactly as it had early in the summer before he went off to Asia with his grandfather.

The first thing he did when he reached the sidewalk was to turn and look at his own house, and after sufficiently taking in the sight of it with a smile playing on his lips, he began to count eight houses down from his, first to the right, then to the left, and then he saw it, just around the bend of his street, a house with two cycads in front. He looked at his watch and saw that it was nearly time for school to start. He would be late to classes, but he figured after being late for the start of school by about a couple of months, a few more minutes wouldn't make much of a difference. He headed straight for the house with the two cycads. When he was at the door, he pressed on the doorbell. Within a moment or two, it swung open, and the person who opened it for him gasped.

"Kyle?"

Chapter 28

Is that you?

"Yes," Kyle responded.

"Kyle Lin? The one who's been missing?" the woman who had opened the door said with disbelief. She was a middle-aged woman who was still very youthful, her glimmering blonde hair wrapped up in a neat bun. Looking out at him with crystal blue eyes, she was not what Kyle had expected. Tai did say she was in foster care.

"My name is Cindy, and I suppose you're here looking for Tai."

"Uh…yeah, is she here?"

"No, she's already gone off to school."

"Oh I see," Kyle said, relieved to find out that Tai was okay and back in this world. Then he was curious. "How did you know I was looking for her?"

"Your grandfather told us what happened. You see, I'm a member of the Tian Yi Society, albeit an unwelcome one by most of the others," Cindy smiled.

"I see, so…you're Tai's foster mother?" Kyle hazarded out of curiosity.

Cindy heaved a sigh and looked a little sad.

"No, I'm actually her mother, though not her biological one. My husband and I adopted Tai when she was an infant. She's still telling people she's in foster care?"

Kyle nodded uncomfortably. Cindy seemed like a really nice lady, so it didn't make sense to Kyle for Tai to distance herself from her adoptive mother by saying she was in foster care instead. He wondered if it was her way of getting attention or sympathy from others, although that didn't sound like the Tai he knew at all. Cindy seemed to sense his questions.

"Tai is…complicated. You have to understand, it's a wound that never goes away, being abandoned by your own parents. Even though I have a Ph.D. in psychology, I can't get her to change her feelings or the way she wants to live her life," Cindy said with another sigh. "Psychology isn't magic or mind control, but it does help me understand and respect where she's coming from, even if I can't relate." She seemed to be talking to herself at this point.

Kyle nodded more to show that he was listening than to indicate that he understood.

"How long has she been home? I mean, she wasn't missing like me for five months, was she?" he asked.

"No, she wasn't missing at all. In fact, according to your grandfather, you were the only one who disappeared the day of the Crossover."

"WHAT?" Kyle couldn't help but raise his voice a bit in surprise.

"Yes, apparently it was proof enough for everyone at Tian Yi Society that you were the fated Chosen One, not Tai."

"Oh boy," Kyle said while shaking his head. "But she wasn't…I mean she came with me, she was there with me the whole time…"

"I know, she told me. But no one there would believe her, thinking she was just making it up to prove she was still the Chosen One. No one that is, except for your grandfather."

"Do you know where my grandfather is?"

"Yes, yes I do. He's still in Asia actually, looking for you, or some way to look for you. He's been very worried since Tai told him that you were kidnapped by the First Child."

"Can you…"

"Right away, but right now, you should go to school," Cindy said with a bright smile. "Tai will be happy to see you."

Kyle gave a wry smile. “Somehow, I doubt that.”

“Then you got to know her pretty well over a short period of time,” Cindy laughed.

“Maybe,” Kyle smiled a bit. “Thank you for your help.”

“No thanks needed. I heard how you took care of her when she needed help. I should be the one thanking you.”

The memory of blood and a nasty slash across Tai’s back flashed through his mind.

“She saved my hide enough times. I was just returning the favor.”

“Here,” Cindy turned around and reached out to a small table behind her in the hall. “My card.”

Kyle took it respectfully with two hands, the way his parents had taught him to do.

“Thanks.”

He looked at it. *Cindy Tan, Ph.D. Clinical Psychologist.*

The walk to school was uneventful for Kyle, but he enjoyed the peacefulness and normality of the little trek. When he arrived, he stopped for a moment at the entrance before entering, breathing in the smells of school and taking in the sight of the red bricks and blue doors that were characteristic of his high school’s architecture.

“You’re late.”

A security guard posted at the front gate of the school gave Kyle a stern look. She was a woman of large build with short hair and a tight frown.

“I’m sorry, this is actually my first day of school. You see, I’ve been…”

“OH, I know. I recognize you. You’re that kid that’s been missing. Your picture’s still hanging on the wall in the office. So you finally turned up, huh?”

"Yeah. My name is Kyle Lin."

"Where have you been?" she asked as she jotted down a note on her clipboard.

"It's…a long story."

"Well, go on in, go on in. Get yourself registered." The guard waved her hand, indicating for him to go to the front office. He was glad she didn't want to hear the long story.

After quickly texting his mother an update that he was at school, Kyle walked onto the quiet campus. First period had already begun, and everyone was in class. The high school was a series of single-floor buildings spread out across a wide flat area. The school pool and gym were straight ahead, football field and band rooms were to his left, and classrooms were to his right. In the middle of the large courtyard surrounded by everything was a medium-sized school library. The front office was adjacent to the entrance to Kyle's right.

Kyle turned, put a hand on the door knob of the large and heavy blue door, and pulled. When he walked inside, he was greeted at first by nonchalance, which gradually turned into shocked looks as people started to recognize him. There were office managers, administrators, counselors, and student assistants, and all the business they were engaged in slowly stopped to a grinding halt as they turned to stare at him.

"Can I…help you?" a girl at the front counter said. The brunette gave him a peculiar look.

"My name is Kyle Lin. I'm…uh…here to register for classes."

"KYLE!"

Kyle looked up at the outburst and saw a ways into the office a pair of glimmering blue eyes under a pretty head of blonde, flowing hair. A young girl was running towards him clad in a flattering, short-skirted pink dress with shiny red high heels clicking against the floor despite it being thinly carpeted. Her lips were red with a thick, glossed up lipstick and her mascara covered eyelashes batted as she blinked in surprise.

"Rose!"

Rose Tracy came up to him and gave him a hug. He awkwardly accepted, remembering with shame and embarrassment the last time he had 'seen' her.

"Oh my gosh! Where have you *been*?! Everyone's been so worried about you!"

"I…it's…it's…kind of a long story," Kyle stammered.

"I just texted Matt! When did you get back? How come there was no announcement, no news, nothing! You just showed up out of nowhere!"

"Yeah, I kinda did. Just got home late last night…"

The door he had just come through swung open, and Kyle turned around to see his best friend bursting in almost completely out of breath. He looked like he had just run a hundred yard dash at top speed.

"KYLE!" his friend bear hugged him and picked him up like a rag doll. Unlike Kyle, who was more on the medium height and lanky side, Matt Lee was tall with broad shoulders and strong facial features. Most people would assess after one glance that Matt was probably considered the most attractive male student on campus. Most of the female students on campus would agree.

"Hey Matt…" Kyle almost squealed out as his strong friend squeezed him without mercy.

"You're okay! What happened? Where'd you go? Look at your arms! You're so buff now! And tan!"

Kyle looked down at his arms. He hadn't noticed, but the training and travel had browned his skin even more and developed his muscles. Although still on the lanky side compared to Matt, his shoulders had broadened and his build was overall more substantial. He'd been too busy to notice the changes in his body.

"Yeah, I've…been out in the sun a lot."

"What?! Here we are all worried to death about you and you've been chilling out on some tropical beach surrounded by hot babes?" Matt said with a slap to his best friend's shoulder.

"Uh…not exactly," Kyle said, scratching his head at his friend's hyperbolic joke.

"Well, you're going to have to tell me EVERYTHING, okay? Man, is it good to see you! We posted pictures of you everywhere in town and on the internet!"

Kyle was surprised to see tears pooling in his friend's eyes. It was hard to imagine seeing such a burly, strapping young man near tears. He couldn't remember the last time he saw Matt in tears. Rose held onto Matt's large wrist with her supportive hand, looking up at him with empathy.

"What's your schedule man?" Matt asked.

"I don't know. I was just about to register for classes."

Rose went to the head office manager's filing cabinet and pulled out a small slip of paper with a list of classes, classroom numbers, and times. She brought it back to Kyle.

"Here you go," Rose said with a friendly smile. "They kept your class schedule on record. Just in case!" She grinned widely.

"Thanks," Kyle said as he looked down at his schedule.

"Figures," Matt said, looking at Kyle's schedule. "You're in all of those AP classes already. Regular honors is never good enough for you, huh? The only class we have together is the only AP class I'm taking, AP Chem, 3rd period."

"And basketball, too," Kyle pointed out the last item on his schedule, which was listed as "P.E. Athletics".

"Nice." Matt's smile was priceless as he held his fist up to Kyle, and Kyle raised his fist and hit it lightly against his friend's in a gesture of their close friendship.

"Okay kids, sorry to interrupt, but I need to talk to Mr. Lin here for a minute."

The three of them looked up and saw that they were looking up at the principal. He was a large man with hair that had gone completely white. He looked at them with kind yet stern hazel eyes, his face somewhat past middle-age which matched the old yet sturdy gray suit that he wore.

"Mr. Lee, I got a call from your first period U.S. History honors teacher that you had run out of class without a word of explanation. I've explained the situation to her, but I think you owe her an apology for disrupting the class."

"Sorry Mr. White. I'll be sure to tell her I'm sorry."

The principal nodded with approval and turned to go back to his office.

"Well, alright man, I'm gonna get back to class. I'll see you in third period!" Matt gave him a friendly punch to the shoulder as he left.

"I'd better get back to work, too," Rose said. "It's great to have you back. Matt's been so worried about you." She gave him a kind smile before going back to her workstation.

Kyle followed the principal into his office and closed the door behind.

The principal sat down in his large, black chair and leaned back, the chair creaking under his weight.

"So, Mr. Lin, where have you been?"

Kyle was starting to get really tired of everyone asking him that, especially when he didn't know how to explain what had really happened to him.

"It's hard to explain, Mr. White, but I arrived back home late last night. My parents know I'm back, and they know I'm here at school today. They're at home right now, but they're probably asleep since they had a sleepless night."

"I'd imagine. Well, it is good to know that you're back safe and sound. Are you sure you feel up to starting school already?"

"Yes, sir, I'm feeling fine."

"Well then, alright. You'll need to get your textbooks and then head to your second period class since you've missed most of first."

"Thank you sir."

Kyle left the office and went around the corner to the textbook room. After he had picked up all the extremely large AP textbooks and filled his backpack and duffle bag with them, the school bell rang, shrill and loud, and students began pouring out of every classroom, filling the empty halls with noise, laughter, and movement.

Kyle looked down at his schedule. First period was over. Second period was AP Calculus. He headed for the only building on campus that was white and two stories high, the math department. Climbing the concrete stairs, Kyle moved through the crowd largely unnoticed by his peers who were too busy with their own little worlds to notice him pass by them. He wondered where Tai was and if she was going to be in any of his classes. He tried to think about how he would locate her, aside from searching for her randomly through the crowds of students. He couldn't help but notice that many of the girls wore a similar shade of lipstick as the one Rose was wearing and were also clicking around school in rather high, shiny red high-heels as well. He gathered it must be the latest fashion trend among the girls, and then he realized that would make it all the easier for him to locate Tai. There was an incredibly high probably that she would be one of the few girls who was not in high heels or wearing red lipstick.

When he made it to his destination, a large and brown room on the second floor of the math building, he stepped in, and the response of the few students already in class was like a snowball effect. First one student noticed him and called out his name, then another and another came up to him. His classmates in the AP classes were pretty much the same from the year before, since most of the students who were taking almost all AP classes had pretty much the same schedule as he did. As he talked to his friends and tried to field their many questions, he was searching around the room to see if Tai was anywhere in there. The chairs and tables in the classroom were the kind that were joined together, so that each chair was attached to a small corresponding table, and these units of desk-and-chair were lined up in four rows all facing forward toward the front of the classroom.

He saw some students here or there that he didn't know very well; they were at their seats but looking over at him and talking to each other. There was one, however, that seemed to be unaffected by all the talk about his arrival. That particular teen sat at the very back of the room wearing a large non-descript black sweater and loose-fitting blue-jean pants with a tan baseball cap. The lid of the cap covered up the student's face almost completely as the student was in the down into heavyweight Calculus textbook open on the desk. If Kyle hadn't been searching, he knew he would have completely missed that silent figure in the back. The tardy bell rang, pulling him away from the crowd of classmates and questions, and though he couldn't even tell for sure if the student in the back was male or female, he quickly moved to sit strategically right in front of that student on a gut feeling.

Everyone took their seats as the teacher set up his overhead projector for the day's lecture and lesson.

"Welcome class. Before we begin, I just received a message from the principal that Kyle Lin, who had been a missing person up until yesterday, has just resumed classes as of this moment. Welcome back,

Mr. Lin."

The class erupted into applause, and Kyle, not knowing how to respond to so much attention, waved awkwardly at everyone in thanks. The teacher flipped the switch of his overhead projector, the light brightened the screen at the front of the class, and lessons went underway as usual. Kyle however, was not listening. He pulled out his binder, undid the rings with one quick snap, and pulled out a new piece of line paper. He thought of ripping the paper into parts, but then decided to leave it whole, leaving space for a response to his question:

Tai, is that you?

Folding it up carefully while the teacher droned on with his lesson, Kyle quietly slipped the note onto the table behind him. He heard it being picked up off the table and opened rather roughly. Then, he heard it being crumpled up, and the next thing he knew, it hit the back of his head. Kyle smiled.

Chapter 29

A Normal Day

As soon as the bell rang, Kyle spun around in his seat only to find that Tai was already on her way out of the classroom. He swept everything on his table into his open backpack, zipped it all up hastily, and was after her.

"Tai!" he said insistently as he caught up to her while she went quickly down the stairs. She ignored him, her eyes hidden under the lid of her cap. "Come on, we've got to talk."

"There's nothing to talk about."

"What do you mean there's nothing to talk about?" Kyle said, losing his patience. "I've suddenly become missing for five months when to me, it was only yesterday that you came popping out of that pool in the mountain with your staff ready to do a major smack down on the First Child demon."

Kyle easily matched her fast-paced stride. There was no getting away from him.

"Don't you have a class to go to?" Tai spat out impatiently.

"Depends. What class are you going to?" Kyle said, not even trying to hide the triumphant smile on his face. If Tai was ranked top in their class the same way he was, there was a 99.99% chance that she had the exact same schedule as he did. That and she did say she chose her classes based on his schedule.

"AP Chem," they both said in unison, to Tai's annoyance. Even though she knew very well that they had the same schedule, it still annoyed her.

They were closing in on the classroom already, down the hall past three red-bricked buildings and then three blue doors to the right. The blue lockers lined some of the walls, the metal clang of their opening and closing filling the air with a sort of random rhythm.

"Look, where do you usually eat lunch?" Kyle pressed.

"I don't."

"Don't lie."

"I had a big breakfast."

"Okay, whatever, but I'm not leaving you alone until we've talked." Kyle was going to get to the bottom of this. If his parents and friends had to suffer not knowing where he had been for five months, he was going to at least know what had happened to him, not to mention he was just intensely curious as to where he'd been for almost half a year.

"Fine."

They entered the next classroom before he had a chance to press her again for where she was going to be for lunch, and his thoughts were interrupted by a call of his name.

"Hey! Kyle! Over here!"

It was Matt. His friend was sitting with a large, toothy grin and a twinkle to his almond-shaped brown eyes. He motioned for Kyle to join him, and Kyle watched Tai sit down in a seat far in the corner of the room, as far away from the teacher's desk as possible. *Some star student,* he thought. *Why is she always hiding in the back?*

Matt noticed Kyle's eyes following Tai as she moved to the back, and after his mouth dropped open a bit in mild surprise, he suddenly got up out of his seat and grabbed Kyle by the arm.

"On second thought, let's move over here."

"What?" Kyle said in surprise as his friend pushed him to the back of the room and sat him down next to Tai. The desks in this classroom were actually large, black lab tables with four stools around each of them, naturally organizing the students into eight groups of four students each. Tai was sitting next to the wall on the inner seat of one of such black tables, and Matt had sat Kyle right down on the stool next to her while he took the seat right across from him.

"Hey Matt! What's up dude?"

A young man waved at Matt as he walked into the classroom. Matt's friend took the empty stool seat right in front of Tai, who had pulled a large textbook from the wall shelf labeled "Organic Chemistry" and started flipping through it as if she were the only sentient being at the table and that textbook was the only object nearby worth her attention. The tardy bell hadn't rung yet. Kyle looked over at her. When he had first met her, she had challenged him to a fight and punched him in the face. Why was she being so quiet and aloof?

"Jake, you know my friend Kyle, right?"

"Oh yeah, hey, the guy who's been missing? Everyone's talking about you man. So what happened to you?"

"Uh, I was just traveling and got lost," Kyle said.

"Yeah, I heard you were in Asia. Taiwan was it? What were you up to? Getting in touch with your roots or something?"

That was an interesting question. Kyle thought about his journey away from home, how foreign everything had been for him, how homesick he had felt, and he answered with a smile, "Naw man, my roots are here."

Matt smiled and gave him a high-five in agreement.

"Right on," Jake said with little real care in his voice. With his thick black hair, strong build, and prominent features, Jake Chang was one of the few other boys at school that rivaled Matt in popularity among the girls, but he wasn't much like Matt other than that. Kyle knew of Jake and his reputation, and he was always irritated by Jake when he saw him.

"Jake joined the basketball team this year, Kyle," Matt said, friendly as always.

"Oh yeah? That's great," Kyle said with as much courteous enthusiasm as he could muster.

"Hiiiiii Jake!" a gaggle of girls that had walked by their table said together in a little, coquettish chorus. They all had their lips covered in red lipstick and all wore matching red high-heels that clicked like a stampede of tiny hooves on the linoleum classroom floor.

"Hi ladies! Lookin' hot as always!" Jake winked at them and flashed them his handsome smile. The girls exchanged sparkling looks and giggles as they settled down at the table next to theirs. Kyle turned as he tried to hide his rolling eyes. Now he remembered why he always felt irritated when he saw Jake, although secretly, Kyle had been envious of Jake's smooth ways with the other gender. No gaggle of girls ever said hi to Kyle like that…or at all for that matter.

Jake pulled out his chemistry lab booklet and flipped it open. He shrugged his shoulders at the blank page.

"I guess I forgot to fill it out. Hey, psss…" Jake suddenly turned on Tai who was still flipping through the organic chemistry book. She was already more than halfway through the thick volume. "Hey, you look smart. Can I copy your lab?"

Kyle was about the burst out laughing but held his composure. Asking Tai to help you cheat was like asking a hungry tiger to share its fresh kill. He waited for Tai to react, hoping it had something to do with her large textbook and Jake's face.

To Kyle's total astonishment, Tai quietly reached a hand into her bag, pulled out the matching lab book made of thin sheets of grayish paper saddle-stitched together, and slid it across the table to Jake.

"Thanks for being such a doll!" Jake said as he happily opened her lab book and started copying her answers over into his book.

Kyle was flabbergasted. Why would Tai help Jake? Why would she help this slimy creep cheat? Was she as susceptible to his manly charms as the other girls were? Maybe Kyle didn't know her as well as Cindy had thought, or as well as he had thought. He couldn't understand it, but he felt a welling anger inside him as Jake scribbled gleefully away, copying Tai's work. Kyle felt like something was being taken away from him, and he was filled with a sudden burning desire to snatch Tai's lab book away from Jake and smash his face in with it.

Jake slid the lab book back to Tai.

"Thanks, babe, you're the best!"

Kyle felt like he was about to explode. *Babe*...the word made his stomach turn inside out. Tai was still looking through the organic chemistry textbook, now nearing the end of it. She finished flipping through the last page, and then looked up and met Jake's eyes with her own from under the tan baseball cap lid she still had on.

Kyle watched her with intensity, looking for some sign of sparkle or giggle in her eye as she looked at the handsome young Jake. But there was no sparkle, no giggle, only a dull boredom.

"No need to thank me. It's mildly amusing to me, helping you amount to nothing."

The tardy bell rang before Jake or anyone else at the table had a chance to comprehend what Tai had said. She had spoken with such an uninterested, monotone voice lacking any malice or mischief that the stripped language had fallen upon their ears like a dryly delivered history lesson no one wanted to pay any attention to.

As the teacher started her lecture, Jake was slowly parsing through the words that had been said to him, and though he finally came to the overdue conclusion that he had been slighted, the moment had passed, and if he were to say anything now, it would only come out slow and awkward, much like a lumbering garbage truck making a shamefully delayed dump at the trash yard. So he left it at that and decided there were easier, less confusing fish to trap in that little pond of a chemistry classroom for his next homework snatch.

Kyle was just as slow as Jake in figuring out Tai's words, but his reaction was quite different. He found himself trying not to burst out in erratic smiles or laughter the more he understood what Tai had just said. At some points, he had to cover his face with his hand to pretend to be rubbing his eyes or wiping his mouth clean of something in order to hide his smile. He turned to steal a glance at Tai at one point and saw that she was flipping through the organic chemistry text again, her fingers stuck in multiple spots in the pages of the book, as if she were cross-referencing some of the information or making note of important parts. He didn't notice that Matt had been observing him the whole time.

When Kyle and Tai walked into their next class, he didn't realize that he was following her until he found himself sitting next to her again at the back of the room and looked up to see a scowl on her disapproving face. Amused, he met her scowl with an amused smile and said in a quiet voice, "Remember? Lunch time, talk."

This classroom was set up much like his second period AP Calc class had been, with rows of connected tables and chairs all facing forward towards the front of the classroom where three large panels of white board covered the wall. The tardy bell rang again, and the students took their seats. It was then that Kyle looked up to notice the AP U.S. History teacher standing at the front.

She was a young looking teacher with her long, silken black hair pulled up in a modest bun. Her blue, almond-shaped eyes were protected by some silver metal framed spectacles, and her smile was sweet and beautiful. Kyle stared at her with brow furrowed, trying to figure something out. She looked extremely familiar, but it couldn't be her, could it? The teacher noticed his intense and probing stare and gave him a friendly wink.

After the bell rang and everyone had settled, she said, "Good

morning class! I see Mr. Lin is able to join us today. It's a pleasure to meet you. I'm Dr. Snow."

Kyle's jaw dropped a little, and then he managed to raise a hand in a mediocre greeting as he sputtered out a 'hi'. Snow gave him and his classmates a brilliant smile, one that softened the moods of everyone in the class. Her class was a daily favorite of many.

As if Kyle's brain wasn't already bubbling with enough questions, a whole new pot of them started brewing, and he felt as if his mental capacity was spilling over and out onto the cold classroom floor. What was Snow doing in this world?

Snow divvied up the class into discussion groups, and as the discussions came to an end, Snow collected all the papers, assigning the chapters to read for the next day's discussion. As the bell rang and Kyle was on his way out, he passed by a smiling Snow and managed to say, "How…"

"We'll discuss it later. Have fun at basketball!" Snow said and shooed him out with the rest of the brood.

Fourth period AP Computer Science passed by without incident, and Kyle actually focused on catching up with the level of familiarity the rest of the class already had with programming language. Again he sat next to Tai, to her renewed annoyance, and again she seemed bored and appeared to be reading some advanced level book and doing some sort of independent project of her own while everyone else worked frantically to complete the given assignment.

Finally it was lunch, and Kyle was walking next to Tai even though she wasn't saying a word to him. He thought of asking her where she was going, but then decided just to follow her to where ever she was headed.

As they were walking, Kyle noticed that quite a few people were looking at him, pointing, and then whispering. It looked like word of his return had fully become the top story of the day on campus. Kyle felt uncomfortable being under so much public scrutiny. He looked over at Tai. She was still wearing the tan baseball cap, and her face was pretty much hidden under its lid.

"Dude, Kyle!"

Matt's voice caught Kyle's attention, and he looked over at his best friend and waved.

"Aren't you going to have lunch with us over here?" Matt asked. He was with Rose and her girl friends, a number of guys from the basketball team, including Jake.

"Sorry," Kyle called back. Tai took the opportunity to quicken her pace and speed ahead of him in hopes of losing him, but Kyle tried to keep up as he responded. "I have a…a meeting to go to. I'll see you at practice!"

"Okay man!" Matt responded with a slightly goofy grin. "Have fun at your meeting! And we're going celebrating with pizza after school okay? Bring your new friend!"

Although Kyle was pretty sure Tai would say no to his invitation, he could only manage to waive in affirmative as he sped up to catch up to Tai. He followed her as she headed to the front of the school library, a spot that was quiet and secluded from the bustle of lunch time, and she sat down on a wall in front of it. Kyle sat down with her and watched as she pulled out a brown paper bag with a peanut butter jelly sandwich, whole grain wheat crackers, string cheese, an apple, a banana, a carton of orange juice, and a carton of asparagus juice. Then Kyle realized he had nothing with him, and that he actually felt hungry.

With the food in her hand, Tai looked at him and paused for a moment, as if remembering something, and then she broke her sandwich in half and handed it to him with the banana and the orange juice.

"Here, you'll need your strength," Tai said.

"Thanks."

They began on their food, and Kyle began his questions.

"So…what happened?"

"What happened when?" Tai said back.

Kyle thought for a moment. Where did he want her to start?

"What happened after I disappeared from inside Phoenix Mountain?"

Tai chewed and swallowed.

"You and the First Child disappeared into thin air right in front of me. Then I went back in the pool and ended up back where we started, and Jade and Snow were there looking for us. I told them what happened. Then Jade took us back to Jun Bao."

Tai fell silent for a moment, her expression suddenly heavy with some thought. Although Kyle was dying to know what happened next, he felt the suddenly solemn mood and decided it would be best to wait for Tai to continue when she was ready. Tai seemed to suddenly snap out of her mood and notice he was there again.

"The mountain top was like a battle field. Trees were uprooted and torn to shreds, his home was demolished, oven and pies and all, but Jun Bao stood in front of the peach tree. It was stripped bare of its blossoms." Tai stared blankly for a moment, seeing the image as if it were right there before her. "Apparently he had protected it from an onslaught of Yehren. There were corpses everywhere."

Kyle shivered. Even the mention of the twisted human creatures horrified him and reminded him of what he'd rather forget.

"That's not even the strange part," Tai said, suddenly rather involved in telling her tale as it relived itself in her mind. "There were living people there, too. People who had been Yehren but that had been turned back."

"Turned back? How?"

"That's what I asked, but they all remained quiet and unwilling or unable to tell me. Jun Bao, Snow, Jade, even the people themselves. All Jun Bao said to me was 'There are ways to return to paradise.' It was like a funeral, and then I noticed that the people were slowly bringing the dead to the word for compassion that Jun Bao had carved into the ground." Tai got out her notebook, flipped to a blank page, and wrote out the character. It was as if she felt the compulsion to practice writing it all of a sudden.

"When the bodies were placed there, they evaporated like stardust, like that one we fought by the ocean."

Kyle flinched involuntarily at the mention of that incident.

"I'm not sure what it all means," Tai said, "but maybe this character is the key to undoing what the First Child has done. Bringing peace to tortured souls, or something like that."

They sat in silence for a moment, eating their food pensively.

"Then what happened?" Kyle finally prodded.

"Then Jun Bao explained to me that the First Child must have used you as a portal to Crossover into this world from that one."

"Used…me…" Kyle said, remembering how the Demon had looked just like Tai but not like Tai. How she had…his face turned a little red. "I see."

"After that, Jade and Snow told me I had to Crossover and take them with me. They told me that if the First Child had come into our world, it meant disaster for everyone here and that we would need their help."

"And that was five months ago?"

"Yes, at least from our perspective."

"I see…"

"When we arrived back, I found myself in the same place and time right before you and I had left, except you were gone. Everyone took that as the sign that you were the real Chosen One, and no one except for your grandfather believed me, and they didn't even notice that Jade and Snow weren't there before. Pathetic, narrow-minded people," Tai added with disgust.

"And then you all came back here?"

"Yes. The Society was useless, so we decided to go where we had the most resources to search for the First Child."

"Have you found her?"

"No. Apparently, she's like a chameleon, so we can't tell who she is or where she is. She could be anywhere. She could be anyone."

"So where do we start looking for her?"

"Nowhere. Unfortunately, the first move is hers."

"That's bad news."

"I know.

"So where's Jade?"

"He's your basketball coach."

"Okay…"

"So you'll see him later on today."

Kyle shook his head. At least it wasn't going to be another strange surprise. He'd had enough surprises to last him a lifetime by now.

The bell rang, indicating the end of their lunch, and they headed out to AP Human Geography and then AP Psychology after that. The work piled on at an insane rate, but instead of fretting over it and turning into a little stress ball like he did in the past, Kyle kind of just accepted it all. He wrote down the long list of his assignments in his book and then almost felt like shrugging at them with a feeling of 'sure, why not' instead of 'I'm a dead man' like in the past. His mind was largely preoccupied with the extraordinary events that keep popping up in his originally un-extraordinary life. His less anxiety-driven approach to school surprised him a little bit, but he figured after being attacked by dragons and demons and twisted human creatures, fretting over homework like his life depended on it seemed, well, rather silly.

They went back to classes, and when the bell rang for the end of 6th period and it was time for him to go off to basketball practice, Kyle turned to Tai.

"Call me right now."

"Excuse me?"

"You have a cell phone, yes? Call me right now."

"Why?"

"So I have your number. With the First Child running loose somewhere out there, we should be in contact at all times, you know, just in case. Right?"

Tai thought about it for a moment and then pulled out her cell phone and dialed the numbers he gave her. He received the call and then saved her contact information.

"There. What are you doing after school?"

They walked out of the classroom and into the busy hallway.

"Training. Which is what you'll be doing too."

"Training? Where?"

"At my foster home."

Kyle gave her a look.

"What?"

"Nothing. I stopped by there today looking for you."

Tai raised an eyebrow at him before continuing.

"Jade and Snow will be there. They've been teaching me how to use qi script."

"Qi script? We…we can do that here?" Kyle said, surprised yet again.

Tai smiled for the first time that day, and her eyes glowed a bit. Kyle noticed that glowing faintly on her forehead was the Chinese character that meant "water" written in what looked like calligraphic strokes of light.

水

Then Tai held up her hand for Kyle to see. A small pool of swirling water formed in her hand, and then it stopped and fell into her palm and dribbled through her fingers.

"No way!" Kyle exclaimed, astonished at both what she had done and that she could do it.

"Yes way," Tai confirmed. "You have a lot of catching up to do."

Kyle rolled his eyes with mild exasperation.

"Don't I always? Anyways, Matt has something planned for me after school at the pizza place down the street. You wanna come?"

"No."

"Yeah, I figured," Kyle shrugged. "You know where it is, right?"

"Yes."

"Okay, well, I'll be there right after basketball practice if you change your mind. I'll be at your house as soon as I can."

"My foster home."

"Yeah, yeah, that. Wait for me, okay?" Kyle said pointing his index finger at her meaningfully before turning to run off to his basketball practice, heavy backpack and duffle in tow.

Tai walked on alone, and lost in thought, she didn't realize that her pace of walking was slowing down. Eventually, she came to a full stop. The flow of the student traffic went past her, barely anyone noticing that she had stopped in the middle of the hallway as they went along their busy way. They curved and ducked around her as naturally as water streams around a rock waiting forever in the river path.

Chapter 30

A Plot Hatches

"Hey Kyle! Coach Yu!"

Matt's cheerful voice rang through the pizzeria, full of youthful masculinity. He was sitting with the rest of the basketball team, and Rose was by his side with her friends. Rose was with her cheerleading crew, Mandy, Mercedes, Robin, Soo, and Kyra, all wearing vibrant colors of lipstick with matching nail polish making them look like an assortment of candy from a bag. Together the young teenage basketball players and cheerleaders took up the longest contiguous row of tables and chairs in the whole restaurant. The white and red plaid table cloths were covered with large pitchers of bubbling soft drinks and a number of large round and freshly-baked pizzas dripping with mozzarella cheese, tomato sauce, and a variety of toppings. Baskets of buffalo wings drenched with savory and spicy red sauce filled the spaces in between everything else. The aroma that floated through the air was mouth-watering. Kyle and Jade, or Coach Yu, waved at the group and headed towards them. Two seats were left empty in front of Matt and Rose for them. Kyle was glad to see that Jake was nowhere in sight.

"Where's your friend?" Matt asked eagerly, looking around hoping to see the girl emerge from the crowd somewhere. Rose and the rest of the girls looked around with anticipation, too, but Kyle didn't really take note of their interest.

"Oh, uh, Tai? She couldn't make it."

Matt and Rose exchanged a disappointed look, and the other girls looked a little let down, too.

"Are you hungry?" Rose said amicably, motioning to the food.

"Starved," Jade said as Kyle nodded in agreement. They dug into the greasy goodness of the local pizzeria.

"So who's this Tai? How come I never saw you talk to her before?" Matt asked.

Kyle couldn't really explain how he got to know Tai. Chosen One? Crossover? Qi script? He'd be locked in a room with padded walls in no time if he told everyone about all of that.

"She…uh…I met her on my trip to Asia with my grandfather. And…and she helped me get back."

"Really? Then we owe that girl," Matt said with a disbelieving shake of his head. To Kyle's relief, his friend didn't pursue asking him about his time away. "So did she just start at our high school today?"

Kyle looked up at his friend to see if there was any sign of joking on his face, but Matt was asking the question sincerely and seriously. Apparently, Tai had be in one of his classes and walking around school all this time but it seemed Matt had not noticed her. In fact, it seemed that no one had noticed she was there. When he had first met her in that temple courtyard where they had their first face off, he hadn't recognized her either, but she had known him. She seemed to have a way of blending in with the background. It was like she was invisible. He wondered why that was. Then he wondered if that was a lonely way to exist.

"Oh, no, she's been going to school…in this area for a while. She's just a quiet person that keeps to herself."

"You seem to know a lot about her," Rose said with a beautiful red-lipped smile.

Kyle shrugged self-consciously. In the background, the latest pop songs were playing on a popular radio station that was always blaring out of the small speakers hung on the walls. As was usual with pop songs, the hackneyed chorus of the newest hit seemed to blare extra loud and stick itself inside Kyle's head like gum to the underside of a table.

I just want your love and devotion
To set our destiny in motion
Is it so bad that I want your heart?
Make it shine or break it apart?
Sweetening you up inside and out?
Come on n' see what Kandi's all about

Unconsciously, Kyle and his friends moved foot, finger, or head in time with the beat. It was one of those songs that really got stuck in your head.

"She sure didn't seem like the quiet type today," Matt commented.

"Huh?" Kyle wondered what Matt was talking about.

"You know, what she said to Jake today."

"Oh yeah," Kyle said and laughed a little without realizing it. "Well, he was kind of asking for it."

"What happened with Jake?" Kyra asked. Everyone knew Kyra was obsessed with the good-looking Jake. The other girls perked up too, to Kyle's mild annoyance, since they all thought Jake was quite the hottie as well. Only Rose smiled serenely sitting by Matt's side.

"Jake was copying Tai's homework today in chem and then Tai kinda dissed him. Doesn't seem like something a quiet girl would do, don't you think Kyle?" Matt explained with a wry smile at his good friend.

"Aw, but Jake is so hot! I'd let him copy my chem notes any day," Kyra crooned as the other girls nodded, their brightly colored lips smiled in agreement.

Kyle took a big bite of pizza and chewed away in silence, now fully annoyed at Rose's friends in a way he never was before. Funny, he wondered, it's not like the first time he'd heard them drooling over Jake.

Before, he'd feel a reluctant envy of Jake, having so many girls at school swooning to his every charming smile, but this time, all he felt was…irritated.

"So tell us more about Tai, Kyle," Rose pressed on.

"Oh, um, I don't really know her that well. I just met her about a month ago."

"A month ago? So you met her at the end of your trip?"

"No…I mean yes. It's all a little blurry to me actually," Kyle laughed uncomfortably.

"I wonder what her favorite color is," Kyra wondered out loud, her bright pink lips in a little pout.

"Yeah, I wonder what Kandi color lipstick she'd like," Mandy wondered with her peach shade lips.

"What's her favorite color Kyle?" Rose asked him directly.

"Black," Kyle said without thinking. The strange little get-to-know-each-other conversation he had had with Tai had started playing itself out through his mind again when he heard Kyra's initial musing about Tai's favorite color. He missed seeing Matt and Rose exchanging a smile when he answered.

"Black? I don't think they have a Kandi color black," Soo said with lavender lips.

"I think they might," Rose said, "Like licorice maybe? Maybe we can find one for her."

"That might look kinda emo, though," Soo commented.

"What's a candy color?" Kyle asked, wondering why they would be interested in buying Tai some lipstick. If they knew her, they'd know the last thing she'd want was lipstick.

"Kandi color is the latest thing, Kyle," Kyra exclaimed.

"Seriously, all the girls have it," Mandy backed.

"It's a popular make-up and fashion line," Rose cleared up Kyle's confused looking face.

"Oh, I see," Kyle said.

"Yeah, it's a new line of products created by the singer Kandi," Mandy added.

"Candy?" Kyle was lost again.

"Yeah, Kandi as in K-A-N-D-I. Her song was playing just now. You know, *I just want your love and devotion…*" Soo sang a bit with a beat-keeping bobbing of her head.

"Kandi's pretty hot, especially in that one music video," one of the basketball teammates said with a resounding chorus of agreements from his male peers, sparking some feelings of envy in the girls.

"Hm, I wonder if Tai likes to read," Robin asked with lips shimmering in a pearl gloss.

"She does," Kyle answered again without realizing it. He drank some soda and took a bite of his pizza.

"She does?" Mercedes said. "Ooo, I wonder what she likes to read."

Remembering his conversation with Tai again, Kyle swallowed and answered, "Probably everything."

They chatted on, eating pizza and buffalo wings while washing it all down with soda, the pop radio station continuing to blare just above the din and noise of conversations in the room. The conversation at Kyle's table somehow kept coming back to Tai. Kyle noticed it, but he pushed aside his wondering of why this was so. When it was time to go, everyone got up and walked out, and the distinct clicking of the high heels against the ground caught his attention. He looked down and saw that all the girls wore different colored high heels that matched their lipstick and nail polish color, all of which complimented the peppy and stylish clothing they wore. He then noticed marks of embellished *K*s on the clothing, similar to those on European designer items so popular in

Asia and elsewhere.

"There should be black Kandi heels, right?" Rose asked Kyra hopefully.

"Oh yeah, there are definitely black Kandi heels," her friend responded.

"Let's go to the mall this weekend and look for some," Rose said excitedly.

"Totally! O-M-G! Shopping trip!" Robin exclaimed and all the girls nodded in shared excitement.

"I wonder if we can invite Tai," Rose wondered, looking at Kyle expectantly.

"I don't think she'll want to go," Kyle shared honestly. It was an understatement to say that he got the feeling that Tai wasn't the shopping type.

"Aw, I'm sure she'd come with us if we invited her. She just needs to get to know us," Rose said optimistically.

"You'll all get a chance to get to know Tai over the next few days," Jade said.

"You know her Coach Yu?" Matt puzzled. Kyle looked up in surprise at Jade.

"Yes, she's been my student for some time."

"You teach her basketball?"

"Not exactly. Just been her physical fitness trainer in a sense."

"Uh, so, is she going to be training at school or something?" Kyle asked with piqued curiosity. What did Jade mean when he said they'd get a chance to get to know her? He couldn't imagine what sort of situation would allow all of these people who seemed so out of Tai's universe to get to know her better. Training qi script at school wouldn't exactly be a low-profile affair.

Jade smiled mischievously and said, "I'll let it be a surprise."

Chapter 31

There Goes the Neighborhood

Kyle entered the house with two cycads in front, Tai's home. They were let in by Cindy. Jade's hair was black instead of its usual green, probably to be less conspicuous, and he was wearing a blue polo shirt and navy blue shorts, his muscular body showing quite prominently even through the thick fabric of his clothing. Kyle felt like a shrimp of a man next to him, and he could tell that the rest of his basketball team, including even Matt, felt a little intimidated by their new coach even though they'd worked with him longer than Kyle had by now. Their coach last year had been the average high school coach, middle-aged and roundish but fatherly and supportive. Jade, on the other hand, appeared a young man in his prime, and knowing Jade wasn't even human, Kyle wondered if Jade was picking the best male specimen human form out of vanity. However, remembering the rippling muscles across Jade's powerful dragon form, Kyle figured Jade's manly form was just the human equivalent to his dragon body. The other guys seemed to like him well enough as a coach, and Kyle's first basketball practice this school year had gone by smoothly and pretty routinely.

In contrast to the pizza place, the house they were now in was cool, quiet, and tranquil. Cindy showed them to the backyard where Tai was training in the early evening light. The sight took Kyle's breath away. Tai was sitting in the middle of a yard of lush green grass bordered by a variety of large deciduous trees covered in leaves glowing with the warm browns, oranges, and yellows of fall. Many of the autumn leaves were drifting down to the ground and scattering across the green grass creating a beautiful miniature landscape of colors. Having grown up in Los Angeles where there were really only two seasons, summer and not-summer, the autumnal flavor by itself was enough to bring a sense of wonder to Kyle, but that wasn't what took his breath away. Tai was on her knees, sitting with her legs folded under her, and she wore a simple black t-shirt over long black yoga pants. Her hair was tied up in a high pony-tail as usual, and on Tai's forehead glowed the character for "wind".

風

Just as Kyle stepped out into the sunlight again from the darkness of the indoors, Tai looked straight at him with the qi script glowing gently just above her glimmering eyes, her expression one of calm concentration, the amber glint of her light brown eyes more apparent in the waning evening light than ever. A light breeze touched him right away, and the colored leaves began to stir off of the ground and float lightly back up into the air as if the hands of time were being turned backwards. They twirled and danced in the air as they floated, their paths becoming circular as they formed a gently swirling curtain around Tai who was in the center of it all. The whirlwind was soft and pleasant, bringing a cool briskness to the whole yard, and just as smoothly as it had begun, the soothing wind and the tender dance of the leaves settled back into calm and quiet.

"Excellent!" Snow said breathlessly. It was then that Kyle noticed that she was there with them, apparently the one who was coaching Tai on her qi script manipulation techniques. "That was the best you've done! You've really learned to moderate your use of your qi script and honed your mastery of it!" She stepped forward to her student and continued with her praise. "Just the right amount, just the right control, and you were able to create the most delicate of winds, enough to move but not to break…"

As Snow, continued to praise and coach Tai, Kyle figured out that it must be more difficult to conjure up a gentle wind than it was to produce a rough windstorm. It made sense to him, since moderation in almost anything was usually a lot harder than uncontrolled bursts. He remembered the little demonstration Tai had given him at school, the small swirl of water, and wondered if that must have actually taken a lot more skill to produce than he had understood at the time. He watched as Tai listened to Snow's comments, nodding here and there in acknowledgement. He didn't know if it was the sunset glow that caused it, but he noticed a tender radiance of warm light emanating from Tai, as if she were her own sun, and wondered if it was a residual effect of her qi script use.

Jade leaned over to him and said in a low voice, "She's a lot more cheerful today than she usually is."

Kyle looked at Snow and didn't think she looked any more cheerful than she usually did.

Before Kyle had a chance to think any more on that topic, he was called over by Snow.

"Kyle, come over here."

He walked over to where Snow and Tai stood in the middle of the large sized yard, stepping gingerly over the beautiful autumn leaves.

"You both have a lot of work to do," Snow said with a smile.

Kyle and Tai both nodded in agreement. There was no question. If the First Child demon was here in their world, they knew that whatever conflict ensued, whatever forces came forth to battle this strange and dangerous creature, the odds were more likely than not that the two of them would be right in the thick of it all. Kyle prepared himself for some serious training with Snow and Jade, possibly two of the most powerful beings existing in their world at that moment.

"Kyle, you know you have much to catch up on. You must prepare yourself to go through the rigorous training that Tai has just spent five months in. You may also need to master it in a shorter amount of time. Who knows when the First Child will strike? Tai, you have really made us proud with your progress. There is nothing more for us to teach you in terms of your qi control and physical prowess, and you will have to rely on your own efforts now to push yourself beyond where you are, beyond even the capabilities of your teachers. And that is the greatest joy of a teacher, to see her student surpass her," Snow said with proud smile. "However, Tai, your training is not complete. You lack something that is not easily taught, and only through experience and willingness on your own can you fill the gap you have as a warrior. In fact, it is something that Kyle has in abundance, this quality you lack."

Both Kyle and Tai turned to look each other at that moment. Kyle's face showed disbelief. How could there be something he was good at that Tai wasn't? By all accounts, she had him beat on everything. Speed, agility, intelligence, strength, focus, self-confidence…the list went on and on. Tai's face showed agitation. It was clear she didn't like hearing that there was something that she lacked and even more so that Kyle had what she lacked. Kyle was not surprised at her reaction and took no insult by it. Tai after all was just being Tai.

"Tai, we give you three tasks that will further your training in a way that we cannot do as your teachers alone," Snow said with an amiable smile that had a hint of good-natured mischief in it. "First, starting from today, you will be in charge of Kyle's physical training and qi script development."

Kyle looked at Tai again, but Tai didn't look at him. She was clearly not very pleased with the news.

"Second, you will join Kyle in his basketball practices."

Snow paused here. The silence grew as the seconds ticked by, and Kyle didn't look over at Tai, already able to feel the pressure of her growing displeasure at this second piece of unhappy news. Kyle swallowed as he realized this was what Jade had meant earlier at the pizzeria when he said that everyone was going to get a chance to get to know Tai. After what seemed like an eternity of silent awkwardness, Tai said, "Can I join the swim team instead?"

"Unfortunately, no," Snow said with a small laugh, clearly amused by Tai's annoyance. "Swimming is not a sport that will be conducive to what you need to improve on."

Tai fell silent again. Kyle wondered what the third task would be. With the trend of things, he feared his new trainer might explode in one way or another.

"Third, you will be joining the cheer leading team at your school."

Kyle looked at Snow in complete bewilderment. Cheerleading? Basketball he understood to some degree. Snow and Jade probably wanted Tai and him to develop more synchronicity in their work together as a team. But cheerleading seemed to come straight from left field. It seemed like a random torture that they thought would be amusing to inflict upon Tai.

"May I ask what I'm supposed to…gain from joining cheerleading?" Tai said in a controlled voice. Kyle could tell she was doing her best not raise her voice.

"Life has many lessons that can only be learned on your own," Snow said. "Here, this will help point you in the right directions."

She put a reassuring hand on Tai's shoulder to ease her student's vexation and handed her a scroll. Tai took it with a respectful bow, and when she unfurled it, she read the contents aloud in Chinese.

三人行必有我師

"Three people walking, one must be my teacher."

Tai took a deep breath that bordered on a sigh. She nodded in acquiescence. Then she turned on Kyle as Snow joined Jade on the sidelines.

"You'll have to begin your training immediately. We've got no time to lose."

She motioned for Kyle to take her place in the middle of the yard. Kyle hesitated a moment, and then decided to take the same kneeling position that he had seen Tai take when she had sat down, resting his hands on his knees as he tucked his legs underneath himself. He looked up to see Tai looking down at him with a look that was all business. He tried not to gulp.

"Your training plan will focus on calligraphy, qi control, solid defense, and strategic offense. Those are your primary weaknesses. We should also improve your sword-handling skills."

With the character for wind glowing upon her forehead again, Tai made a sort of casual sweeping motion with her hands, and the wind swept together a small pile of the fallen leaves in front of Kyle.

"We'll start with the basics. Fire."

He understood her simple command. He was to set the pile of leaves on fire. He looked at the pile of fall leaves framed by green lawn grass and remembered what he had learned in the other world about how to perform qi script without brush and paper. With his mind, he drew the character for fire out onto the image he saw of the pile of leaves.

火

From his perspective, the character glowed in his line of vision, and he realized from the perspectives of others, the Chinese character must be glowing on his forehead. The pile of autumn leaves burst into flames.

"Good. Now water."

Kyle repeated the same procedure but with the character for water this time. A swirl of water formed above the flames and fell, leaving a heap of wet, burned leaves.

"Now, fire again."

She gestured to the leaves that lay scattered across the yard. Kyle paused. He realized she was asking him to now set fire to multiple targets simultaneously. He made his attempt and succeeded in only setting a couple on fire at the same time. These leaves burned up quickly and the small flames extinguished when their fuel was eaten up. Tai's nod indicated to him that he was to next attempt to increase his number of synchronous targets. After a number of attempts, during which Tai waited and watched patiently standing a ways in front of him, he was able to increase his number to setting eight leaves on fire at the same time.

Tai's forehead glowed again with the character for wind and the remaining leaves in the yard suddenly began to swirl around them as they had earlier.

"Again."

Kyle figured now she was asking him to hit moving targets. At first his impulse was to look at the moving leaves, swinging his head this way and that, his eyes focusing here and then there.

"Focus here," Tai instructed him, holding her hand up in a classic sword gesture with two fingers pointing up right in front of her face, "and then…focus everywhere." She let her hand drop to her side.

In the midst of trying to master the task, Kyle figured out what she meant. Instead of trying to look at each moving leaf individually, it would be more efficient to focus his vision forward and then expand his attention to try to encompass everything within his sight at the same time and then enact the qi script technique. He succeeded in singeing the corners of some of the leaves in motion.

"Predict."

Kyle looked at her for a moment, seeing the Chinese character still glowing on her forehead which made her eyes glimmer in an otherworldly way, and then he nodded in understanding. For moving targets, it would be best to predict their movements and aim your attack at their foreseen trajectories. Two leaves burst into flames in mid-air and fell as ash to the ground.

"Good. Now increase your target capacity."

This went on for a while, and the sun was fully set by the end of the session. The glowing qi script executed by the two young warriors in their training glowed all the more brightly in the dark night environment. Their session was ended by the voice of an old man.

"Kyle."

It was his grandfather.

"Ah-gong," Kyle said as he got up from his sitting position and stumbled a little, not realizing that his legs had gone a little numb under him while he had focused on his qi script training.

His grandfather walked straight up to him with a big smile on his tired looking face. At first he embraced him with affection, and then he held Kyle by the shoulders and examined him as if sizing him up. He nodded in approval.

"Better, Kyle. Much better."

Kyle didn't really get what his grandfather was talking about, but he had enough of an idea to smile at his Ah-gong's words of approval.

Later on that night, Kyle and Tai were alone together in her study. It was a small room of warm colors with wooden bookshelves and desk complete with a green shaded lamp. Every inch of wall was covered in books from every subject. It was like a piece of a university library had been cut out and placed into this house. A loudly ticking grandfather clock stood in the corner of the room. Tai pulled out her books and binders, and Kyle did the same. It seemed like it was going to be a normal enough homework session, but that changed when Tai pulled out some phoenix paper. The sheets seemed to glitter and glow even more than Kyle remembered. The material seemed almost eager.

"Uh, what's that for?" Kyle asked dumbly. He couldn't imagine they would waste phoenix paper on calculus homework.

Tai gave him a stack.

"Save these for last resort. We don't have an unlimited supply of them. You remember how to use them?"

Kyle nodded, remembering Bao and his use of the brush to turn this rare paper into a dreamy fluttering of butterflies.

"Now that you can do qi script without a brush, you can use that technique on these phoenix feather papers to enhance the magnitude of your power. KYLE!"

Tai's sudden outburst caused Kyle to look involuntarily up from the phoenix paper to her, and then to his horror, he realized he had drawn the character for fire on Tai's face. Just in the nick of time, the character for water glowed on her forehead and the flame that appeared was extinguished quickly with a blast of water.

"Holy…I'm so sorry!" Kyle exclaimed.

Tai sighed. "Just be careful."

"I…I don't understand. What just happened?"

"The more you train in qi script, the more it becomes second nature, like instinct. When I told you that you could use the brushless technique on the phoenix paper, your mind automatically began executing it, and when you looked up at me, the technique was directed at me instead. When I realized what was happening, I figured it would be better if my face got a little burned than if you blew up this entire neighborhood."

Kyle's jaw dropped. He didn't realize how powerful and how dangerous his new ability was. Blow up the entire neighborhood? Is she kidding? But Kyle knew by the look on Tai's face that she was dead serious.

"Remember that time I experimented with 'swift' in the forest?" Tai asked.

"Yeah, what about it?"

"Well, we can do that too with brushless qi script. Try it now with me."

"How do we use qi script on ourselves?"

"After some practice, you'll get a sense of how to target yourself naturally. But what helped me at first was using a mirror. Here."

Tai handed Kyle a small pocket mirror. He opened it and looked at his face in the small reflection of himself.

"On three, ready? One, two, THREE."

Kyle heard the ticking of the clock and couldn't help but be distracted by Tai who suddenly blurred and disappeared from his sight. Realizing he'd missed the starting mark, he looked back at the small mirror reflection of himself and qi scripted the character for swift:

快

Tai suddenly blurred back into his view, but she was no longer standing by the table anymore. Instead, she was sitting and already almost done with a detailed outline of a chapter of one of their textbooks, hand written based on the instructions of the teacher. The tick-tock of the clock had stopped.

"Took you long enough," she looked up after finishing the outline. Apparently the couple of seconds of delay on his part set him behind Tai by almost an hour. He sat down and started work on his homework assignments. After finishing one, he moved on to the next. He heard the clock tick once.

"This is kind of awesome," he said out loud.

"Well, there is a price. When the qi script you've activated wears off, you'll feel exhausted. Just like what happened to me back in the forest."

"Oh yeah, that's true. So we'll end up having to rest longer to recover from the strain?"

"Precisely. So in essence, there's not really time saved. We're doing this primarily to build up our qi stamina."

They continued with their homework silently. Occasionally, Kyle looked up at Tai to see what she was doing, but each time, all he saw was a girl busy at work. After a while, he grew a little weary of the dull busywork that made up most of their assignments, and his curiosity about Tai got the best of him.

"Tai?"

"Mmhm?" She didn't even stop to look up at him.

"Why is it that you hide from everyone at school? I'm only asking, you know, because we should know more about each other if we're going to work together." He threw her a sideways glance.

"Hide? I don't hide. I'm in plain view at all times," she continued unbothered with her work.

"Yeah, but nobody notices you. I know you were playing a 'game' with me, but that's just me, right? 'Cause my grandfather told you to. I mean, it's not like you're a shy person or anything."

"Let's work on calligraphy."

Tai ignored his question and pulled out a black stone plate and an ink stick with a golden dragon painted on it. She tossed a brush at Kyle and began grinding the ink with water into the stone, creating a dark black liquid mixture. Rolling out some paper, they began. Kyle was kind of glad for a change in activity, and Chinese calligraphy took on a different meaning now that he could apply this training to qi script. Tai dropped some classic Chinese texts in front of him and instructed him to start copying. He began with the Dao De Jing, a central book of Daoist philosophy.

The feel of the brush and the smell of the ink, the sensation of watching as the paper absorbed the black liquid with his every stroke, all under a warm light, made Kyle feel sadly nostalgic. He had spent many a night like this with his grandmother back when he was a child, before she passed away. He felt her spirit lingering in his heart and mind and even in the strokes he made with his brush. He smiled. She was a part of him, a past that made him what he was today, a soul that had nourished his own, a cherished heritage.

Then he looked up at Tai and wondered what it must be like to not know one's real parents, to not even know where one came from. Kyle knew his grandparents and parents had been born in Taiwan, that his family had immigrated to the United States in search of a better life, especially for him, their only son. From the looks of Tai, she most likely had at least some heritage from the same geographic gene pool that he had derived from, but her features weren't that simple to categorize upon closer inspection. She looked like she was generally of Asian descent, but at the same time there was a brown in her hair, a shade in her skin, and a curve to her features that showed something else, and she could have easily been placed in a number of categories of ethnicity. The golden glint in her eye was something he had never seen before. Kyle pondered back on her virtual invisibility at school.

"So why doesn't anyone ever notice you?" he asked, looking her way and then looking back down at his calligraphy work. "Matt thought you were a new student who started school just today, but you've been in his class for months. What gives?"

"Well, people have a lot of mental blind spots."

"Mental blind spots?"

"Yes, they don't notice what doesn't stick out or what doesn't fit into what they already know."

Kyle scratched the side of his head with the handle of his brush.

"And you like to hide in those blind spots?"

Tai looked up at him with a blank stare.

"I don't hide." She looked back down to her work. "Besides, you make it sound like it's so hard to not be noticed at school. High school students aren't the sharpest tools in the shed, and I simply minimize unnecessary interactions."

"Unnecessary?"

"Yes. Our…peers aren't exactly the most stimulating people to interact with. What can someone like me gain from them?"

Kyle felt the condescending attitude in what she was saying, but at the same time, he had to admit she had a point.

"Their mental blind spots are so massive, it's actually hard *not* to be hidden in them," she continued. She threw a glance at the school homework they had just finished. "They're like worker bees busily sustaining a hive that produces no honey."

"Then why do you stay? In high school I mean?"

It seemed to Kyle that maybe Tai should skip high school altogether and go to college or something beyond that. She obviously felt like she wasn't getting anything of value from her high school experience.

"Your grandfather told me to stay. He said for someone like me, it was important to take a 'normal' road and understand the life of the average person, that that was a sort of 'education' in and of itself."

"Wow," Kyle said shaking his head. "He's always trying to get me to quit high school and go training with him on a mountain or something."

"Sheesh," Tai laughed, "I wish."

Kyle laughed as well. He was beginning to understand why Jade and Snow had given her the three tasks they had.

Chapter 32

Basketball Practice

Kyle was worried. Today was going to be Tai's first day at basketball practice. Out of the corner of his eye, he kept watch on Tai as she bent down to one foot and then the other to tie up her new, generic white high tops. She wore a pink mesh women's basketball jersey with black game shorts. *Pink?* Kyle had wondered. It seemed like a very unlikely color for Tai to choose. It had only been the day before that she was given her 'special assignments', so he wondered how she had gotten a pink jersey so quickly. Tai finished tying up her shoes and caught Kyle staring at her.

"Dr. Tan bought it for me," Tai answered a bit irritably, reading his mind. He smiled, thinking that Cindy, or Dr. Tan, must have known it would mildly annoy her to wear pink while practicing with an all-boy basketball team. Jade walked into the gym.

"Hey, peach blossom! You look ready to roll!" he laughed as he saw Tai in her basketball gear. Tai's eyebrow twitched.

Soon the rest of the straggling team members were out on the gym floor along with Kyle, Tai, and Matt. Jade started everyone off with stretching and a few laps jogging around the faded yellow gym. They began drills, the orange leathery basketballs bouncing and echoing through the vast gym as they did lay-ups and other exercises. Kyle watched with surprise as Tai fell into line, doing all the drills as if she'd been playing basketball all her life. Maybe he'd been wrong to assume. After all, basketball was an extremely popular sport, and the women's team at their high school was one of the top in the area, too.

"Hey, you played basketball before?"

"No. I read up on it last night and watched some instructional videos on the internet."

For some reason, something in Tai's tone of voice worried him. Maybe he was just a little nervous about her coming into the territory of male basketball, but what also bothered him was this strange look she had in her eyes, that hint of amber glimmering brighter than usual. There was something penetrating in the way she was observing everyone, and he seemed to be the only one aware of it. Matt was trying his best to be friendly and welcoming with Tai who responded to his affability with civil yet emotionless remarks. Kyle thought how lucky it was that the fast pace at which Jade kept the warm up and drills gave little time for conversation. He believed even the out-going Matt would run out of patience with someone like Tai.

"Hey Kyle," Matt said during a little breather.

"Yeah?"

"You seriously need to tell me what you've been doing while you were gone."

"Yeah?" Kyle responded uncomfortably.

"Yeah, you've upped your game dude. You're like faster and stronger. You jump higher, too. I'm having a hard time keeping up with you."

"Yeah?" Kyle laughed nervously.

Soon they were splitting up into teams for a practice game. Kyle gravitated towards being on Tai's team, mainly because he thought he could keep a better eye on her that way. Why he was keeping an eye on her, he didn't know, but he just felt the impulse to. He got the feeling she was up to something, but he just didn't know what yet.

The first half of the practice game went by smoothly. Tai played her part and turned out to be a pretty decent player. When Jade had announced to the group that she would be training with them for a few weeks, the other guys muttered a little about why she couldn't just train

with the girls' basketball team instead, but since her presence didn't seem to have any impact on their usual routine and she wasn't holding practice back in any way, they soon paid little attention to the flash of pink here and there. In fact, they found it kind of admirable that she was able to at least hold her own on the court amongst all the boys. Kyle was glad so far that no one had told her she was pretty good for a girl. He was sure she wouldn't let that sort of insult pass her by without a basketball slammed into someone's face. Though he still had the distinct feeling that Tai was watching everyone very closely, he felt himself letting his guard down as the game continued on without incident.

After half time, the two playing teams switched sides on the court, and the team that Kyle, Matt, Jake, and Tai were on together had possession of the ball. Matt took the ball and stood out of bounds, passed it to Kyle, who passed it back to Matt as he stepped onto the court, starting off their offensive play. However, right before Matt's fingers even had a chance to touch the ball again, a pink blur shot through the not-so-wide space between Kyle and Matt, and before either of them had a moment to comprehend what had happened, they heard the dribbling of the ball across the court, and they watched Tai pressing forward with perfect ball handling, the orange and leathery ball moving between her hand and the ground as if she had a telekinetic hold over it. She stopped for a split second, surveyed the obstacles in the battle field before her, and then pushed forward again, her heart clearly set on the basket. The opposing team barely had time to recover from their shock in time to guard her. Kyle, Matt, and the other two players on their team were bewildered, but they soon began heading towards supporting their unexpected shooting guard.

Tai got around the defense expertly, able to predict each of the defensive players' moves, effectively faking them out and slipping around them. Then when she neared the basket, she found an opening and leapt up off the ground, soared unbelievably through the air, and slammed the ball in. She dropped to the ground, landing much like a falling cat on her feet, and then she held out a hand and caught the falling basketball like a warrior would catch a weapon. She stood up and turned around to unapologetically face the other players, and then handed the ball to the closest member of the opposing team.

Kyle's jaw dropped. *So this was what she was up to.* He realized that she had spent the first half of the game observing and analyzing every player's moves, storing away a mental card catalogue of each of the boy's strengths, weaknesses, and preferences. And now she was exploiting everything she knew to utterly defeat every player on the court, whether they were on her team or not. She was quickly making enemies.

On the sidelines, Jade sighed quietly to himself. Matt gave Kyle a befuddled look, and Kyle responded with a sheepish shrug. The other players began to scowl at the little pink addition to their basketball practice. The ball was passed back into bounds, and the next play was on. As soon as the offensive player on the other team began to push forward, he passed the ball to a player on his right, but Tai intercepted the ball in midair, as if she had known it was going to be thrown there all along, and raced down the other end of the court before anyone had a chance to catch up to her. With no one to block her, she did an easy lay-up, and after the ball bounced lightly off the backboard and then swished through the basket ropes, Tai again caught it before it hit the ground. She handed the ball over to the opposing team, and she was not smug or even excited about her success. She just looked satisfied.

The next play was on, and again the other team had the ball. Tai simply hung back, watching what was going on, and Kyle hoped that she was done with her antagonistically anti-social behavior for the day, but he knew Tai enough to know his hopes would soon be dashed. Sure enough, after his team got possession of the ball and all the players were heading down to the other side, Tai intercepted Jake's dribbling, tapping the ball out of his grasp, and stopped as everyone was still moving forward with the momentum of running. Then she made a jump shot. *Swoosh!* Perfect shot.

Jake gave her an angry glare which she met with her unperturbed eyes; it didn't faze her at all. Jake must be doubly angry, after being slighted by her the day before. Kyle rubbed his forehead with his fingers as if staving off an impending migraine. This time Tai's humiliation of Jake wasn't so funny because she was doling out insults to everyone on the court. It was destroying the group morale and making the game extremely unpleasant to be a part of. Matt looked at a loss as to what to do to ease the situation.

Another pass in of the ball, another steal by Tai, and this time, with the players onto her aggressive ways, she was being double teamed with two from the opposing team guarding her. Though this deterred her from making as easy a shot as in previous plays, it took her only a little time to figure out how to outsmart the two, doing a double fake to the left then to the right that caused them to get tangled in each other, allowing her to slip past them to the left and slam the ball into the basket for a second dunk. The score was four shots out of four for Tai, zero for everyone else.

"Time out!" Jade called. All of the players went to drink from their water bottles and wipe their foreheads with towels. Many were giving the new pink addition to their team annoyed looks. Kyle felt extremely uncomfortable. On the one hand, he felt rather defensive of Tai, afraid that the guys might get angry enough to be moved to violence against her. She wasn't just bruising their egos, she was annihilating them, and the feeble human mind can only take so much beating on their fragile egos. On the other hand, he was afraid that if they did decide to gang up on her in any way, he might end up calling 911 for medical assistance when the gym floor was littered with wounded high school basketball players. Kyle sighed. Why did he have to be in the middle of this?

Jade gave Kyle a meaningful look and motioned with a nod of his head that he should probably go talk to Tai. Kyle was irritated at having to be the one to handle the situation that was Tai. What was he anyway, her babysitter? He walked over to where she was, on a corner of the bleachers, isolated from everyone else.

"Hey Tai, what's going on?"

Tai looked at him with uninterested eyes.

"Nothing. What's going on with you?" she threw back at him.

"You're playing this game as if you're the only one on the court."

"And?"

Kyle tried hard not to lose his patience. He tried very hard.

"Well, basketball is a team sport."

"Is the object of this game to win?"

"Well, yes."

"Then if your teammates are inferior to you, isn't it logical to take control of the situation to optimize the chances of winning?"

He was a little stumped by her clean reasoning. It did sound logical, but at the same time he wasn't quite satisfied with it.

"Yes…and no. I know it seems efficient to just take control of the situation and do it yourself, but don't you think there's more potential to win if you can work well with everyone else?"

Tai raised an eyebrow with interest, and Kyle wondered where these words of wisdom he had just spoken had come from.

"Possibly," she conceded to Kyle's amazement and relief.

"Just think of it like you're training them, like how you're training me right now. You've obviously got the basics of basketball down, so work on how you can manage the strategy of an entire team of players, like in chess, but don't treat them like pawns. They've got to want to work together and with you to make a good team."

Tai gave him a slight nod, showing agreement in trying out his suggestion. He gave her a knowing smile, remembering how she had punched him in the eye when he had first met her in that faraway courtyard. This was Tai all right; it was just the way she was with people. She expected others to step up or step out of her way.

He made his way back to the rest of the group that was now hydrated, rested, and ready to finish this practice game.

"Hey man," Jake said with a scowl, "did you tell your girlfriend over there that she had better chill out?"

Kyle felt a surge of anger and an intense need to come to Tai's defense, but he was able to keep it cool. He knew his teammate had a right to be angry but at the same time he knew that anger also largely sprang from a fragile self-concept. He laughed out a bit and put on a smile before he spoke out loud enough for all the other players in the vicinity to hear. Tai was still off in her isolated corner taking gulps of rejuvenating water.

"First of all, don't tell her you called her my girlfriend or she'll kill us both. Second, she might seem like a pro at this, but this is the first time she's ever played. She's just tends to be really good at everything she does, so maybe we should just try our best to step up our game." He took another drink from his water bottle. "Come on, let's show her how this is really supposed to be played."

As he walked back onto the court with everyone, he caught Matt's eye, and they both smiled at each other. Matt gave him a solid and approving pat on the shoulder.

The practice match continued again, and this time Tai did not go around intercepting and stealing the ball from all the players, she simply hung back for a bit, allowing the other players to do their thing. Kyle noticed this and quickly found an opportunity to pass the ball to her. Immediately, the opposing team began double teaming her again, with two players guarding just her. They had clearly learned to go on DEFCON 1 whenever Tai had possession. Her eyes met Kyle's briefly, and then she did a quick chest pass to him. As he received, he saw her slip around the two players that had been blocking her as their attention followed the ball to him. Then, when she was clear of the two, her hands came up again, ready to receive again. Kyle got the message and bounce-passed it back to her, and she took the ball up for another slam into the basket. Matt whistled.

"You sure do like to show off your slam dunks," he commented.

"It's not for show. It has the highest percentage for accuracy in close-quarter plays, especially since I'm the shortest player on the court."

"Oh, I see. My bad." Matt saw the no-nonsense look on her face and realized that she really wasn't trying to show off anything. Instead, she was just playing the best strategy for herself with great skill. He was still amazed by her ability to do something that most basketball players her height could only dream of. "How the heck do you jump so high?"

"Years of practice."

When they were back on the defensive, Tai easily predicted the movements of the opposing team's point guard and, using her lower height as an advantage, practically slipped between the legs of her taller, male counterparts and intercepted the ball mid pass again. At first, it looked like she was back to her old tactics as she maneuvered her way back to the scoring basket, but as she was pushing towards the goal, she suddenly passed the ball to her left, and it ended up in Kyle's hands. Since the other team's players were all focused on her, they had little time to recover and redirect their attention, but they were still close by, and hands were already reaching out to grab the ball or block a shot, and

Kyle realized he'd have drive that ball as close to the basket as possible to ensure a score. Surprising even himself, he jumped and twisted his body and smashed the ball into the basket in a back-handed dunk.

"NICE!" Matt said as he gave Kyle a congratulatory pat on the back. "Dude, I didn't know you could dunk!"

Kyle looked over at Tai before looking back at Matt and saying, "Uh…neither did I." It was the first time he had ever dunked.

"See! I told you! Upped your game!"

As they prepared to continue the game, Kyle took a quiet moment at looked down at his own hands and feet. Was he really that much stronger? That much faster? He knew he had been training, but still, how did that happen?

Kyle and Tai continued to tag team and effectively work around all the players, and soon, Matt, Jake, and the other players on their team caught on to their patterns and began to place themselves in supporting positions, often open and making shots of their own when assisted by either Kyle or Tai. Assists, helping others score, was Kyle's specialty as a basketball player, and Tai had taken quick notice of that and started to incorporate his techniques into her own repertoire. As a result, their team, which had originally been playing pretty much head to head up until half time, won the game by a landslide in the second half.

At the end of practice, Jake turned to her and said, "Hey, good game." She had passed the ball to him plenty of times when he was open for a shot and had scored many points as a result. He was also of course pleased at the outcome of the game. Jake liked to win. He shook his head and added, "I can't believe this is the first game of basketball you've ever played. You seriously play like a pro."

Tai looked over at him and he noticed the strong, feminine confidence and poise emanating from her very presence. She was unaffected by his compliments but seemed to be contemplating a thought while looking at him. After she looked like she had decided on something, she said, "You'll need to handle the ball much closer to the ground. Your height makes it easy for shorter players like me to take the ball from you mid-dribble. Also, you favor your left side too much. You should work on strengthening your right."

Without waiting for a response, Tai turned and walked to her bag. She picked up her things and headed for the girl's locker room. She left Jake a little flushed and red-faced but not from anger. Kyle was in the middle of packing away his water bottle when he saw this exchange, but instead of feeling glad that Tai had taken his advice to work with the other players and 'train' them, he felt a surge of upset. He suddenly felt the impulse to ask her not to talk to the other players anymore, even though that was logically a very unrealistic request to make, but he wasn't really thinking with his head at that moment.

Chapter 33

Cheerleading Practice

"Hi Tai! Coach! Over here!" Rose called out to her with an energetic wave of her hand. The other girls in varsity cheer waved and smiled as well. All of them had their hair tied back in pony tails with colorful scrunchies covered in patterns of the letter "K". They had matching blue workout shorts and red tank tops with white shoes, their school colors. Tai also wore the same clothes and had her hair tied up in a high pony tail as well, but hers was tied with a simple black hair tie that was pretty much invisible unless seen up close. Rose had handed her the workout clothes at lunch earlier that day when Tai was dragged over by Kyle to meet her new cheer squad-mates at lunch. He had bought her a chimichanga and carton of milk from the lunch line, mumbling something about paying her back for lunch.

Rose and the girls had gone about trying their best to befriend her, and Tai had replied in a civil and polite manner, but not with much enthusiasm. There was a fine line between manners and pretense, and Tai didn't like to pretend she was excited when she wasn't. She had declined their invitation to the shopping trip that weekend, citing the fact that she had a major project underway and had no leisure time to waste. It was true, what with training Kyle on top of alternating between cheer and basketball practice every day, but she also wasn't at all thrilled at wasting a whole day of her precious time wandering through the mall making purchases of vanity. They hadn't pressured her too much, since they knew her schedule was loaded with AP classes while their own was mostly just honors classes sprinkled with only one or two advanced placement courses. They had thought that it was her heavy academic load that was keeping her from going to the mall.

Snow walked out onto the empty grass field, one of many fields around the school, wearing long blue sweat pants and a red t-shirt, her hair also tied up. She looked so young that if she had been dressed like the girls, it would have been hard to tell that she was the coach and not just another cheerleader on the squad.

"Rose, lead the stretch."

As team captain, Rose gave her a little salute as she ordered the girls to line up and start their stretching session. After that, they did a couple laps around the field and then moved on to drills in jumps. Then they moved onto their cheer routines. Tai followed along with the routines as if she'd been practicing them for years, doing the moves better than anyone on the varsity team. She jumped and kicked higher and with more precision than anyone Rose had seen in person, and she had been to a number of national cheerleading competitions with different teams for over five years. Kyle had warned her about this.

"This might be her first time in cheerleading, but just don't be surprised if she is really good at it. I mean like *really* good at it. She's really physically fit and learns fast."

Rose had nodded in acknowledgement of his admonishment, but seeing it for herself was something else. Her existing squad members were really great, but she was excited as she saw the potential in Tai to take their team to another level. At the same time, she also noted that Tai also looked kind of bored with everything they were doing.

"Hey, Coach, would it be ok to work on stunts today?" Rose asked Snow.

Snow smiled at hearing the eagerness in Rose's voice. It was clear Rose wanted to see what Tai could really do. She nodded to Rose.

"Sure."

"Tai, would you be interested in trying out some stunts as the flyer?" Rose said perkily, thinking Tai would be happy to show off her stuff as the girl flying high at the top of some cheerleading stunts.

"No," was Tai's flat and uninterested response.

"Aw, come on, why?" Rose coaxed. She couldn't help but feel a little hurt by Tai's response. Tai saw the flicker of bruised feelings in Rose's eyes. She let out a little sigh. It was always hard for her to talk to people because they always took things personally.

"It's just that I'm not fit for that position," Tai tried to explain.

"But we can see you'll be awesome for it," Kyra said followed by encouraging nods of agreement from the other girls. Their friendliness made it clear why they were the most popular girls at school.

"I would be better as one of the bases because I'm strong and heavy," Tai said.

"You can't be heavy, you're about my height, and I'm usually the flyer," Kyra said, thinking that telling Tai she didn't look heavy would make her happy.

"How much do you weigh?" Tai asked without hesitation.

"118," Kyra said a little startled by Tai's direct question about her weight.

"I usually weigh over 140," Tai said.

"That's impossible…" Kyra said. Tai was fit and slender and really was Kyra's height. It didn't make any sense to her that Tai would be so much heavier.

Tai raised her left arm and flexed it, and her bicep bulged out quite pronounced and solid. It had been clear to the girls that she had a more athletic body that they had, but it wasn't really until she explicitly flexed her arm in front of them that they realized how much of a difference there was. She wasn't ripped like those massive body builders on those muscle magazines, which was part of why it was easy to overlook her athleticism, but she was definitely cut. She pointed to her impressive bicep and explained, "Muscle is much heavier than fat, and I have a lot of muscle."

She didn't have an ounce of bragging in her voice, and it was more that she was stating a simple truth. The girls were left with mouths a little agape in surprise.

"Which one of you is the heaviest?" Tai asked next, to their greater astonishment.

"Um…I guess maybe I am? I'm 130," Soo said with a tentative raise of her hand. She was the tallest in the group. Without another word, Tai walked towards her, and Soo stepped back in initial alarm and surprise.

"Here," Tai said, holding a hand out to her. Soo looked over at Kyra and Rose with a little apprehension in her brown eyes, and the two girls nodded in support. She reached out her hand to take Tai's. Next she felt Tai's other arm slide behind her knees, and then the hand that had taken her hand slid behind her back, and before she knew it, she was cradled in Tai's arms. Standing effortlessly with Soo in her arms, Tai explained her demonstration, "I can hold and probably throw up any one of you by myself, so what you may want to do to optimize your resources here is to keep your existing base-spot-flyer teams and assign me to be a single base supporting a flyer on my own."

"Oh…" Rose did want to see what Tai could do, but this wasn't what she had expected. "I see what you mean. You know, you're right, that's a good idea." She quickly recovered back into her friendly and cheerful self again. "How about me? I'm usually not a flyer since Kyra and the other flyers are smaller, but I've always wanted to try." She finished off what she said with a bright smile.

"Fine with me," Tai said with much less excitement. Rose felt slightly disappointed at Tai's lack of interest but bolstered herself up with the fact that at least Tai was involving herself in it more than just mimicking their existing routines. They ran through some of their

stunted routines making adjustments to where Tai would single-handedly hold up Rose with a spotter standing to the side just in case, but Rose had never experienced a more steady and solid base holder than Tai. Tai had been right. She was better for the base position of stunts than as the flyer girl that's usually held up or thrown up in stunts.

Two days later, after Tai had spent a day at basketball training with Kyle and Matt again, she was back with the cheerleading group. Practice went along as usual, but Rose was still on a quest to make cheerleading more exciting for Tai. It was her way to be proactively friendly and nice, which was why so many people at school liked her.

"What would you like to try out in cheerleading? You've obviously got all the routines down pat," Rose offered.

Tai looked at her with a flash of interest that gave Rose a little hope.

"I was watching some instructional videos on baton twirling, and I'd like to try it."

Rose's face fell a little. There was a reason why their team didn't have much baton usage in their routines. She was never very good with them.

"Uh, sure, Coach Snow, do we have any batons?"

"Let me go get some in the storage."

"Bring enough for two per person," Tai requested.

Rose tried not to gulp audibly.

When Snow came back with a bag full of batons, the girls put their hands on them eagerly, excited to do something out of their normal routines. Some began twirling them, doing hand to hand passes, and behind the back and neck combinations. A few even threw them up for a catch. Rose did a few timid figure eight twirls to warm her wrists up while trying to stay cheerful.

Coach Snow directed everyone to line up, and she went through basic drills and routines. As expected, Tai handled her baton like a pro. Everything was fine until they got to the throw, and that was when Rose's baton flew out into the field.

"Sorry!" she exclaimed as she ran after it. She came back, and the next few throws showed that Rose really had a lot of trouble with projectiles. When the drills were over, she looked at Tai to see if there was any disappointment, but Tai just looked the way she always did, uninterested. They took a little break mid practice.

"That was pretty fun," Kyra commented.

"Yeah," Mandy agreed. They went off to drink some water together with the other girls.

"How did you like the batons?" Rose asked Tai good-naturedly.

"It was somewhat interesting but unsatisfying," Tai shared honestly.

"Unsatisfying?"

"Yes, it just isn't too exciting twirling and tossing a stick around without purpose."

"Oh, but you're so good at it! Kyle told me you're a fast learner. I wish I could pick it up so quickly. I've always had trouble with batons."

At the mention of Kyle's name, Tai raised an eyebrow at Rose.

"It's not really that I'm a fast learner. It's just that I learn new things by making use of what I've learned before."

"Oh?"

"Yes."

"But how? You said you've never handled a baton before today."

"Today may be the first time I've picked up a cheerleader's baton, but I've been training to handle weapons like the baton since before I could walk. So really, I didn't just learn it today. I just applied what I already knew really well to something new, and what I've learned before about how to handle a stick is much more complicated than just baton twirling and throwing."

"What did you learn before that helped you with batons?" Rose asked with genuine interest.

"Have you heard of a martial arts style from the Philippines called arnis?"

"No…"

"It's a weapons focused fighting style that is often characterized by the use of a pair of baton-like sticks in battle."

"Sticks?"

"Here, I'll show you."

Tai picked up four batons, tossing two of them at Rose who caught them last minute. Tai held a baton in each hand, and Rose did the same.

"In arnis, you can use the stick as a striking weapon from many angles, but here are the basics. Diagonal…horizontal…and vertical."

With each word, Tai was demonstrating the strike with her two batons, swinging them each diagonally, horizontally, and then vertically. Rose tried her best to imitate the simple movements, not sure how she had suddenly ended up in a one-on-one martial arts training session.

"Swing with your whole body…that's it…follow through like a batter in baseball," Tai instructed.

With the slight adjustments based on Tai's directions, Rose felt the baton cut through the air in a satisfying slicing motion. The firmness and effective control of the baton in her hand felt powerful and good.

"Let's try a basic drill. First, hold the baton in your right hand up as if you're about the hammer something. Tuck your left hand with the other baton under by your waist like this…"

Tai showed how Rose how to position and then walked her through the six-hit pattern. Then she showed her how to practice with a partner. Soon, their batons were hitting each other in a regular rhythm. When the other girls returned from the water break, they saw Rose and

Tai clacking their batons against each other in way they had never seen batons used before. They asked them what they were doing, and soon, Tai had the whole cheerleading squad using their batons as arnis sticks, and the sound of baton hitting baton filled the open air of the grassy high school field. As they practiced, Rose had an idea for a new and original cheerleading routine her squad could try out.

Chapter 34

Boring

Kyle had barely run across mid court when he jumped and jettisoned the ball through the air. *Swoosh!* It was clean and precise. He had earned another three points for his team.

"Dang, what have they been feeding you over the summer?" Matt said as he gave Kyle a high five. Usually it was Matt or one of the other taller players that were the star players, but at this game, Kyle was stealing the show. Though he smiled, satisfied with his performance, he shook his head in disbelief. He'd never been this good at basketball.

Kyle picked up his water bottle at half time and savored the refreshing feeling of pouring the clear liquid into his parched mouth. It was a big game with the team from a rival school across town, but unlike previous years, Kyle's high school basketball team was beating the other team by a landslide, and there was no way for the other team to catch up. They had always been better than the other team, but the games were sometimes a close call. Clearly, Kyle and his team had stepped up their game this year, and he knew that it was most likely because the boys on the team had been challenged to the extreme by their talented part-time, pink-clad player who split her school extracurricular schedule between basketball practice and cheerleading. Tai had an uncanny way of finding each player's weaknesses and using them to her advantage which had forced each of the players on the team to work heavily on compensating for those holes in their game play. The result was a much stronger defense in the team overall and a more dynamic offense.

The gym they were in was packed like it hadn't been in a long time. Basketball usually had a pretty decent draw at his school, but today's audience volume was unprecedented, at least since Kyle could remember. There was a positive and lax feel in the air, the sort of mood that came with a game that was clearly going to be a win for the home team. Despite the lack of intense excitement that usually comes with a close game, there was still a stir of expectations because the basketball game wasn't all that they had come to watch that cool Southern California afternoon in a gym that was faded yellow with decades of use.

Standing on the sidelines with the other players, Kyle watched as the varsity cheerleading squad lined up for their routine. When his eyes fell on Tai, he looked away before looking back at her again. When she had walked in before the game started with the cheerleading squad, she was wearing the same uniform as the rest of the girls. It was a red and blue tight-fitting, sleeveless top that was cut midriff, exposing both her tone and cut arms and her quite prominent six-pack stomach, something the other girls, though slender and athletic, didn't have. The matching blue and red pleated short skirt barely provided coverage for her buttocks, revealing her muscular legs. She didn't look like those bulky professional body-builders, but her relatively petite body clearly had no excess, every muscle, bone, and sinew strengthened and trained to its highest potential. What Tai was wearing today revealed more of her body than that first night at the Lin Gui village when she had danced in the Assassin's Charm performance dressed as an otherworldly sprite, and it had made Kyle's face turn magenta to see her in her cheerleading get-up. He had to turn away from Tai to hide his reaction, but not before Matt had a chance to notice his red face and poke him in the ribs saying, "What's the matter? See something you like?"

In actuality, Kyle was annoyed with himself, but he didn't quite understand why he was annoyed. He only knew that he somehow felt gullible. He remembered how angry Tai had been when he had complimented her on how she looked that night in the forest in that faraway world.

"Hey Tai! You look hot today!" That had been Jake, who probably felt some kind of camaraderie with Tai since they had been in basketball practices together. In response, Tai had thrown Jake a look of utter disgust and contempt, which had stunned the usually undaunted lady's man into silent confusion. She acted as if he had thoroughly insulted her. Many onlookers noticed the exchange, and the many female admirers of Jake in particular couldn't understand what was so insulting about such a coveted compliment.

As Tai and the other girls got up to set up their half-time performance, many were afforded a clear view of a large scar that ran diagonal down the course of her back. The sight of it made Kyle bow his head in shame. He hadn't forgotten about what had happened in the Ocean Palace, how Tai had protected him when he was paralyzed with fear and confusion at the attacking Yehren. He had thought a lot about what happened, and he realized it wasn't just the terror inspired by the Yehren that had frozen him; it was also the knowledge that it was a human being, or at least what had once been human, that was attacking him. It was knowing that killing another Yehren was killing another human being. He didn't want to do that ever again. Still, it was his hesitation that had caused Tai's injury, and the evidence of it was now forever marked on her back.

"Hey Kyle," Matt had said when he noticed the scar. "You know where she got that scar?" Matt wasn't the only one asking, a lot of people were whispering about it.

Kyle wanted to shrink away say that it was nothing, but that would disrespect what Tai had done for him, cheapen how she had risked her life to protect him. He didn't want that.

"She got it protecting me."

Matt's eyes had widened in shock.

"From what?"

Kyle paused before he answered, his eyes glazed over for a moment with a passing terror that surprised Matt.

"A wild animal."

Loud, energetic music, with a touch of grooviness to it here and there, filled the gym as the cheer squad began their routine. At first the routine was pretty basic, consisting of attitude, dance, and shouts that assertively proclaimed victory and school pride. There were plenty of impressive flips, jumps, and kicks. At what seemed like the end of the routine, there were some acrobatics in which three girls were lifted into air, standing on the supporting arms of others, and then thrown and twirled as they fell down into catching arms. Then there was a whole group reformation in which the three girls were again held high with arms stretched out in the V shape of victory. In front of the group formation stood Tai and Rose, and everyone watched in surprise as Tai, who stood behind Rose, put her hands on the waist of her golden-haired teammate and, with a quick jump-start momentum, threw her up in a controlled twirl and supported Rose on her shoulders. Rose's fists shot out in the victory sign. It was an incredibly hard stunt to pull off, and in response, the audience was cheering, hooting and shouting with approval.

Then, there was something like the sound of a vinyl record stopped in mid-play, and the music took on a louder and more epic quality as each cheerleader picked up a pair of batons. A series of twirls, kicks, and jumps ensued, and then each cheerleader let her batons slide in her hands until she held them by the ends. The girls turned to each other and shouted the word "FIGHT!" with great enthusiasm and, to everyone's surprise, began an intricate series of strikes and blocks with their batons as if they were weapons and not just performance props. The sound of the metal batons hitting each other echoed off of the walls of the gym, filling the large structure with a sound akin to a heavy rainfall.

When they finished this, each cheerleader began to hit her own two batons together in a steady rhythm as they commenced in a chant of "Warriors! Let's do it!" As they chanted and hit their batons together, they moved to line up in a scattered formation on the basketball court, and suddenly everyone realized that one girl had exchanged her batons for a basketball and was dribbling to the end of the court, placing herself under one of the baskets. It was, of course, Tai, and the other girls formed a sort of obstacle course across the court. With the ball in a tightly controlled dribble, she began to make her way to the basket at the other end of the court, dodging and spinning around the other cheerleaders as she went, controlling the ball with clear expertise, and as she passed each cheerleader, that cheerleader would stop hitting her batons together and throw up the batons in a twirling action above her head and then catch them again, creating an effect that was reminiscent of a water spray show set to music. Near the other basket was Rose, standing between the basket and the free-throw line. As Tai approached her, Rose stopped hitting her sticks together and held them to her sides, twirling them like a visual drum-roll, and Tai jumped over Rose, flying over her head, and made a slam dunk into the basket. As she did during practice, she landed on the ground like a cat, her small falling form emphasizing the ten feet that stretched between the ground and the basket rim, and her right hand came up again, effortlessly catching the ball.

The audience exploded into an uproar. Again, there were whistles, shouts, and hoots of approval. People were stomping on the bleachers or standing up and applauding. Some were shaking their heads in disbelief.

Kyle also clapped, but although he was as impressed as everyone else was with the new cheerleading routine, he had been distracted the whole time by Tai's smile. Throughout the routine, Tai had a bright look on her face, one that matched those of all the other girls on the squad. It conveyed a cheerful and friendly personality, but Kyle knew Tai well enough to know that it was a fake smile. Just like the sweet and flirtatious smile she had worn when she performed the Assassin's Charm with the Lin Gui, it was a clear to him now how much of a sham it all was. He watched as she stood up and beamed at the audience again, mimicking the other girls as they jumped and kicked enthusiastically with encouraging shouts. And when it all ended, Kyle confirmed his conclusion as he observed the smile wipe from her face like a peeled off mask, and Tai once again looked expressionless and bored with a touch of mild disapproval for all those around her. As she walked with the other cheerleaders off the court, people were approaching her and congratulating her, trying to talk to her. She responded civilly to everyone, thanking people for compliments and answering questions. While turning to talk to another person, she caught sight of Kyle staring at her, and with a raising of her eyebrows, she asked him silently what he wanted, and he just shrugged and shook his head, looking away. He was relieved when the game was called to resume.

The game ended easily with a clear victory for the home team, and crowds of teens made their way to the local pizza joint to celebrate. At the restaurant, Matt and Rose set it up so that Kyle was sitting next to Tai.

"Tai, you look totally cute in that uniform. You should wear skirts more," Kyra said, her pony tail a cascade of black silken curls that she had carefully styled with an iron. She sat on the other side of Tai.

"Yeah, you should dress up more often," Rose nodded, smiling agreeably.

"Nah, Tai's the kind of girl that doesn't care about what others think," Robin said with a nod of approval, but then she added, "but you'd look totally hot in the latest Kandi wear. Just sayin'." She gave Tai a wink with her deep brown eyes.

"Everyone cares about what they look like, whether they admit it or not," Kyra waived, dismissing Robin's comment. Robin rolled her eyes at her friend in mild annoyance.

"Actually, I care very much about what I wear and what people think about it," Tai said as she took a bite of the pizza Kyle had just put on her plate after some prodding from Matt. Everyone, including Kyle, looked at Tai with a bit of surprise. Tai came to school every day with a make-up free face and wearing a baseball cap, a plain t-shirt or sweater and nondescript pants. She was as plain as plain can be, not the sort of girl that seemed to put a lot of care and thought into what she wore.

"What do you mean?" Rose was the first to break the silence.

"I choose what I wear carefully to attract the least attention possible," Tai said.

"The least attention?" Kyra said. She was so used to choosing clothes that attracted the most attention possible that she couldn't understand why anyone would do the opposite. She thought getting people's attention with her clothes was the whole point of wearing them.

"Yes, the least attention."

"But why?"

"I don't want anyone's attention."

Kyra looked at her with a perplexed expression that was mirrored to different degrees in the faces of everyone else there. Tai could see they wanted more explanation.

"It's just troublesome," Tai shrugged. Kyle remembered how Tai's first basketball practice was heading towards a meltdown situation and nodded in understanding. That hadn't stopped her from holding back on the guys, but Kyle guessed that was part of the problem. Tai didn't pull punches. Anything she did was done with full force and dedication. That usually made people feel inferior, and there's few things more troublesome people with bruised egos.

Feeling the conversation would probably turn in a bad direction if pursued further, Rose changed the subject.

"You like to read books, right Tai?"

"Ooo, Robin and I read like sooo much," Mercedes said.

"Mm-hm, getting through a big book is not a problem for me. That's why Mercedes and I both score perfect on anything language arts. What kind of books do you like, Tai? I've got a taste for romance and murder-mysteries myself," Robin said.

"I like fantasy and romance books best," Mercedes said. The two bookworms looked at Tai expectantly.

"I enjoy reading really useful books," Tai said.

"Like what kinds? How to books?" Robin said.

"If they're useful, yes."

"What was the last book you read?" Mercedes asked.

"*Deterministic Chaos in Anatomical Systems*," Tai said.

"Woah, what's that?" Robin said.

"It's about the application of a theoretical model common to physics and mathematics to a biological system."

"What?" Mercedes said.

"Wow, are you like super smart or something?" Mandy said.

"Yeah, seriously," Soo said.

"Aren't you ranked first in our class Tai?" Rose said, glad to emphasize people's accomplishments to keep the conversation positive and pleasant.

"Yes," Tai said, "but so is Kyle."

Kyle looked over at Tai's unimpressed expression and said, "Yeah, and so are like a dozen other people. I've lost count of how many potential valedictorians we have."

"We've got so many smart people at our school!" Soo said to the nods of agreement amongst the other girls.

"Not really," Tai said as she took another bite of pizza, making people feel kind of uncomfortable with her comment. Kyle tried not to shake his head at the situation. It was Tai's nature to stick to the truth as she saw it, not to make people feel good about themselves. Still, Tai could do with a little social finesse. She was quite the challenge for Rose who decided to try another tactic to change the topic of conversation yet again.

"So Kyle, how did you and Tai first meet?" Rose ventured to direct the attention towards Kyle, whom she knew would try his best to keep a friendly conversation going despite his usual silence in social situations.

"Huh? Oh, I was just visiting a place with my grandfather, and I met Tai there."

"Oh yeah? Tell us about it!" Mandy asked with interest.

"Well, I said hi to her and she…uh…"

"Punched him in the eye," Tai finished for him.

"What? No way, really?" Matt interjected, bewildered.

"You're such a violent girl, you know that?" Kyle said dryly, giving Tai an equally dry look. Couldn't she have just let him tell the story in a less controversial way? His annoyance at her wiped away any self-consciousness he had had.

"I am not," Tai stated as if it was simple fact and not a defense on her part.

"You attacked me, physically."

"I don't strike others with malice."

"You hit me."

"Out of respect."

"What?" Kyle gave her a look of disbelief. "How is hitting someone respectful?"

"When I hit you, it was as a martial artist testing your skill. I attacked you out of respect for your skill. If I thought you were weak and defenseless, I wouldn't have attacked at all."

"A punch is a punch," Kyle said with a bit of open irritation.

"True," Tai said and then stopped talking. Kyle waited for some sarcastic response on Tai's part, but she didn't say anything. He had apparently 'won' the argument, and although he wanted to feel triumphant in his rhetorical skill, all he felt was awkward. An uncomfortable silence filled the conversational space again.

"How long have you been learning kung fu Tai?" Matt asked, taking his turn to keep an amicable ambiance going.

"As long as I can remember."

"I took tae kwon do when I was a kid," Matt said.

"Oh, me too!" Robin exclaimed. "I'm a black belt."

"I've got a black belt in karate," Mercedes added.

"Maybe we should spar sometime," Matt offered Tai. "I used to go to regional competitions."

"Yes, maybe," Tai said, not seeing Kyle turn to Matt with wide eyes while slightly shaking his head no.

"So what do you think of Kyle's game today? He was totally MVP," Matt said, and some of the teammates gave Kyle a fist butt or a high five. "I'd never seen him score so many points in one game."

"And he was throwing some killer assists, too," Jake added with an approving nod. "He was barely looking on some passes. That's pro dude."

"Yes, much better," Tai repeated Kyle's grandfather's words and nodded in agreement. Although he had easily received props from his other peers with no discomfort, Kyle suddenly felt bashful after hearing Tai praise him. She even turned and offered him a rare smile of approval, but it had a touch of mischief. "Maybe next time you can avoid getting punched in the eye."

His timidity was wiped away by indignity.

"You're so kind," he said sarcastically with a roll of his eyes.

Tai shrugged with a slight smirk. "I just call it as it is. If you don't like the facts, then change them."

Chapter 35

Little One

"Why can't you train today?"

It was a Friday night, and Tai had just informed Kyle that she wasn't going to be training with him this evening. He had grown so accustomed to training with her every day that a break in routine bothered him.

"I told you, I'm busy."

"Busy with what?"

"None of your business."

"I think I have a right to know, you know, since we're preparing for a battle with the First Child demon." Kyle was grasping for a logical reason to push events into the direction of his original plans. At the same time, he spoke sincerely. It bothered him, gnawed at the back of his mind, that somewhere in this world, in his world, was an evil being running around unchecked, wreaking whatever havoc she pleased. This was the same being that had killed off all the adults of the Lin Gui village, had murdered the Dragon Queen, and had twisted the bodies and minds of people in Tian, turning them into Yehren… Yet they had not the slightest idea where this demon child was. There did not seem to be any big event of terror or tragedy that pointed them in her direction. She seemed to be hiding somewhere.

"I have to help Dr. Tan with something at her university," Tai said to appease him.

"Oh."

"We'll resume training first thing tomorrow morning."

"Uh…okay."

Tai closed her front door on him, and Kyle stood for a moment, staring at the closed door, feeling miffed at being kept in the dark regarding Tai's activities, and then he wondered why he was miffed at all. Isn't it a good thing to get a day off from training? Maybe he could play video games or watch a movie or just bum around at home for the evening and relax. He resolved to have a great evening without Tai as he turned around and walked down the small path between two bright green lawns to the spacious sidewalk of their suburban neighborhood. It was nearing the end of November, the following week being Thanksgiving, and though it had rained a few days before, the sky was bright blue and the sun was shining past some gorgeously fluffy white clouds. The temperature was moderate, the sort of extremely pleasant near-winter weather that was common in the Southland.

Kyle felt his phone buzz in his pocket. He took it out and saw that he had received a new text message.

> Tai 8pm @ University Café, 61998 Campus Drive. bring friends. ^_~ Cindy

It was a text message from Tai's adoptive mother. Kyle smiled, realizing he was being invited to witness whatever it was that Tai would be doing at the university that evening without Tai knowing. He was looking forward to seeing the look on her face when he showed up with…everyone. He proceeded to quickly forward the text to Matt, Rose, and others.

Soon he got texts back from people.

> me + the girls r so there! My momll drive us. – Rose

> kool! wat is it? can ur mom give us a ride? - Matt

Kyle was sure his mother would be more than happy to give him a ride to the local prestigious university. She'd been driving him there to walk around since he was a baby, telling him he would go there one day. He text-replied back to people and also texted his mom, coordinating the trip. In the end, to accommodate for the basketball team and cheer squad plus some miscellaneous tag-alongs, there ended up being about five minivans full of teenagers with designated parental drivers that were wondering why these high schoolers were suddenly so keen on hanging out at a college campus scene. Smirking a little inwardly, Kyle felt a little smug to be crashing whatever party Tai was going to be at, a touch of pay back for her earlier dismissal.

When they had arrived in the college town area, it was buzzing with life and activity with plenty of local resident patrons, tourists, and college students enjoying their Friday evening socializing with friends before the onslaught of finals that was looming over the horizon. The trees were covered in lights, and laughter and music poured out of every doorway. Kyle and his peers added to the festive cacophony, talking excitedly as they headed towards University Café. They arrived at their destination about ten minutes before 8pm. It was a quaint but roomy coffee shop, designed in a way that was somewhat reminiscent of a rustic American living room with warm colors and prairie wild flowers. There were paintings of faded sunflowers and daisies, old book shelves and cabinetry full of dog-eared books, and large and plush couches of warm colors that lined the walls. Motley wooden tables circled by unmatched wooden chairs that seem to have each come from a different dining room set filled the sizable main floor area. The coffee and tea bar area was off to the left while across the room from it, to the right, was a small platform. To the side of the platform were stacked some tables and chairs that had apparently been moved to clear the raised dais as a little stage. On that stage was set up a beautiful instrument made of a deep red

wood with a rare array of twenty-one strings made of twisted silk. It was a Chinese guzheng. To the side was a stand that held a microphone hovering over the guzheng.

Kyle suddenly realized what was going on. Tai was going to be performing live in this coffee house. He looked around for Tai and saw instead that the establishment was packed. Every inch of couch and every chair was occupied, and he and his high school classmates had to line up in the back near the entrance next to some other late comers who were eagerly waiting on their feet without complaint. As he scanned the crowd, he saw a flash of blonde hair and realized that Tai's adoptive parents were waving at him and giving him approving thumbs up at the group he had been able muster for the occasion. Tai's adoptive father, Mr. Tan, was a large and tall man with a strong build and heavy set jaw, but his almond-shaped eyes were gentle, and although he dwarfed Dr. Tan, their affection for each other was serenely apparent. Sitting at the table with them were Snow and Jade, looking like a very normal and attractive young couple. No one would have guessed they were the oldest ones in the room. It seemed like everyone had been invited except for Kyle. He waved back as Snow and Jade waved too. There was no way for Kyle to make his way over to them without stepping over a number of people, so Kyle just stayed put and waited for the performance to begin.

"Good evening everyone," a young woman with bright red hair, glimmering green eyes, and a welcoming smile got up on the little stage and bent over to speak into the microphone that hung over the instrument. "Thanks everyone for coming out to this Indie Music club event. I know you're all as excited as I am for tonight's special performance. We all saw her last time and are ecstatic that she's agreed to come back and perform her unique music for us again today. It's my pleasure to introduce Tai performing her original music on the guzheng."

There was a flurry of welcoming applause as Tai stepped out from behind a group of people that were crowded up near the stage. She wore a simple black t-shirt over blue jeans, and her hair was flowing loose on her shoulders. The sight of her hair untied reminded Kyle of the first night they spent with the Lin Gui sharing a room together, her face lit by the warm light of the candles she was extinguishing. She bowed her head a bit in polite acknowledgement of the audience, and when she looked up, her eyes met Kyle's and she raised a questioning eyebrow. He shrugged and smiled impishly, and then Tai gave her adoptive mother a quick look to which Mrs. Tan feigned an innocent smile. With a shake of her head, Tai sat down in front of her instrument. She moved up to the microphone placed in front of her.

"This first piece is an instrumental called 'At the Gate of Heavenly Peace'."

Tai raised her hands, her fingers at the ready like the bamboo leaves poised to dance in the wind. It was then that the audience could see that there were silver ringlets with sharp points on the tip of each of her ten fingers. As her fingers began their frolic over the strings, the sounds of the instrument filled the air like a cascading waterfall singing in a hidden oasis. As Kyle listened, he felt transported to a place filled with greens and blues, where fresh air and gentle breezes reigned and clarity and purity pervaded the mind and soul. As Tai played, her body and head swayed with both the music and the physical movement of her playing, her hair swaying forward with her motion, sometimes covering her face. The beautiful piece went on for what seemed like too short a time, coming to an end to his disappointment.

When the last shimmering note faded in the air, the audience began applauding enthusiastically, and Rose gave Kyle a look and silently mouthed the word 'wow' to him.

"This next song is entitled 'Little One'."

This song was markedly different in mood and style from the first composition. The first had followed a more classical style of guzheng music, and this one fell more in line with modern guzheng compositions in that it had a melody. Also, the music expressed a melancholy emotion at the beginning, as if it was grieving. And then Tai slightly startled everyone when she raised her lips to the microphone and sang, her voice intermingling with the guzheng.

Take of my flesh
My blood can make
Gray cheeks rosy again
Take of my voice
Let your wandering soul
Speak through it

Little one

Let us dance together
In these flames
Spread your wings
and sing with me
let them all hear you
from beyond the grave
burn little phoenix
in the broken light

Oh, little one
Abandoned little one
Murdered little one

Tai's voice was piercing yet clear, angry and sad, the song like a snapshot of a moment in her perception of the world, the music emanating from the guzheng matching in mood and tone. The keen musician familiar with both classical Chinese styles and modern American styles would be able to discern the skill in which Tai had integrated both into a new form of musical quality.

Kyle tried to enjoy the music, and he did find it beautiful and moving, but he was distracted by the fact that he felt uncomfortable with everyone there, listening to her as well. There was something very intimate and sharing about her songs, and he suddenly regretted bringing everyone along with him. He couldn't understand this selfish feeling, this unwillingness to share with others. He thought wistfully of the time when he had enjoyed Tai's musical performance in more private settings.

She finished the song and went on to another, and after a five-song set, she finished. She stood up and bowed politely to loud, approving applause, and stepped off stage. Her adoptive parents moved quickly to start putting away her large instrument as Tai was flooded again with people who wanted to speak with her. Apparently she was quite the hit amongst the college students. Kyle suddenly found that he and the other high schoolers had to wait in line to even talk to her, and he felt even more removed from her than he did when she had refused to tell him her plans for the evening. When they finally had their chance to talk to her, she graciously thanked them for attending, but Kyle saw the weariness to her polite smile and could see she was just humoring all the people who wanted to speak to her.

"That was amazing!" Rose said.

"Thank you," Tai said.

"I take it you don't like pop music since you're into this world, indie stuff huh?" Robin said good-naturedly.

"No, music is music. I like pop music same as any music."

"Cool, glad you're not one of those snooty musicians. I'll burn you a mix of my favorites then, cuz I love pop music," Robin smiled.

"Sure, thanks."

"Hey, where'd you learn to play like that?" Jake sidled up next to Tai from behind Kyra. As Tai answered his questions, Kyle felt some tension in his chest, dark stirrings he didn't understand, and he muttered something about the bathroom and excused himself. It was a natural reaction to remove himself from an uncomfortable situation.

There was a line at the small, bathroom at the back of the café, and as Kyle took his place behind a blonde haired woman, she turned around and smiled at him. It was Cindy, Tai's adoptive mother.

"Hi Dr. Tan," Kyle smiled back politely despite his negative mood.

"Hi Kyle, I'm so glad you could make it. Did you and your friends enjoy the show?"

"Yeah, it was really good. Tai was really good."

"It's nice to see Tai interacting with people her own age, even though I know she doesn't enjoy it."

Kyle laughed, knowing exactly what Tai's mother was talking about, but still, he wondered.

"Why is that anyway?"

"Well," Dr. Tan sighed heavily, "you've probably figured out that Tai's not your average high school teenager."

"That's the understatement of the century," Kyle laughed. Tai's mother laughed, too.

"You see, it's a pretty well documented phenomenon that prodigies tend to feel isolated from their peers."

"Prodigy…" Kyle thought the title fit Tai pretty well.

"Look at it this way. Have you ever heard of Plato's Cave?"

Kyle knew who Plato was, but he'd never heard about his cave. He shook his head.

"The story is that there are a bunch of prisoners chained in a cave in a way so that all they can do is look at shadows projected on a wall from a fire that's behind them. The shadows are all that these prisoners have ever seen, so to them, the shadows are reality. Now, imagine someone who isn't chained, someone who can see the shadows, the fire, the prisoners, and even leave the cave to see what's outside. Then imagine that free person trying to talk to the prisoners. Imagine that person trying to explain what the sun is to the prisoners who have only known the shadows."

Kyle stood silent and let the ideas sink into him. A person who completely believed that shadows were reality probably wouldn't even be open to believing that something like the sun could actually exist.

"It would be like talking to someone who doesn't speak your language," Kyle finally said out loud.

"Yes, very much like that, except worse. At least with language differences you can get a translation. It's a lot harder when not even your *ideas* match with what others know and believe. There's no way to even translate in that situation."

"Can't people just try to understand those ideas?"

"Can or cannot are definitely questions to be considered, but so are will or will not. If you've believed the world is flat all your life, and someone comes along and says it's not, how likely are you to change your mind?"

"Not right away, that's for sure."

"Well, what if someone came along and told you that the world was actually flat, and we'd been wrong about it being round this whole time?"

Kyle let out a short laugh. The idea was too ridiculous to even consider, and yet Tai's mother was asking the question very seriously.

"I'd say I'd probably never believe that," Kyle admitted.

"Right or wrong, we tend to stick to what we know. It's just natural to the human mind. When Tai was seven years old, she got into a huge argument with her fellow second graders when she told them that three was divisible by two."

Kyle looked at her in surprise and said, "But it is."

"Yes, but the teacher had just explained to them that day that only even numbers were divisible by two."

"Oh…I see. So what happened?"

"Well, needless to say, you know how stubborn Tai is. She wouldn't budge from her argument, of course. The group of kids got angry at her, and the situation unfortunately escalated to some violence."

"Violence?" Kyle's eyes widened.

"Yes, they started to throw rocks at her."

Kyle's heart sank. He could just imagine a defenseless little seven-year-old version of Tai being bullied by a group of her merciless classmates…wait, *defenseless*? That didn't sound like Tai.

"Was she hurt?"

Dr. Tan smiled. "No, she dogged and blocked every rock effortlessly, and then the teacher noticed, and all of those kids were sent to the office."

Kyle laughed and shook his head. "I'm surprised she didn't kick their butts."

"Well, that's the thing. At seven years old, she understood. When the teacher asked her why she didn't tell on the kids right away, she said, 'They just didn't understand what I was saying.' She didn't take it personally. She just understood them, but they, they didn't understand her."

Kyle thought back to his own simple and carefree childhood where the biggest concern of the day was whether or not he got his green card pulled for talking out of turn in class. Then he remembered what Tai had said about not wanting to draw people's attention because it was 'troublesome'. This little story about her childhood gave the word 'troublesome' a whole new meaning for Kyle.

"In middle school, at eleven years old, Tai had come across a group of eighth grade girls picking on a sixth grade girl. Without even a word to anyone, she locked an iron grip on wrist of the ringleader of the bullies who was twice her size, dragged her into the principal's office, explained the situation, and then left. I had to go in with her after school to sign a witness form," Dr. Tan shook her head and laughed.

"Geez," Kyle said shaking his head.

"You see, Tai just doesn't play by the same rules as everyone else because she understands the rules better than any of her peers. But that means she's really completely alone…in a way you and I can barely imagine."

"Wow, you've really got her figured out," Kyle said with a look of awe and admiration.

"Maybe." Dr. Tan looked up at a painting of a sunflower on the wall that was faded with time. "I've got a daughter who won't call me 'Mom'. I try my best to understand why." She turned and gave Kyle a sad smile that made him rather irritated at Tai for being so distant from someone who clearly loved her so much.

The evening wrapped up quietly, and the café emptied and quieted down. As Kyle and the other teens headed out, the girls clip-clopped along in their stylish Kandi heels, sounding like a herd cattle, while Tai walked beside them in her black running shoes, padding along, silent as a panther. They bade their last goodbyes and congratulations to her, and she waved to them politely before she turned and padded silently away to meet back up with her parents. Watching as she tied her loose hair back up into a serious high pony-tail, Kyle kept staring at her until she disappeared behind the closing doors of the café.

The next morning, Kyle was jogging alongside Tai, their white sneakers hitting the pavement in a regular, synchronized beat with their steady breathing. They followed the concrete path as it headed up a hill for a while and then turned into a park situated at the top. Their path ran up the edge of the park, giving them a panoramic view of the San Gabriel Valley beyond a row of eucalyptus trees. They passed by a baseball field, a soccer field, a basketball court, and clusters of park benches. Grass stretched far and wide creating a green and well-groomed landscape.

When they reached the highest point, they found themselves at the edge of the park where the green lawns were on one side of the concrete path while the other side was lined with natural tall and browned grasses of the hillside swaying golden in the early morning breeze and sun. They followed a dirt path that turned off to the side and led a ways into the tall grasses to a set of metal bars held up by sturdy wooden poles. As soon as Tai and Kyle reached the bars, they jumped up and grabbed both hands onto the bars and began to do reverse-grip pull-ups. Their foreheads were covered in perspiration from their efforts, and they pulled their young, athletic bodies up, doing one pull up after another in perfect unison. Tai counted off their last few reps out loud.

"Twenty-eight, twenty-nine, thirty."

After the last pull up, they let go of the bar and dropped to their feet again, breathing hard and wiping the sweat off their faces with their shirts. The Southern Californian sun was already starting to warm the hillside. The sky was a perfect blue. Taking a drink from the water bottles strapped to their waists, they shook out their limbs to keep their muscles from going stiff.

They looked out at the view of the valley below patterned with an orderly patchwork of suburban homes, clean and well-tended, each its own domain, yet identical to all others. The hillsides close to the park, however, were wild and untamed, covered in long grass and flowers, a last vestige of the natural environment that reigned here before the layers of concrete and asphalt were laid over them.

Kyle looked out at the neighborhood where he had grown up; it was all he had ever known. He thought of his family, his friends, his schools, and even the local supermarkets and restaurants, all that he had taken for granted. He looked over at Tai whose breathing was calming down as she stared out at the same view.

"It's good to be home, isn't it?" he said to her.

Tai looked over at his smiling face and then back out at the view. She shrugged.

"It won't last you know."

"What won't last?"

"This." Tai gestured out toward the view of their suburban neighborhood. "Nothing is permanent. Change is inevitable."

Kyle looked out and imagined what it would look like if all that he saw before him was destroyed. He thought of the First Child Demon. He remembered why he was training, what he was protecting.

"Maybe."

"No, not maybe."

"Well, not if I can help it."

"You can't stop change. For better or worse, it'll come. In fact, it's always changing. Cling to it, and you'll suffer."

Kyle looked out at the neighborhood. It looked exactly as he'd always remembered it.

"It looks the same to me."

Tai looked him in the eyes.

"You're young."

He realized she had a point. He'd only been alive for less than two decades. Of course it would look the same to him. Still, he felt like arguing with her.

"And you're not?"

She shrugged again in response. She started to stretch her arms and legs, and he followed her lead. He looked back out at the view of the orderly homes and lawns and remembered what Dr. Tan had said about Tai and about Plato's cave of shadows.

"Your performance last night was really good."

"Thanks."

She didn't really sound appreciative of the compliment. In fact, Kyle noticed compliments seemed to bore her.

"What was that one song you wrote? The second one I think."

"Little One."

"You really write that?"

"Yes."

"Where'd you get the idea for that song? It was pretty intense."

He noticed that she looked down a bit before looking back out at the view again and stretching her arms.

"Dr. Tan goes on a lot of trips to research conferences all around the world. She takes me with her whenever she can. One time, in the summer before sixth grade, we went to Beijing and visited the Forbidden City." She paused as she switched to stretching her other arm. "Right when we got off the bus by Tiananmen Square, I saw a phone booth on the sidewalk, and inside the phone booth, on the floor, was a small bundled up baby."

Kyle's mouth opened a bit in surprise. Tai looked over at him with a deep sadness and pain in her eyes that he couldn't comprehend.

"It was the middle of winter. It was snowing. She wasn't breathing."

"She?"

Tai looked away into the distance again, as if seeing the scene all over again.

"A crowd had already started to form, and a police officer was shooing people away." She looked down at the dead and dry wild grass nearby. "And I thought, 'That could've been me.' So I wrote the song. To remember her."

Kyle contemplated a patch of dead grass Tai was staring at. They stood in silence for a moment, motionless.

"But you're not her, are you?" he said suddenly, surprising even himself. "You've got a mom and a dad and friends. Heck, you've even got me to kick around if you need cheering up."

Tai looked at him, taken aback, her eyes wide. Then she let out a small laugh despite herself, shaking her head.

"Here," Kyle said, taking a step towards her and sticking his face up close to hers while pointing a fist up to his right eye. "You can smack me one here again right now if it'll make you feel better."

Tai brought a hand up and gently pressed it against the side of Kyle's face, pushing him away. It was almost playful. Almost.

"Don't be stupid. If I can kick you around, then I wouldn't be doing a very good job as your trainer."

Then she smiled at him. Framed by the bluest sky and the faded greens and beiges of the surrounding eucalyptus trees, the morning sun reflected golden off of her face as she smiled the most beautiful smile Kyle had ever seen. Clear, pure, and true.

Chapter 36

Winter Formal

"Why don't you ask her to the winter formal?" Matt asked, giving Kyle a punch in the shoulder and then putting his large backpack down as he started to unfurl a large white sign made on butcher paper asking Rose to be his date to the winter formal dance.

"Are you crazy? Do you want me to *die*?"

Kyle tried to laugh it off. The question made him uncomfortable. He already knew Tai would say no. High school was a bore to Tai. High school teenagers were, too. A high school dance full of teenagers was the perfect recipe to bore her to tears. Probably the only way he could get her to go was to convince her that the First Child demon would be there. Or maybe that there would be a dragon there. Yeah, that would do it. Not counting Jade of course. But it wasn't the fact that she would say no to him that bothered him.

"She's waiting for *you* to ask her. Come on, I just know it," Matt pressed on. "You'd better ask her before someone else does."

This made Kyle laugh out loud. And it wasn't because he thought no one was interested in Tai. It had only been a few weeks since Tai started training with varsity boys basketball and varsity girls cheer, and talk of her had already spread through the school. To add to that, the last game and the amazing cheer routine she had been the star of easily made her the talk of the entire school. Also, Rose, the darling of the school, was going around non-stop jabbering about Tai and how skilled she was.

All the while, Tai and Kyle had continued their training in qi script. He couldn't imagine how people would react if they *really* knew everything she was capable of doing.

Kyle definitely had a better appreciation now of why Tai had kept low key before. For someone who had little patience for high school and high school students, having everyone at school constantly paying attention to her and trying to socialize with her must be annoying to say the least.

She had, however, managed to keep everyone at a distance with her easily frigid demeanor. As was usual when a girl drew the attention of many people, there were a few boys at school who developed a shallow interest in this overnight school celebrity, and some had been brave enough to even approach her, probably to try to ask her out to the winter formal or something, but she had given them a look of such intense disapproval that they had simply slunk away. Even sharks knew to steer clear of a killer whale.

"Here, can you help me hold this up? I think I made this sign too big. I'm gonna need you to help me," Matt explained as he handed Kyle the rest of his unfolded sign.

"Uh, okay," Kyle agreed as he took a hold of the sign. They were standing in the main lunch courtyard area of the school in a row with about twenty other gutsy guys who were holding up signs asking girls to go to the dance.

Someone had started this tradition years before they were students there, and it was a public declaration of feelings for a girl. Many of them were guys who were asking their steady girlfriends out, but some were going out on a limb and proclaiming their interest in a girl to the whole school, risking public rejection.

It was something that Kyle knew he would never have the guts to do, so he had some respect for those guys and hoped for the best for them. In fact, Kyle had never asked a girl to a dance before. He usually just tagged along with a group.

"Hey, Kyle, the part you're holding up isn't fully rolled open. Can you get that for me?"

Kyle pulled the rolled up butcher paper fully open so that he was holding the corner of the paper.

"Thanks man, I put a lot of effort into this poster, so I don't want Rose to miss any part of it."

Kyle nodded to his friend who was flashing him a big toothy grin.

"Look, there they are!" Matt said merrily. "See? Tai's staring right at you! She totally wants you to ask her out to the dance, dude. Why aren't you asking her?"

At the other side of the yard, Rose and Tai were emerging from the buildings where the classrooms were housed. The two of them began walking towards Matt and Kyle looking very much the mismatched pair. Tai wore a simple white t-shirt over loose-fitting blue jeans and black sneakers. A black baseball cap with a stiff rim blocked the light from reaching her light brown, amber-glinted eyes.

Rose, on the other hand, was clacking away in the bright in-style pink high heels with tight, hip-hugging purple jeans covered in patterns under a bright pink sleeveless blouse. Everything Rose wore was part of the pop star Kandi's very popular fashion and make-up line. Her red lips and shading-enhanced eyes were like a glowing beacon compared to Tai's plain, unembellished face.

Kyle turned to Matt with a dry look on his face. "She's not staring at me. She's glaring at me. There's a difference, and she's probably thinking about how inferior I am compared to her," he said with a shake of his head.

As Rose and Tai made their way towards the two boys across the yard, Rose saw the slight scowl on Tai's face. She'd grown accustomed to Tai's less-than-friendly ways, but she still couldn't help but feel the need to ask her what was wrong. She saw that Tai was looking directly at Kyle who had just turned to talk to Matt about something. "Is there something wrong Tai?"

"Nothing. I was just thinking about how inferior Kyle is compared to me."

"Oh come on Tai," Rose coaxed.

Tai sighed as if this sort of misunderstanding of her words happened all the time.

"It's not a personal attack. I am just stating the truth."

"Aw, Kyle's such a nice guy, and I can tell he really likes you."

At this, Tai raised an eyebrow and looked at Rose, remembering something that happened not so long ago in a faraway world.

"I am sure that you are mistaken, Rose."

Rose was a little taken aback. She could feel that Tai put some weight into saying her name at that moment, although she didn't have the faintest idea why.

They approached the sign that Matt had made. Rose smiled and went up to Matt to give him a big hug while Tai stared blankly at the poster.

"Thanks for the poster! You're so sweet! Of course I'll go with you to the winter formal," Rose said with an appreciative smile to Matt. Then they both turned to expectantly look at Tai who was staring intently at the poster. A few people started gathering around as they noticed the drama that was unfolding right before their eyes. They saw what Kyle still couldn't yet see.

Kyle stood there holding his corner of the poster, starting to feel very awkward and uncomfortable, but he couldn't quite understand why.

"Oh, hey Tai. So is training at five again today?" he tried to make normal, useless chit chat to fill in the strange silence. Of course training was at five again.

Tai ignored his pointless question as she finished staring at the poster he held and then shifted her gaze up at him. She looked a bit irritated at him, and he knew he should be used to it by now, since she was often irritated around him, but there was something pressing about this time that he couldn't quite put his finger on. "What? What is it?" he asked with a nervous smile.

"No," Tai said.

Kyle looked from side to side. What was she driving at?

"Uh, no what?"

He noticed Matt and Rose's eager smiles and then everything suddenly clicked into place for him. He quickly looked over his hands and down at the corner of the poster he was holding, the part that Matt had handed to him partially rolled up, and saw that painted on that one strip of the butcher paper, the part that he was holding, was the message:

TAI,
WILL YOU GO TO THE WINTER FORMAL WITH ME?
-Kyle

His jaw dropped, and he wished with all his might that a black hole would suddenly open up where he stood and swallow him so that he no longer existed, or at least not at this time and place. But of course, he had no such control over the space-time continuum.

Seeing his bewilderment, Tai calmly examined his changing facial expression as Kyle panicked, trying to figure out what to say next. He had two choices, fake having written the message himself and take the public rejection from Tai graciously or announce that it had been Matt's doing but risk insinuating that he didn't think Tai was a girl worth asking to the dance. Under the intense strain of embarrassment at the moment, there was only one thing he could think of doing—tell the truth.

"He did it," Kyle said, pointing a finger at Matt and let go of the poster. It drifted to the ground.

"AW man! Come on! I set it all up for you! Tai, come on, just go with him. It'll be fun. Rose is going, Kyra and Jake are going together, and everyone else will be there," Matt tried to persuade Tai good-naturedly.

"Yeah, Tai, come with us. It'll be fun!" Rose backed her boyfriend.

These entreaties fell on deaf ears.

"I don't have time for it. I'll see you all at practice," she said nonchalantly. Tai took one more look at the shell-shocked Kyle and then turned to go.

"How about a competition?" Matt said as a last minute resort. Tai stopped, and Matt felt triumphant at just having caught her attention. Over the last few weeks in basketball, he got the sense that Tai liked a good challenge, and Matt knew there was no one on campus who could give her that aside from Kyle.

"What sort of…competition?" Tai asked as she turned around slowly.

"How about you and Kyle have a duel, a face off, you know, in martial arts or something. If he wins, you go to the dance with him. If you win, you don't go to the dance. How does that sound?"

Tai looked intrigued by the idea.

"Let's have the match today, at basketball practice. I'll talk to Coach about it," Matt added.

Kyle looked at Matt with a look of utter perplexity and mouthed, *What?!* He turned back and saw Tai with a look of self-satisfied certainty on her face.

"I accept."

"Ah?" Kyle was apparently temporarily stripped of the ability to utter comprehensible speech.

"I accept the challenge."

Kyle could have sworn he saw a sadistic smile dance over her lips just before she turned and walked away. He turned to Matt and Rose.

"You really do want me to die."

"Don't be so melodramatic, man," Matt waved away his comment.

"No, seriously, you guys just don't understand what she's really capable of…I…am a dead man." Kyle massaged his temples in a futile attempt to calm down.

"You'll be fine, Kyle," Rose said, giving his arm a supportive shake.

"I'll ask Coach to get you guys boxing gloves, okay? That should protect you from mortal danger," Matt laughed.

Kyle was dazed and confused. His best friend just signed him up to battle against a girl who was probably one of the most formidable martial opponents on the planet, what with her ability to use qi script and the fact that she'd been training in combat arts since probably before she could speak.

"You have no idea how much mortal danger I'm really in right now."

Chapter 37

Ready? FIGHT!

The gym was packed with people. Apparently word of the little joust planned between Kyle and Tai spread throughout the school, and anyone who could get away to attend the event had done so. They filled the bleachers to the brim, and people were even standing on the sidelines and in the nooks and crannies. It was rarely this filled up, even at school pep rallies or at popular sports events held in the gym. Although all this attention did make Kyle feel a little like a monkey in a cage about to be let out to dance a crowd-pleasing jig, he was too afraid for life and limb to really feel self-conscious. *At least I won't die unnoticed and forgotten*...was his futile attempt to console himself.

"No gloves," Tai had refused, but she was busy winding white support tape around her hands and wrists. Kyle gulped and started to follow her example, winding his own hands and wrists in the same material. Her winding of this support material around her wrists made him very nervous indeed. She looked like she was preparing for a serious beat down. Maybe this was her chance to go all out and let out all her pent up aggravation against him. He felt his stomach go queasy again. Goodbye cruel world.

Matt, Rose, and the others were wishing them both luck and encouragement, but since Kyle looked a lot more perturbed by the whole affair, they focused on bolstering his confidence a little more. Their words did little to comfort or unwind him from the stress-ball he was now tangled up in.

"Just do your best Kyle and you'll be fine!"

"Just be yourself!"

As Kyle and Tai walked onto the court, their awaiting battlefield, wearing their basketball practice jerseys over long, loose blue pants with a white stripe running down each leg and low top sneakers (Tai had complained the high tops would restrain her movement too much), Tai spoke as she rubbed her left fist with her right hand in anticipation.

"Your friends give bad advice."

Kyle looked up at her straight in the eyes, a little irritated by her words and defensive of his well-meaning friends.

"If you're going to beat me, doing your best won't be enough," Tai continued to goad him, pulling on her high pony-tail to tighten it.

"Oh, is that so?" Kyle was feeling a little combative now with her provocation. They both reached the center of the court and turned to face each other.

"Don't just be yourself. Be better," Tai said with some intended smugness.

"Don't regret your words," Kyle threw back with his own haughty smile. He didn't know where his newfound confidence came from, but he decided to just go with it.

"I never do."

Jade came up to them and asked, "Are you ready?"

Without taking their eyes off of each other, Kyle and Tai nodded.

"Very well, let's begin." He raised his voice a bit for the next part as he took a few strides backwards away from them. "First to land a solid blow wins the fight."

The milling crowd settled and quieted at the sight of the two of them getting into ready positions on the basketball court. Kyle stood with a right jabbing fist forward. Tai looked more relaxed, shaking out her hands.

"Ready, FIGHT!"

Jade's voice had barely finished its echo when Kyle saw something faint glowing on Tai's forehead. It was the character for swiftness, barely noticeable and recognizable if Kyle wasn't so used to seeing it night after night of training with her. She was boosting herself with just a bit of qi script. Instinctively he activated his own qi script to matching intensity. If she was going to play that way, so was he. This happened in a split second, and in the second half of that second, which seemed to the audience to be instantaneous to Jade's audible mark of the beginning of the fight, Tai's body immediately surged forward and she was up in the air with a flying kick to Kyle's head. She moved with a speed that was just a notch below inhuman, and the clear power of her onslaught was most apparent when Kyle lifted his arms to block and was pushed back about five yards. That gave Tai enough room to land and then launch into another attack. This time, she jumped up from the ground high up into the air over Kyle's slumped form and began bringing her right leg down on him, heel first, in a massive ax kick. Kyle flipped backward and out of the way before being totally crushed, and the audience was in silent awe, everyone thinking they had imagined the clear rippling waves that seemed to pulse through the air from where Tai's leg had come down towards the ground. Matt whistled now, understanding where Tai's ability to do the very difficult slam dunk came from, since what she was doing now made the slam dunk look like child's play, and Rose saw why the cheerleading kicks had looked so effortless for Tai. They also both understood now why Kyle had acted like he was in real mortal danger. Any one of those kicks would have done serious damage had they hit their mark, and it was finally clear to them that Tai wasn't one to pull any punches.

Kyle saw an opening to jump into the offensive. Shaking his open hands into fists, he brought on a quick and relentless series of grounded punches and kicks at Tai, varying his points of attacks and alternating unpredictably between leg and fist. Nevertheless, Tai matched every strike and blow with block and parry, the power of every one of Kyle's hits diverted away from its mark. The movement of their precise little dance looked like an incomprehensible flurry of motion from the audience's perspective, and it was a wonder to them that the two combatant's arms and legs didn't get tangled with each other.

In an intense moment, one of Kyle's powerful punches aimed for Tai's face, and she turned to the side, just in time to get out of his fist's way, ending up in a position where she was looking right at the assaulting fist from the side, its air displacement causing her loose hairs to blow away from her face. Her hand that was farthest away from Kyle grabbed firmly onto the wrist of his punching hand, trapping him place, and the other coiled up across her own stomach before it swung out for a decisive, back handed strike at his stomach. It was a simple yet coordinated little move, and it would have been the solid blow that won the fight if Kyle hadn't realized in time what was happening and thrust his free hand in between the back of her fist and his stomach. Her fist struck his arm instead, and the with a deft twist of his wrists, Tai suddenly found her two wrists held firmly in *his* hands as he pulled her arms in a cross motion and began to twist them as if he were tightening up twist-ties on a bag of bread. Tai had three choices at that moment. She could let him continue to twist and break her arms, bend to the force of his motion and let herself be thrown to the ground, or jump and spin faster than his twisting of her arms and untangle herself from situation. She chose the last option. She jumped and kicked herself into a twisting, spinning action, looking like she was doing an in-place butterfly twist.

Breaking free of his grip, it was Tai's turn to throw a flurry of punches and kicks at Kyle who found himself now on the defensive. At the end of the sequence, she threw a powerful and high round-house kick to his head, which he ducked just in the nick of time, and then in one smooth motion she turned, spinning flawlessly as she dropped to the ground and attempted to sweep him off his feet with the back of her leg.

She spun back up to a standing position and continued an onslaught of kicks until Kyle suddenly timed his movements just right and, with a quick turn of the body, began to return her kicks with his own. He used the same combo of round-house kick and then low sweep on her, forcing her to duck and then jump, but instead of just spiraling back up to a stand, he took advantage of his grounded position and sped up just fast enough to bring an upward thrusting sidekick at her while she was still in the air.

Tai blocked the assault with both arms, but being off the ground, she was thrown back high up above the gym floor. It looked like she was going to fall on her back, which would have made the blocked kick a solid blow and costing her the match, but instead she leaned back into the momentum of the kinetic energy moving her body, flipped backwards in midair and landed on all fours like a panther on the gym floor.

The two contenders stood about ten yards away from each other, the distance evidence of how potent Kyle's kick had been. Tai stood up slowly from her crouched position. Both were breathing hard from the exertion, and both were rubbing their forearms that were sore from all the blocks and parries. Kyle's eyes met hers, and he saw a faint smile spread across her face as she looked at him. Then he realized that he had the same expression on his own face. Despite his exhaustion, he felt an acute sense of clarity permeating throughout his mind and body. There was no more fear, no more self-consciousness, no more stress, no more uncertainty. It was as if all the exertions of the last few minutes had burned away everything that was unnecessary in his existence. He was aware of the air, of the faded walls of the gym, of the audience sitting in stunned silence, of the way the lighting made them all look washed out, but most of all he was aware of this girl in front of him who he knew was preparing in every way to fully bring on the pain if he didn't hold his own. He let out a quick, single-breath cathartic laugh.

"Let me guess, there can only be one?" Kyle joked, thinking of some old action films he had seen.

Tai broke out into a full smile, "A Chosen One."

"I think it might be me," he threw back at her.

"You speak too soon."

Kyle smiled back.

"Oh yeah? Watch my stance!"

Ignoring the aching in his arms and legs, he put up his fists again with solid emphasis, indicating to Tai that he was ready to finish this. Shaking out her fingers first, Tai pulled them quickly into her own solid fists. However, quickly after, they unfurled into open hands, her slender fingers opening a little to look more like flower petals than knives. She also took what looked like a softer stance, looking more like she was about to flow into a traditional Chinese dance instead of a martial form, but she bent her knees and sunk much lower to the ground, erasing any misunderstanding that her movements were only decorative.

Originally in a standing, boxing-ready position, Kyle took the cue from Tai and slid his front leg out, sinking into a stance almost as low as hers as he opened his fists out as well into open-handed preparation.

They moved forwards toward each other again, but this time there wasn't the straight jabbing thrust that Tai had used to literally kick off their fight. Instead, their feet moved in a circular pattern and so did their arms and hands. When they met, they didn't start throwing vicious strikes at each other like before. Instead, their initial meeting in this round consisted of both of their feet sliding forcefully up next to each other on the floor and their two forward open hands pushing against each other, wrist to wrist. For a moment their hands pushed against each other, drawing a circle in the air between them. It looked as if they were getting each other's bearings, feeling for the weight of the other before engaging in battle, but in fact, they had begun combat before they had even touched. Each had been redirecting and gathering up the momentum and energy through their movements, and now that energy was swirling between them in an unapparent exchange, each trying to redirect that energy to strike at the other. Occasionally there was a punch or strike thrown between them, and they even moved their feet in kicks that looked soft and gentle at first but ended in a clear point of energy focused attack. Energetic jumps and kicks ended in soft landings that would shame the most agile felines.

Most of the onlookers had no idea what type of fighting they were looking at, but they were mesmerized by the fluid movements nonetheless, amazed at the flawlessness in which they seemed to predict each other's movements in a choreography that seemed practiced a thousand times over instead of the fresh and dynamic interaction unfolding between two fighters before them. Few were consciously aware of a light breeze that had begun swirling around inside the gym.

Out of a rolling movement, Tai threw a sharp elbow strike at Kyle that he pushed away and retaliated with a fist which Tai also successfully redirected away. Their punches were rolling off each other in a fluidity that seemed too beautiful to be hostile, yet, they were clearly still trying to land that one solid hit that would finish the match. It was a wonder to be engaged in such a heightened exchange. Suddenly there was a quickening of their joint circular motion, the both of them throwing twirling kicks at each other, jumping, and then landing as light as falling feathers, and before anyone could realize it, Tai and Kyle both had a hand firmly gripped on the other's throat.

"DRAW!"

As the crowd broke out into applause, the hands that gripped the other's throat loosened and slid off gently in a motion that was almost a soft and tender caress. Each was breathing hard again from the exertion, and people who were watching started to pour out onto the basketball court, talking to each other excitedly or wanting to congratulate the dueling pair.

"That was the most awesome thing I have ever witnessed in my life!" someone in the crowd exclaimed.

Rose and the girls went up to Tai first as the boys on the basketball team came up to talk to Kyle.

"See! You weren't in mortal danger! Come on, you totally matched her blow for blow!" Matt exclaimed.

Kyle nodded in modest acknowledgement, but he was pretty amazed with himself. Tai was not one to go easy on someone; he had a punched eye to attest to that. And he had stood his ground against her.

He then noticed that the crowd was shifting, with all the girls moving over to him and all the guys moving over to Tai. He suddenly found himself in a sea of teenage girls, their stylish high heels clicking against the ground around him, their eyelashes batting invitingly, and their lusciously covered lips lauding him.

"I've always noticed you in AP bio last year but I didn't know you could do those things!"

"Huh? Oh, well, I couldn't do a lot of this last year, not really," Kyle tried to field the conversations and comments politely.

"When are you going to do this again?"

"Oh my gosh, you should totally have a match with the school kickboxing team!"

"I know! Right? That would be like so amazing!"

"You should take on two or more of them at a time."

"Haha, yeah, that's sounds interesting," Kyle tried to muster some enthusiasm. He looked over to see a group of guys asking Tai some questions, and motioning with their fists, emulating some of what they saw earlier. Her smile was gone, and her face had fallen back to her usual, uninterested expression, but she responded to their questions and comments in a very instructional manner. Jake, who was sidled up close to her, started talking to her, made a slight punch to her face, which she brought a hand up to block by grabbing his wrist and pushing the assault out of the way, then she twisted his arm and applied pressure on his shoulder, forcing him to cry out a little in pain. Then the other guys broke out into applause and approval at her little demonstration, smiling and laughing, and then asking her some more questions. Another guy put his hand on her shoulder to get her attention, and she turned to address him, with her back towards Kyle.

Kyle excused himself quickly, mumbling something about needing the restroom, and headed out of the gym. The girls who had been circling him started moving their attention over to Tai and the circle of boys around her. The peaceful, calm, and even happy state Kyle had had during their fighting had evaporated away, and all he had left was a sinking feeling and stirrings of dark emotions.

Chapter 38

First Date

Kyle lay in his quickly darkening room on his bed. The Liquid Blade was leaning against the wall next to his bed as if it were a baseball bat instead of a mystical blade of epic magic and wonder. It glimmered like water in the waning sunlight that stole in through his small bedroom window, but Kyle was too moody to notice its beautiful presence.

His eyes were wide open, and he was staring at the ceiling. He tried closing them again, hoping he would fall asleep, but the quiet, growing evening reminded him of his first night in the Lin Gui village, when he had shared a room with Tai, and she had gone around blowing out the candles in their room wearing the simple brown village clothes with her hair let down and her face clean. That memory kept replaying itself over and over in his mind, like a song that kept resurfacing in his consciousness.

He heard the doorbell ring. The door opened, and he could hear the ensuing conversation through his thin door that was placed right at the top of the stairs by the front door of their house.

"Is Kyle here?" It was Tai's voice.

"Yes, he's upstairs in his room. Is there something wrong? I thought he was supposed to be training with you right now," his mother responded.

"Yes, he is supposed to be at training with me right now."

"Did something happen?"

"We had a fight today."

Kyle slapped his hand to his forehead. He knew his mother was misinterpreting Tai's words. Not that kind of fight.

"Oh, I see. Well, come in."

"May I go upstairs and speak to him?"

"Sure, you go on ahead. Do you want something to drink?"

"No thank you. I'm fine."

Kyle pulled his covers over his head in dread when he heard the creaking of the stairs under Tai's weight as she made her way up to his room. A rather loud and obnoxious knock came on his door. He tried to pretend he was asleep. The knock came again, only louder and more intolerable.

"What?" Kyle called out irritably, still not ready to come out of his cave of self-pity.

"Open up," Tai demanded.

There was a moment of silence before Kyle finally replied. "It's unlocked." He turned so that he was facing the wall. Tai came in, welcomed only by Kyle's blanket covered back. Some of the light from the rest of the lighted house slipped into his darkening room.

"Why weren't you at training?" she demanded.

"I didn't feel like it today," came Kyle's muffled response.

"Why did you leave school without telling anyone today? We still had basketball practice."

Tai closed the door behind her and towered over Kyle on the bed with her fists on her hips. The room fell back into shadow with the closing of the door.

"I just didn't feel like doing anything today. It's Friday. I'm just tired from the fight, that's all. Why don't you just go ahead without me today?"

Tai stood silently for a while, observing him and trying to understand why he was being so moody. Then, giving up, she turned around and sat down on the ground by his bed with her back leaning against it. Kyle felt the slight shifting of the bed, the solidity of her presence.

"I'm supposed train you. So I can't do anything without you there."

They sat there in silence for a while, the sound of crickets outside Kyle's window announcing the night. He knew she was right, and he knew that his childish behavior was causing her, causing both of them to lose valuable time. He felt bad, but at the same time, he wasn't willing to let go of the grumpy emotions he cradled inside. Kyle turned around in his bed so that he was now facing Tai, but she kept her back to him, showing no reaction to his movements on the bed. He was close to her, enough so he could feel the warmth emanating from her body, his own forming a sort of semicircle around her back where it leaned against the mid-section of the bed. The insect chirping filled the silence.

"Sorry."

He felt Tai shrug in the darkness in response.

"You fought well today."

"So did you."

"I always fight well," she shrugged again. Then a pillow came crashing down on her head, knocking her baseball cap off and ruffling up her ponytail. Unseen by Kyle, a gentle smile spread across her face in the dark.

"You're so full of yourself," Kyle laughed as he pulled himself up to a sitting position.

She pulled the hair-tie off and let her long hair fall all over her shoulders again. Kyle watched as she gathered it all back up and tied it into a high pony tail, the image of her going from candle light to candle light at the Lin Gui village playing again in his head. He noticed her exposed neck, and then he looked away, feeling a little flushed in the face.

"You mere mortals always misinterpret truth for ego. I'm just stating facts." She put her baseball cap securely on again, pulling her pony-tail through the fastening hole in the back of the hat.

"Hey, I had a piece of that special peach pie, too, so I'm immortal now, like you."

"You wish."

"Whatever."

Kyle had the impulse to hit her on the head again with his pillow, but realized it might knock her hat off again, so he refrained. They sat for another moment of extended silence.

"So…uh, since we had a draw, what's the deal with the dance then?" Kyle asked, looking furtively at the back of her head.

"A draw nullifies the agreement. We go back to the original plan."

Kyle tried to remember what that was.

"Uh, what original plan?"

"I said I wasn't going."

Kyle couldn't help but feel a little crestfallen at her words even though he logically knew that she hadn't said that she didn't want to go with *him* specifically. She just didn't want to go to the dance itself. Period.

"You know, it might be fun if you give it a chance. It's not that bad."

She turned and gave him a look of disbelief.

"Okay, yeah, they're kind of boring. Matt's dragged me along to a lot of them. But dancing is fun, right?"

"Not that kind of dancing. Not for me anyway."

Kyle forgot he was talking to a professional dancer who had performed in front of draconian royalty.

"Girls seem to like dressing up for them…" Kyle began, thinking about Rose and her friends, but realized he was being an idiot since Tai clearly wouldn't find that at all fun. "So what do you like to do for fun?"

"Train."

"Besides that."

"Study."

"Besides studying. I mean, don't you ever just hang out?"

"Hang out?"

"Yeah, just spend time with friends."

"Sounds like a huge waste of time."

"Well, we're kind of 'hanging out' right now. Is it a waste of time?"

Tai thought about this for a moment. "Maybe."

Kyle laughed and shook his head.

"Look, it's Friday night. There's no school tomorrow. What do you usually do on Friday nights besides training and studying?"

Tai was quiet for a moment before she responded, "Once in a while I watch science fiction or horror shows on TV."

Something sparked in Kyle's head. "I got an idea. Come on, get out of my room, I need to change."

Tai went out into the hallway, and Kyle came out a few moments afterwards, dressed to go outside.

"Come on," he motioned to Tai. Kyle called to his mother, "Mom, can you give us ride to the mall?"

When they arrived at the busy, large white structure that housed all sorts of commercial units, Kyle and Tai got out, and Kyle poked his head back into the car and talked to his mother for a bit before she drove off. They walked in through glass doors, and Tai followed as Kyle headed toward the movie theater.

"Here we are," he announced. "Wow, I haven't been to a movie in like forever. What do you want to watch?" He looked up at the list of what was playing. He was a little surprised with himself. Here he was at the movies alone with a girl that he had invited to come. By traditional definitions, this was like a first date, but he'd spent so much time with

Tai, both alone and with others, that it didn't feel like anything in particular. It just felt natural.

"What's that one about?" Tai pointed to the movie title *Quantum Assassin.*

"Perfect. I saw the preview online. It's about a time traveling ninja."

"That sounds ridiculous."

"It's just a movie. It's just supposed to be fun."

Kyle purchased the tickets and soon they were off to theater eight for a twilight showing of their film of choice. In the dark, the two of them sat next to each other with their arms crossed. They watched quietly, fully immersed in the film. Sometimes Kyle was laughing, although he noticed Tai wasn't when he was. Occasionally he stole a look at her, and each time he did, he saw her looking intently at the big screen, as if she was trying to figure something out. After it was over, they exited and went back into the mall.

"Well, how did you like it?" Kyle asked.

"Unoriginal plot line, poor acting, overly dramatic camera work and editing, clichéd characters, and simplistic martial arts choreography. It was clear the actor who played the main part hasn't had any martial arts training. It was bad."

"Don't you mean awesomely bad?"

"Awesomely bad?"

"Yeah, like so bad that it's good."

"Is this a Daoist trick question?"

"No, I mean that you appreciate the movie because of its shortcomings. You can't watch a movie named *Quantum Assassin* and expect it to be *good* or take it seriously. So you watch it because you know it's going to be bad. Awesomely bad."

"I see, I think."

They started to walk around the mall while Kyle explained some more about how the bad parts of the movie made it good because they were bad. The high-ceilinged halls of the commercial catacombs that they walked through were brilliantly white with bright lights glittering everywhere. It wasn't until their discussion about the movie thinned out that they started to notice what lined the shimmering walls of commerce. Every shop that sold clothing, especially the ones that featured women's clothing, had a display of the popular line of fashion by the pop star named Kandi. The accessory shops featured her make up line as well. Shoe stores displayed the multi-color high-heeled shoes that were all the rage. Almost every available ad space in the building was covered with an image of her, and Kyle and Tai stopped at one of the larger ones.

"So this is the Kandi that everyone is talking about," Kyle mused out loud. On the large full-bodied ad poster, the pop star was winking with her brown, almond-shaped eyes, her silken black hair flowing about her shoulders in shiny curls. Her lips were a glossy bright red, and she had beautifully long eyelashes. Looking like she was somewhere in her late teens or early twenties, she wore a flirtatious short-skirted, red spaghetti-strapped dress that showed off her womanly figure. On her feet were lustrously bright red high heels. Her presentation had an exquisite mix of glamour and beauty with a touch of innocence. Under her name was the tagline:

Be as beautiful on the outside as you are on the inside!

"Do you think she's beautiful?"

Kyle turned to look at Tai, a bit startled by her direct question. He looked back at the poster. Kandi seemed the epitome of feminine beauty as he understood it. She was tall and thin with long legs and soft smooth hair. She exuded playful flirtation and alluring glamour all with a simple smile and wink of the eye. But he just didn't react to it the way he used to. He knew a few months ago, he would have been drawn to this image on a more emotional level, but today he looked at it more from the perspective of an observer than a participant.

"I…guess so," he answered uncertainly. Before they had a chance to discuss the issue further, they were interrupted.

"Tai! Kyle!" Jake's echoing voice reached them from down the hall.

Kyle's stomach sank. He wasn't happy to see Jake, but he tried not to show it.

"Hey Jake, what's up? What are you doing here?"

"Hey dude, are you two on a date here?"

"Huh? What? Us?" Kyle was put in another really awkward position. It was a double edged sword. Say yes and risk angering Tai. Say no and risk angering Tai. It was a lose-lose situation for him.

"We just went to go watch a movie," Tai answered unbothered.

"Yeah, just taking a break from routine, you know how it is," Kyle added, trying to sound natural and relaxed.

"Totally. Hey, what happened to you at practice? You like disappeared. Matt was looking all over for you."

"Well, I was feeling kind of out of it after the fight."

"For sure, man, for sure," Jake nodded, then turned his attention to Tai. "You were fighting the ultimate blooming rose of the martial arts world over here." Jake moved to put his large hand on her shoulder but Tai maneuvered herself out of his reach with a single and very natural looking leaning from one leg to the other. Jake's hand went through air. He seemed unbothered by what happened, thinking it was just a coincidence that she moved away at that moment. He looked up at the poster.

"I see you're checking out Kandi over here. Isn't she hot like there's no tomorrow?" Jake elbowed Kyle who nodded casually in polite agreement. "I heard she's having her first live concert soon."

"Oh yeah? That's cool," Kyle said, not really paying attention to Jake's banter because he was too busy wishing he would leave.

Jake looked around and then said, "Well, I gotta go. Got a sweet date waiting for me at the theater. Catch you two later." He gave Kyle another elbowing and then winked at Tai before he turned and took off toward the theater.

Kyle watched Jake's back for a moment as the tall, dark and handsome teenage boy headed away from them. He looked over at Tai who was also looking at Jake.

"What about you?" Kyle asked.

"What about what?" Tai asked.

"Do you think he's beautiful?" he asked with a wry smile, pointing to Jake.

Tai looked contemplatively back at Jake's shrinking figure.

"I'm not sure."

Kyle's ego felt like a whoopee cushion that just got sat on. He had been hoping for a flat out 'no' from Tai, so a 'maybe' was very disappointing to him. Despite this, he was able to ask, "What do you mean?"

"Well, for one, I don't think I really understand what beauty is yet. That and I think Jake is more confused than anything else."

The whoopee cushion partially re-inflated itself.

"Confused?"

"Yes."

"In what way?"

"I just don't get the sense that he knows who or what he is."

Kyle thought about this for a moment and then answered honestly, "I don't think I really know who or what I am either."

"You're still looking. Jake is like a lot of people; he's settled for an easy answer, so he isn't searching anymore."

"How do you know?"

Tai shrugged, "I don't know if I really *know* it. I'm just calling it as I see it. That's all."

They wandered around the mall some more, quiet most of the time. At one point, Kyle's hand had accidentally brushed against hers, and she pulled hers away instantly and shoved her hands in her pocket. He snuck a look at her face and then turned back towards the display windows of the stores. Then his gaze drifted down at the white floor as he wondered if he'd every measure up to Tai's standards.

Kyle's phone rang, and when he answered it, it was his mom, waiting at the front of the mall to pick them up. They hurried to meet her.

Chapter 39
Eye Kandi

"Dude, heard you were out on a date with Tai last Friday," Matt said to Kyle with a big smile plastered on his face.

"It wasn't a date. We just went to watch a movie."

"Alone, just the two of you?"

"Yeah, well, that's no big deal. I'm alone with her a lot anyway."

"Oh *really*?"

Kyle wanted to smack himself in the head. He was giving Matt too much ammunition.

"Look, Matt, you wouldn't understand why I'm always with her even if I explained it to you. You wouldn't *believe* me if I did."

"Try me."

"No way."

"Come on."

"Okay, fine. You asked for it," Kyle took a breath and then continued. "The truth is that Tai and I are warriors chosen to battle a demon that's going to wreak havoc and destruction on our world, and we've been spending a lot of time training together for it."

Matt gave him an incredulous look.

"Is it really that hard for you to just admit that you like her?"

Kyle threw his hands up in exasperation as he walked down the hallway with Matt early on a Monday morning, right before homeroom started. As he thought about girls in general and about liking them, he remembered his attraction to Rose and the incident at Phoenix Mountain. Then he realized that those feelings just weren't there anymore, that they had evaporated like a mist burned away by the morning sun. He looked over at his best friend, feeling remorse, and wanting to make things right. He felt he should tell Matt and apologize for his coveting, for his envy. But Kyle didn't feel this was the time and place, and instead he said,

"You know, come to think of it, I really don't like any girl in particular right now."

"That's because you've already got a girl," Matt said, giving him a shake of the head and wry smile. He gave Kyle a sure pat on the shoulder. "Look, I gotta head off to video broadcasting. I'm going on-air in five minutes. See ya in Chem."

"See ya."

As soon as Kyle walked into his homeroom, he immediately saw Tai and naturally made his way over to her and sat down in the empty seat next to her.

"Morning," he greeted.

"Morning," she nodded back. She was busy flipping through the pages of the biography of a well-known political figure.

"Is that for history class?" he inquired.

"No."

He should have known. Tai was always engaged in 'extracurricular' reading. He realized now her habit served two purposes. One was that she simply was just a voracious consumer of knowledge. The second was that her intense engagement in the reading activity deterred people from approaching her. He remembered what she had said about her peers being uninteresting company and of the observations of Jake she had shared with him the other day. He remembered what her mother had said about her. Despite becoming well-known at school, she still kept to herself, turning away from the social overtures of others. By all accounts, it seemed she was antisocial on purpose, but he couldn't imagine it being pleasant being at school day in and day out never interacting with anyone there. Then he wondered if she really *chose* not to talk to anyone or actually *couldn't* talk to anyone.

Turning his attention to the classmates around him, he suddenly felt an odd sense of distance from them. Like him, all of them were top students at the school. They were heavily involved in school activities and often in leadership positions and were highly eligible candidates for college, poised to succeed at the future profession of their choice. Nevertheless, he suddenly got the distinct sense that there was a lack of substance in everything he saw in them, as if they were all puppets dancing around to someone else's song with a false sense of purpose.

The clicking sounds of high heels against the floor suddenly got his attention again. He saw again the lusciously painted lips, the carefully styled hair, the flirtatiously designed clothing and accessories marked with 'K', all to imitate the sort of glamorous flirtatiousness he had seen in the poster ads at the mall of the pop star Kandi. There was a sort of desperation in their attempt to mimic the pop star, and the boys in the classroom gave their approval with interested smiles and garrulous attention to all the girls wearing the latest 'hot style'. He realized that what he used to find interesting and attractive now felt plastic and dull. He felt the make-up actually made the girls look like clowns, and the boys attracted to it all were like Pavlovian dogs, drooling at the sound of a bell.

He looked back at Tai, her eyes hidden in the shadow of a baseball cap, another way she blocked out her high school peers. Although she did a good job of blending in and going unnoticed before, now that people were aware of her, she was the one that clearly stood out from the rest, and that was another way of saying that she stood alone. He listened to the sound of her turning a page in her book. His girl? He looked away. Remembering the carbon copy of himself that they had fought at Phoenix Mountain, he felt again the distance between him and Tai. He wasn't the strong and confident warrior that Tai had wanted him to be. Hadn't she called him a disappointment that day?

The TV screen in their homeroom classroom flashed on, and to everyone's surprise, the pop star sensation Kandi's biggest hit single music video, *Eye Kandi*, started blasting out of the speakers, and the video started with a shot of Kandi's lusciously glossy red lips singing with a seductive mix of charisma, confidence, and innocence.

Listen
Time to show off my stuff
I'm an artist
A real diamond in the rough

The name's Kandi
Nothing like you've ever tasted
Start the party
Not a moment to be wasted

I'll show you
My many different flavors
If you'll give me
All I want to savor

I just want your love and devotion
To set our destiny in motion
Is it so bad that I want your heart?
Make it shine or break it apart?
Sweetening you up inside and out?
Come on n' see what Kandi's all about

Come on DJ start the mix
Come on get your Kandi fix

Kandi was dancing, moving with intense precision and enthralling style, her team of dancers mimicking her every move, falling out of line and coming back in sync with pristine isolations. Kandi was mesmerizing, and her dancers were like extensions of herself, enhancing her presence with every twist, sway, and turn. Kandi herself flirted with the viewer with body, mind, and soul.

Kyle watched, mesmerized. The movements with the beats of the music were intoxicating. Kandi's blushing cheeks, batting eyelashes, and glistening lips coupled with her sleek body and alluring hair evoked emotions that seeped through him from an internal source like a hormonal stimulant. She was assertive and attractive yet submissive and timid all at the same time.

As the video came to a close, Kyle became aware of everyone else's comatose staring at the TV screen, realizing he must have looked the same just a fraction of a second earlier. Then he realized Tai was staring straight at him. He looked over at her, into her eyes which looked out from under the rim of her baseball cap. She had a look of disappointment on her face he had never seen, and he looked away from her, down at the table, more than a little humiliated.

"Good morning boys and girls!"

Kyle and Tai's attention were both pulled back up to the TV screen by the clarion voice full of feminine charm. Their classmates started making exclamations.

"Is that really her?"

"It looks like it's her!"

"I can't believe this, is this for real?"

"She's *here*?"

"She hardly makes *any* public appearances!"

"This is bizarre!"

"No way! This is totally cool!"

On the TV screen was Kandi herself, apparently standing in the media broadcast center of their high school campus. In back of her was the usual broadcast stage they were used to seeing every day, with a wall covered in the red, white, and blue, their school colors painting out their school name and mascot.

"Kandi here wishing you all a sweet and delicious day!" she winked characteristically. "Now, you might be wondering what I'm doing at this quaint little suburban high school of yours. Well, I'll let you in on a little secret. I've got a huge crush on the hottest guy on this campus, and here to set me up with him is his best friend."

At this, Matt Lee walked onto camera with her. It was Matt, but he didn't seem right. He was staring at the camera with glassy eyes, as if he had fallen asleep with his eyes open, but he appeared to be able to move with no problems although he seemed subdued overall. He didn't say anything and just stared blankly forward. Kyle went into utter shock and his whole body went numb. The ground seemed to fall out from under him.

"Kyle Lin, if you're out there, which I'm sure you are, I still remember our sweet first kiss. It seems like you've forgotten all about me, though, since you've been fooling around with that other girl. You're such a naughty little playboy, breaking my heart like that. Just to give you a little reminder that I'm still here pining away for you, I'm gonna give you a little punishment for neglecting me. See ya soon babe!"

A glowing horizontal line seemed to burn itself across the TV screen as if it was being carved there by a knife, and then five more strokes of light appeared simultaneously below it.

死

It was the Chinese character for 'death' written in qi script. Too engrossed in watching the TV, no one noticed as Kyle suddenly blurred out of sight, and almost immediately afterwards, Tai did as well. But just before she went into hyper speed using her qi script, she caught a glimpse of an invisible force demolishing holes through the red-bricked walls between their classroom and the media broadcast building as the other students sat helplessly confused, unable to understand what was happening around them.

As Tai launched out of her seat after Kyle, everything around her slowed down to a halt. All the students looked like mannequins, frozen in time as she ran past them, following Kyle's path of destruction through demolished school walls and broken classroom furniture. Miraculously, he had left the people unscathed as she pressed on after him. Dust clouds literally hung thick in the air because they were still slowly falling. As she ran, a million thoughts flooded through her mind. The First Child Demon had been all around them this whole time, and Tai silently screamed at herself over not picking up on the scent earlier. And now the demon had made her first move. The qi script for death they saw on the television screen could only mean she was going to kill Matt…if she hadn't done so already. When Tai came near the media center, she heard Kyle before she saw him.

"WHERE ARE YOU DEMON!"

The media center was no more. Its remains floated in the air as suspended debris. The remains of brick, wood, and machine seemed to float in midair. Kyle had annihilated the building in his search of Matt. He flung around wildly at the pieces that were still falling slowing to the earth, and each time he touched a piece with his flailing fists, it sped up in the direction it was hit, and then floated to a near stop as it was resynchronized with the normal flow of speed.

"Kyle!"

Tai barely had a chance to look into his angry, glowing eyes before she noticed through the suspended dust what character glowed on his forehead.

摜

It was the Chinese character for 'smash'. Kyle was attacking her, and had she not reacted out of pure survival instinct, she might have joined the mess of debris.

盾

With the qi script for 'shield', she conjured up the protection just in the nick of time to block his onslaught, but the force of his attack still threw her off her feet, and she flew back more than a few yards. The throw knocked some air out of her. As she shakily stood up, she shook her head to recover from the shock, but the next thing she knew, Kyle had grabbed her by the throat and had lifted her up in the air with a physical strength she had never seen in him before.

"WHERE IS HE?!" he screamed at her. Her hands came up to hold on to the hand that held her by the throat.

"Kuh…Kyle…" was all she could manage to choke out. But it was enough. The anger on his face collapsed as he realized what he was doing, and he lowered her to the ground. Tai coughed and choked as she breathed again, and Kyle fell to his knees, pressing his fingers against his skull as if he were trying to hold it together and keep it from exploding.

"No no no no no no no no no no…" he whispered to himself as if saying the word repeatedly could change the reality of everything that had just happened. Tears started streaming uncontrollably down his

cheeks. It was heartbreaking to watch.

Tai dropped to her knees with him.

"Kyle, if she used qi script to…we can use qi script to bring him back…" Tai offered weakly. But she looked around and could see nothing. There was no way of knowing in which direction Matt had been taken. The First Child demon had thought this through. Yes, if she had killed Matt using qi script, they could possibly revive him with qi script, but every moment that passed lessened the possibility of this happening.

"I can't…I can't find him. I can't…It's all my fault…" Kyle sobbed helplessly, an internal, high-pitch screaming ringing in his ears, in his mind. Tai could only sit there powerlessly and watch him grieve. Then he suddenly collapsed, falling forward, drained by the explosion of qi script he had just used, and she caught him in her arms.

Chapter 40

Blame

Kyle awoke from a dreamless sleep, disoriented and groggy. It was night time and dark, and the shades were drawn on the window, blocking whatever light was outside from coming in. He turned his head and felt unfamiliarity with the bed he was on. This wasn't his bed. This wasn't his room. He sat up to get off, and a slightly metallic creaking filled the silent and cold room. Something rolled across the floor, and he felt a slight tugging of something attached to his wrist. His bare foot touched the cold, carpetless floor as he fully got off the bed.

"Kyle? Oh thank goodness you're awake!"

He turned to the sound of the voice.

"Mom?"

A lamp clicked on, filling the room with a subdued yellow light.

She came up to him and embraced him.

Kyle looked around still confused, seeing faded green curtains, the stack of cards and flowers on a worn old stand by the hospital bed, and a small cushioned chair that his mother had apparently been sitting on. A needle was in his wrist, its full length embedded in one of his veins, and it was held firmly in place by some clear tape. Kyle looked at it, and his eyes followed a long tube attached to the needle that led to a large, hanging transparent plastic bag full of clear fluid. It was an IV. He realized he was in a hospital room.

Then all the memories of what happened flooded back into his mind, and Kyle felt a massive singularity forming in the heart of his soul as all the pain and grief threatened to drown his spirit for good. His first reaction was defensive: denial.

"Mom," tears welling up in his eyes, "Why am I in the hospital?"

He covered his face with his hands as if he could block out reality like that. He wanted her to tell him that he had just eaten something bad and that it had all been a nightmare.

"I was just about to leave for work Monday morning when Tai suddenly showed up on our doorstep carrying you on her back. You had lost consciousness. You've been out for over three days. We were so worried."

Kyle waited in dreadful silence for her to finish.

"I'm so sorry Kyle…they…they found Matt's body on his front lawn…He's…he's dead," his mother was barely able to say through a quavering voice as she was overcome by grief for Matt and the suffering of her only son.

His knees went weak again, and he couldn't stand anymore. He fell to his knees, the IV on the metal stand clattering to the floor near the bed. The events of the last few months rushed through his mind like a torrent of madness—the Crossover, the Lin Gui, Phoenix Mountain, the First Child Demon…in his mind everything fell into place and led step by step up to Matt's death. He would never forgive himself.

"It's all my fault Mom…"

His mother embraced him.

"Don't say that. There's nothing you could have done."

But Kyle knew that was not at all true. The warmth and love of his mother's embrace broke him down completely and he was crying out the full extent of his pain, his body convulsing as it was ravaged by the anguish of loss and remorse. His fingers were crushing into his skull, as if only that held his mind together.

Outside in the dark hallway, Tai sat on a small, thinly cushioned bench with a small laptop open in her hands as she listened silently to Kyle's grief with sad, glistening eyes.

The next morning, Kyle was wearing a black suit and sitting at the front row of a spacious chapel with a ceiling made of wood beams that crisscrossed in a mesmerizing pattern. The air inside was cold, and the gentle browns of the walls, wooden pews, and large floor tiles were soothing. The front of the chapel was made almost completely of glass, giving a full, three-story high view of cumulus clouds floating through a cerulean sky. It was like a gateway to heaven. At the base of this was a dark coffin, and in it was Matt's body. He lay there in a black suit, his high school basketball jersey folded and neatly placed next to him, a favorite childhood stuffed animal tucked in on the other side. Matt looked like he was just sleeping there, as if his almond shaped brown eyes would flutter open at any minute and he would sit up and start being as friendly as he'd always been. But he lay there, still and silent. The large chapel was filled, so much so that there were even people filling up the extra folding chairs placed to extend the pews and others were piling up in the balcony above. Everyone there was shell-shocked by Matt's death, which was compounded by the strange circumstances of his passing. Kyle was numb inside and out, as if blocking out all feeling could block out the reality around him.

As Kyle sat with his parents, his grandfather came up and calmly took a seat next to him before the ceremony began.

"Kyle," he said, "I'm so sorry."

"You should be!" Kyle snapped back in a quiet rage. "If you hadn't taken me to Asia, none of this would have ever happened! Why couldn't you have just left me alone?"

Through Kyle's mind swam all the what-ifs and could-have-beens, the normal life he could have continued to lead if the Crossover hadn't happened, if he had just stayed at home, if he had just been less gullible…or stronger…

His grandfather was silent for a while in response to his beloved grandson's outburst. He was stung by Kyle's anger and words, but he also understood.

"Kyle," he spoke quietly yet steadily, "The demon would have found a way into this world eventually. Don't blame yourself for this."

Ah-gong placed a hand on Kyle's shoulder, but Kyle violently shrugged it away. His grandfather heaved a heavy sigh, and then stood up to leave, knowing his presence would only serve to aggravate his grandson in this time of grief.

"Don't lose sight of what you need to do. I have to travel again. The Tian Yi Society is in an uproar." Ah-gong left, looking weary and old.

Kyle felt both glad his grandfather was gone and guilty at the same time. He knew deep inside that he was taking it out on Ah-gong, but he was still drowning in blame and felt compelled to share it. It was too much to bear on his own.

When the ceremony and presentation had finished and people had had a chance to line up and see Matt one last time before the coffin was closed, the event was moved outside to the plot of land where Matt was to be buried. On the way out, Kyle saw Tai standing just outside the door of the chapel, wearing black slacks and a black blouse with long sleeves, her hair tied back high up on her head with no baseball cap on. The sight of her was too much for him to bear. She represented everything that had happened to turn Kyle's world upside down, a change that had led to the death of his best friend Matt. Tai was looking right at him, and their eyes met for a fraction of a second. Then he looked down and away from her. He said nothing to her, walking by her as if she had nothing to do with him.

On the open hillside, the bright and sunny weather over cheerfully green grass belied the dark grief that threatened to burst inside Kyle like a gluttonous sac of poisonous bile. He lined up with the others to place a rose on Matt's closed coffin, and then he looked on wordlessly as the coffin was lowered into the open ground. After it all, people remained, milling around a bit, and with a few last goodbyes to Matt's grief-stricken family, Kyle and his parents started heading for their car.

"Kyle?"

He didn't want to turn around, but he did. It was Rose. She was in a black dress with sunglasses, her black, slightly heeled shoes clopping across the ground, the sound grating against Kyle's ears like fingernails scratching on a chalkboard.

"We'll meet you at the car," his mother said, giving his arm a reassuring squeeze.

Kyle noticed the light pink lipstick on Rose's lips, and he gave them a look of contempt. Holding a large and brown paper shopping back to her chest, Rose was taken aback by the intensity of the hate that just flashed across his face. Then as that look quickly passed, another replaced it, one of great remorse. Kyle was silent as Rose spoke.

"Kyle," she tried to muster a weak smile that trembled here and there, threatening to break into a sob, but she kept composed to deliver her message and her package, "Matt and I got this for you. It was supposed to be your Christmas gift. He picked it out. Here, open it."

She handed the paper bag to him. Kyle unrolled the folded top of the bag and found that there was a large white shoebox inside. Pushing the shoebox lid off while it was still in the bag, he reached into it and pulled out a pair of black basketball high tops with red trim. They were the latest, most stylish top-of-the-line shoes for basketball, the ones that Matt had had. Without a word, Kyle took off the black loafers he wore and slid his feet into the new shoes, putting his loafers into the shoe box. He tied each shoelace firmly.

"How do they fit?" Rose asked.

"Perfectly."

Rose smiled. Kyle couldn't look into her eyes. He stared down at his new shoes.

"Rose…there was something I wanted to tell Matt, to apologize to him for…"

Her smile faded and it was replaced with a look of concern. She could see that Kyle was barely able to compose himself.

"Yes?" she said in the most comforting, encouraging voice she could.

"I've always been jealous of Matt…he always seemed to have everything I didn't have…and I always wanted what he had…including you. I wanted to apologize to him, but I…can't now. So I wanted to apologize to you."

A few tears stole their way down his cheek, sincere and heartbreaking.

Rose had no words to comfort him with, but she lifted her arms and embraced him. He let himself be held, feeling the regret so deeply he thought it would kill him as it hollowed him from the inside out.

As she pulled away from him, she mustered another weak smile.

"You guys really are the best of friends," Rose gave him a squeeze on the shoulder. "Every moment of your life is a gift, Kyle. Don't waste it."

As Kyle stood there in silence, still staring at his new sneakers, Rose's words rippled through his mind, filling his consciousness, and a sense of urgency flooded through him. He suddenly looked up at Rose but then looked past her and saw Tai standing alone by a tree silhouetted against the blue sky. The look on her face surprised him. She looked…hurt. And then she was gone, as if she hadn't been there. He blinked, almost wondering if he had imagined her there.

"Tai."

Rose wanted to smile at the sound of him saying her name, knowing how happy Matt would have been if he had been standing there with her, but there was a worry in Kyle's voice that made her respond otherwise.

"What's wrong?"

"I don't know, I thought I just saw her. And she looked…upset."

Suddenly, Rose remembered what Tai had said to her right before the winter formal poster ordeal. It clicked in place for Rose that Tai had known about Kyle's feelings for her. Then she realized that Tai had probably just watched her giving Kyle a present and hugging him.

"Kyle, we've got to find her." Rose spun around, and the two of them searched the quickly diminishing crowd for her but found no sign of her at all. He pulled out his cell phone and pressed the speed dial to Tai's number. It rang, and rang, and rang some more. No one picked up. He tried again, with no luck. He began to text her.

where r u? -Kyle

He tried calling again. This time, the phone rang only twice before someone picked up.

"Hello?"

It wasn't Tai's voice; it was Cindy.

"Hi, Dr. Tan, this is Kyle."

"I'm so sorry about your friend, Kyle."

"Yes."

"Is the funeral over?"

"Yes, yes it is."

"I guess Tai forgot her cell phone at home. I heard it ringing in her room and picked up. I could have sworn I saw her take it with her this morning. You wouldn't happen to know where she is?"

"I was going to ask you the same thing."

"That's strange...She's supposed to bring you here. Jade and Snow are waiting here for the both of you. They have some important information to share with you. You have my number yes? Call me when you find her."

As he hung up, Rose looked at him expectantly and asked, "Any luck?"

"No. She left her phone at home."

The floodgates of Kyle's emotions were fully open, and so many intense thoughts and feelings arose in his consciousness, but two conflicting ones stood at the forefront. He had an intense ache to be where Tai was, be with her wherever she was, to know she was safe, and only her presence could quench this thirst. Contrasting with this yearning he had never known before was another extreme emotion—a seething dark hate boiling up inside him that could only be soothed with the ecstasy of vengeance. His existence now had only two objectives, to find Tai and to kill the First Child Demon. Although he greatly desired to do the latter first and on his own, his concern for Tai's safety took precedence. If the First Child was to target anyone else next, it seemed it would most likely be Tai. He turned to Rose. She had a right to know, regardless of whether or not she'd believe the truth.

"Rose, Matt was murdered, and Tai could be next."

Rose's eyes widened with surprise, but the seriousness on Kyle's face told her this was no sick joke. She didn't understand what was going on, but she knew she had to act.

"I'll alert the girls." Flipping open her pink phone, she sent a mass text out to all the girls on the cheer squad to be on a look out for Tai. Kyle realized how handy it was having the resources of a tight network available.

code RED grls. We need 2 find Tai ASAP! –Rose

Immediately, she got a series of texts back.

saw her @ chapel but not after. –Robin

im on my way 2 mall. will look 4 her. –Kyra

dont no where she is. wat happened? –Mandy

maybe at school?? @ home. will look 4 her.
–Soo

just got 2 library. dont c her here. - Mercedes

"Where could she be?" Rose showed Kyle the messages.

"If you and the girls can check those other places, I'm going to go home with my parents first. There might be a slight chance that she's there. Then I'm going over to her house. I have a feeling that we won't find Tai anywhere nearby..."

"I don't understand Kyle. Matt was murdered? By who? Why?"

"You saw it didn't you? On the school broadcast system. Kandi."

"What? But on the news they confirmed it was an imposter. Kandi had an alibi. She was preparing for her live concert. There were witnesses."

Kyle shook his head. It's possible the First Child demon was only imitating the popular celebrity, but Kyle remembered his first encounter with her in the cave back at Phoenix Mountain, her vanity mirror surrounded by makeup, the image of Kandi on the poster, the music video and the song itself, and it was all enough to give him the gut feeling that this 'pop star' Kandi was the First Child Demon herself.

"Kandi *is* the imposter. No, it was her. I'm sure of it."

"But how do you know…?"

Kyle looked at Rose and cringed. Matt's death was really his fault. He had Crossed into the other world. He had let the First Child Demon get the best of him, and she was here because of him. She had killed Matt because Matt was his best friend. A dark look spread across his face that both scared Rose and made her sad. Innocence was lost.

"I'll explain everything to you. Come on."

Chapter 41

A Score to Settle

Kyle stepped into his house as the sound of his parents driving off to work faded behind him. The cool quiet of his home was somewhat soothing, but the rage and anxiety inside him still burned strong.

"Tai?" he called out.

He was sure she wasn't here, but he couldn't help but hope she was. He went straight up to his room. He opened the door, wishing that Tai was there, sitting by his bed the way she had been just a few days ago, but his room was empty and quiet, his Liquid Blade glimmered expectantly against the wall. He quickly changed into workout clothes, long blue track pants with red stripes running down the side of the legs under a plain white t-shirt, and then slung the sword over his back, his modern American clothes contrasting with the ancient Chinese weapon. Writing a quick note to his parents and leaving it on the kitchen counter, he whispered a quick sorry to them because he knew he was about to be a source of worry yet again. Kyle rushed to Tai's house.

When he arrived, the first thing he asked Snow and Jade was, "Is her Soaring Staff here?"

"No, we looked for it when you called and we found out she was missing. She must have slipped by us," Snow said.

Jade began, "We think that she-"

But Kyle finished for him, "-went after the First Child on her own."

The missing Soaring Staff confirmed that without a question. Tai wasn't one to sit around wallowing, doing nothing. She had taken matters into her own hands. *Damn it Tai. Why are you so stubborn?*

"Where?" Kyle asked.

"We don't know," Jade responded.

"We've been scouring the internet and media since Monday trying to find something. We've even made inquiries to the company producing Kandi and visited office locations, but there're no leaks on her whereabouts. All we have to go on is the public announcement that this Kandi will be having her first public concert tonight, but we don't know where. It's some kind of publicity stunt. They released four possible locations for the concert, San Francisco, Las Vegas, New York, and Miami. Supposedly it's part of the 'hype marketing' surrounding Kandi, but we think it's just the First Child's way of making things harder for us," Snow said, putting a worried hand to a furrowed brow. "Tai's been searching on the internet for leaks on the concert, too, so we don't know if she found something that she hasn't shared with the rest of us. Did anything happen? Why would she leave without us? It's suicide."

"I'm not sure, but I think she's upset with me. I haven't really been…available," Kyle admitted.

"Understandably," Jade said heavily. He figured it prudent to say nothing more than that about Matt's death at that moment. "Well, we have to figure out where to go. I don't think it's a good idea to split and go to all four cities. I'll whisk all of us there as soon as we know."

"Tell me what I have to do."

Kyle couldn't help but regret asking that because he was assigned to do reconnaissance through watching entertainment television. Nothing could be more frustrating than being forced to sit in front of a television set watching inane entertainment gossip reporting when he was in the perfect mood to go out there and kick some demon butt. The entertainment channel was flashing in front of him on the large flat screen TV in Tai's home, maddening him with gossip about pointless minute details of the lives of celebrities. More than ever, he could care less about who spilled coffee on whom and who was caught on camera doing something scandalous.

He did, however, pay attention, when there was any mention of Kandi. He wanted to know everything he could about her, so that he could destroy her from the inside out. He sat at the edge of his seat when a major A-list actor came on, talking about Kandi.

"Devon Blair, we've heard rumors that you and Kandi are an item now. Is it true?" a female reporter asked, thrusting a microphone in his face at a red carpet event while the camera cued in on the handsome and attractive young actor. About five other pairs of cameras and microphones lined up to catch the juicy news. Devon raised his hands in a gesture of surrender, his gorgeous hazel eyes sparkling with the lights of fame as he flashed a perfect smile. A few locks of his sensuous auburn hair brushed across his face.

"What can I say? I can't hide it. I'm in love. Kandi is the most brilliant, intelligent, and drop-dead gorgeous artist on the face of this planet. No man can resist her, and I'm lucky enough to have her sweet eyes on me right now. All I want is her love and devotion, to set our destiny in motion," Devon said in a corny, lovesick reference to Kandi's hit pop song. He exited off camera, and the reporter took her position.

"You heard it here first folks. Hollywood heart-throb Devon Blair is head-over-heels for pop sensation Kandi. This is Kristine Mercado on Gossip Hollywood."

Kyle leaned back in the couch in disgust. Occasionally a commercial for Kandi's products would flash across the screen, and Kyle had to refrain from throwing the remote controller he had in his hand at the TV. Awhile later, a special program came on. A young woman with long black hair and brown eyes wearing a revealing red suit sat at a clear glass table with a series of large screen TVs behind her.

"Now bringing you special coverage of the highly anticipated first concert by pop-sensation Kandi. Publicists had previously released to

the media that the concert could potentially be put on in four locations: New York, Miami, San Francisco or Las Vegas. News update is that Los Angeles, Washington D.C., San Diego, Chicago, and Austin have been added to the list. This brings the total of potential concerts up to nine locations. The fans at the new cities on the list are ecstatic. Tickets for all event locations were sold out as soon as they went on sale. The concert will be broadcast live to all the cities. Cameras have also been set up at each concert venue with the announcement that a direct feed of the video footage will be going to Kandi herself. It's a chance to have an audience with Kandi, easily the hottest celebrity in the world right now. Fans have already started gathering at each of these cameras to show their love and devotion to their pop star darling, many of them sporting her clothing or make-up line and blasting her music."

Behind her a series of images of massive crowds of people filled each of the large TVs. The view zoomed in on one of them.

"I LOVE YOU KANDI! YOU'RE SO AMAZING!"

"YOUR MUSIC IS SO AWESOME!"

"YOUR LOOK HAS CHANGED MY LIFE!"

"KANDI!"

"THANK YOU FOR MAKING ME BEAUTIFUL!"

As the screen showed footage from the different cities, the fans were screaming at the top of their lungs in full hysterics. A cold shiver ran up Kyle's spine. The First Child had only been in this world a short time and already she had infiltrated the consciousness of almost every sentient being on the planet. It didn't make any sense. He thought that as a demon she would want something like world domination or mass murder and destruction, instigate wars or carry out genocide. Why a pop idol of all things? It seemed like such a benign position to take compared to all the options available to a powerful being, and yet the screaming and totally entranced hordes of fans showed him there was a powerful side to something as seemingly harmless as a pop star idol. He had no idea what this could mean, but he knew it wouldn't be anything good.

"We'll be back soon to bring you another update on this hot event."

Kyle closed his eyes, trying to calm himself. He couldn't lose control, especially not when he had qi script power at his disposal. After all that training with Tai, the qi script was so tied to his consciousness now that it was volatile, susceptible to his change in mood, emotion or thought, as his destruction of his high school buildings had shown. If he didn't keep himself under mental control, who knows what he would destroy next. Pulverizing the neighborhood wasn't going to help him find Tai or the First Child Demon. He had to control his mind, quiet it so that he could focus, concentrate, and prepare. His hands reached out involuntarily, his left grabbing onto a backpack full of supplies for the journey, his right grabbing on the Liquid Blade. It was torture not being able to *do* something.

His phone rang.

"Hello?"

"Hello, Kyle?"

"Yeah, Rose."

"Any luck finding Tai?"

"No."

"Are you still at her house?"

"Yes."

"I'm outside. Can you open the door for us?"

Us? Kyle wondered who else could be there. He went to the front door and opened it to find Rose and her five best friends from the cheer squad all wearing long blue track pants striped in red along the side of the leg and zipped up in matching jackets with the words 'WARRIORS', their school mascot, printed across their chests in large white letters.

Their faces were uncovered, no longer hidden behind a layer of makeup. The most surprising member of the group was Jake, who wore track pants with a basketball jersey. Kyle gave Jake an openly hostile look that surprised everyone, especially Jake. They had long been accustomed to the timid and reserved Kyle. The young man of raw emotion that stood before them was a Kyle they had never seen before.

"What are you all doing here?"

"We want to help. Jake was with me," Kyra answered, feeling she had to speak for Jake given Kyle's adverse reaction to his presence.

"Yeah, Matt was my friend, too," Jake said with sincerity.

Kyle looked at Rose.

"I explained what's going on to them."

Kyle raised a questioning eyebrow with a severe look in a way at them that reminded them all of the way Tai looked at people she was criticizing.

"And you all believe her?"

"We don't know what to believe, Kyle," Robin said honestly.

"Yeah, but we're a team," Mandy added, "and we're going to stand by Rose. She trusts you, and we've got her back."

"Besides, we all saw the video on the school broadcasting system," Mercedes added.

"Yeah, I can't even look at my Kandi merch without feeling sick now," Soo shivered.

The girls all nodded in agreement.

"Well, there's not much we can do now…" Kyle said with great frustration.

"Kyle! Look behind you!" Rose exclaimed.

Kyle turned around, not sure of what to expect, but there was no demon there, no Yehren, just the TV. On it were crowds and crowds of ecstatic people. Kyle, Jake, and the cheerleaders crowded in.

"I repeat! Kandi has just arrived at Phoenix Mountain, the newest, hottest, and most expensive and luxurious hotel in Las Vegas, opened by Kandi herself! I repeat! Kandi is in Las Vegas!" the news reporter announced with glee.

"Snow! Jade!" Kyle called out and the two quickly came from the study to join them all. Tai's mother and father also came into the living room from the kitchen, and all eyes were expectantly on the television as the camera zoomed in on a limousine that had just pulled up to a red carpet. Police forces and large security personnel in yellow shirts were lined up on both sides of the carpet creating a human wall that held back a flood of fans, flashing cameras, and microphones. The limousine door opened and out stepped the dancers from the music video. After about a dozen of them had come out, Kandi followed with red high-heeled shoes coming out first, and when the rest of her emerged, she was as gorgeous and flirtatious as ever, wearing a lustfully red Chinese silken qipao or cheong-sam, the tight-fitting and sleeveless kind that was a hybrid east-west exotic fashion created when Europe held her spheres of influence on China's shores. Kandi waved and winked, smiled and threw her silken black curls of hair around her shoulders as the crowd went wild, almost breaking through the security lines. Devon Blair stepped out after her and held his arm out for her. As she slipped her arm onto his, the dancers formed a protective wall around the couple, all of them wearing qipao dresses that matched Kandi's, except theirs were pink. All of the dresses were slit high up their legs, seductively exposing the sides of their thighs and long legs.

The camera flashes and yells from the crowd were nonstop as Kandi and her entourage reached the white backdrop covered in sponsor logos a few steps away, and suddenly there was a scream in the crowd and all the girls, including Kandi herself, looked up calmly, unperturbed by what had caused the scream. A figure in all black suddenly jumped over the mob, launching herself across and off of the shoulders of the unsuspecting crowd, running over the people like an insect across a pond of water, and then it came crashing down right in the center of the pop star's entourage, aiming a large silver staff at Kandi. The dancers and the diva, however, stepped aside out of harm's way in perfect unison, as if they had been expecting the attack all along. Devon Blair was saved only because he had been pulled out of the way by Kandi. Missing its target, the staff smashed deafeningly into the ground, ripping the red carpet.

The attacking assassin lifted the silver staff with a battle cry and began to twirl it and strike in all directions at the dancers that were now closing in, preventing the dark figure from coming close to Kandi who backed away with an amused smile on her face. The dancers jumped and dodged the strikes of the silver staff and soon got close enough to neutralize the attacker, first by grabbing hold of and pulling away the staff and then pinning the assaulting arms to the figure's side. Kandi came up to the now captive assassin and pulled off the black face mask revealing Tai's face which was showed clearly on the news camera. Tai struggled to get out of the grip, but there were hands that pinned her arms behind her and others on her shoulder holder her at bay. Her attempts to kick were met with painful jabs by the dancers knees and elbows into her ribs. There were too many of them and they were apparently too strong for her. Kyle watched as her eyes seemed to glimmer with a light as she attempted to use qi script, but another elbow to the ribs caused the light to go out as she cried out in pain. Her head hung as she tried to recover from the shock. She breathed hard, her eyes full of fire as she tried to fight off the pain in order to focus. Kyle's fingers twitched as he tried hard to compose himself.

"Well, well, here all by yourself are you?" Kandi said on camera with a smirk on her face. Tai looked up, visibly upset by Kandi's snide little comment, her face twisted up in anger and hate as she continued to breathe hard from the pain of the blows she'd just received.

"Are you alright ma'am?" one of the security guards asked Kandi. The fans, reporters, and security were clearly all very anxious over what was happening.

"Yes, yes, just fine. No need to worry everyone," Kandi said, looking into the cameras that were all pointed at her, flashing a gorgeous smile as her cascading black curls bounced playfully, "this is just a little stunt to promote a new movie project I'll be working on."

Her words caused the whole crowd to relax.

"Let me introduce you to my supporting actress. Tai, say hello to your new adoring fans," Kandi said smiling sweetly.

"MURDERER!" Tai was able to yell in between gasping breaths, and she received a punch in the stomach which caused her to cry out in pain again, but the fierceness on her face was not knocked out.

The audience looked to Kandi for guidance. "Always in character," Kandi laughed. "Tai's a real professional actress. I only want the best for my artistic endeavors." She winked at the crowd who, though they all thought the punches seemed pretty real, all preferred the easier path of following along with what Kandi was saying. The reporters quickly got to work.

"When is this new film coming out Kandi?"

"What is it called?"

"Devon Blair, will you be in the film, too?"

Amidst the questions, Tai was dragged away.

A hand on Kyle's shoulder tore his eyes away from the screen. It was Tai's adoptive father. Kyle looked up at his large, muscular form and noticed that he had two broad swords slung over his back. He handed him the white porcelain jar and the willow branch that had been gifts from the Goddess of Mercy. Kyle put them away in his backpack.

"Las Vegas. Target confirmed. Come on, let's go rescue my daughter."

They all filed out into the front yard. The daylight had mostly faded away, leaving a dark blue sky that was quickly turning black.

"How are we going to get there?" Robin asked. "Drive or fly?"

"Fly," Kyle answered, "but not in a plane."

"What?" Robin said.

"Just watch."

The cheerleaders and Jake watched as Coach Yu, or Jade, as everyone seemed to be calling him, suddenly stepped out onto the small suburban black asphalt road that was wide enough to let two cars pass by each other with plenty of room to spare. His black hair now looked more green, and his eyes glimmered like emerald gems, making the high school students wonder if the dull, yellow street lamplights that lit the street weren't playing tricks on their eyes. He was shirtless while wearing a sleek and slick long green jacket tonight, not the sporty clothes they were used to seeing him in. Out of his pocket, he pulled out a large pearl, and without warning, he turned and threw the pearl right at the group. The uninformed high school students lifted their arms up protectively, expecting to be hit by the huge pearl, but when nothing made contact with their arms, they all lowered them and found that they were trapped inside a large glass sphere.

"What…what's going on?" Kyra asked bewildered.

"Don't worry, we're safe in here," Kyle reassured her. "Don't be afraid by what you are about to see either."

The girls and Jake all looked at Kyle and then followed his gaze towards Jade whose body was starting to elongate in a sickening way. They could see that his bones were growing and rearranging themselves in a way that looked immensely painful. The coat morphed into scales. Before long, he took the shape of what looked like a long and massive snake.

"Wh…what is he?" Mandy said with fear.

"He's a dragon," Kyle said firmly, "taking on his true form."

They all turned to look at Kyle and Snow.

"Don't worry," Snow said with an understanding look. "Kyle and I are both human."

To their terror, the large reptilian creature with eyes facing forward and flowing flesh strands extending from his face turned towards them, opened its mouth, and took the clear sphere they were trapped in into its bone-crushing jaws, his dagger sharp teeth making a ghastly ring around them. They couldn't help gasping or letting out a squeal of fear as this happened, but then the falling away of the ground as they were suddenly lifted up into the sky stunned them into a frightened silence. After a few moments of adjustment, they all calmed down and noticed the grim expressions of Kyle and the adults, and they sat down as if to catch their mental breath from the shocking events that had just occurred. The twinkling lights of Los Angeles County rolled away beneath them, and very soon they had gone over the mountains and were floating above dark lands. Above them, the starlight was revealed, an infinite ocean of diamonds in the deep black sky.

Some of the girls started to crouch down and huddle near each other. Rose remained standing next to Kyle.

"So it's true, isn't it?" she said, now fully buying into Kyle's tale of other worlds and demons and qi power. "Kandi, she's really a demon, and she's the one who murdered Matt."

Kyle's fists gripped so tightly his knuckles went white.

"Yes."

Rose closed her eyes, squeezing out a few tears of anger and grief. She let them slide down her cheeks. Her bright blue eyes opened with a look of determination.

"Then I've got a score to settle with her." Kyle nodded.

Chapter 42

An Artist's Monologue

Tai sat with her head bowed in a room of excess and opulence. It was the presidential suite of the newest, most expensive hotel in Vegas opened by Kandi herself and properly named Phoenix Mountain. Everything in the spacious accommodations shined with a golden glint. The couch she sat on was upholstered in a silky white fabric made gold by the lighting.

There were mirrors everywhere to amplify the effect. Some walls were completely covered in mirrors while others had large, picture-framed mirrors hanging on them. The tables and counters were lined with small mirrors of all shapes and sizes standing or lying flat. Tai was sick of seeing reflections of herself, so she looked down in her lap, where there were no mirrors. She was no longer wearing her black assassin clothes. Instead, she wore a pink qipao dress that matched the ones the back-up dancers wore. Her hair had been let down, and it flowed about her shoulders like a shiny black silk fabric.

Kandi walked into the living room from the bedroom carrying a medium-sized pink box with tiny "Ks" covering it in an intricate pattern. Tai did not look up as the First Child Demon sat gracefully next to her on the couch and placed the pink box on the coffee table in front of Tai.

"Men are so fickle, aren't they?" Kandi said sweetly. She started to undo the latches on the pink box and opened it to reveal a collection of make-up and jewelry all marked with the letter "K". The lid flipped up to reveal yet another mirror. "This is one of my best selling products, the Kandi Beauty Core. I'm going to make you as beautiful on the outside as you are on the inside, Tai."

The demon removed a small jar of foundation make-up. She

reached out and lifted Tai's head with a little pressure from her fingers under Tai's chin, and then she began to dot the perfectly matched foundation over Tai's face with her finger tip. Next she used a small, circular sponge to smooth out the coloration evenly on Tai's face. Pulling out implement after implement, she worked on Tai's eyes, then her cheeks, and finally she held a slender, golden tube in her hand and pulled off its cover revealing a bright red lipstick.

"You don't need him. When I'm done with you, you'll have men falling at your feet begging for your attention. You'll forget all about that puny little boy when you've got all the hottest guys at your beck and call." Kandi began to apply the red lipstick. "You'll see. You and I are going to have so much fun together. Like BFFs. Right?"

Outside in the sky above soared the Dragon Prince Jade as he approached Las Vegas from over rolling mountains black and blue from the night, the silhouette of his massive, serpentine body crossing the full moon with the large crystal sphere in his powerful jaws glowing in the moonlight. Kyle looked down as the glowing city drew near; its glimmering lights and massive gleaming buildings looked like luminescent gems jutting out of the flat and dark desert floor. He and his parents had gone to Las Vegas on many occasions ever since he could remember. His memories of the place were filled with bright lights, elaborately patterned carpets, and an endless sea of gambling machines and tables.

Although the lights were shining and flashing as they always had, Kyle noticed something unsettling. The streets were deserted. There was no movement in the cars that lined the roads. This contrasted sharply with the teeming streets full of people they had seen on TV wanting to catch a glimpse of their pop queen, not to mention that Vegas was always filled with people. As they got closer, Kyle noticed that the sudden ghost town quality of this usually thriving city was everywhere, in the sprawling suburbia and city around as well as on the main strip where all the main hotels stood. His peers and the adults stood looking down at the strange sight in awe as well.

"Where is…everyone?" Jake said out loud. Nobody answered because no one had an answer. Jade headed down towards the Phoenix Mountain hotel complex. The whole building glowed with a golden glint. There was a massive crest with a golden phoenix at the top of the building. The front part of it was an intricate Chinese garden complete with an impressive gold pavilion and a pristinely white bridge that extended over a large, man-made pond filled with shimmering fish. This garden had nothing of the contemplative beauty of nature and thought that made up the soul of a classic Chinese garden. This glamorous abomination was reminiscent more of Midas than of Laozi. They saw the red carpet they had seen on television set up near the hotel entrance, even the rip in the carpet where Tai had struck it, but it was completely deserted.

Kyle pulled out the willow branch that had been a gift from the Goddess of Mercy. Its leaves were still green and the wood a healthy brown. He held it up and watched as an invisible wind moved it, causing it to wave and point straight at the topmost part of the building where there looked to be a sprawling penthouse suite. Jade headed for the rooftop of the building. When he reached it, he first gently placed the large sphere onto the rooftop as he floated above it, and then he transformed back into human form, his body shrinking and his bones shortening and rearranging unpleasantly under his scales that were smoothing out into skin. The teens couldn't help but look at him warily, and his hair and eyes were very obviously green and otherworldly, making them wonder how they ever saw him as just a regular high school coach.

The rooftop was typical, plain and gray with running ventilation pipes and openings. It was not made for the guests of the hotel to visit.

"There," Kyle said as he pointed to a gray service door. They went through it and down some stairs lit by white lamps on every flight. Kyle went down just one flight and burst through the first door he saw. He found himself in a long golden hall in front of some shiny elevator doors. At the far end of the hallway were large double doors. He ran towards them, pulling his sword out of its sheath as he ran.

摜

The character for 'smash' appeared across his forehead as his eyes glowed, and the doors were reduced to splinters.

"Tsk, tsk, so violent Kyle. Didn't your mother ever teach you any manners?"

Kandi sat there, luxuriating across a golden couch in her high-slit, sleeveless red qipao dress. Behind her was a large glass mirror that reflected the image of Kyle and all of his companions as they came into the room. The mirrors all around reflected large and small images of the unfolding events. Sitting on the ground by the couch and by her feet was Devon Blair. He was gently massaging her bare feet, looking at her with adoring eyes. Next to the First Child Demon stood Tai in a pink qipao designed like her mistress', the only thing that made it clear that she was Tai was the fact that she held the silver Soaring Staff. If it had not been for the staff, which she held protectively by Kandi, she would have been unrecognizable to Kyle under her thick make-up and lustrous hair; she looked just like one of the backup dancers that he had seen subdue her earlier on television, soullessly robotic.

The sight of the two women inspired such conflicted emotions in Kyle that he could scarcely make sense of the storm. Hate and anger raged against the First Child while a deep and sad longing reached out for Tai. The sight of her done up the way she was right now was like poison, corrupting mind and soul.

"No…" Kyle breathed. Tai's parents went pale.

"Oh goody, I believe it's time for my monologue. This is the part where I say 'Foolish mortal, you've had your chance to win her heart, but now her soul is mine.' How do you think that sounds, Devon darling?" Kandi said.

"Brilliant, babe, you're going to do great in your first film. It's going to be a blockbuster *and* critically acclaimed," Blair answered with approval.

"I know, right?" Kandi laughed.

"What do you want…" Kyle began, not knowing what else to say. They couldn't attack, not knowing how the demon would exploit Tai if a battle were to break out. The others stood behind him, tense but ready.

"Want?" Kandi said, her giggle like a playful bell echoing one too many times, tempting madness, "I'm an artist. All I *want* is to *express* myself."

"An artist?" Kyle asked, genuinely puzzled, but then he added with some sarcasm, "What kind of art could *you* possibly be capable of?" Kyle thought of art as expression of beauty. He found nothing beautiful about the demon diva he saw before him.

Kandi gave him a coy smile. It took all of Kyle's self-control not to use qi script to smash her face in. "A true artist knows no boundaries." She sat up, pulling her feet away from Devon's tender attention. "My dear mother molded creatures out of clay and gave them life. I'm simply following in her footsteps, but taking it to the next level."

She gestured to Devon to give her something, and he handed her one of her classic red Kandi high-heel shoes. Kyle looked at the shoe, pained and bewildered, trying to understand how a fashion statement could somehow be related to Matt's death.

"I make music. I dance. I sing. I design. My mother molded clay, made flesh and blood bodies, and I have made my medium for my art the human spirit. Take this ravishing creation. It is one of my favorites," she said as she fingered the smooth and shiny red high-heeled shoe. It was the same one that Rose often wore. "You know what I did when you brought me to this lovely world of yours, Kyle? I read. I love reading. And I read, well, everything. I learned all about your history, every empire, every war, every struggle for freedom or pride or country, for family and love. Your peace keepers and your warmongers, your murderers and your saints. All of the religions and all of the laws ever written. All of your greatest literature and all of your trash. Riveting, all of it was, really. I wanted to, you know, get to know my audience before I began to mold you."

"Mold us? How could you possibly mold us?" Kyle spat out.

"Well," Kandi tilted her head thoughtfully, "let's just say I simply help you petty little creatures reveal your true selves. Art is about truth, is it not?"

"Truth? There's no truth in anything you do," Jade said, a carefully controlled fire burning in his eyes.

"Yours is a selective reality. You're missing the whole picture," Snow said. Her voice was calm but aggressive at the same time.

The demon ignored them. She slid the red high heel shoe onto one of her feet as she gestured for Blair to give her the other one. She held up that one now, examining it the way a sculptor would examine a finished piece.

Kyle wanted to take that red abomination and shove it down her throat. The only thing that kept him from doing so was the fear for Tai's safety. He glanced over at her, but she showed no signs of acknowledging that he was there. She stared blankly, the way Matt had stared blankly forward on the school broadcast TV.

The demon continued explaining, more like she was thinking out loud than really trying to help them comprehend. She even seemed a little bored.

"There was this one cultural practice that particularly intrigued me. Something called foot-binding, where a woman's feet were disfigured with tight wrappings. I found it amusing that you pathetic humans found something as stupid as that attractive in a female. However, as an implement of torture, it was too crude, too obvious. It lacked elegance to its design. And then I found this," she held up the red high-heel shoe for emphasis. "Isn't it lovely? I just had to design one of my own. It's so refined, so graceful, and so delightfully devious. The most wonderful part about it is how easily the human spirit embraces it, loves it, even though it is so obviously disfiguring. It's not as crude and obvious as foot-binding, making it much easier for the human mind to deceive itself into accepting it, a welcomed torture for the body and mind, its victim choosing to subject herself to its torment willingly, even joyfully. Have you ever seen the x-ray of a pair of bound feet? Let me show you. It's beautiful!"

Everything she said made almost too much sense to Kyle, so much so that he began to slightly doubt himself. He was speechless as he watched the demon slide the other shoe on and then walked around to the back of the couch, her hips swaying sassily as the high heels limited her stride. She pressed a button causing the large mirror to slide up, revealing a large, embedded flat screen as high as the wall and twice as long. She gingerly tapped on the screen, and it came alive with little icons lined up across the middle. She touched the icon of the camera, and it exploded into a splash of pictures that looked like cards thrown across a table.

"Now let me see, where is it…" she caressed the screen with her fingers, shifting through the pictures, taking her precious time. She tapped on one black and white photo, and the image expanded to a large size, its contents clearly visible to everyone in the room.

“There, see?” The image was a black and white x-ray of a pair of feet that looked like they had been bent up vertically at the middle. She pulled off one of her red high-heeled shoes and held it up next to the x-ray image. “Bound feet look just like human bone fashioned into high-heel shoes! Exquisite! Don’t you think?”

Then Kandi laughed. Out of context, it would have sounded like a particularly normal laugh, the sound of a young woman enjoying a well-delivered joke. But in the current circumstance, it sent shivers up the spines of Kyle and his companions, with Rose and her girls looking down at their feet with no small measure of shame and horror. Kandi, the pop sensation that they had worshiped with thousands of dollars spent on all her products and creations, was laughing…at them.

Kyle looked over at Tai, desperately willing her to snap out of it, to take that staff in her hand and smash it into the First Child or at least demolish the screen with that awful xray of disfigured bound feet on it. But Tai didn't move a muscle and continued to hold the staff in a way that protected her new mistress. It didn't make any sense to Kyle. Tai was the last person he'd expect to be won over by this evil temptress, and yet here she was, totally under the First Child's control. It made him ache to think how he had played a part in making her vulnerable to the demon's temptations.

“Oh, humanity is so wonderfully pathetic, your priorities so easily rearranged. Spending dollars on lipstick while children starve to death. Watching pointless entertainment while wars rape the less fortunate. I’ve been having loads of fun since I got here. So much more amusing than those silly Lin Gui villagers who refused to play with me,” the First Child Demon said with sadistic glee as she wiped a tear that had escaped her eye from her bout of laughter. She slid the shoe back on her foot.

"You monster…" Kyle said. At the mention of the Lin Gui, he

remembered the crying orphans in the Ghost Village who now had to carry on alone without their parents. Kyle looked at Tai for a reaction, but she just stood there on the other side of the screen like an elaborate mannequin, her long, mascara-covered eyelashes curling upwards while her amber-glinted eyes stared forward and down, looking rather glazed over and lifeless.

"Psh, puh-lease, Kyle baby, you act like it's all my fault. You shouldn't give me all the credit. As if it's really that hard to Twist people. Just look at your precious Rose and all her little friends who threw money at my feet. They voted for me with every dollar they spent on me, on themselves. Isn't that one of humanity's prized concepts? What's it called again? Democracy? Here, let me show you all my supporters. Devon darling, can you turn the feed on for me?"

"Sure thing, sweetheart." Blair was clearly completely enamored with her. More than that, there was something wrong with him. Kyle suddenly realized that the famous male celebrity looked feverish, his hair a little damp from sweat, and he wiped his brow constantly, ignoring his state of discomfort. Blair got to his feet a little unstably, and went to the wall behind Tai. He turned a knob, and the sound turned up.

"I LOVE YOU KANDI!"

The large screen divided into about twenty smaller video feeds. The fans screamed their enthusiasm for the demon diva. Each of the screens showed oceans of people at different cities all around the world, all gathering for the live concert promised that night by their beloved pop queen, Kandi. Her eyes narrowed in disgust as she looked upon her adoring masses.

"As if their puny little minds clouded by self-deceit could understand what true love really is." She turned to Kyle. "It's not like they don't deserve what they get. In fact, they ask for it, *beg* for it. Can't you see?"

The camera in one screen zoomed in on one particularly zealous girl donned in all Kandi attire and make-up.

"Oh my gosh! Thanks to Kandi's make-up line, I was the prettiest girl at my sister's wedding!"

Kyle looked away from the screen in disgust. Was she right? Did humanity even deserve to be saved? A sharp pain of regret shot through him. It was Kyle's gullibility to the First Child's feigned feminine charms that had allowed the demon to use him as a bridge to this world. It was his fault that Matt was now dead. Maybe he was no better than that stupid, nameless girl ranting ecstatically on the screen, consumed by her own vanity. Rose was the one who stepped forward and said something.

"I don't understand. Why Matt? What does Matt have to do with any of this?" she said, tears brimming in her eyes, her voice quavering dangerously near a sob, but she gritted her teeth angrily.

Kandi appreciatively looked with her almond-shaped brown eyes at the pretty blonde-haired and blue-eyed cheerleader. Then she walked over to the center of the screen, the video of the hundreds and thousands of adoring fans from all the major cities looking like multi-colored maggots squirming and writhing behind her. She demurely looked at Kyle.

"You can thank your secret admirer over there for that. Matt was just a little piece in another art project of mine—another human spirit I wanted to mold. So what's it going to be Kyle baby?" she winked at him and giggled playfully as she put her hands on her hip and struck a flirtations pose reminiscent of her poster advertisements. "Didn't you know? I did it for you, babe. With Matt out of the way, you can have Rose all to yourself."

The next thing he knew, Kyle had flung his sword at Kandi. There was a sudden spray of electric sparks that mingled with a piercing scream. It was Rose who screamed. She fell to her knees and covered her face with her hands and began sobbing uncontrollably. The rest of her friends stood there in shock, unable to accept what they saw. It was Snow who fell to Rose's side and tried to comfort her, a grave and sad look on her own face.

Kyle stood with tears slipping down his face. He looked down at his now empty hand; it was trembling with what it had just done. He brought it up to cover his face, both in a futile attempt to steady it and to hide his mortified expressed from the world, from himself.

Kandi was still leaning against the wall-sized screen that now buzzed with blurring white noise, but she was now impaled with the Liquid Blade that struck right through her torso and into the screen behind. Kyle had flung it at her in a fit of rage, her words hitting the sorest spot of all in his tattered soul. But in losing himself to his rage, he had let her win, let her Twist him into a violent creature of vengeance.

Though the blade clearly cut through her dress and pierced through her flesh, there was no blood. She slumped forward. Devon Blair was now too engulfed in a fever to notice that his beloved had been struck down; he was groping his way to the couch and fell on it, sweating and breathing heavily in delirium.

After Rose's sobs had subsided somewhat, Jake broke the silence.

"Is that it? Is it over?"

He was immediately sorry he spoke, for something horrifying responded to him. The slumped figure of Kandi suddenly stood erect, still skewered to the wall.

"It's never over!" the demon said and then laughed again. Her features began to melt, as if she were made out of dough that was quickly losing its form. The sight was not only grotesque but disturbing to the nth degree, her laugh gargling like someone choking on their own vomit as her mouth and larynx lost shape. Soon, all that was left was a pile of white mush that buried the red high-heels, and the now-empty red qipao hung still pierced by the Liquid Blade, bits of the white gunk still dripping out of it.

Tai moved, and that's what brought Kyle's hand down again and drew his reluctant gaze back up towards the sword he had just speared the First Child Demon with. He watched with dismay as Tai put a hand on the sword and pulled it out of the wall, letting the red qipao fall to the ground. Then, still with the glazed and lifeless look in her eyes, she turned and pointed the sword at them in an antagonistic gesture. The pile of mush at her feet bubbled slightly.

Kyle looked at her, realizing that Tai, like Matt, was another piece in the demon's sadistic art project to Twist his soul. Tai stood with the Soaring Staff in her left hand and the Liquid Blade in her right, the tip of the blade pointed straight at Kyle. Her hair was long and silken, flowing loose about her shoulders, and the tight fitting, sleeveless and high-slit pink qipao highlighted the femininity of her young body. Her immaculately embellished face was aglow with the golden light in the room that was enhanced by the many mirrors. She looked like an A-list celebrity in her own right, an alluring symbol of glorious excess in humanity's long standing conceptions of artificial beauty.

But to Kyle, she was just an empty shell. All he could see was his Tai lost behind a veil of lies. Where was that beautiful smile full of truth he had seen? Where was the real Tai? A flood of thoughts and things to say came to his mind. Clearly it was another one of the First Child Demon's sadistic jokes to pit the two of them against each other. Kyle didn't want to fight her, and he felt at that moment that he would rather perish at Tai's hands than raise a hand against her, but he couldn't stand by and watch her attack everyone else nor would he be of any use in saving her and bringing her back if he were dead. There was still hope. Didn't she say that they had been able to turn even Yehren back to humans again, even after they had been Twisted by the First Child?

He didn't know what to do. Then he remembered what she had said when they had dueled in the gym. *Being yourself won't be enough,* she had said. *Don't just be yourself. Be better.* He realized he'd have to defeat this possibly demon-enhanced Tai if he had any hope of saving her. But something in him still resisted.

"Tai...please. Don't be on her side."

He heard the sound of his own pathetic voice and words come out before he was even conscious of the fact that he had spoken. However, it seemed enough to catch the attention of the seemingly possessed Tai. She looked up at him from under her thick, fake eyelashes and feature-enhancing eye shadow, and he couldn't help but search her eyes. Something in them gave him a glimmer of hope. And then she spoke.

"I never said I was on anyone's side."

Chapter 43

The Cleansing

"Tai? You're okay?" Kyle said, in disbelief.

"Of course I'm okay. You'd think I'd let myself be a pawn of that stupid demon so easily?" Tai said.

"Why didn't you say anything earlier?" Kyle said annoyed.

"And how would that have helped? She probably would have just killed me on the spot if she knew I was unaffected by her. You heard her, she wants to toy with your mind and spirit. If she didn't think she could use me to play another mind game on you, killing me would be the next best option. She seems to have taken a special liking to you," Tai said as she turned the Liquid Blade's sharp point down, walked around the couch to Kyle, and held out the hilt to him. He took it from her, feeling the brush of her red-nail polished finger tips against his. She kicked off the pink high heels that plagued her feet. Despite all the emotional trauma he had just gone through, he wanted to smile at Tai, happy that she still had her wits about her and was still uncorrupted by the demon's allure. But the look of distress on her face kept him from smiling.

"Kyle, I don't know how we're going to defeat her," she said with a genuine worry he had never seen on her usually confident face. "She's invincible."

Kyle looked over at the pile of dough that was left over from his attack. "What was that?"

"Just one of her doppelgangers. Her entourage of backup dancers is made of the same stuff. Like her goddess mother, she can mold clay and give it some semblance of life, but she uses the ability to make minions instead of truly living creatures. After I was dragged into the hotel away from the crowds, I broke free and took down one of them with great difficulty. I even attacked the First Child herself, but there was nothing I could do to touch her. She let me land some punches on her, but all she did was turn and smile at me after I'd hit her with all the qi-script enhanced strength I had. She blocked everything with her own qi script, and her mastery of qi script is beyond what you and I can even imagine, Kyle. She seems to have a limitless source of qi, too. She's an unrelenting force."

"We have to try," Jade said.

Trembling, Tai's mother and father came up to her, some color coming back into their faces that had gone pale earlier with fear. Tai turned to them, surprised at first at the pained looks on their faces.

"Mom, Dad…I'm sorry," Tai said.

"You're always so stubborn…" Cindy said, her crystal blue eyes gleaming with tears. "Don't ever run off like that again, you hear me?" There was a moment of silence as her parents hugged her, saying something quietly to her and smiling through worried expressions.

A moan of suffering interrupted the touching family reunion and brought all of their attention to Devon Blair. He was slumped on the couch and was sweating profusely. More importantly, there was something about his features that didn't seem quite right. He was turning pale, and his arms and legs seemed strangely longer than normal. His teeth were markedly sharper than before, and his brown locks of hair were starting to fall out, strands and patches of it littering the couch. The black pupils of his eyes were growing larger and larger, as if they would engulf his vision in a terrifying emptiness.

"He's Twisting," Snow said. "Quickly Kyle, Guan Yin's jar."

Kyle quickly pulled out the white jar and placed it in Snow's hand. She lifted the warping celebrity's face up and poured the pure water into his mouth, and then she poured it all over his face and head, as if she were baptizing him with holy water. Almost immediately, his heavy breathing and sweating subsided, and his troubled features were soothed. They watched as his body visibly changed right in front of their eyes and returned to a more human state of being.

"Twisting? Into a Yehren?" Kyle asked, clearly afraid.

"What's a Yehren?" Mercedes asked with a timid voice.

"Humans Twisted by the First Child into monstrous creatures," Snow explained.

"I don't like the sound of that," Robin muttered.

"Is it contagious? Are we going to turn into what he was turning into?" Jake asked anxiously. He looked at Tai suspiciously.

"Only if you allow yourself to be," Tai said. "The demon can't corrupt you unless you're willing."

"But who would want to turn into a monster?" Kyra asked incredulously.

Dr. Tan put a hand on Kyra's shaky shoulder.

"Human society is always on the edge of insanity. It doesn't take much for us fall off of this delicate balancing act. Our history full of conflict and betrayal is more than enough evidence to show how true this is," she tried to explain to Kyra who still gave her an uncomprehending look. "It didn't take much to convince you to buy into Kandi's image and products, did it?"

At that, Kyra understood, if only a little, putting a hand to her forehead to stave off a headache borne of her reluctance to face the truth.

"You mean I could have turned into one of these Yehren? If I hadn't known?" she finally said.

"Yes," Tai answered gravely, "and all those people you saw on the TV…"

Rose gasped, "Oh no…"

"Exactly," Tai said. "Which is why we have to hurry. We've got to stop her concert at all costs. We might not be able to defeat her, but at least we can delay the Twisting millions."

Then a new, more terrifying chill ran up Kyle's spine. "Wait, is that why Vegas is deserted right now?"

"It's not deserted," Tai said with a bit of wild panic in her eyes. She threw Devon Blair a wary look before she went into the bedroom and quickly came back with black pants and shoes on under her pink qipao, the neo-ethnic wear over the sporty black pants making her look like a video game character more than ever. She tied her hair up in a high ponytail, ready to get down to business. Grabbing her Soaring Staff, she headed for the door.

"Wait," Kyle said, stopping Tai in her tracks. She looked at him impatiently. They had no time to wait. Kyle hurried over to the elaborately set up dining room table and grabbed one of the white cloth napkins. Then he held his hand out to Snow who knowingly gave him the white jar. He poured the pure water onto the napkin. "Let's get that gunk off of you first."

Kyle went up to Tai with the cloth and started to gingerly wipe her face. Kyra opened her mouth to protest, wanting to say something about how make-up removal needs a special cleanser fluid, but the stuff came off easily as Kyle wiped it away. Also unaware that nail polish usually required special, alcoholic remover, he wiped the polish off of each of her red nails as well, holding Tai's hand as he clean each finger, and it too came off with ease.

"You wouldn't want me to punch you in the face accidentally thinking you were one of those dancers, right?" Kyle laughed.

"You're all talk. You couldn't hit my face even if you wanted to," Tai gave him a dry look with her now clean face. Kyle shook his head, smiling to himself.

Kyle cleaned off the last of the polish and make-up. It gave Kyle some solace to see Tai without the clown's mask covering her face.

"Where's the concert going to be held?" he finally asked.

"On the other side of town in the new concert hall."

They all headed back to the rooftop, and Jade pulled out his large dragon's pearl and encased them all inside the clear sphere again. He transformed and took them soaring back up into the sky. They soared above Vegas again, and the streets still looked deserted from above.

"Down there, where the flood lights are," Tai directed, pointing at a large building with streams of lights coming out from its roof and perimeter. It looked like a large black cube with glowing red edges, like Pandora's Box about to burst at the seams. They landed in front of the building by a large, modern style water fountain made of square rocks with cascading falls coursing over them, and when they were released from the sphere, Jade turned quickly to his human form as they immediately began running over a red carpeted path to the front entrance.

When they reached that entrance, though, they stopped in horror. Out of the darkness seeped a putrid smell of rotting flesh that poisoned the air as people came out of the dark shadows, people that were half twisted into Yehren. They still looked human, but their faces were distorted, some with one eye bigger and darker than another, some teeth like razors while others were only just starting to sharpen, all in the same mouth. The Twisting people limped and staggered out on their limbs that were apparently elongating at different rates, hissing and growling and yelping like hyenas, their viscous drool dripping down their chins as their ripped and torn clothing stretched and hung on their bodies that were turning into triangular torsos.

Kyle and Tai were shaken, seeing so many Yehren again. One was bad enough, but an ocean of them? And these half-Twisted people were all the more terrifying because of how human they still looked. Rose and the others were visibly lost in utter terror. Never had they witnessed such horrific creatures in their life.

"What do we do?" Kyra's voice trembled no small measure of hysteria.

"We have to fight our way through," Tai said, trying her best to give Kyra and the rest of the girls a reassuring nod. She held up her staff to them with emphasis, and the girls took the hint and pulled out their batons and held them out at the ready. "They're not fully Twisted, so they're probably weaker than full Yehren. Look at the way their limbs are uneven. That should limit their mobility and effectiveness."

What Tai said made sense, but it didn't make what they were looking at any less petrifying.

They backed away slowly from the mass of Yehren, only to hear the same sickening sounds from behind. They turned to find a horde of them coming towards them on the street as well. They were pouring out of the buildings to the left and right, filling up the street, moving towards them like a creeping death.

"There's…there's too many of them!" Mercedes said, a clear panic in her voice.

"Here," Jade said, gesturing to Kyle. "Give me the jar." Kyle quickly pulled it out of his backpack and placed it firmly in Jade's hand. He pulled Snow into his arms and gave her a deep, passionate kiss, and held up the jar. "I'll be right back."

Jade transformed back into his dragon form, the Yehren falling back as his body formed and encircled the group protectively. He took a few sweeps with his massive, five digit claws at the nearby Yehren, knocking dozens of them unconscious. Then with a terrifying roar that scattered and drove many of the monstrous creatures back into hiding, hissing in the dark, he took flight and was soon soaring into the sky in a wingless flight. With the dragon gone, the Yehren reemerged slowly from their shadows and began to approach them again. A group of particularly intrepid ones launched into the air at them.

Kyle and Tai stepped forward together instinctively, engaging in battle with the half-Twisted humans. Tai knocked the ones who jumped into the air and Kyle took the ones that were pushing towards them on the ground. With his Liquid Blade, he began slashing with precision at them, aiming for their legs and sometimes the tendons in order to immobilize them while trying not to kill them. Despite their repulsiveness, they were after all human beings, and he wanted to avoid killing anyone if he could. He took five down in one swoop, the creatures screeching and hissing in pain and anger as they lost mobility and writhed on the ground, red blood spilling from the cuts. Tai was on the move too, knocking the Yehren off their feet and unconscious with her Soaring Staff. The two of them fell into a natural complement to each other in their efforts to keep the onslaught of Yehren at bay. They fought in a sort of alternating movement, with one to the left when the other was right, one fighting high while the other attacked from below. Together, with the help of their weapons made of dragon scales, they brought down wave after wave of the twisted and wild human abominations. It was clear the two of them had come a long way since their first fight with the Yehren by the ocean in the other world.

Just a beat behind the two youths, Tai's father pulled out his double broadswords and began to follow Kyle's lead. He slashed at the creatures with the trained handling of his two swords, the blades emitting a piercing metallic vibration as they sliced through air and flesh. His wife pulled out a three-sectioned staff from what looked like a yoga bag and began to wield this difficult weapon. She was abloom in a swirl of wood as she twirled the three sections of sticks connected at the joints with metal chains in front of her, behind her, above her, knocking out Yehren from every angle imaginable.

Snow let fly a Chinese meteor hammer, a large melon-shaped metallic ball tied to a five-meter-long rope that had been wrapped inconspicuously around her body and hidden behind cloth. She swung the hammer around her body, striking a number of Yehren down, but as she swung, she seemed to be entangling her body within the ropes. Just when it looked like she was fully wrapped up in the ropes, the hammer continued to swing out and build momentum, now unwinding from her torso. With a few more circular swings, she was shooting out the bone-crushing weapon with explosive and accurate attack power. She was creating her own heap of half-twisted Yehren.

The trained warriors fought on, but wave after wave of the zombie-like creatures came. There was no end to them, and even though these more experienced fighters were trying to protect the untried teens, they couldn't keep up that pace indefinitely. Jake, Rose, and the other cheerleader girls at first stood in a protective center, encircled by the other more experienced warriors, but it was inevitable that the protective line would be breached, and as the others were pulled away from them with the onslaught of the terrifying human-creatures, a few slipped in and began crawling maliciously towards them.

"Get behind me," Jake tried to say bravely to the cheerleader girls, although he had no idea how he was going to fight off these inhuman attackers. He put his hands out courageously as a shield for the girls behind him, but when one of the Yehren that were closing in suddenly leaped into the air at him, flashing its long fleshy claws, he involuntarily moved his arms to cover and protect his face. He closed his eyes, bracing himself for the slashing of his forearms by those disgusting, flesh claws, but instead, he heard a most unexpected series of battle cries. He lowered his arms to the view of the six cheerleaders with a baton in each hand, hammering away methodically at the attacking claws, bashing in a few teeth with the hand-held weapons. They dodged swipes from the creature with skilled back flips and high jumps. When the opportunity arose, they let loose a series of coordinated kicks that knocked the creature unconscious onto its back.

Emboldened by their small victory, the girls turned quickly to face other monsters that had made it past the front lines. Their acrobatic experience made the picking up of some basic martial arts kicks a simple addition to their callisthenic repertoire. Alone, each one of them would probably have been easily overrun by the half-twisted Yehren slipping in through the front lines, but together, they were a well-coordinated force to be reckoned with, fighting off and taking down their small share of the creatures. Jake tried to help with the throwing of a few fists here and there, but, though his attempts were admirably noble, his untrained efforts kept faltering, and the cheerleaders covered.

Up in the sky above, Jade twisted and turned in figure eights and cyclonic shapes as he brewed and stirred the moisture from Guan Yin's jar of pure water into large storm clouds. They grew heavier and darker with the water he kept feeding into them.

A flash of light and the sound of thunder reached those fending for their lives below, and they caught a glimpse of the clear night sky that now had gathering black storm clouds that blocked out the moon and whatever visible stars there were. The lights of Vegas reflected off the dark clouds, making them look hellish. Another flash of lightening gave everything a white, washed out look for just a fraction of a second before rain started to shower down on them in large quantities. The Yehren out in the street that were exposed to the rainfall suddenly all fell and writhed, a massive sizzling sound filling the air, mixing with the steady patter of the rainfall. Exhausted, the group watched with relief and amazement as the Yehren being drenched by rain suddenly melted away into raggedly dressed men, women, teens, and children, unconscious on the ground.

"How is this happening?" Rose said, breathing heavily from her exertions.

"The pure water from the Guan Yin's flask helps to reverse some of the corruption," Snow explained, and then shook her head sadly, "but it can't cleanse the human spirit. The First Child Demon Twists people's spirits by amplifying what's already there. The rain of pure water can only stop making them obvious monsters, but what they are on the inside is a totally different matter."

"Does that mean if it stops raining, they might turn back?" Soo asked, her hands gripping her batons tightly. Her weapons were scratched up badly from the battle, but they were still ready deal out more blows.

"Possibly," Snow answered.

"Look!" Mercedes pointed. Inside the concert building, where the rain could not reach, were half-twisted Yehren, screaming and hissing and baring their horrible teeth, unable to come out but protected by the indoors. Rose looked out at all the other buildings.

"There must be thousands of them in all those buildings," she said with a shiver.

"We've got to defeat the First Child. Stop her and everything will turn back to normal," Tai said decisively, but then added, "which will have to do for the time being."

"I agree," Kyle said, and with the Liquid Blade firmly in his grip, he led the way to the front entrance of the large concert building which was brimming with half-twistedYehren.

Chapter 44

The Darkest Hour

Kyle and Tai stood in the rain at the front entrance to the large cubical concert building. The falling drops splattered on them, soaking them through, droplets stealing down their skin and their weapons. Jade had rejoined them in his human form, and the others all stood expectantly behind the pair, each wielding their respective weapons. The Yehren milled about inside, hissing and growling at them, baring their teeth and showing their claws menacingly. There was a thick wall of them that blocked the way inside.

Tai looked at Kyle who gave her a nod back, both of them thinking the exact same thing. Both of their foreheads glowed with the character for water, and the falling raindrops suddenly began streaming steadily into the building through the open doors, causing the Yehren to screech in agony as the pure water made them fall to the ground like their counterparts outside in the street. They too began to transform back into recognizable human beings, covered in the ragtag remains of their clothes.

They stepped in cautiously over the unconscious and fallen people, and when they reached one of the double-door paths to the main concert area, they opened it up to a ghastly scene. The massive 20,000 person venue with stadium seating was filled past maximum occupancy with Yehren. The creatures were jumping up and down and yelling at the stage like rabid animals. The spacious front stage was the only space free of them, and across it stood the backup dancers all information, wearing long red hip-hugger pants matched with sleeveless midriff tops that all sparkled in the stage lights. The backdrop of the stage was a series of massive, two-story tall mirror panels that faced this way and that.

"Welcome to Kandi's first live concert everyone!" the pop star's voice filled the hall through gigantic speakers placed on either side of the stage. The raving mad audience of half-Twisted Yehren snarled and howled in response.

She came walking out onto stage as the mechanized cameras on lifts came zooming in on her. She wore short shorts and the same top as her dancers, but her red fabric didn't sparkle, it gleamed like the smooth hood of a luxury vehicle. She wore red, high-heeled boots to match. The stage exploded with indoor fireworks and flashed some automatic light displays.

As soon as Kandi spoke, a path was blown clear by a great wind rushing through the center of the ocean of Yehren. In walked Tai and Kyle with glowing eyes, and soon after, the rain front outside came streaming in, soaking every last Yehren in pure water. The cameras burst into flames, cutting off the live broadcast, and the smoke from the flames caused the sprinkler system to come alive.

The broadcast had been stopped, but how much damage had been done already, Kyle and Tai could not know. Behind the pair followed their companions, each hammer, sword, or baton ready for the upcoming fight. The First Child Demon, however, was unimpressed.

"You think you've won or something? That you've saved humanity from an apocalypse? You haven't saved anything!" the demon jeered. "I don't Twist the human spirit. There's nothing I could do that could be worse than what you all do to yourselves. All I do is make you all as beautiful on the outside as you are on the inside! Is it my fault that you're all really just monsters hidden under the guise of civilization? Please, a little bit of vanity and dash of ego and you'll be selling out your parents to the next highest bidder. You just keep repeating the same history over and over again. It's hilarious just to sit back and watch."

She laughed girlishly again, hollow and empty, her voice echoing with the sort of cruelty that teens often dole out to their peers when they disapprove of them. "Pathetic. You have no concept of how truly useless you all are," she added with a dull air.

The water from the sprinklers were falling on the stage as well, covering the First Child and her clay minions, but it didn't wash them away the way water usually washes away clay.

With a wave of her hands, the backup dancers jumped off stage and made their way towards them.

"You know, I'm sort of bored of you guys and your pointless plight. Girls, get rid of them so that we can start the real party," the demon said casually as if asking someone to take out the trash.

The lifeless girls moved in quickly. In a way, they were more disturbing than the Yehren. They looked fully human but were completely empty, creepy like porcelain dolls with glassy eyes. Kyle and Tai braced for the onslaught, but they were surprised when everyone behind them suddenly rushed ahead of them and engaged the girls in battle. Jade landed the first real strike, hitting one of the girls squarely in the head with his fist, but in an incredibly sickening way, her head flung backwards, the neck stretching a bit as it went, and then it sprung back up. She counter attacked, and Jade was soon blocking instead of doling them out. Snow's meteor hammer was swing around, hitting one girl and then another, but it only served to slow the mindless creatures down, doing no apparent damage to them. Even Tai's father landed some cuts on the girl he was facing, but there was no blood, and the cuts he had made on their bodies filled in, like rising dough. Rose and her girls were landing blow after blow with baton and leg on another girl that they had engaged in battle, but their strikes seemed to bounce back, leaving no marks on the clay dolls of the First Child. Even Jake had picked up a heavy broom stick and was trying his best to whack at the back up dancers in a baseball bat fashion, but it was no use. It was all they could do to slow down the clay creations and avoid being killed.

All the while it was raining inside, the sprinkler system sending forth an unrelenting fall of water. The fights caused sprays of water to burst from the ground or splashed falling water in curving trajectories. It gave the rather grave situation an almost tragic theatrical ambiance.

Tai and Kyle realized that these counterfeit women, these clay-made creatures were undefeatable and indefatigable while their human opponents would eventually tire out. The efforts of their companions would only serve to slow down and distract these mindless puppets. The two of them realized what they had to do. They darted forward past all the fighting and jumped up on the stage, heading straight for the source of it all. For a moment, they stopped before her, and she stood with hands on sassy hips, cocking her face at them, unperturbed by the falling water that streamed down her hair and body. The strange thing was that the water was clearly on her, but she looked dry still, her hair still in vivacious, shiny curls, and her clothes un-soaked. It was like she was covered with a thin, clear, and seamless force field that protected her from the water around her.

"Hate to spoil the ending for you, but there's just no way you can defeat me. I'm sure you've figured out by now that I'm immortal and invincible, especially relative to you. Go ahead, try your best. You're not going to get anywhere," the First Child said matter-of-factly.

Tai began spinning her staff around her body in a motion that built momentum and force. Kyle burst forward with the Liquid Blade straight at the demon girl while Tai swung her Soaring Staff high above her head and jumped up for an aerial attack. Their strike pierced through the falling water, causing the streams of droplets to splash aside to make way for the force of their attack.

The demon held one hand out in front of her and one above her head, easily intercepting both strikes, her bare skin pressed against both staff and blade, causing a painful jolt through Tai's and Kyle's joints as the shock of the cut off momentum radiated back into their arms. Responding to the pain, they let go of their weapons and cradled their arms into their bodies. The First Child held both weapons out in front of her, her bare hand on the blade of the sword, and with an effortless little squeeze, the weapons shattered and fell to pieces on the ground. She shrugged at Tai and Kyle.

"Told ya so," she said with the jeering sing-songy voice of an insolent child. "I crushed a Dragon Queen before with my bare hands. What makes you think weapons made of dragon scales would be any good against me?"

Sharing a look of both alarm and anger (for it was Jade's mother that the demon spoke so casually of), both Kyle and Tai shook out the pain in their arms and stood back up to fight. This time, their eyes glowed as they struck with every qi script assault they were capable of, starting first with elemental attacks of fire, water, metal, earth, and wood.

With the fire strike, the demon child burst into flames despite the drenching water still streaming down on her. She looked down at her hand that was aflame and then gave them an impatient roll of her eyes. Next, the water around her crept up and enveloped her in a spherical liquid prison. She seemed to be at ease as she blew a few bubbles out of her mouth the way a child with a bubble blower would play. Metal pieces broke off of the awning over the stage that held lights, and they shot towards the demon as she was released from the watery prison, but as the metal pieces hit her, they seemed to melt immediately upon impact into a molten mess.

Finally, the earth shook and cracked open beneath her, splitting the stage in half, and from the cracks sprouted forth wood vines that twisted and wound around the demon from the ground to the ceiling and then solidified into stone-hard petrified wood. For a moment, the First Child seemed contained, but then the strange wooden edifice began to shake, and then it shattered to pieces, the demon stretching her arms as if she'd just awaken from a nap. She yawned purposefully in mockery. Then she turned sharp eyes on the two of them.

"I'm nothing like you. You grow and change and die. I am immortal and eternal. I am a god."

"Forget this," Kyle said in frustration.

"Kyle…" Tai called to him, but he had already rushed forward without her, fists at the ready. All she could do was run after him and try to synchronize with his attack the best that she could. He, of course, reached the demon first and threw punches straight at the smiling woman's face, and she easily moved out of the way, bending slightly to the side or taking a small step this way and that, leaving Kyle's punches hitting only open air and falling water droplets. She seemed to be able to predict his movements perfectly, as if she knew what he was going to do next before he did.

Tai slipped around behind the demon and initiated a series of kicks at the First Child's legs, and her kicks hit their mark, sending a force straight into the backside back of the knee joint, but it was as if Tai had hit a wall that wouldn't give, and her efforts left her limping in pain. The demon looked back at her, and Kyle finally landed a punch against her face, the blow turning her to look to the other side. The impact hurt Kyle's fist as much as Tai's kick had hurt her leg, but he was too furious to care, and he gripped his other fist and struck again, and again, and again, each blow causing the demon girl to turn her face to one side and then the other. He stopped when he could not move his arms anymore from the pain.

The demon had her face turned to the right from the last punch, and she slowly turned her face forward again to look at him with a mild look of amusement playing across her lips, showing that none of his hits had affected her in the least. Tai hobbled over to his side and pulled him back away from her by the arm. He looked over at Tai's pained face with a moment of worry before he turned his glare furiously back at the First Child demon, as if he believed his hate alone was the last resort power he could use to destroy the vile demon.

摜

The character for "smash" glowed on his forehead, the destructive power of the blow causing the light and air around the demon to ripple outwards, but all it succeeded in doing was cause the First Child's still immaculately curled hair to blow backwards away from her face, as if it had only been a light breeze that had caressed her skin and not an attempt to annihilate her.

"Excellent. I love that look on your face, Kyle darling. It's quite becoming of you. You know what? You've been so much fun to play with, I'll give you a little hint on what might give you some teensy tiny chance to stop me."

She stepped toward them, and though Tai and Kyle had the impulse to step back away from her, they stood their ground.

"You're gonna to love this! All you have to do to prevent me from turning all of humanity into the drooling feral morons they already are," she rolled her eyes, "all you have to do is forgive me, forgive me for everything that I've done."

Kyle's look of pure hate wavered a bit. Was this just another one of her games? Or was their some truth to her words? Even if it were true, the concept of forgiving the First Child had *never* crossed his mind before, not even for a nanosecond. The very thought of it made him sick to the stomach. Kandi could see his thoughts as clear as day.

"Come on, I'll help you. Repeat after me: 'Kandi, I forgive you for murdering my best friend for no good reason.' It's not so hard right? Your little brain can handle those itty bitty words, can't it?"

Kyle was visibly shaken now, torn apart at the deepest core of his being. They were clearly no match for this demon in any way, shape, or form. He and Tai and everyone else were probably only moments away from defeat, total annihilation or transformation into Yehren, and there was nothing they could do about it. But here the demon offered him a sliver of hope to defeat her, and even if it was just another one of her mind games, the possibility couldn't be ignored. It was worth a try, but nothing could be farther from his capabilities at the moment. Forgive her? For killing Matt? For all that she had done?

"I…I can't…"

"Aw, the pwoh wittle Kyle is having a wittle twouble, is he?" the demon giggled. "Here, how about I make it a little easier for you." With that, her face and body morphed and distorted, and she no longer looked like Kandi, the pop diva that had taken the world by cultural storm. Now, she looked the spitting image of Kyle's mother. This infuriated Kyle. His eyes burned with seething hate as he looked upon this abomination.

"Please Kyle," the demon said in his mother's voice. "I'm so sorry about what I did to Matt. Can you every forgive me?"

His hands trembled and his eyes twitched. It was too painful to see.

"No good? Hmm, let's see, how about this?" Again the demon morphed and changed, her brown eyes transitioning to blue, her black hair turned to gold locks. Now she looked like Rose.

"Kyle, I didn't mean it," the demon now spoke in Rose's voice. "Can't you find it in your heart forgive and forget? Then you and I can be together forever."

"SHUT UP!" Kyle screamed.

損

The qi script to smash activated involuntarily in him, sending a blow at the demon that actually pushed her back a few steps. She laughed with Rose's voice, deceptively friendly and light-hearted.

"You're too easy, Kyle. You should play harder to get, you know? It's all part of the game of love. Don't you know the rules?" the demon Rose said. Again she changed and distorted. She now looked exactly like Tai.

"Don't you remember the fun we had at Phoenix Mountain when we first met Kyle?" the demon said using Tai's voice. "For old times sake, can't you forgive me this one little time?"

Kyle looked at this ghost image of Tai with anguish in his eyes. This was the guise he had fallen for that allowed this demon to come to Earth. His heart thumped heavily in his chest, pounding against his bones, and he could feel the sound of it echoing through him. It was hopeless. The demon Tai laughed in delight.

"FAIL!" she laughed as if someone had told the most hilarious joke in the world. "Where's the noble human spirit now? Huh Mother? Look at what you gave your life protecting!" the demon seemed to be yelling out to no one in particular. "NOT even when I look like THIS Kyle? SERIOUSLY? There really is no hope for humanity. I don't even know why you bother *trying* to save your pathetic race. Right?"

Kyle was at his wits end. He looked past the demon Tai at the massive mirrors behind her and saw his own reflection staring back at him. He really was pathetic, and there was nothing he could do to change that. At this moment when his soul was put to the truest test of tests, and he knew what the right answer was, he still couldn't choose it. He looked down and away from his sorry reflection, and he resolved that if he could not defeat the First Child Demon, he would give his life trying to at least delay her, one last act of destructive defiance. He braced himself to rush forward and throw everything he had at the monstrous demon, even if it meant blasting out a qi script attack that drained every ounce of his life energy. But it was then that he felt Tai's hands tighten on his arm, and then her hand slipped into his, her fingers interlocking with his. He turned in surprise to look at her, and saw the pain still creased into her brow. Then she spoke.

"Whatever happens, Kyle, whatever you choose to do, I'm with you."

Tai's words were like a clear bell that chimed through his soul. Suddenly, the explosive turmoil inside of Kyle abated, and the tumultuous waters of his hate and anger smoothed out into a calm pool with a clear reflection of himself and the situation at hand. Tai's solid presence comforted him, and his hard stare softened as he looked upon her loyal and caring eyes, those eyes so full of honesty and truth that he had grown to love. He watched as they began to glow, and upon her forehead, glowing in strokes of brilliant light, was the character for compassion.

He then realized that his own eyes were also aglow with the soft light of his own qi energy, and on his forehead glowed the same reflected Chinese character, holding within its patterns the heart of thousands of years of human thought and feeling.

Kyle and Tai smiled gently and knowingly at each other in their sudden shared understanding, and then they turned their eyes towards the First Child Demon.

The demon looked at them with genuine surprise, and then her eyes unwilling began to glow like theirs as the character for compassion appeared on her forehead as well. She reacted to it as if it were hot brand burned into her flesh. She began screaming and tearing away at it, as if clawing at the calligraphic strokes of light on her forehead could rip it off of her face. Instead, her features, which were still a mimicry of Tai's, began to melt and deform. The demon fell to her knees as her body, too, lost form, the still falling water from the sprinklers now soaking into her hair and matting it down.

The light faded from Kyle and Tai's eyes, and at first, it seemed like the demon would dissolve completely away the way the doppelganger had back at the hotel penthouse. Then they noticed tiny hands holding a small head emerging from the viscous, dough-like clay that was quickly being washed away. It was a young girl, looking like she was only about seven or eight years old. The little girl's eyes continued to glow, the Chinese character for compassion still glowing on her forehead, and suddenly, Kyle and Tai realized that there were images running across her eyes, making them look eerily like miniature television screens with the video footage playing on fast forward. The images flashed and flashed, one after another, unrelenting, and all the while the child was wailing and screaming, looking up at the ceiling with wide open eyes, unable to close them, unable to even blink. Her head trembled under the strain of whatever was happening to her, and finally with one last convulsion, she fell to the wet ground, a small and pathetic sopping mess. The child curled up into a ball, still holding her head as she whimpered.

"Mama…mama…" she sobbed on.

Kyle and Tai stared in disbelief.

"What…who is she?" Kyle asked out loud.

"She is the First Child," a voice said. Kyle and Tai looked up to the source of the voice and saw that the large mirrors originally meant to be props and amplifiers for the pop star concert had now turned into a sort of vertical liquid wall, and through it stepped Guan Yin, the being known commonly as the Goddess of Mercy. She was again in her plain yet pure white clothes, and she walked with the grace and gentleness that emanated from the core of her soul. With a wave of her hand, the falling waters ceased. As Guan Yin walked across the wet surface, the water rippled outwards in a large circle at each step she took. "Created by the Nu Wa to enjoy the beauties of the world, the First Child was lost while playing in the Phoenix Mountain. When she re-emerged centuries later, long after Nu Wa had given her own life to save the world from being destroyed in a battle of gods, the First Child found that her beloved mother had not only passed away but had created many brothers and sisters for her, a fact she was not pleased with. Her natural mischievousness easily transformed into a childish sadism as she took joy in tormenting the other inhabitants of the world her mother had created. Kyle, Tai, you have just taught the First Child to experience her first mature emotion—remorse."

"Remorse?" Tai echoed.

Guan Yin walked up to the First Child and picked up the young girl gingerly in her arms, cradling her small form in a way she really didn't deserve after all that she had done. Rose, Snow, Jade, Cindy and the others, no longer fighting the unbeatable clay dolls that now lay in piles of formless matter, came wearily yet curiously up to the stage. Guan Yin passed kind eyes over the other weary warriors, and then looked back towards Kyle and Tai.

"Right now the feeling is too overwhelming for her. That is why you see her so distraught. She still doesn't understand what it means to feel sorry for what she's done. She's trying to deal with the pain of knowing suffering from the eyes of others."

Kyle didn't know what to feel right now. Here this tiny child was the source of all his misery. Her actions had taken the life of his best

friend, had killed and hurt so many others and broken so many hearts. And yet here she was, just a little kid. He couldn't forgive her, and he couldn't understand how he had been capable of stopping such an unstoppable force, when he couldn't even muster an iota of forgiveness.

"I don't understand. How did Tai and I do this..." Kyle trailed off as he looked at the detestable yet pathetic little girl still crying 'mama' in the arms of Guan Yin.

"The First Child opened up to you two, especially to you Kyle, and that small crack was all that was needed to break through to her. You'll understand one day, Kyle, what you and Tai accomplished here, but, like all true paths to enlightenment, it is an understanding you must come to on your own," Guan Yin said as she took a step backwards. "It is time."

After Guan Yin nodded to Kyle and Tai, she turned and walked through the liquid portal, Crossing back over to the other world, Jade and Snow stepped forward on the stage, joining Kyle and Tai.

"You both really came through today," Jade said putting a proud hand on Kyle's shoulder.

"Yes, on so many levels, you came through," Snow smiled, as she gently placed her hand on Tai's shoulder.

"We couldn't have done it without your help," Kyle said, still not quite sure what it was that he had done.

"Thank you," Tai added.

"Till we meet again, then," Jade said, and hand in hand, the Dragon Prince and the fisherman's daughter stepped through the liquid portal. It rippled and then smoothed out into a clear reflection, showing Tai and Kyle, standing hand in hand.

Chapter 45

First Kiss

When Kyle, Tai and the rest of them filed wearily out of the front of the concert building, they found that the rain had stopped, but they quickly were blinded by bright floodlights pointing right at them, the deafening sounds of helicopters and sirens blaring.

The entire Las Vegas area was busy with National Guard and police, paramedics, and firefighter forces from nearby small towns and cities, with some even having flown in from San Diego and Los Angeles areas. Tens of thousands of people were disoriented and injured, requiring medical attention and shelter areas for recovery. It was as if a natural disaster like a hurricane or a flood had hit Las Vegas, but no one fully understood what had really happened.

At first, Tai, Kyle, and the others were questioned with intensity, but none of them knew what kind of answer to give and just shook their heads in exhaustion. All around them, other people in tattered clothes were being questioned as well, but they only had confused musings to share and faint memories of a dark nightmare that they couldn't quite remember the details of.

When it seemed like the ruckus was calming into a steady routine, a fleet of about twenty helicopters came flying in. Kyle and the rest looked up to stare at the incoming aircraft, noticing that there was some writing on the sides. It wasn't until the first of this new batch of helicopters turned a bit to land on an unoccupied strip of road nearby that they could see the words "Tian Yi Society" on the side.

As soon as they touched down, a flood of people in light blue uniforms and matching caps poured out and began to quickly and efficiently unload crates of what looked like emergency food supplies. A

National Guard soldier went up and began talking to someone who stepped forward to meet him. That someone was Kyle's grandfather.

Recognizing him, Kyle began running towards him with Tai and her parents following. Rose and the others hung back, accepting emergency blankets from workers. Ah-gong was handing some papers to the officer.

"Everything looks in order. It's a good thing you came. We were short on water supplies to hand out. Got a whole city to take care of here."

The soldier walked off as Kyle reached his grandfather.

"Ah-gong," he started, wanting to apologize for the cruel words he had thrown at his grandfather at their last meeting. But before he could say sorry, his grandfather took him in a firm embrace.

"Well done, Kyle, Tai," he said. He released his grandson and gave him a look of relief. "I'm so proud of you, both of you." Ah-gong looked over at Tai and put a firm and approving hand on her shoulder.

"Thank you Grandmaster Lin," Tai said and bowed to him with right fist in left palm, which caused Kyle to look over at her and mouth 'grandmaster' with a question mark, to which she replied by mouthing 'what'. Their little silent exchange was interrupted.

"Kyle!" a female voice called out that made him wince, although he wasn't sure why.

They turned to see Mei, the girl who had been his hostess at the Tian Yi society, running up towards him with sparkling eyes, hair tied up a cascade of silky black curls, and lips covered in pink lipstick. She moved to embrace him, but, almost instinctively, he stepped back and held an arm out to stop her. Only a little disoriented by his deft little block, Mei easily shifted to just holding his arm in an imploring fashion. "Is it true? Can you really do it?"

Kyle looked down at her eager eyes, not understanding what she was asking.

"Can you do it?" Mei continued in her foreign-accented English. "Qi script? Is it true?"

He was a little surprised that she knew about qi script, but he realized that if she was part of the Tian Yi Society, she must know more about it than the average person. Not understanding the significance of her question, he nodded slightly in affirmative.

Her response was immediate. Tears welled up in her eyes as if she were witnessing a dream come true—or a miracle.

"I knew it! I knew it was true! I knew you would be the one to Awaken us all!" She moved forward towards him, but found herself still held at bay by his extended arm.

Too enthralled by the news to really be disturbed by his distance, Mei raised his hand up her lips to kiss it, but he pulled his hand away before her lips could touch it. Mei looked up at him, a fleeting question in her eyes, but then she just bowed and said, "Thank you, Chosen One." Her voice was full of reverence and a joy that she could barely contain. With that, she turned and went off to join the others in passing out the water supplies.

Kyle looked up at his grandfather, full of questions.

"What does she mean by 'awaken' Ah-gong?"

His grandfather sighed wearily. "There are those in the Tian Yi Society that believe that the Chosen One will revive the ability to use qi script in this world."

"Revive?"

"Yes, there is much to explain Kyle. You see, you are descended from the original Crosser, the first person to come over to this world from Tian. *My* grandfather."

Kyle recalled some mention of it when he was at the Tian Yi Society, but he had excused it as irrelevant cult mumbo jumbo. Now, he was keen to understand.

"What does that mean?"

"It means," Tai was the one to jump in, "that you're a descendant of the Lin Gui people of Tian."

Kyle looked at both of them, dumbfounded.

"Tai is correct. My grandfather was able to use qi script, and he did many great deeds with that power in this world, but he refused to pass on the ability to others. He told me he believed people were not ready. He also knew of the threat of the First Child demon, which is why he formed the Tian Yi Society. But I believe he was right not to pass on qi script skills to others. There are those who are not ready for it, and those who would use it for selfish reasons. I tried to keep the qi script you and Tai were able to perform a secret from the Society, but of course, now, that can no longer be hidden." Ah-gong shook his head wearily. "I'm not sure what this Awakening will mean for this world, but I suppose we will just have to wait and see."

It was a lot to swallow. He remembered the Lin Gui, the Ghost Village, and the other world. Was it really where he was *from*?

One of the Tian Yi Society workers came up to Ah-gong and handed him some bottles of water. Each bottle had a label marked with the Chinese character for 'sky'.

Ah-gong held one of the bottles in his hand and looked at it thoughtfully before he handed one to each of them.

"Drink this carefully," Ah-gong said, "for it might cause you to forget all that has happened over the last few days."

"What?" Kyle looked at the bottle. It seemed like a pretty normal looking plastic bottle of water to him.

"It is a special clear tea. It will help people to forget if they want to."

"Forget? But why?" he looked around as he saw Tian Yi Society workers handing the water out to everyone, including Rose and her friends. He felt a sudden urge to run to them and knock the bottles out of their hands. His grandfather put a steadying hand on his shoulder.

"It won't hurt them, only test their resolve."

"I don't understand. Why are you trying to help people forget?" Kyle shook his head. Memories of Matt smiling at basketball practice, laughing at lunchtime, and flicking folded paper footballs at him in class streamed through his mind. "They shouldn't forget. They should remember."

"Kyle, not everyone is ready to remember. All the people in this city, are they ready to live with the memories of what happened tonight? Are they prepared to face what they almost became? What they are? Plagued by nightmares to the point where they can't function in their lives anymore? Sometimes, revelations can do more damage than good when a soul is not ready."

Yet again, it was too much for Kyle to understand at once, but it made some sense to him at least. He looked down at the bottle he held in his hand.

"So you're saying that if I drink this, I'll forget about everything that happened? The First Child, Matt, everything?"

"No, you'll forget only what you want to forget. It is a test of your resolve."

He looked at the harmless looking bottle. The memory of Matt's death was still wrenching his insides, tearing at his soul with guilt and self-hate. His anger towards the First Child was not gone. It still seethed there inside him like a venomous snake, writhing and impatient to strike.

All the turmoil inside him made him wonder how he had been able to conjure up the qi script for compassion at all at that crucial moment.

Forgetfulness seemed like an enticing escape from all the tumult that now lived in him, that sprung from his inner core. But he realized he could not turn his back on it, despite it all. He looked up at his grandfather with resolve.

"I don't want to forget…any of it."

His eyes met with Tai's, and he saw a look of sureness and determination in them. He realized how rare it was to see eyes like that, felt so appreciative that she was there with him. He returned her look of determination with one of his own. The two of them lifted their respective bottles, uncapped them, and then began to drink the tea of forgetfulness until they had consumed every last drop. They recapped the now empty bottles with a look of defiance, as if daring the liquid to make them forget. Tai's parents also drank theirs to show their solidarity. There was no fear on their faces. They knew what they were doing.

"Why did you drink it?" Ah-gong asked quietly.

Kyle wiped his mouth with the back of his hand rebelliously.

"To prove that nothing will make me forget."

With a sad smile, his grandfather said, "Remembering is a hard path to walk."

Looking up at his grandfather with eyes that now reflected the depth of a new way of life, Kyle said, "I know."

The night wore on, and Kyle and Tai and their companions had been given emergency blankets and other supplies and left to their own devices. The Tian Yi Society passed out crates and crates of the drink of forgetfulness. Rose, Jake, and the girls were glued to their phones in calls to their families, reassuring them of their safety and trying their best to explain what had happened and why they were inexplicably in Vegas without parent knowledge or permission. Reports of some mysterious outbreak or disaster in Vegas were all over the news, and that had many of their parents in hysterics.

What a couple of them found odd was that as they tried to tell their parents about what had happened, they found that parts of their recollections seemed to slip away from their conscious grasp, like liquid soap under running water. The more they tried to hold on to what they thought they remembered, the more those memories unraveled, and finally they just had to settle for telling their parents that they must be too tired to talk about it.

Rose sat by herself, holding an empty Tian Yi Society bottle and speaking calmly into a phone with her parents. She didn't forget a thing.

Tai's parents had gone off to find food and to organize a means of transportation for them back to their suburban homes in the Los Angeles County. Their dragon ride was no longer available.

Left alone for a quiet moment, Kyle sat on the edge of the large water fountain in front of the concert building where they had defeated the First Child Demon. He had a flimsy yet effective silver emergency blanket draped across the back of his shoulders. His right hand held the blanket loosely in place. He gazed out into the cool, damp night, watching numbly as rescue workers guided the distraught people to designated shelter locations; some were carried on stretchers with broken limbs and slashed legs. Guilt shot through him and he looked down at the ground.

Inside, Kyle felt empty. Matt was dead. Nothing could change that. There was a deep hollowness inside him from the grief. It made him feel so empty that he wondered if he was even really alive, if he even existed, or if he was just an illusion, a fabrication in someone else's dream. But the cold of the night, the smells of the exhaust from emergency vehicles, and the sounds of people helping people gave him some grounding.

Kyle had stopped the First Child demon from Twisting everyone in this world into Yehren. He tried for a moment to understand what had happened, how he and Tai had been able to defeat such an invincible creature, but he was too tired to really think on it with much clarity. He also had a feeling that even when he was well rested and had all his wits about him, he'd still be baffled by this strange puzzle. He decided he would have to let that understanding brew and wait, let it emerge in due time.

He stared down at his black sneakers with red trim. This pain, this loss, would never be gone. He didn't want it to be gone. It wouldn't be right, not to Matt, not to anyone. His mind was numbing from emotional and physical exhaustion. Then, from the blurring surroundings, a fresh Fuji apple was held in front of his face.

"Here."

It was Tai. Still soaking wet and bedraggled from their battle, she looked as beat as he felt, but the sight of her triggered something in him that gave him one last spark of energy for the evening. A moment had presented itself. Without taking the offered apple, he stood up, the silver emergency blanket falling as a glittering mass from his shoulders. Kyle's hands reached up and gently held Tai's face as he kissed her.